STEELHEART

A MEDIEVAL ROMANCE

BY KATHRYN LE VEQUE

Kathryn Le Veque Novels

The Savage Curtain (Lords of Pembury)

The Fallen One (De Reyne Domination)

Fragments of Grace (House of St. Hever)

Lord of the Shadows

Queen of Lost Stars (House of St. Hever)

Lords of Thunder: The de Shera Brotherhood Trilogy

The Thunder Lord

The Thunder Warrior

The Thunder Knight

Highland Warriors of Munro

The Red Lion

Time Travel Romance: (Saxon Lords of Hage)

The Crusader

Kingdom Come

Contemporary Romance:

Kathlyn Trent/Marcus Burton Series:

Valley of the Shadow

The Eden Factor

Canyon of the Sphinx

The American Heroes Series:

The Lucius Robe

Fires of Autumn

Evenshade

Sea of Dreams

Purgatory

Other Contemporary Romance:

Lady of Heaven

Darkling, I Listen

Multi-author Collections/Anthologies:

With Dreams Only of You (USA Today bestseller)

Sirens of the Northern Seas (Viking romance)

Ever My Love (sequel to With Dreams Only Of You) July 2016

Note: All Kathryn's novels are designed to be read as stand-alones, although many have cross-over characters or cross-over family groups. Novels that are grouped together have related characters or family groups.

Series are clearly marked. All series contain the same characters or family groups except the American Heroes Series, which is an anthology with unrelated characters.

There is NO particular chronological order for any of the novels because they can all be read as stand-alones, even the series.

For more information, find it in **A Reader's Guide to the Medieval World of Le Veque**.

Contents

AUTHOR'S NOTE

Finally, David's story!

Well, this is quite a yarn, I must say. This has taken a very long time to come to fruition because David's story is a complex one. Much of it weaves around his older brother's story (RISE OF THE DEFENDER), and David plays a very large part in that novel, so it was a matter of constructing a story that is completely from David's perspective. That's a tough job when the last time you wrote about the guy, in this particular period of his life, was twenty years ago!

A few things to note before we start – Windsor Castle plays a part in this novel, as it did in RISE OF THE DEFENDER. At this point in time, Windsor was a royal residence but not the favored one. It was big, of course, but a good deal of it was still made of wood. It wasn't until later in thirteenth century that the entire structure was built in stone. The motte was apparently poorly constructed and had a lot of 'sinking' issues until it was reinforced in later years. For the purposes of the story, however, I have advanced the architecture slightly and made it more like the castle we know today.

Also, there is no Earl of Canterbury – only an Archbishop of Canterbury, but Canterbury itself was never an earldom, so that too is a fictitious title.

A tournament figures in this tale. Something interesting to note about tournaments in general – the term 'melee', used to describe the mass, mock fighting that was a staple of tournaments, wasn't widely used until the 16th century. Before that, it was known as the 'mass competition' or 'the mass'. Don't be confused when you see that term in the story.

Something very important to note in this story – you will see sections of text in italics, adding an additional point of view to this story. Since David's story intertwines so much with his brother's story in RISE OF THE DEFENDER, I have included sections from ROTD to help explain what is happening in David's world from Christopher de Lohr's perspective. David is in much of Christopher's story so it is only right that Christopher is in much of David's, so the italic sections are meant to help the reader understand what more David was dealing with outside of his story with Emilie.

There is also a good deal of politics happening which I choose to explain from Christopher's perspective, not from David's. RISE OF THE DEFENDER was politics-driven. STEELHEART is not. David is involved in the politics, of course, but his story is more about his relationship with Emilie rather than the political dealings of his brother. There are also times when Emilie makes an appearance in ROTD, which I have tried to include as well. You will see her in some of the Italics also. Because David was in and out of ROTD so much, there are times when I must include paragraphs from ROTD simply to explain what is going on in David's life at that point in time so there aren't big gaps in David's story as a whole. This really gives a lot of dimension to David's story, showing us that there was so much more to him at this point in his life than his relationship with Emilie. But, since this novel is *about* his relationship with her, that is where the focus is.

You will, however, see many peripheral characters that were in RISE OF THE DEFENDER that make appearances in this book – Christopher de Lohr (David's brother), Edward de Wolfe (father of William de Wolfe of THE WOLFE), Leeton de Shera, and Marcus Burton. Marcus, Christopher's best friend, had a very complex relationship with Christopher and essentially lusted after his wife, Dustin, who is also marginally in this novel. See the list of characters following this note to get a sense of who everyone is. I don't normally do a list of characters, but in this case, it was necessary.

David story parallel's ROTD most of the way so some of the angst from ROTD is here as well in certain scenes. Just to explain this situation a little – David had a very hard time with Marcus from that perspective. There is a good deal of animosity there, which you will see as you read. All I can tell you is this – if you haven't read RISE OF THE DEFENDER yet, then I think you can figure out by now that you really, really should! It's not essential to understanding this storyline, but it will open up a whole new world of understanding for David's novel.

Also, as we know these days, the Richard I's crusade to The Levant (or the Holy Land) was kind of a lesson in vanity from the standpoint of the Christian armies. There is the mention of the massacre of Ayyadieh in this novel, which really happened. You can read about it here:

https://en.wikipedia.org/wiki/Massacre_at_Ayyadieh

So those are things worthy of note for STEELHEART. This book has been such a long time in coming that I really hope you enjoy the complexity of it and the detail of it. It was a difficult book to write but a rewarding one. I'm so glad to see David come to life again. He's a personal favorite of mine.

Hugs,
Kathryn

LIST OF CHARACTERS

Sir David de Lohr – The hero, second son of Myles de Lohr (WHILE ANGELS SLEPT)

Lady Emilie Hampton – The heroine, eldest daughter of the Earl of Canterbury

Lord Lyle Hampton – Earl of Canterbury

Sir Brickley de Dere – Captain of Lord Hampton's troops, sworn to the House of Hampton

Lady Nathalie Hampton – Emilie's sixteen-year-old sister

Lady Elise Hampton – Emilie's fourteen-year-old sister

Lillibet – The nurse to the Hampton girls; she is known as "Mother"

Sir Christopher de Lohr – Richard I's champion, known as Defender of the Realm (hero of RISE OF THE DEFENDER)

Sir Edward de Wolfe – knight sworn to Christopher; father of William de Wolfe (THE WOLFE)

Sir Leeton de Shera – knight sworn to Christopher; once married to a daughter of the Earl of Derby

Sir Brentford le Bec – knight sworn to the Earl of Derby

Ralph Fitz Walter, Sheriff of Nottingham – ally of John Lackland

John Lackland, Prince of England – Richard I's brother

Sir Marcus Burton – knight sworn to Christopher originally; formerly best friends with Christopher and David

William de Ferrers, the Younger – heir to the Earldom of Derby

William Marshal – part of Richard I's council of regency, also custodian of England for Richard I.

Dustin de Lohr – wife of Christopher de Lohr

Baron Sedgewick and his wife, Lady Anne – friends of Christopher and Dustin

Sir Philip de Lohr – Uncle of Christopher and David; older brother of Myles de Lohr. Philip is lord of Lohrham Forest, the de Lohr ancestral home. He also had a son very late in life, which meant the boy would inherit the de Lohr estates – not Christopher or David.

Knights from Christopher de Lohr's stable who make brief appearances or are briefly mentioned: Max and Anthony de Velt, Jeffrey Kessler, Nicholas de Burg, Sean de Lara, and Guy de la Rosa

Kieran Hage – mentioned in passing. He is the hero of KINGDOM COME and THE CRUSADER. He fought with David and Christopher under Richard's command.

Zephyr – Christopher de Lohr's horse.

PROLOGUE
~ THE WARNING ~

Windsor Castle
October 1192

*I*N THE GREAT HALL *with revelers and music in the background, two men faced each other in the recesses of the room. They had come there for privacy, unheard and unseen from the crowd, sheltered by a supporting pillar the held up the arched ceiling. An older man, with yellowed eyes and a face line with sorrows, faced a younger man, very big, who possessed a neatly combed crown of blond hair and a neatly trimmed beard. As the minstrels played in the background and the smell of meat and too many unwashed bodies filled the air, the older man spoke.*

"Chris, we have just received word from Palestine," he said softly. *"There is no easy way to tell you this, lad, so I shall come out with it. Richard is missing."*

Christopher de Lohr, Richard I's champion and defender, faced William Marshal with a furrowed brow. "Missing? What do you mean?"

"He sailed from Acre to the coast of Corsica and simply disappeared," the earl replied. *"His general believes him to be traveling across the continent incognito, trying to reach his Duchy of Normandy*

before crossing to England, but no one is certain."

"Damn," Christopher hissed, relaxing against a massive oaken table. "Why would he do that when he knows Duke Leopold of Austria is out for his blood? Not to mention Emperor Henry, or Philip Augustus. Christ, they are all out for his hide. Why would he chance such a stupid action?"

"Richard is a wise man, Chris," William replied, as perplexed as the baron was but trying to remain confident in Richard's ability. "He must have damn good reasons whatever they might be. The fact remains that John is going to run rampant with this knowledge."

Christopher's handsome face was grave, his eyes dark. "What do you suspect?"

The earl shrugged, examining a particularly fine chair. "He's already amassed quite a mercenary army, you know."

"I know, but how large? My sources tell me conflicting stories," Christopher said. "And how in the hell is he paying these cutthroats?"

"His loyalists," William said frankly. "He has some very wealthy backers, Chris, and they are feeding their wealth directly into his coffers. Believe me, he has the means to pay an army. A massive army, nearly ten thousand men as near as we can gather."

Christopher nodded. "I'd been told that," he said. "But I have not been returned from the Holy Land long enough to verify the information myself."

"You have had other things to attend to," William acknowledged, then fixed him with a reluctant gaze. "But that's not the only problem. 'Tis rumored that John is trying to establish an alliance with Philip Augustus which, if successful, will supply him with almost limitless power and men."

Christopher sighed heavily, studying his boots for a moment. "I fought with the French king in Palestine," he said. "He and Richard were like two roosters, each vying for the dominant position. There is no love lost between them and he will surely find allies in Richard's enemies. Leopold is out for Richard's blood for what he did to him at

Acre," he shook his head slowly. "Richard is in danger of losing his throne, isn't he? With his disappearance, 'twill be easier for John to claim the kingdom."

William nodded. "I am afraid that is what it will come down to," he said quietly, sitting in the chair he had been examining. "Richard has very powerful allies, his largest being the church. But if he is missing and presumed dead, then there is no use defending a kingdom for a dead king. John will rule."

Christopher stared thoughtfully at the floor for several long, pregnant minutes. Neither man spoke, the severity of the situation sinking in and a great cloud of doom settling.

"Does John know yet?" he asked.

"When I sought you, he had yet to be informed," William replied. "But that may have changed since then."

Christopher sat still a moment longer before pushing himself off the table and crossing his arms. "It would seem to me that if Richard is missing, then someone should go looking for him. As his champion, it must be me."

"Nay, lad, not you," William said firmly. "As his champion, it is important you stay here and control the crown's troops so that John cannot use them. If you leave, there will be no one to stop him. You cannot appoint your own replacement – only Richard can do that."

"We cannot simply sit here while Richard may be in grave danger," Christopher said passionately in the first real display of emotion. "He very well may require assistance."

"There is nothing you can do," William said. "Even if you were to find him, 'twould be you and he against the whole of the continent. You said yourself that Leopold and Henry and Philip were out to get him. You alone could not defend him against every troop on the continent, formidable as you are. And most certainly if he is traveling in disguise, don't you think that Richard's champion riding into France and Germany would attract attention?"

Christopher looked at him a moment, hard, before turning away in *frustration. He kicked at the floor, scuffing his boots. "So what do we do, my lord?"*

"At the moment, nothing," William replied. "The justices will be meeting on the morrow regarding this crisis, I am sure. I go now to deliver the message personally to all of them."

Christopher turned to him. "'Twill take you all night. Allow me to assist you in this so that we may both be in bed before the sun breaks the horizon."

"I would be grateful," William admitted, rising. "I am not as young as I used to be, not as young as you."

Christopher snorted. "At thirty-five years, I am hardly young. Richard is a mere three years older than myself."

"You are young," the earl insisted with a weary smile. "When you reach my age, you will know what old is. By the way, Chris, I have not had the chance to congratulate you on your marriage to Lord Barringdon's daughter. A fine match."

"Thank you, my lord," Christopher mumbled.

William moved for the door, eyeing Christopher. "You know, if I were you, I would return her to Lioncross. 'Tis not safe for such a beautiful woman here in John's court. The prince will set his sights on her, if he hasn't already."

Christopher's jaw ticked. "I am well aware of the prince's lust," he replied. "As for returning her to Lioncross, I feel better able to protect her here. My knights are with me and she is never alone, whereas at Lioncross, there is less protection."

William's hand rested on the door latch and Christopher stopped, facing him in the dim room. "Chris, before John makes his move to seize Richard's holdings, you must leave Windsor and return to your keep if you expect to preserve your life. He shall go after everyone loyal to his brother, especially ranking officials such as you and myself."

"I can handle John's mercenaries," Christopher said confidently. "Yet in faith, the only thing that concerns me is if John does indeed ascend the throne. My only hope is that he will allow me to live out my

life in England in peace, although I have grave doubts that that will be the case. I fear I may find myself fleeing to Ireland or Scotland."

"All of us, lad," William smiled wryly and opened the door. "'Twould make a fine commune living amongst Richard's ousted loyalists. Now, I shall deliver the messages to the clergy justices. That leaves you with the nobles."

Christopher nodded curtly. "Most of which are at Windsor, except for a very few. I should be done by midnight at the latest."

"Waste no time," William said. "I will see you on the morrow."

Christopher left the marshal and made his way back to the fragrant and stuffy dining hall. His great sense of foreboding was overshadowed by the urgency he felt. The feast had finished and the orchestra was filling the hall with a lively tune, and realizing that John had already left the hall caused his sense of urgency to multiply.

Later that night, the attacks against Richard's supporters began.

Hell began.

PART ONE
AND SO, IT BEGINS....

"There to perish by judgment meet,
Dying a villainous death of shame."
~ Song of Roland c. 1040 A.D.

CHAPTER ONE

I T WAS AS dark as sin in the corridor, that sooty blackness of night that not even the torches, burning low and heavy in their iron sconces, could erase. In the corridor of this black and inky building, a sea of darkness in the dead of night, he knew that they were up here. The anticipation in the air was palpable.

He could feel it.

Sir David de Lohr stood at the top of the stairs, his sky-blue eyes gazing off into the darkness beyond. Just within the past several hours, news had reached London that Richard, King of England, had been declared missing on his journey home from the Levant, and that information seemed to spur his jealous brother, John Lackland, into a series of actions against Richard's loyalists. With Richard gone, there was nothing between John and the throne of England. Nothing but the House of de Lohr, and even in that, John was determined to remove that very large obstacle.

In this past hour, he'd gone after David's brother, Richard's champion and a man known throughout England as the Defender of the Realm. They even called him the Lion's Claw, for a lion's deadliest weapons were his claws, and Christopher de Lohr was quite deadly. He was a great man, no doubt, and a worthy target for John's hatred. In fact, there as probably no one in England more worthy of being John's target.

But, like the poor marksman he was, John had missed the mark. The man had struck Christopher's wife in an ambush meant for the husband and had injured the woman. David had been present at the ambush and he'd fought off a horde of John's personal guard who had been trying to wipe out anything with the name de Lohr attached to. A young knight, who was the cousin of Christopher's best friend, Marcus Burton, had fallen beneath the steely blades of John's assassins. Christopher's wife had also been injured. In truth, it had been a bloodbath begging for vengeance.

And David would answer the call. As Christopher had gone to check on his wounded wife, David had left the apartments in search of the lowly scum who had committed the atrocity. Not the prince, of course, but his personal guard, a group comprised of the lowliest scum and assassins England had to offer. That was the putridity that John surrounded himself with. David's offensive was completely without Christopher's knowledge, of course, for Christopher was preoccupied with his wife and not with vengeance at the moment. Christopher tended to plan more appropriately for things like this, a time and a place for his revenge, but not David. His reaction was instantaneous. Therefore, David and several of Christopher's soldiers had gone on the hunt.

It was time for John to pay.

Backtracking from the section of corridor where the ambush had occurred, David and his men had followed footprints, tracks of several men running off from the residential block where Christopher was staying. It headed towards the south end of Windsor where there were some old timber outbuildings that served as knight housing, now serving as housing for the collection of barons that were in attendance for John's coming tournament and feast. Wherever the pack of jackals had been heading, it was in that direction.

As David and his men had crossed the dark middle ward of Windsor, heading to the lower ward, they came across two knights that David recognized as allies – Sir Stephen Marion, a bachelor knight of great skill and wealth, and a knight who served the Earl of Derby by the name of Brentford le Bec. David knew the men, and they knew him, and when they saw David crossing a darkened bailey armed to the teeth, they didn't hesitate to join him when David explained what had happened to Christopher's wife. Soon, David had two skilled knights at his disposal and the odds against John's guard were mounting.

David and his men then ran all the way to the old building that had been constructed by the Duke of Normandy over one hundred years before, a two-storied wooden structure with about twelve rooms total. The lower ward of Windsor was dark for the most part, with weak light emitting from the old wooden structure, enough light to cast upon a party of riders outside of the building and what seemed, the closer they came, to be a struggle going on. David and his men could hear the clash of swords as they approached.

They could also hear the frightened yelp of women. Sounds like that always spurred men onward and as David and his men rushed up to the skirmish, he could see that some of the combatants were wearing the dark green and black tunic that John's guard so proudly donned. The connection was unmistakable and David even recognized one of the men as having been part of the earlier ambush against Christopher's wife. Realizing they had come into yet another fight perpetrated by the very men they sought, David's sword was unsheathed in the blink of an eye and, feet first, he plunged into the melee. He didn't even care who John's men were fighting; even if it were an enemy of the House of de Lohr, the greater enemy was the prince's personal guard. Like the praetorian guard of old, fearsome men who used to the bidding of the great leaders of Rome, John's guard had the power of fear and pain.

But, then again, so did David.

The addition of David, two knights, and eleven de Lohr soldiers turned what had been a grunting, clanging fight into a maelstrom of blades and blood. Because it was so dark, it made the situation all the more dangerous because of the limited visibility. Men ended up fighting their allies before they realized it, and as David was fast as lightning, he narrowly missed cutting down one of his own men in the darkness. Still, he managed to regroup and cut down two of John's men in quick succession. He could see Marion and le Bec fending off multiple enemy guard but over to his left, in the lightless haze, he could hear another female yelp. Instinctively, he moved in that direction.

As he passed around the side of the carriage, sword wielded defensively, he was set up on by another sword. Leaping back to give himself room in preparation for a battle, he brought his sword around and caught a glimpse of an older man in the weak light. It was only a brief glimpse but in that flash, he thought he recognized the man. He avoided striking a heavy blow against the man as he stood back, out of range, and tried to get a good look at him.

"My lord?" he said, squinting in the darkness. "Lord Hampton?"

Lyle Hampton, Earl of Canterbury, was in the fight for his life and the somewhat friendly voice in the midst of the battle threw him off. But not too far off; he managed to stop his sword and peered at David in the darkness. When recognition dawned, his eyes widened in relief.

"De Lohr!" he gasped. "David?"

David nodded. "It is I," he said, gesturing to the carriage. "What are you doing, my lord? I thought you only arrived this morning?"

Lyle nodded. "We did," he said, grasping David by the arm with fear in his expression. "I brought my daughters with me to Windsor but when I heard the news of Richard's disappearance, I thought to remove them immediately and take them to my sister's home closer to London but it seems I was not soon enough. John's men have found me as they have found so many others this night. Have they set upon you as well?"

David nodded. "They have," he said. "They injured Chris' wife.

You say they have hit upon more of Richard's supporters?"

Lyle nodded. "I was told by a harried servant that the Earl of Bath has taken a blow," he said. "That was when I decided to take my daughters and leave. Now I hear they have struck de Lohr, whom no one in their right mind would strike out. John is out for blood."

David sighed with disgust. "He is feeling empowered with news of his brother's disappearance," he said. "I was tracking the men that struck at my brother when I came upon your party. Did you see Fitz Walter with these men who attacked you?"

Lyle shook his head. "I have not seen the Sheriff of Nottingham," he said. "But the truth is that I do not expect to. He would not dirty his hands with something as mundane as this."

David wasn't hard pressed to agree. Ralph Fitz Walter, the prince's second-in-command who bore the title Sheriff of Nottingham, was usually the one who planned dirty events such as this, but he did not participate usually. He was a coward that way. David peered a bit more closely at Lyle, seeing that the man was greatly troubled.

"Have you suffered great damage, then?" he asked.

Lyle nodded, his features strained. "Emilie," he said. "They took Emilie. I was just going after her when you came around the side of the carriage."

David frowned. "Your wife?" he said, looking around swiftly. "Which direction did they take her?"

Lyle shook his head. "Not my wife; my eldest daughter," he said hurried. "You've not met her yet. They took her back into the residence and, I fear, that mayhap they intend to take her to the prince. You know of his savagery for female flesh. David, please help her – John must not have her!"

David was already flying into the two-storied structure, dark and cold inside as he paused, listening for any sound that would point the way to an abducted daughter. He thought he heard something up the stairs but when he started to move, he realized that Lyle was right with him. David threw out an arm to prevent the man from following.

"Nay, my lord," he said quietly. "You have other womenfolk to protect, do you not?"

The fear on Lyle's face was turning to panic. "Aye," he said quickly. "My other daughters, Elise and Nathalie. But…"

David shook his head, pointing back out to the carriage. "Go to them," he commanded softly. "If you see Marion or le Bec, send them to me. Go, now; I will find your daughter."

Lyle was very reluctant to leave but the sounds of the skirmish in the darkness outside and the frightened cries of his two remaining daughters drew him back outside. David was right; he had to protect Nathalie and Elise and trust that David would find Emilie. Sweet, blond, and delicately fair Emilie was his heart. He was terrified for her. But he knew David de Lohr and knew the man's reputation; he knew that if anyone could save her, David could.

As Lyle raced back to the carriage containing his remaining daughters, David bolted up the stairs. It was as dark as sin in the corridor, that sooty blackness of night that not even the torches, burning low and heavy in their iron sconces, could erase. In the corridor of this black and inky building, a sea of darkness in the dead of night, he knew that they were up here. The anticipation in the air was palpable.

He could feel it.

He stood there a moment, accessing the situation, before crouching low, listening for any sound from any direction. It wasn't any time at all before he heard something heavy fall and scuffling, like running, off to his left. He took off at a dead run because that was what David did; the man charged full-on into situations, sometimes before thinking, and only his incredible speed and skill with a blade had prevented those rash decisions from costing him his life.

Even now, he ran off down the hall, sword in hand, heading for the direction of the sounds with his only thoughts being that of what needed to be done, not what could possibly happen to him. It was a bravery that few men possessed. When he heard another large thump behind a door at the end of the corridor, he charged towards the door and leapt up into the air, kicking the panel open with a flying leap.

Wood and pieces of old iron hardware exploded in all directions as David crashed through the door. The chamber was dark except for a slight glow given off by the dying hearth, but it was enough light for David to see at least two of John's guards and one small woman. He only knew it was a woman because of the clothing; heavy skirts and a cloak, he thought, and she was trying desperately to climb a massive wardrobe as both men tried to yank her down. There were upturned chairs and a table on its side, and the room in general was in disarray. Knowing that the woman as in grave danger, David launched an offensive in the dark.

One man rushed him while the other continued to try and yank the woman off the wardrobe. David had to duck as the man charged him, narrowing avoiding being sliced in the neck, and came up under the man with his blade to catch the man in the soft belly. As the first guard grunted and fell away, David threw himself at the second guard trying to pull the woman down from the wardrobe.

Unfortunately, the woman had a good grip on the furniture and the guard had a good grip on her. When David charged the man, the guard refused to let go of the woman's foot, so David ended up yanking her and the wardrobe off of the wall and everything went crashing to the floor, as David tried to avoid being smashed by the falling furniture. He managed to escape, with his arm around the neck of the guard wearing the black and green tunic, but the woman fell on top of both of them.

In the crash, David's sword went flying. Now, he was in trouble. The woman's torso had mostly fallen on him and she was shrieking, struggling to get away, but the guard still had her by the ankle. David was getting kicked in the head as the woman struggled and, at one point, she brought her knee up and kicked him straight in the nose.

Seeing stars, David could feel the blood start to pour and it was getting all over her skirts as she fumbled, still trapped by the guard. He knew he had to free the woman, and subdue the guard, because he was fearful of what would happen should the man have colleagues come to his aid. Whatever he was about to do, he had to do it quickly. There was no time to spare. With that thought, David began to squeeze the man's neck as hard as he could.

David was strong; unusually so. He had big arms, fuzzy in the forearms with blond hair, that were significantly muscular. Therefore, the guard was in a very bad position when David began to squeeze. He used his other hand to brace up the arm that was doing the squeezing, grunting with exertion as the woman over his head struggled and fought. Sometimes her fists found David's skull but he couldn't pay any attention to that; he was more concerned with killing the man in his arms. It was either kill or be killed. Mercifully, the man in his grip quickly weakened.

Bootfalls were suddenly in the doorway and due to the fact that David had a woman on his head, he couldn't see who it was. Fearful it was one of John's men, he suddenly shifted so that he ended up flipping the guard in his arms over so that he was now in the dominant position. The action caused the guard to lose his grip on the woman, who scrambled to her feet now that she realized she was free.

Without the encumbrance of skirts covering his head, David could see that indeed one of John's soldiers was in the doorway, and when he saw David he charged with a yell. David, now on top of the guard he was wrestling with, yanked the guard up to use him as a human shield as John's soldier charged them both. The guard in David's arms took a sword to the gut meant for David and David let go of the guard, long enough to lash out a big fist and catch John's charging soldier in the face. The soldier fell back, face shattered, and the guard with the sword to the gut fell to the floor dead as David leapt to his feet, grabbing his own sword a few feet away.

There was blood all about the room with two dead men and furniture smashed on the floor. David turned to the woman, who was standing fearfully by the door at this point, but she suddenly ran off, fleeing him as he chased after her.

"Lady!" he called. "Lady, wait! Do not go outside!"

The woman wasn't listening. She was a little thing, and very fast, and she raced down the steps and out into the darkness where she had last seen her father and sisters were. David was on her heels, taking the first two steps of the staircase before planting his buttocks on the banister and sliding all the way down to the bottom in a swift, slick motion. It was a much faster way to descend the stairs but by the time he got there, the woman was already out in the ward beyond.

As David barreled out of the building, he could see Lyle several feet away with his arms around the woman. There were also several bodies on the ground but there didn't seem to be any more fighting going on. The skirmish was oddly still. David was still holding his sword defensively, blood smeared on his face from his bloody nose, as he made his way cautiously into yard. He could see le Bec and Marion in the darkness, instructing David's men to gather their wounded.

"David!" Lyle called over to him. "You have my thanks. I am indebted to you for saving my daughter!"

He was indicating the woman in his arms and David pointed at her with his sword. "Is she well?" he asked.

Lyle nodded, greatly relieved. "She seems to be."

David simply nodded, his gaze moving over the blond figure being smothered by Lyle, before his mind moved to his wounded soldiers and away from the woman he'd just saved. His thoughts were moving on to the prince and his cohorts, and what more havoc they would wreak that night.

"I would suggest you retreat to your rooms and not try to leave this night," he said to the earl. "It is not safe for travel. Consider it in the morning if you must but for now, take your daughters back inside and bolt them in. Put your men out in the corridor on watch and do not let anyone up those stairs that you do not know. If you need assistance, send one of your men to me or to Chris. We will come."

Lyle was still holding the young woman tightly, looking at the carnage around them. "It is like this with all of Richard's supporters this night," he said, dread in his tone. "I have been fortunate and I pray that others are as well."

David was looking around, too, watching as his soldiers helped the two of his men who seemed to have been wounded. He nodded wearily. "As do I," he said. "I am on to check on William Marshal and others, including Derby and Bath. I fear what may have befallen them this night. Oh… and, my lord?"

Lyle paused to look at him. "What is it, David?"

David lifted a pale eyebrow. "Reconsider leaving Windsor altogether," he said. "Now, more than ever, we must band together. If we do not, we weaken, and John will succeed gaining ground against Richard. Send the women away if you must, but now is not the time for you to leave."

Lyle knew that but he was concerned with his daughters. Still, David had a point. "I will consider it," he said.

That wasn't good enough for David. "There is a tournament on the morrow," he said. "That is when we must show John his attempts to weaken us have failed. He must know that he cannot defeat Richard's supporters. *You* must be there."

Lyle understood the logic behind that. It was why he had come to London in the first place, to attend the tourney in support of the king. Even though it was John's tournament, it was essential that Richard's presence was heavily felt and now, with the king rumored missing, it was more important than ever. Reluctantly, Lyle sighed.

"Very well," he said. "I will be there."

With a curt but reassuring nod, David fled. Lyle watched the man go, still hugging his daughter, who had been struggling to pull herself together. She was a strong lass, but still, the events had shaken her. Now, she stood quietly as she watched the powerful young knight and his men move off into the darkness. They were heading back to the middle ward, back to where some of Richard's supporters had been lodged. She sniffled.

"Who *was* that, Papa?" she asked.

Lyle watched David walk away until the darkness swallowed him. Then, still clutching his daughter, he went to the carriage and opened the door, ushering out the younger pair.

"That was David de Lohr," he told her. "You will remember that I have spoken the name. His brother, Christopher de Lohr, is the king's champion and, mayhap, the most powerful knight in the realm right now. He and his brother have recently returned from the Holy Land and John is not pleased by this. He was hoping that Christopher and David would never return."

Two young women, heavily wrapped in expensive cloaks, climbed from the carriage as the earl's men began to gather around them, collecting baggage, preparing to move the earl and his family back into their lodgings for the night. Even though the battle was over, the sense of fear had not left them. The group was moving swiftly, back into the old residence block. They were determined to make it back inside as de Lohr had instructed, to safety, until John and his assassins had their fill of whatever blood they were seeking and crawled back into their dark and savage holes for the night. Quickly and quietly, they moved.

"Must we really leave, Papa?" one of the younger girls asked. "You only just brought us here. We have never been to Windsor before and I do not want to leave so soon!"

Lyle, who still had Emilie in his arms, looked at his daughter in horror. "Your sister was nearly ravaged, men were injured, and still you do not want to leave?" he scolded. "Are you truly so foolish?"

The middle daughter, at sixteen, hung her head sheepishly as soldiers hurried the family back into the building, back to the four rooms they'd been assigned when they arrived. There was no more talk at that point, only the desire to reach safety. Lyle managed to usher his three daughters back into the single chamber they shared, a rather small room but cozy. It was good enough for the three girls with a very big bed to sleep on.

Once the women were safely away, Lyle retreated to a sitting room to discuss the events of the night with his men and plan for their future at Windsor, if any. Lyle fortunately hadn't lost any men in the attack but there were a few who were wounded; mostly gashes that were tended. As he talked, his men listened, and eventually they prayed, grateful for their lives that night.

It could have been much, much worse.

As the men prayed and talked in the antechamber, the three girls who were now back in their chamber were laboring to calm themselves after their harrowing experience. As Nathalie and Elise retreated to the big bed and hugged each other fearfully, Emilie lingered over near the window that overlooked the darkened lower ward.

Emilie....

A lovely girl with a little nose, small but curvy lips, and brown eyes of enormous proportion, she was very doll-like and porcelain in her appearance. She had a decidedly delicate façade but behind that angelic beauty was the heart of iron and a will greater than that of the king himself. She had proven that only moments ago when John's guards had tried to ravage her. She fought and kicked, and would not let them have their way. Emilie Adalind Letizia Hampton, in spite of her size, was nothing to be trifled with.

Along with the will of iron, she had steady nerves as well. She wasn't easily rattled. As her sisters huddled together, frightened, Emilie simply stood by the window as she reflected on the events of the evening.

That knight....

Emilie lingered on the warrior who had saved her, a man she'd never seen before until that very night in the heat of battle. Of course, she'd heard the name de Lohr from her father, many times, as one of the greatest houses in England, but she'd never actually seen a de Lohr. They were elusive and legendary, these de Lohrs, mythical men like Arthur and Galahad. Not that she'd seen much of her savior in the darkness other than cropped blond hair and a lightning speed she'd never witnessed in any man. When he'd burst into the room where she'd been trying to evade John's men, she'd caught an indication of that impressive flash of movement. Even in those quick actions, there had been something different about him. Mayhap even something intriguing. Too bad she's run from him before she'd realized who he was.

David de Lohr. Odd how just a brief glimpse of the man was enough to peak her interest. Even in the midst of a mortal crisis, she had been drawn to something about him. Emilie had known her share of suitors and she'd even encouraged one. Or maybe even two. But there had also been the de Grez brothers from Rochester. Aye, she'd definitely encouraged them as well, so that would make at least four suitors she had encouraged. But she hadn't been serious about them, much to their dismay. She'd never been serious about any man.

Until now.

Mayhap this night would see that particular opinion changed in the form of David de Lohr. Odd how so brief a glimpse, and in a violent situation nonetheless, has changed it.

In spite of the aggression they'd suffered that night, and in spite of the fear in the air, they weren't leaving Windsor. There was a tournament on the horizon that her father had promised to attend in order to show support for Richard. David de Lohr would undoubtedly be there. He'd suggested sending the women away, but Emilie wasn't going to let that happen. If David was attending, she would be as well. A power-mad prince wasn't going to change that.

She wasn't leaving.

Smiling, Emilie turned away from the window.

CHAPTER TWO

The next day

*T*HE MORNING DAWNED *bright and clear, unusual for the time of year but very pleasing to the occupants of Windsor. There was a cool breeze lifting the banners about the tournament field as the grounds came alive with knights and servants, groomsmen and squires, all preparing for the exciting day ahead.*

Christopher de Lohr had risen and bathed in the antechamber so as to not wake his wife. His squire and two other young boys sat in the corner polishing the rust from his armor. His wife's monkey, George, ever curious, had followed Christopher into the room and sat perched on a chair as the baron bathed, screaming a monkey scream when Christopher flicked water at him and drawing laughter from the boys.

Christopher donned his breeches and heavy linen shirt, pulling on his boots, as one of Dustin's maids brought the morning meal into the room, followed closely by David. His brother had brought his own squire and soon four boys sat in the corner polishing two sets of armor.

"How is Dustin?" David yawned, breaking apart a hunk of cheese.

"Still asleep," Christopher replied, drinking a warmed mulled wine brew. "What about you? Did you get any sleep?"

"About an hour," David replied. "Marcus probably didn't sleep at all. He is devastated with his cousin's passing."

Christopher grunted in sympathy, sipping at his cup. "David, I made some decisions last night," he said. "With the uncertainty of Richard's future, I have decided to leave Windsor. I am afraid that last night was only a foretaste of what is to come."

David nodded. "That is wise," he said. "Dustin shouldn't be here with John and Ralph on the prowl. They came for her last night, you know. She belongs back at Lioncross."

"She's not going back to Lioncross," Christopher said, noting the expression of surprise on his brother's face. "David, when John goes through with his plans to seize the throne, and have no doubt that he will, Richard's loyalists will be his first targets. Lioncross is too close to London to be safe for my wife."

"So… what?" David wanted to know. "Where will you send her?"

Christopher took a healthy drink of his brew. "With Marcus to his home of Somerhill."

David eyed him warily. "Chris, what are you talking about?"

Christopher sat forward, his expression grim. "David, John is raising a mercenary army and the justices believe he intends to forcibly seize Richard's holdings, especially now that Richard is missing," he said in a lowered tone. "Obviously, if that happens, you and I and all of Richard's troops will move to halt him and civil war will ensue. I intend that Dustin should be as far away as possible, with Marcus, at Somerhill."

"Marcus will not be fighting with us?" David demanded, his emotions running high as usual.

"With his arm useless? I would not allow it," Christopher said.

"But you will allow him to protect your wife, to be with her day in and day out, while you defend Richard's throne?" David hissed. "You may save your king's throne, but you may also lose your wife in the process. Think on it, Chris. Marcus loves Dustin and in your absence, you know what could happen."

"It will not," Christopher snapped quietly, eyeing the squires in the corner. "Dustin is my wife and she loves me. I will have to trust them both, David. What else can I do?"

"*Send her to Lohrham. Or to Bath,*" *David insisted.* "*Jesus, Chris, do not send her into the wilds with Marcus. You shall never get her back.*"

Christopher sat back in his chair, his expression icy. "*I have made my decision, David. I must do what's best for my wife.*"

David acted as if it was his own wife being sent away. "*You are wrong.*"

Before they could argue the subject further, the door to the bed-chamber opened. The men turned to see Dustin, Christopher's wife, standing in the doorway.

"*You are back,*" *she said, her focus on Christopher.* "*I thought I heard your voice.*"

"*Dustin,*" *Christopher said as he got out of his chair.* "*You shouldn't be up, sweetheart.*"

She met him halfway, throwing herself into his arms. He hugged her deeply and then tried to swing her into his arms, but she protested with a grunt of pain.

"*I am sorry,*" *he said gravely, lowering her back to the ground.* "*I did not mean to hurt you, sweet.*"

"*I am fine, really,*" *she said, but she was pale. Then she glanced over at David.* "*Good morn, David.*"

Before David could answer her, Christopher lifted her gingerly. "*Back to bed with you, lady. That leg requires rest to heal.*"

Her brow furrowed. "*The physician said it is not too deep and I do not feel like staying in bed. The tournament is today.*"

"*No tournament for you,*" *he said firmly, swinging her back into the bedchamber.*

"*But, Chris,*" *she protested, gripping his neck tightly to prevent him from laying her down on the bed.* "*My leg will heal. The physician stitched it and wrapped it tightly, and I can walk on it. I must get ready for the tournament.*"

David listened to them argue, hearing Dustin challenge and com-plain and cajole in response to Christopher's firm denials. When

Dustin got mad and called him a less-than-ladylike name, David shot a reproachful glare to the gigglers in the corner. The sun rose steadily and the fight ensued, much to David's amusement.

As he sat there listening to his brother's wife rant, it occurred to him how much this woman had become a part of their lives. Not just Christopher's, but his as well. It was as if she had always been a part of their lives and he almost could not remember what it was like before she graced them with her light.

His infatuation with her had banked to respectful appreciation, but he had to admit he was fiercely protective of her when it came to Marcus. Mayhap it was jealousy, but whatever the case, he didn't trust Marcus where Dustin was concerned, and he thought his brother's intention to send Dustin north with the new baron to be foolish.

The door to the bedchamber suddenly slammed shut with a re-sounding noise, rattling the utensils on the table before him. Even with the door closed, he could hear Dustin shouting and Christopher's even responses. David took a last swig of wine and rose, going across the room to see how his armor was coming along. The squires, proud of their work, displayed the shiny pieces for him.

Something banged heavily in the other room and he heard Dustin yelling loudly. He couldn't really make out her words, but whatever they were, they were angry. Casually, he held his arms out while his squire pulled his hauberk on, acting as if there was nothing unusual occurring at all. But the young squires had big eyes as the banging and shouting continued. David thought it all rather comical.

He finished dressing, including the tunic bearing Christopher's colors. This was a newer tunic, made a few days ago when he had tunics made for Marcus, Dud and Trent. David wondered if Marcus would even be wearing colors today, even though he would be acting as Dustin's escort. And he had no doubt Lady de Lohr was coming, although he pondered the question of whether or not she would award trophies.

Time was passing and they had to get to the tournament field to begin preparations. He knew that the other knights were most likely already there, but he hesitated to leave without Christopher. The fight coming from the bedchamber had grown suspiciously quiet and he suspected it was either because Dustin was crying or because Christopher was making mad love to her.

David waited about as long as he dared, finally donning his helmet and heading for the door just as the bedchamber door opened and Christopher exited, not looking the least bit sheepish.

"Well? Is she coming?" David demanded, fumbling with his gloves.

Christopher shot him an impatient glance as he went to his squire. "She is," he said, forcing the words out. "Go and make sure the preparations are complete. I shall escort my wife down to the field."

David snorted and Christopher glared at him menacingly, conveying silent threats of pain and death to his brother should he laugh at him. David bit his lip and feigned a serious look.

"Edward and Leeton are at the field, I am sure," he said, fighting off a bad attack of the giggles. "I shall wait for you and your lovely wife."

Christopher ignored him as his squire helped him with his armor. Dustin's two fat maids bustled in and out of the bedchamber, carrying in hot water and linens and other things. The young squires sitting against the wall watched with great interest as the women scurried in and out, back and forth, digging into the massive wardrobe in the antechamber at one point and retreating with a pile of cloaks.

"How is her leg?" David asked, watching the competent young squire handle Christopher's leg armor.

"'A mere scratch, she says, to quote a more experienced warrior," he replied, shaking his leg to adjust the greave. The armor settled down over his boot. "If she bleeds to death up in the lists, then it is her own fault."

"Are you going to let her award trophies?" his brother inquired.

Christopher tugged at the tunic as his squire straightened his breastplate. "I already told her that she could," he said, looking at

David. "As much as I loathe the idea of her anywhere near John and Ralph, there is naught they can do to her with Marcus by her side or with thousands of people as witness."

David stood with his legs braced apart, arms crossed, watching the squire finish his brother's dress. David had seen his brother in armor for as long as he could remember, and words that came to mind this day were imposing... indestructible... power... fearless. Defender of the Realm and Richard's Champion. His brother was all of those and more.

"Chris, with all of the excitement, I forgot to tell you that Deborah is here," David said after a few moments. "I saw her in the dining hall last eve. She's a damn woman grown; I never would have recognized her if she hadn't come to me first."

"Deborah?" Christopher looked surprised, then nodded with sudden understanding. "Of course; how could I have not realized? The Earl of Bath is here. Christ, I shall have to seek her out and see if your words are true. How old is she now – seventeen? By the way, have you seen anyone from Lohrham?"

"Nay," David answered. "They probably arrived late yesterday, as did the rest of the competitors who weren't already here." He grinned suddenly. "It shall be a rout, Chris. Lohrham's knights are all old warriors who fought with father and Uncle Philip. There are only a few worthy knights in the contest worthy of your skills, most of them having recently returned from the quest."

"And not even they can defeat me," Christopher said with customary arrogance, as casually as if he were discussing the weather. "You are correct in your observation, little brother. This tourney will be a rout for Richard's forces."

His squire was securing his sword when Dustin entered the antechamber. All male eyes in the room, young and old alike, were glued to her like flies to honey. She wore a surcoat of rich royal blue silk, the same color as Christopher's tunic. The flattering lines along her bosom and shoulders brought out the beauty of her neck and torso, and she *had pulled her hair back softly to reveal her heart-shaped face.*

She smiled as she approached her husband, noticeably limping. "Do you like it? It matches your colors."

Christopher was deeply pleased. He smiled faintly, touching her gently under the chin. "The color makes your eyes as dark as storm clouds," he said softly. "Aye, I like it a great deal. Never have my colors looked so good."

She grinned triumphantly and Christopher had to chuckle; she was always as happy as a child when she got her way.

"Thank you, my lord," she curtsied coyly, lowering her lashes. She was becoming quite practiced with her feminine gestures, for they came naturally to her.

Christopher grinned openly at her, holding out his hands for his squire to pull on his gauntlets. Dustin stepped back as the tall lad silently and deftly pulled on the gloves. She eyed the young man curiously, now at close range. She had never been this close to him before and she was interested.

"I have never met your squire, Chris," she said. "Would you introduce us?"

Christopher looked as if the idea had never occurred to him. The squire stopped what he was doing, his cheeks flushing bright red as he looked up at his liege.

"Darren, this is my wife, the Lady Dustin de Lohr." He looked at his wife and turned the boy to face her. "Dustin, this is Darren Ainsley, son of Lord Robert Ainsley. Darren served with me three years on the quest. His father served Richard."

Dustin nodded to the embarrassed young man. "Is your father still in the Holy Land?"

The poor squire looked as if he were going to die from sheer fright. "Nay, my lady, he perished over a year ago," he answered, his voice cracking.

"How terrible," Dustin said sincerely. "Then it would seem that you and I have something in common."

"Aye, my lady," the boy nodded rapidly, his eyes too shy to meet hers.

"How old are you, Darren?" she asked.

"Seventeen, my lady," he replied, then added, "I was sent to foster at Lohrham Forest when I was seven years old. Lord Christopher took me as his squire when I was twelve."

Dustin smiled at him and Christopher felt the boy sway under his grip. As amusing as it was to witness Darren's abject terror, time was pressing.

"If you are ready, then, we shall proceed to the field," Christopher said.

As Dustin nodded, he let go of Darren, positive the lad would collapse without the support. He didn't, but bolted for the corner as if he had been burned, gathering Christopher's weapons and shield hastily. Christopher had to smile to himself; he barely remembered the same fear when he had been a lad barely over the threshold of manhood, speaking to a beautiful woman for the first time. But no woman he had ever seen nor spoken to had ever compared with his wife, so he felt doubly sorry for Darren on that account.

"Do you think I will need my cloak? I do not think I will need it." Dustin was chattering at David, who simply shrugged.

"Bring it," Christopher ordered. "The day may grow chilly."

"But the sun is shining," Dustin pointed out, "and this silk is heavy. I will not need my cloak."

Christopher picked up the deep blue cloak and threw it at her. "Take it."

She dropped it on the floor purely from spite, smoothing her surcoat primly. "I do not want to," she said disagreeably. "The silk is warm enough. Besides, it will cover up this lovely dress and I want to show it off."

He glared threateningly at her, about to suggest that her surcoat gave an ample view of her lovely breasts and that the cloak would cover her from lustful eyes, but he didn't want to upset her. Instead, he *sighed heavily and picked the cloak up.*

"Take it or you do not go," he said in a low, even tone. She scowled but took it, for she was wary of the level of his voice.

The squires preceded them from the room, the boys laden with Christopher and David's shields as well other implements. Dustin fastened the cloak around her shoulders and took David and Christopher's arms. Outside in the hall were a full company of soldiers lining the walls, snapping to attention when they exited from the antechamber and Dustin startled at the loud salute as they greeted the baron. They were all Christopher's troops, their sharp blue and gold tunics indicating such, their mail polished to a sheen.

It was extremely impressive, even to her. Twenty-four soldiers escorted her, Christopher and David down from the apartments and through the bulk of the castle. There were very few people in the castle, most of them either getting ready for the tournament or already down at the field, and the cadence of synchronized bootfalls echoed loudly in the cavernous halls as they made their way outside.

Dustin gripped the elbows of the two knights, almost running to keep up with the pace that had been set, and her chest was swelling with the enormous pride she was feeling. She could not keep the cocky smile from her lips.

She glanced up at her husband, so tall and strong and powerful, that he was nearly surreal. His helmet was on and his visor lifted and it was impossible to see most of his face, but she stared at him anyway. She could not describe the pride filling her veins, proud that he was hers, that all of this loyalty was theirs, that her husband and his knights were the envy of the whole of Windsor.

"How's your leg?" his helmeted head looked down at her.

Truth was, it ached a great deal but she forced a smile. "Not too bad."

"Are we walking too fast for you?" he asked.

She didn't want to be a bother, especially when she had put up such a fuss earlier. But her expression gave her away and before she could answer he was barking orders at the sergeant to slow the pace. Slower, and much better for her, they continued on to the arena.

The lists were already filling up with women in gaily decorated dressed and men with brightly colored tunics and shoes. The royal box was decorated with flowers and ribbons and silks, but John and Ralph were nowhere to be seen.

THAT WAS WHERE DAVID had departed from his brother. As soon as his brother's wife was settled in the lists to watch the coming spectacle, that was David's clue to go about his business. Dustin was with Marcus, precisely where she should not be, while Christopher pretended that is best friend did not lust after her. But in David's opinion, while Marcus watched over Dustin, someone needed to watch over Marcus. That was his fierce protectiveness of her talking again.

But he kept his mouth shut about it. It was frustrating for David to watch, as his priority was his brother. He only wanted the best for the man but it seemed as if Christopher resisted him at every turn these days, as if nothing he could say or do was right. Once, Christopher had even accused his brother of being jealous of the relationship between Christopher and his wife. Perhaps that had been true once. Perhaps it still was; David infatuation had banked to a healthy appreciation but it wasn't gone completely. Still, Dustin had enough attention from Burton. She certainly didn't need David's attention, too.

David headed down the stairs of the lists, moving out into the avenue that was busy this morning because of the coming games. He was coming to think that he was the only one seeing things clearly these days, but his brother didn't think so. Christopher was caught up in too many things at the moment, a new wife being the least of the issues. As they had seen last night, John was starting to make his grab for power now that Richard had been declared missing. It was only a matter of time before things grew worse.

They would have to be on their guard constantly from now on.

And that included the tournament slated for today. David never even had the chance to tell his brother what had happened with Lyle Hampton the night before, but he supposed it really didn't matter in the grand scheme of things. What mattered was the tournament that the prince had scheduled before he even knew of Richard's disappearance because they were all coming to suspect the prince would now use the event to display his might and mastery of England. He would display what kind of ruler he was about to become, a ruler who found gladness in his brother's absence.

A man who was ready to conquer.

And that meant conquering Richard's loyalists, who had come to London for the tournament, the biggest of its kind in many a year. Everyone would be here, competing, and it would be a particular showcase for the House of de Lohr. Being so closely linked to Richard, a man whom both David and Christopher considered a personal friend, it was inevitable that all eyes would be on the big blue de Lohr lion banner as the king's champion took on the prince's henchmen. David was ready for the competition and he hoped his brother was, too. But he feared the man's attention would be divided with a new wife in the lists. And divided attention could be deadly.

Women.

David shook his head at the idea of just how much a woman could distract a man. Of course, he wasn't *that* kind of man. There was no woman on earth beautiful enough or luscious enough to distract him. He had a will of iron and was a knight to the bone, a de Lohr, which meant he came from a long line of knights. including an ancestor who had come to the shores of England with William, Duke of Normandy.

The House of de Lohr went way back, into the age of Darkness, into that time when men fought men with disorganization and raw brutality, men who ruled their own small kingdoms amidst a land that was ruled by many such men. Even then, in those dark days, the House of de Lohr of Forneaux-le-Val was a powerful house to deal with, and even the Duke of Normandy, a man known also as William the Bastard, took notice. It was William who coaxed the de Lohrs to follow him, and follow they did.

They were still following William's descendants. The House of de Lohr and the crown of England were synonymous with each other. Therefore, unlike his brother, David wasn't apt to let something like a woman get between him and his duty as a knight. The mere thought that a de Lohr should be so distracted was shocking.

Lost in thought, David walked down the avenue. As he walked, pondering what was to come this day, he happened to catch a glimpse of another knight heading in his direction.

David recognized the figure. This October day was cold and bright, and he lifted his hand to shield his eyes from the sunlight as Brentford le Bec headed in his direction. A tall man with dark hair and bright blue eyes, le Bec was an excellent knight and someone David had known for years. That friendship had come in handy last night when le Bec had helped him go after those who had attacked Christopher's wife. David lifted his chin in greeting when le Bec lifted a hand.

"How is your brother's wife this morning?" Brentford asked.

David threw a thumb in the direction of the lists. "She seems to be well enough," he said. "She is already in the lists, waiting for the tournament. Chris is talking about sending her away from London after this, someplace safe, until this situation calms. He fears for her safety with John's unpredictability."

Brentford cocked an eyebrow. "From what I hear, your brother and the Earl of Canterbury were lucky last night," he said. "I heard this morning that the Earl of Norwich and the Earl of Warkworth both lost men last night. Norwich's sister was even badly injured."

David grunted unhappily. "Jesus," he cursed softly. "What of your liege, Lord Derby? Did he suffer serious damage?"

Brentford shook his head. "Fortunately, we did not," he said. "And, as you saw last night, neither did Bath or William Marshal. But I have heard that several lesser barons left early this morning, unwilling to compete and in fear of their safety. Today's tournament maybe lightly attended."

David simply shrugged although he was disheartened to hear that Richard's ranks would be low. "Possibly," he said. "I am going to tend to my horse even now and take a look at the field conditions. Maybe we can see just how many of Richard's supporters have remained. Will you come with me?"

Brentford went along. The wind was starting to pick up, tossing dead leaves about in the street as they passed by businesses and homes, as there was a substantial town built up around Windsor. There were other knights in town, men of nobility, moving to and from the castle on their business, and there were vendors in the street trying to catch all of the spectators as they headed to the tournament field. Old women sat on the side of the road, selling cheap favors for the women to give to knights.

In spite of the harrowing night, the mood of the day was somewhat festive. A tournament such as this was rare in these times and there was a steady trickle in from the countryside as people arrived in town for the festivities. As David and Brentford progressed down the avenue to a gated area that would give way to the east end of the tournament field, they were focused on some of the knights of various houses they were seeing, men who had a particularly dark look about them. They were nearing the eastern field gate when they heard a voice coming from behind.

"David!"

David and Brentford came to a pause, turning to see a man with dark hair and golden-hazel eyes jogging up behind them. Sir Edward de Wolfe, also one of Christopher's close friends and a knight in the de Lohr entourage, came to a halt when he reached David and bent over, breathing heavily and coughing. When he stood up, it was with his hand over his heart.

"God's Bones," he grunted. "I have been running all the way from the castle."

David frowned. "I thought you were already at the field," he said. "Who is seeing to the men?"

Edward coughed and gasped. "Leeton," he said. "He has the men in hand. One de Lohr knight is enough. He did not need me there as well."

David was still frowning. "Were have you been, then?"

Edward wiped the sweat from his brow. "Back at Windsor," he said. "God's Bones, I should not have run that entire way. I am not meant to exert myself so."

David shook his head, unsympathetic, and continued walking with Edward and Brentford now following. "Poor Edward," he said sarcastically. "You are not much good for anything. But you had better do well in the tournament today. Much depends on it."

Edward was still out of breath as he followed. "Possibly more than you know," he said. "I've heard rumor this morning that John has hired mercenaries to compete as legitimate knights. He's paying them gold crowns to badly injure or kill Richard's supporters."

David came to a halt, as did Brentford. Both men stared at Edward in horror. "Are you certain of this?" David hissed.

Edward nodded, his mood turning serious as the weight of his message settled. "I just heard it from one of William Marshal's men," he said. "The Marshal will not be in attendance this day. He has business to attend to."

"I suspected as much," David said pensively. "I wonder if he will send word to Eleanor after what happened last night?"

Edward cocked an eyebrow. "She is the mother of both Richard and John, and technically ruling in Richard's stead," Edward replied. "She will want to know of John's attempt against Richard's supporters last night. I cannot believe she would be completely oblivious to his actions, but in any case, William sent one of his men to find Chris to tell him of John's mercenary knights but the man found me instead. That is why I was running to catch up with you and Chris – you both could quite possibly be facing an assassin today on horseback. God only knows what those bastards will do in the mass competition, fighting dirty whilst other men fight with honor. You know that the prince approached Marcus to champion him, do you not?"

David nodded grimly. "Aye," he said. "Marcus told us everything last night before Chris' wife was attacked. I am very aware that the prince has been trying to divide and conquer Chris' men, starting with Chris' best friend."

Edward lifted his eyebrows ominously. "Thank God he has not been successful," he said. "Even so, his subversion has cost Marcus the use of his right hand for now."

Brentford, who had thus far been listening carefully, interrupted. "What happened to Burton?" he asked. "Why did he lose the use of his hand?"

David looked at him. "It is very complex," he said, "but suffice it to say that John wanted Burton's service so badly that he offered him a barony to leave Chris and represent the prince in today's tournament. Burton accepted the offer because it was quite generous, but right after he accepted, he smashed his hand into the wall and broke nearly ever bone in it."

Brentford was shocked. "Sweet Lord," he murmured. "Why would he do such a thing?"

David had distress in his features. "For one very good reason," he said. "He would not be forced to compete against my brother. A crippled knight cannot complete, you see, and the prince, unaware that Marcus deliberately broke his hand so he would be unable to compete against Chris, cannot take back the barony because if he does, it will look as if he purposely bribed Burton with it. Therefore, he cannot rescind his offer or all will know he only gave the man the title to coerce his loyalty."

Brentford listened to the explanation, shaking his head with disgust. "But we all know it was a bribe," he pointed out. "Did he not think Burton would tell others of the offer?"

David shrugged. "Possibly," he said. "But even if Burton tells of the prince's bribery attempt, John will deny it. It will be his word against Burton's."

In that case, it meant that the prince, being royalty, would be believed overall, including a reputable knight. Brentford was appalled. "Is there nothing that bastard won't do in order to see Richard's supporters defeated?" he asked rhetorically. "Now he has sucked Marcus Burton into his scheme and lies."

Edward spoke this time, his gaze moving to David. "Chris' brother will be next," he muttered, hazard in his tone. "He wants you, David. With Marcus out of contention, his next target will be you."

David was unimpressed. "He has yet to approach me because he knows what I will do if he does," he said, resuming his walk to the field. "He will be fortunate if I do not cut his head off before the words are even out of his mouth."

Edward, the most sensible and least likely to act before thinking of the de Lohr stable of knights, glanced at Brentford as he followed David down the sloping avenue. What David said was not a boast; it was the truth. David, more than any of them, was fearlessly unpredictable. He possessed bravery few men did and they all knew it.

"He knows," Edward said quietly. "But be on your guard nonetheless, David. John is displaying his muscle for all to see."

David was well aware of that. "What of Ralph?" he asked. "Has anyone seen him since last night?"

Edward shook his head. "Nay," he said. "No one has seen any sign of Nottingham. I would be surprised if Ralph showed himself to day much less compete on the prince's behalf after the beating Christopher gave him yesterday. And something tells me that John's attacks last night might have also been in retaliation for said beating."

David nodded, remembering the day before when Ralph had not only insulted his brother's wife but had also killed one of her dogs. It had been a nasty confrontation and Christopher, like any good husband, had beaten the sheriff within an inch of the man's life. Yesterday's beating, as well as John's thirst for Richard's throne, all played a part in last night's attacks. The politics of England these days were complicated as well as deadly.

"Aye," he said slowly, with labored thought. "I have considered that as well. Vengeance for the beating my brother gave Ralph."

"I would say that was as good a reason as any to attack Richard's supporters last night," Edward said. "Punishment on behalf of Fitz Walter. In any case, we must all be on our guard. I have a feeling this may get worse before it gets any better."

At that point, there was nothing more to say on the subject. The stakes were higher than they'd ever been and there was a sense of apprehension as well as a sense of determination. The knights all knew what needed to be done. Therefore, David shifted his focus towards the sea of tents to the east of the tournament field. Many great houses had come for this tournament and with Windsor already full, men had taken to creating a tent city in the meadows and marshes east of the tournament field.

David, Brentford, and Edward stood at a fork in the avenues by the eastern gate, a vantage point by which to see the tournament field as it nestled in a meadow not far from the River Thames. With the clear weather, the vista of the countryside was quite impressive, and clear, and they could see dozens of tents off to the east.

Men and horses milled about the tents as great houses such as Derby and Bath, Warkworth, Ashford, and Gloucester prepared. Banners were snapping in the brisk breeze, identifying the different factions, and David realized that most of the standards he saw were of men loyal to Richard. Given what had happened the night before, and what could still happen, he thought it best to venture into the encampments and speak with some of the men. No telling what would come up this day and David thought it best to be prudent.

To warn them.

But what David didn't know was that, at the moment, he too was being watched by a very predatory animal.

A woman.

THE SURCOAT WAS a dark, rich red, the color of currants, made from the finest wool. The bodice was tight, embroidered with golden thread that her nurse had so lovingly stitched. This was the same nurse who would spit profusely when she spoke, spraying everyone and everything within range. Still, she was a loving woman and whenever Emilie wore the garment, she thought of Nurse Lillibet.

Lillibet had been a novice nun before Emilie's mother had acquired her services as a nurse, and she had literally raised Emilie and her sisters. In fact, Emilie had looked upon Lillibet as her mother more than the woman who gave birth to her, a rather sickly woman who died when Elise, the youngest sister, had been an infant. The girls even called Lillibet 'Mother' although she really wasn't.

It was an odd dynamic but it was how they felt about the woman, and no one ever really spoke of Lady Willow de Norville Hampton these days. Her memory was long gone, now an emotionless reflection and little more, although Lyle had mentioned on more than one occasion that Emilie looked a great deal like her. Sometimes Emilie even saw something in his eyes when he looked at her, a hint of the love he'd once had for his Willow. But the look was quickly gone and it was something Lyle never discussed, especially since he had taken Lillibet to his bed and thought his girls didn't know about it.

But they knew. It was impossible not to know in the close-knit world of Canterbury Castle. Lyle had been taking his children's nurse to his bed for as long as the girls could remember, until they were old enough to understand what was occurring between their father and their nurse. Only when an elderly house servant pointed out the obvious were their suspicions confirmed. In fact, Emilie was fairly certain that Lillibet had been pregnant a few years ago because the woman put on weight around her mid-section and then went away for a time, to visit her father she had said, and returned quite slender a couple of months later. But no mention was ever made of any child and neither Emilie or her sisters saw the need to bring it up. It was an open secret they never discussed, for they loved Lillibet very much.

In fact, Emilie's gaze was fondly on Lillibet at this moment as she sat in the carriage that was festooned with regalia from the House of Hampton. Lillibet was sitting towards the rear of the carriage with two big slobbering dogs and Elise, the youngest daughter who had seen fourteen years, pointing out the sights of the village to her. Lillibet would point, spit would fly from her lips, and Elise would simply wipe her cheek off. It was simply a normal conversation when it came to Lillibet, something all of the girls were used to.

"I am so glad Papa decided to remain at Windsor," Nathalie, the middle sister, leaned over and muttered to her sister. "After what happened last night, I was positive we would be leaving this morning. I would be heartbroken to miss seeing all of the knights today."

Emilie's focus came away from the dogs, Lillibet, and Elise to look at her sister. Tall, brunette, and pretty, Nathalie had just turned sixteen years of age in the summer, and at this point in her life everything revolved around men. It was all she spoke of. Therefore, the subject she spoke of was not unexpected.

"Papa is fearful for our safety," Emilie said, looking to her father riding astride his big brown horse up by the wagon driver. "But he promised David de Lohr that he would not leave, so that is why we remained. Also, Papa and Brick very much to compete in the tournament so I think it was difficult to pass on the opportunity to see victory for the House of Hampton in front of the whole of England."

Nathalie leaned her head out of the wagon, looking up to the head of the column where her father's commander, Sir Brickley de Dere, was riding astride his feisty roan charger. The animal was muzzled, and controlled with a heavy bit, but he was still giving Brickley a good deal of trouble. The big knight was wrestling with him. She sighed dreamily.

"I should very much like to see Brick win today," she said to her sister. Then, she leaned in on Emilie. "Do you think he will carry my favor? I am coming to think that he may have some interest in me, you know. He smiled at me this morning and he does not usually do that."

Emilie looked at her sister, trying not to smile at her hopeful tone. "Brick is much older than you are," she said tactfully. "In fact, his son is Elise's age. I do not think he is looking for another wife. I have told you this and so has Papa."

Nathalie would not be deterred. "His wife died six years ago," she said. "You would think the man would be ready by now."

Emilie patted her sister's hand. "You cannot blame him," she said. "It is hard to think of you as wifely material after years of practical jokes on the man. That is what he knows of you, Nat."

Nathalie turned her nose up at her sister primly and looked away. "I do not do such things any longer," she said. "I am a woman now. Women do not do such things."

Emilie knew that wasn't exactly true. Nathalie and Elise were both known to do terrible things to the men of Canterbury Castle, such as pulling strings across doorways to watch them trip or putting bees into the pockets of unsuspecting soldiers. Lyle would yell at them, punish them by confining them to their chambers for a day, but he had never been particularly hard on his daughters in any case. The result was that Nathalie and Elise were much feared among the inhabitants of Canterbury, mostly because their pranks could be vicious, but the earl didn't seem to care.

It was something that Nathalie was trying to outgrow. Sixteen years of age was a pivotal age, a young woman in fact, and she didn't want to be treated like a child any longer. But that childish streak was still in her. Emilie realized it even if Nathalie didn't.

"Give Brick time, sweetheart," Emilie said. "If you are truly serious about him, then it will take time. He must look at you as a young woman and not a child, and that will not be an easy thing for him."

Nathalie wasn't particularly comforted by that. Frustrated, she crossed her arms irritably and looked out over the town, watching the villagers go about their business. It was a colorless little village peppered with business and residences. Nathalie peered at a man with dancing dogs as the carriage lurched past, something even Elise was greatly interested in when she caught sight if it. Elise even pointed out the dancing canines to the two big dogs that sat on either side of her in the carriage, as if the dogs knew what she was talking about. They were spoiled beasts that belonged to the youngest Hampton sister, and they even ate at the family table.

Nathalie watched her sister kiss and hug the big dogs for a moment before her attention fell upon a rather large merchant with all manner of goods hanging on the exterior of his business. Pre-made dresses, cloaks, and other things caught her eye. Along with men, Nathalie was also greatly interested in pretty things. She cried out to her father.

"Papa!" she said. "May we stop, please? Look at that merchant! Look at his wonderful things!"

Lyle heard Nathalie's voice and turned to see what had his daughter so excited. The sun was bright on this clear fall day and he had to shield his eyes from the glare in order to see what she was pointing at. It was then he saw the large merchant with his wares displayed and, as Emilie also asked to stop, he relented without any protest and brought the column to a halt.

Brickley, up at point, directed his foaming beast next to Lyle and, with a few words from his liege, dismounted his horse and handed the reins off to the nearest soldier. The big knight approached the wagon.

"Come along, ladies," he said, unlatching the rear door and shoving the eager dogs aside as they tried to escape. "Come and see if you must. Hurry, now. We have places to go, so do not linger overly."

Nathalie was already up, smiling sweet at Brickley, who took her hand politely and helped her down from the carriage. As she scurried over to the merchant, Emilie was right behind her. Brickley caught sight of the eldest Hampton daughter and his smile turned genuine as he helped her down from the carriage.

"Careful, now," he said to her. "Careful that your sister isn't looking for itching powders or something that magically bursts into flame. She will use that against us."

Emilie laughed softly; she genuinely liked Brickley, a big man, muscular and seasoned, with short brown hair and big blue eyes. He was handsome in a rather mature sort of way and she'd known the man over half her life. He was like family to her.

"I have told you many times, Brick," she said. "Whatever she does to you, you must do it back. No one has ever been brave enough to give her a taste of her own medicine, so whatever she uses against you, give it back to her tenfold. You must learn to fight back."

Brickley snorted. "I would except for the small issue of your father, who might not take kindly to revenge against his daughter," he said. Then, he sobered. "I have not had a chance to ask you how you are feeling this morning after the events of last night. Are you sure you are well?"

Emilie nodded. "I am well," she said, looking at the sorrowful expression on his face. She knew what was on his mind. "Brick, there was nothing you could have done. You were trying to fight off an entire horde of men when I was grabbed. What happened with me was not your fault. I am well, am I not? Everything is fine. You should not feel guilty."

Brickley grunted softly, averting his gaze. "It is my duty to protect you and your sisters," he said. "But David de Lohr had to do it. I cannot help but feel ashamed."

Emilie put her hand on his arm. "Do not," she said. "Let us instead be grateful that we all emerged with our lives. And we should also be grateful that God put David de Lohr in the right place at the right time."

Brickley shrugged; he wasn't ready yet to be comforted from last night's ordeal. As Hampton's commander, he was feeling guilty about the entire thing. He was also feeling the least bit apprehensive about what the day would bring with the prince on the offensive against Richard's supporters. But he nodded because Emilie was nodding. He smiled wanly.

"I suppose you are right," he said. "I did not have the opportunity to thank de Lohr last night. I will do so when I see him today."

The mention of David de Lohr brought back Emilie's interest of the man. In fact, she'd been thinking of him quite heavily this morning, her mysterious savior, and her heart fluttered just a bit at the mention of his name.

"Do you know him, then?" she asked casually.

Brickley nodded. "I knew him before he went on crusade with Richard," he said. "But that was nearly five years ago. I have not seen him since he and his brother returned."

Emilie pretended to be interested without looking like she was very interested. It was a fine line to walk. "Where did you first meet David and his brother?" she asked. "Of course, I have heard the de Lohr name but last night was the first time I ever saw either brother in action. I must say that David was quite impressive when he ran to my defense. He fought of three men with relative ease."

Brickley took her by the elbow and helped her cross the muddy street to towards the merchant stall on the other side, dodging men and horses as they moved.

"David and Chris are younger than I am," he said, watching Emilie grin and then he grinned as well. "I know; *everyone* is younger than I am. That is what you were going to say, isn't it?"

Emilie shook her head. "Of course not," she said. "That would be a terrible thing to say to you."

He cocked a dubious eyebrow. "That has never stopped you before."

Emilie struggled to appear properly contrite although it was all an act. "I know," she said. "I have been very wicked to you in the past. I will try to be better."

He simply shook his head. "Lies," he muttered. Then, he gestured towards the stall. "Go and see if there is anything that interests you. And keep your sister away from anything sharp or dangerous."

He was jesting with her. Emilie glanced at the stall but she was more concerned with their conversation than what her sister might, or might not, be buying to torment the men.

"But you did not tell me where you met David de Lohr," she said. "Where was it?"

Brickley's brow lifted. "Why so curious about de Lohr?"

Emilie didn't want to give herself away, especially not to Brickley. The man was sharp and she was fearful he might tell Lyle, who didn't like the thought of his daughters having interest in any man, not even a knight like David de Lohr. Therefore, she tried to be casual in her reply.

"Because the man saved my life," she said. "I was simply curious to know something about him. Why so reluctant to tell me? Did you meet him in a place you had rather not discuss, Brick?"

He frowned. "Like where, for instance?"

Emilie lowered her voice. "Where you drinking terribly together?" she said. "Were there women involved?"

He laughed. "Nay," he shook his head. "I met David and his brother years ago at a tournament near Kenilworth. In fact, David was not yet a knight at the time; squiring for his brother. It was a very long time ago when Diana and I were newly married."

Diana had been Brickley's wife, a lovely and willowy woman who had died of a cancer. It had been a very sad time for them all, as she had been a sweet woman. Emilie was quite sure that Brickley wasn't over the woman's death, in spite of what Nathalie had said. Sometimes six years wasn't enough to ease the ache, which Emilie was sure of in Brickley's case. He still pined for the wife he lost those years ago.

"A tournament?" Emilie repeated, a glimmer in her eye. "Like the one today? Father is very excited for you to compete."

Brickley grinned as the subject shifted from David de Lohr to him. "I am too old to be competing, but your father is insistent," he said. "I suppose I have no choice."

"Are you not excited about it?"

Brickley shrugged. "I suppose," he said, looking over to the merchant's stall again. "If you are going to look at the wares, you had better do it. Your father's patience is not infinite."

Emilie lifted her shoulders, figuring that he was probably correct, so she turned to look at the first piece of goods hanging on the eaves of the merchant's stall, a heavy brown woolen cloak with a rabbit lining, when she heard Brickley mutter.

"Speak of the devil and he shall appear," he said.

He walked off. Emilie, not sure what he meant, turned to see what had his attention and she caught sight of three knights standing at an intersection several yards away. There was a knight with dark hair, a very tall knight with black hair, and then a shorter knight with cropped blond hair.

She recognized that hair.

Brickley was strolling in the direction of the three knights. *De Lohr!* Emilie thought. Unfortunately, he was far enough away so that she couldn't get a good look at him, just as she couldn't the night before in the darkness. But in spite of that her gaze moved over the man; he was somewhat tall and he was very muscular. He was wearing a dark tunic and leather breeches, with big boots, and no mail or protection of any kind. She could therefore see the size of his arms and shoulders, which were quite broad. He was well-built, to be sure, and the blonde hair glistened in the sunlight. She felt like she was looking at a god of sorts; a pristine, blonde-haired avenging angel that had rescued her the night before.

Emilie very much wanted to meet him but she couldn't be so bold as to ask her father or even Brickley to introduce them. That would be very forward indeed. And she clearly couldn't simply walk up to the man and introduce herself; that simply wasn't done. So she had to think on a way to meet the illustrious David de Lohr without making her look bold or interested or eager. It would have to be natural. It would have to be by chance.

There was truth in the rumor that Emilie Hampton was the most clever and devious out of all the Hampton sisters. She was quite cunning when she wanted to be. She drew on that particular trait at the moment, trying to come up with a plausible but proper way of meeting David de Lohr, before the man moved on and she never had the chance to meet him.

She watched as Brickley approached the three knights, obviously speaking to them, and she watched as David extended a warm hand to Brickley as if quite happy to see the man. Emilie knew for a fact that Brickley would speak to the men a few moments before returning to their party because he didn't like to leave them without his oversight for any length of time. He was very conscientious that way. Therefore, she had to act fast. As she labored to think of something believable, her gaze fell on the dogs in the rear of the carriage.

Elise had left the carriage with Spitting Lillibet at her side, and the two of them were looking over the merchant's wares as the dogs sat in the carriage and gazed forlornly at their mistress. They were insulted that they'd been left in the carriage, when everyone else had climbed out. Passing a casual glance at Elise and Lillibet, she meandered over to the rear of the carriage where the dogs were very happy to see her.

Their names were Cid and Roland, courtesy of Lyle who was himself an educated man, and named the big black beasts after mythical heroes. Cid was slightly bigger than Roland, with a head the size of a cow, but both dogs were from the same litter. Both were as black as coal, and both were loyal companions and great protection for the three Hampton women. In fact, the dogs were much the reason that Nathalie and Elise hadn't been taken the night before when Emilie had been abducted. Emilie had been too close to the door of the carriage and had been an easy target, whilst the other two sisters and the dogs had been further away.

But they were actually very affectionate dogs and they loved Brickley a great deal. Smart as they were, all Emilie had to do was open the carriage door, speak Brickley's name a couple of times, and the dogs ran off for the man.

Pretending they had just escaped, Emilie followed.

CHAPTER THREE

ALL HE COULD see was teeth.

Well, teeth and drool. David realized he was looking into the mouths of two very big black dogs who were running at him, eagerly crossing the avenue, barreling down on him like a couple of runaway horses.

Damnation, those are big dogs!

David's first thought was to leap onto the roof that was just to his left, an overhang of eaves of a business. It was over his head, but in a panic, he could pull himself to safety from the great snarling beasts. He certain didn't want to end up fighting off those two monsters. He wasn't entirely sure he could win.

"Brick!"

A high-pitched female cry suddenly filled the air and Brickley, who had his back to the dogs, suddenly turned around to see the mutts bearing down on him. Unlike a sane man, who would have run, Brickley charged the dogs and grabbed their collars, strips of leather around their necks, in an attempt to control them.

A woman was running up behind the dogs but David and Edward and Brentford weren't paying any attention to her; they were watching Brickley with concern, wondering if they should run away or go help the man, as Brickley wrestled with the dogs who were clearly trying to eat his face off. Or, perhaps they were only trying to lick him. In either case, very big pink tongues were on Brickley's cheeks and the man sputtered in disgust.

"Vile brutes!" Brickley said as he struggled to control the dogs. "How did you get free?"

As Brickley scolded the dogs and David debated whether or not to heave himself up onto the nearest roof, Emilie's train of thought was quite different. Rushing up on the heels of the dogs, she was looking at the handsome de Lohr brother and trying to pretend like she wasn't. Poor Brickley was getting a bath, and not in a good way, as happy tongues assaulted him, but she wasn't much concerned with Brickley. She was more concerned in having David de Lohr notice her. She presented her best flustered appearance.

"I am sorry, Brick," she said, feigning breathlessness as she tried to pull the dogs off her father's commander. "They jumped out of the wagon and ran off!"

Brickley still had Cid, the bigger dog, who was up on his hind legs, so tall that he was nearly eye to eye with Brickley. The dog was happily licking at him.

"They were sitting quite calmly in the wagon when I last saw them," Brickley pointed out to Emilie, who had managed to subdue Roland. "What happened?"

Emilie shrugged as Roland sat beside her obediently. "I do not know," she said. "Mayhap they saw something that attracted them because, quite suddenly, they were running off."

Brickley put his hand on Cid's head and pushed the dog down by the snout. "Smelly, slobbering beasts," he muttered, getting a good grip on Cid's collar. "I will have dog stew for supper tonight!"

Emilie grinned, mostly because Brickley loved the dogs and he was being rather dramatic about his irritation. But her attention inevitably moved to David, who was standing a few feet away with the two dark-haired knights. David's focus was on Brickley, some relief in his expression that the man had the big dogs under control, and Emilie was mildly incensed that his focus was not on her. Hers was certain on *him.*

Emboldened, she spoke.

"You are the knight who came to my rescue last night," she said to David without a proper introduction. "My father told me that it was you. Forgive me for running from you and not thanking you at the time."

David, who had indeed been watching Brickley in case the big dog in his grasp tried to escape, heard the soft female voice. It took him a moment to realize she was speaking to him. His focus then shifted from Brickley to the exquisite creature holding on to one of the charging dogs, who was now sitting politely beside her.

In fact, David was a bit surprised that he hadn't really noticed the woman until now, for she was clearly a sight to see. He hadn't realized who she was until she mentioned the events of the previous night, for it had been very dark and she had been dressed quite differently. But now, in the light of day, he was somewhat astonished, and pleased, to realize that this was Lord Hampton's Emilie.

His focus shifted to her, for good.

Emilie....

"My lady," he bowed his head politely. "My sincere apologies. I did not recognize you in the daylight and without the context of you trying to scale a wardrobe."

He said it with humor and Emilie grinned, flashing the big dimple in her right cheek. She gazed into that handsome face of sky-blue eyes, tanned skin, and square jaw, her heart fluttering just a bit more as the full impact of David de Lohr settled upon her. She was not disappointed in what she saw, the face of a seasoned warrior who also happened to be exceedingly attractive. Her eyes were still on David as if unable to look away as she spoke to Brickley.

"Will you introduce us, Brick?" she asked. "It is rude of me to speak to a man I've not yet been introduced to."

Brickley was forcing Cid to sit beside him, annoyed at the diso-bedient dog. "David, this is Lady Emilie Hampton," he said, not particularly paying attention to the fact that David and Emilie were staring openly at each other. "You were kind enough to save her from disaster last night and we both owe you our thanks. My lady, meet your savior and my friend, Sir David de Lohr."

David was riveted to the doll-like face before him. Such a sweet, sweet face with the most beautiful brown eyes he'd ever seen. Emilie's dimpled smile grew when Brickley formally introduced them and she dipped into a practiced curtsy.

"My lord," she said. "It is an honor to finally meet you."

David couldn't seem to stop staring at her. He couldn't explain it, but there was something magnetic about the woman, something sweet and warm, a beauty that radiated forth that he'd never seen before. All he knew was that she had his attention.

"The honor is mine, my lady," he said. "It is unfortunate that we became acquainted last night under horrific circumstances. I trust you suffered no ill effects?"

Emilie shook her head. "I did not," she said. "Although I am sure were it not for you, the story would be much different this morning."

David simply smiled, modestly, realizing he was very close to blushing. *Jesus, when did I become the blushing type?* Feeling somewhat flustered in the face of her glorious smile and praise, he turned to look at Edward and Brentford, who were looking at him with some amusement. Evidently, his thoughts about the lovely lady weren't something he'd been able to conceal from the look of humor on his friends' faces. They knew exactly what he was thinking.

Damnation!

"May I introduce Sir Edward de Wolfe and Sir Brentford le Bec," he said, trying to take the focus off of him because he was feeling flustered and chagrinned. "Brentford was also of service to your father last night while Edward hid somewhere in fear."

Brentford and Brickley laughed at Edward's expense, who merely rolled his eyes and shook his head in annoyance. Emilie, sensing the jest, nodded politely to both knights.

"It is an honor to meet you both," she said. "And surely, Sir David, you do not mean to say that Sir Edward is a coward, do you? Why, I do not believe such a thing. He looks quite brave to me."

Edward was grinning by now. "You have my gratitude, my lady," he said gallantly. "David often likes to tell stories that are not true. I am pleased that you have the insight to know this."

David looked at his friends, feeling the giddy urge to laugh. He had no idea why, but with Emilie smiling so openly, she was making his heart do strange things. He was usually quite controlled around women, indifferent to them even, but Lady Emilie seemed to have brought something out in him he wasn't aware he possessed – giddiness. *Jesus Christ, I am giddy!*

"Edward is also a silver-tongued devil, so do not listen to a word he says," David said in answer to Edward's insult. "But I am pleased to hear that you did not suffer any ill effects after last night. Your father seemed to be determined to leave Windsor because of it, in fact; I am happy to see that he is still here this morning."

Emilie pointed to Brickley. "My father remained so that Brick can compete in the games and bring great honor to the House of Hampton," she said, her eyes twinkling with mirth at Brickley. "He seems to think he is too old for such things."

Brentford, standing closest to Brickley, clapped the man on the shoulder. "Is this true, old man?" he asked. "You cannot be more than fifty or sixty years of age. That is not too old to complete."

Brickley gave the man an intolerant look. "I have seen forty-one summers," he said. "I can still beat you in the field, joust, game, or street any day of the week, le Bec. Do not test me."

Everyone laughed, even Brentford. Edward, in fact, put up his hands as if to surrender. "That is an excellent attitude, de Dere," he said. "Considering the way these games may go today, you will need that confidence. In fact, we were just heading over to the encampment to see how many of Richard's supporters have remained. Rumor has it this morning that several have already left."

The humor seemed to fade from the conversation. "Do we know how many?" Brickley asked.

David shook his head, answering before Edward could. "We were going to discover the answer to that question, as my brother will want to know," he said. "You are welcome to join us."

Brickley shook his head. "Unfortunately, I cannot," he said. "I am escorting Lord Hampton and his daughters to the lists. Mayhap when they are settled, I will come and find you. I...."

He suddenly stopped, his eyes narrowing as he gazed up the avenue from the direction he had come. The other knights, seeing his change of focus, turned to see what had him so interested but Emilie wasn't concerned in the least; she was still looking at David, trying to figure out what more she could do or say to continue speaking with the man. She had already thrown the dogs at the man, which had garnered her an introduction, but now there had to be something more to keep the conversation going. She knew he had duties to attend to but that didn't seem to override her own wants at the moment. She did so want to speak with him.

But that all changed in a swift moment.

"The prince," David suddenly hissed. Quickly, he looked at Brickley. "You said that all of Lord Hamptons daughters are with you?"

Brickley nodded, knowing what David was going to say before he said it. Reaching out, he took the dog from Emilie's grasp. "Quickly, my lady," he said, already moving with the dogs in each hand. "Back to the carriage."

David shook his head, moving towards Emilie swiftly and reaching out to take her elbow. "Nay," he said. "He has already seen her. Give her to me. Return to your party and make sure the other daughters are swiftly hidden. Edward, go with him and help conceal the daughters. Brentford, remain here and throw the prince off of our trail. I do not want him to send his men to follow when he sees us disburse."

The men had their orders and began to move. David had a natural air of command about him and men trusted him, willing to obey. Even so, the sense of urgency in the air was tangible as the group disbursed. Emilie found herself in David's grasp as he pulled her along the avenue, disappearing into an alleyway behind a row of merchant stalls. One minute, she had been staring at the man dreamily and in the next, he was pulling her along. Lifting up her cranberry-colored skirts so they wouldn't drag in the mud, Emilie skipped after him, gladly and willingly going with the man. They wound their way through a walkway off the alley, moving into an alcove between a couple of structures that had a small bench and an overgrown vine.

It was secluded and private. David finally came to a halt, peering out from the gaps between the buildings that faced onto the avenue where he had seen the prince approaching. Emilie watched him closely as he studied the situation out on the street.

"Will the prince try to attack us again, Sir David?" she asked.

David held up a hand to quiet her, his eyes riveted to the gap between two particular stalls. He seemed very focused on what he was seeing. His gaze was tracking someone, or something, and Emilie could hear muffled voices. But tucked back in this haven with David de Lohr, she really didn't care what was going on out on the street. The Devil himself could be on the very avenue beyond and she wouldn't have much cared. All she knew was that she had been given an amazing opportunity to be alone with a man who had held her attention since last night. It was more than she could have dared hoped for.

But she remained silent because David had asked her to with his hand gesture. Instead, she lowered her bum onto the stone bench and found herself studying David as the man focused on things out on the avenue. As she'd noticed before, he was quite broad shouldered and she could see the muscles on his arms straining through the fabric of the tunic he wore. He wasn't wearing anything that identified him with the House of de Lohr, and even the tunic he wore was simple in design. It was a woolen fabric dyed a shade of brown, and the leather breeches he wore were rather snug. When he bent forward she could see his buttocks, which were perfectly formed, like two round loaves of bread nestled beneath the leather.

She rather liked the shape. Heart fluttering again and she looked away, demurely, even though she was thinking wicked thoughts of the man's buttocks. It was true that Emilie was a maiden, but she had, on occasion, allowed a suitor or two to kiss her. Never anything more than a peck to the cheek, although once she allowed one of the de Grez brothers to kiss her on the lips. Well, maybe she's allowed *both* of them to kiss her on the lips. At different times, of course. And that was the entire reason behind the brothers having a terrible fight outside the gates of Canterbury as Brickley and her father had stood on the battlements and watched with disgust. Although she'd never allowed anything more than a kiss, that did not prevent her from having a healthy appreciation of a handsome man with an attractive form. Like David and his round, tight buttocks.

Grinning to herself, she kept her gaze averted.

"I am sorry for handling you roughly, my lady," David's soft, deep voice interrupted her naughty thoughts. He was still standing over near the gap in the buildings. "In answer to your question, I do not believe that the prince will attack you again but it is best to remove you from his sight."

Emilie was listening with great interest. "But why?" she asked. "I have never met him before."

David lifted a dark blond eyebrow as he turned to look at her, sitting so prettily on the stone bench. "God willing, you never shall," he said. "Have you not heard of the man and his reputation, my lady?"

Emilie wasn't sure what he meant. "I have heard he desires is brother's throne," she said hesitantly. "My father does not speak of him, to be truthful. Why? What reputation do you mean?"

David looked at her a moment before moving away from the gap, heading in her direction. He sighed faintly, trying to determine just how to explain such things to her. Unsavory things for a lady's ear, things of politics and brutality and sexuality that were things even most men didn't want to hear. But it was the reality of the situation with John, unfortunately. David didn't want to overstep his bounds, but the woman had asked a valid question.

"I suppose I should let your father tell you, but given that you are at Windsor in the presence of the prince, I will take the liberty to tell you," he said. "You will forgive me if I say things you may find offensive, but I must be truthful with you for your own safety. The prince has been known to take any woman he fancies for his own pleasure."

Fortunately, Emilie wasn't one to become offended or frightened easily. Still, her brow furrowed with concern. "Is this true?" she asked. "*Any* woman?"

David nodded slowly. "*Any* woman, my lady," he said. "In fact, last night…when I came upon you, I am quite sure that after those men had had their fill of you, they would have taken you straight to the prince. The man is a deviant and surrounds himself with deviants, with one in particular being the Sheriff of Nottingham. You must therefore be very careful when coming into contact with the prince or any of his men. In fact, you must do everything possible to ensure that you do *not* come in contact with him. He would take a beautiful woman like you faster than the blink of an eye and no one, not even your father, could stop him."

A beautiful woman like you. Emilie was deeply flattered, a faint blush coming to her cheeks. But more than his flattery, the message of his statement was having some impact on her.

"Sweet Mary," she breathed, rather shocked by what she had been told. "He would just… *take* me?"

David was standing next to her by now, gazing down at that blond head. He thought it looked quite silky to him and he could only imagine running his fingers through it.

"Aye," he said honestly. "He would take you to his bed, use you, and then toss you away like rubbish. That is why I had Brick and Edward rush to tend to your sisters. It was imperative that we remove the three of you from John's presence before he could see you."

Emilie thought it all rather sweet and heroic of him. "Then it is twice that you have saved me," she said. "It would seem to me that you are probably the most gallant and brave man I have ever met."

David gave her a half-grin, modestly, realizing that he was feeling rather giddy and foolish again.

"It was a pleasure and a duty to be of service, my lady," he said. "I hope you will not find it too unbearable to remain here for a few more moments until the prince leaves the area."

"Alone?"

He shook his head. "I would not leave you alone, my lady."

Emilie was thrilled to hear that. She moved over on the stone bench, clearing a spot for him to sit as if this was any other social occasion.

"Will you sit, then, and tell me of yourself whilst we wait?" she asked. "I would like to know something of the man who has twice saved my life. My father says you and your brother have recently returned from the Holy Land. Will you tell me something of it? I have heard that the entire land is covered with rocks."

David knew he shouldn't sit down. He had to stay vigilant because the prince, and more than likely Fitz Walter and his men, were still in the area. The last he saw, John's entourage had stopped at the intersection of the avenues and Brentford was speaking to them. Therefore, David knew he needed to remain alert to the situation but as he gazed at Emilie's lovely, hopeful face, something was tugging him to sit right down next to her. She was difficult to resist. All angelic beauty and dimpled smile, David was under her spell whether or not he wanted to be.

But this wasn't a social situation. This was something quite serious. David didn't need to have any contact with her more than he'd already had but he couldn't help himself. He was attracted to her. Like it or not, he was inclined to do as she asked. Right or wrong, that was his inclination.

So he surrendered. Holding up a hand as if to beg a moment's pardon, he made his way back over to the gap between the buildings and strained to see out to the avenue beyond. He could see John's litter, an odd chariot-like contraption that was pulled by his personal guard, and he could see that both John and Ralph Fitz Walter were speaking to Brentford now, and it was something of great concern to him.

John's guard, those same bastards from the night before, seemed to be posturing threateningly near Brentford, and the man was alone after David and the others had fled in order to protect the women. Brentford was one lone knight sworn to Richard and John knew very well that le Bec served Derby and, therefore, Richard. David was coming to think that he needed to go stand with Brentford as a show of strength but if he did, it would leave Emilie alone and vulnerable. He wasn't about to do that. Therefore, he had to trust Brentford as the man dealt with the prince. Le Bec was seasoned and diplomatic. David would simply have to let the man work.

Moving away from the gap, he made his way back over to Emilie, who was smiling openly at him. She was also expecting him to sit next to her, which she did, rather stiffly. He suddenly felt very self-conscious and awkward because it had been a very long time since he'd gone through the gentle proprieties of interacting with a lady. There hadn't been much opportunity for that in the Holy Land and he was a bit out of practice. That lack of practice was enough to make him feel like he'd never done anything like this before, ever. He cleared his throat softly.

"It is true that much of the Holy Land is barren," he said to her earlier statement. "We traveled by sea to reach it and I have never seen such sand. Sand everywhere. And the heat... you have never known anything like it."

Emilie was thrilled that he was willing to engage in some manner of conversation with her, although he seemed fidgety. He also seemed distracted, as he kept looking to the gap between the buildings that had his attention. She hastened to keep the conversation going, fearful he would soon lose interest.

"My father took my sisters and me south to Brighton, once," she said. "It was in the summer time and we played in the sea. It was quite warm, as I recall. That is my experience with great heat, although we have been known to have warm summers in Canterbury. I have lived there most of my life. Where were you born and raised as a child?"

David was having a difficult time looking at her because it seemed as if every time he did, his heart seemed to beat firmly against his ribcage. Breathing was difficult. It was an odd sensation that confused and rather excited him. It was wholly strange.

"Lohrham Forest," he said. "It is my family's home in Derbyshire."

Emilie nodded, pretending to be greatly interested. "And your only sibling is Christopher?"

He shook his head. "I have a younger sister, Deborah," he said. "She is a lady in waiting to the Earl of Bath's wife. They are here at Windsor, in fact. I've not seen her for years."

Emilie smiled that pretty, dimpled smile and David caught a glimpse of it. He couldn't seem to take his eyes off her now, thumping heart and odd breathing be damned.

"I should like to meet her," Emilie said. "Being at Windsor is all so exciting to my sisters and me. When Papa received the notice about the tournament, he only agreed to come because Nathalie and Elise begged and cried about it."

"Nathalie and Elise?"

"My younger sisters."

He nodded in understanding. "And you came to Windsor only to find yourself attacked," he said. "That is sad fact."

Emilie shrugged. "It could have been worse," she said. Then, she eyed him. "I suppose the bright side is that I was saved by a legendary knight."

He looked at her full on in surprise, before breaking down into one of those modest smiles that were quite rare for him. Much like his brother, David, too, had a colossal ego. "I would hardly say that I am legendary," he said. "Skilled, mayhap. Talented and seasoned. And I can best any man in a sword fight. Now that I think on it, mayhap I *am* legendary after all."

Emilie giggled. "Of course you are legendary," she said. "And since you have saved me from the prince on more than one occasions, that means I am in your debt. Should you ever need a favor, you need only ask."

David was smiling because she was, but his smile soon faded; she had given him a wide-open statement that could have been taken any number of ways. Were he any less of a chivalrous knight, he could have taken advantage of it. As it was, the possibilities were most interesting but he refused to play on her innocence.

At least, not so soon.

"No debt is necessary, my lady," he said. "It was no trouble, I assure you."

Emilie had flirted with him and flattered him, and each time, he'd not risen to the bait. Therefore, Emilie wasn't sure if he was warming to her or not. She couldn't tell. Usually, flattery would break down even the most stone-faced man, but David was different. He didn't seem particularly impressed by her flattery and she was coming to view that as something of a challenge.

"Do you make it a habit of rescuing women, then?" she asked. "You seem as if you have done this before. I can only imagine what great adventures you have had rescuing damsels from wicked men. Mayhap there is a service you can provide – mayhap you should charge great amounts of money to save foolish women for their desperate fathers."

He was back to grinning again and stood up, thinking that he should check on Brentford to see what was happening. More than that, his face was starting to feel hot from Emilie's close proximity and sweet flattery. The more neutral he tried to be, the more charming she became. He was trying very much to remain proper, as they had just met, but it was difficult when she was being so delightful. A pretty woman who fed his pride was never a bad thing.

"I cannot say that I have rescued more than a few women from various situations," he said. "But you may have a point; there may be money in such a thing."

Emilie grinned. "Of course there is," she insisted. "An average knight could only charge a few silver marks for such services, but with the de Lohr name, you could command thousands. You should think on it, Sir David. It may be a lucrative line of work for you now that you have returned home."

He was becoming upswept in her humor. "It is possible."

"Would your brother mind?"

"Not if I split the profits with him."

She cocked an eyebrow. "Ah," she said knowingly. "The greedy sort."

He shook his head. "Nay," he replied. "He will somehow see it as his due for my privilege of using the de Lohr name."

Her eyebrows lifted in shock of such a terrible brother. "But it is *your* name, too!"

He smiled. "It was his name first."

She laughed. So did he. But he quickly shut his mouth, aware that his snort of laughter had been somewhat loud. And high-pitched. Actually, it sounded silly, like an excitable young squire, and had anyone else made the sound, he would have teased them mercilessly.

Thank God no one else had heard it.

Jesus, what is happening to me?

Turning away quickly, David headed for the gap in the building where he had last seen Brentford and the prince. Now, it was oddly vacant and David wasn't sure if he should be concerned or relieved. The prince was gone... but so was Brentford. Turning to Emilie, he held out a hand to her.

"I believe the prince has moved on," he said. "Come with me."

Emilie bolted up from the stone bench and went to him. His extended hand was meant purely as a gesture but she reached out and took his hand, boldly, and refused to let go. She was thrilled with the feel of her warm hand in his and David looked at her, surprised that she should take his hand like that, but moment their eyes met, he suddenly didn't think it was such a bad idea. He rather liked the feeling of her hand in his, too. With a faint smile, he led her out of the maze of walkways and alleys, out into the avenue where the Hampton party was still situated.

Edward, Brickley, and Brentford had been waiting for David and Emilie to emerge from their hiding place and when the three knights saw David, with Emilie in hand, crossing the muddy avenue towards them, it was a great relief. John had moved on, towards the tournament field, and it was all Brentford could talk about as David released Emilie to a woman who sprayed spittle into the air when she spoke. As the woman happily greeted Emilie, David narrowly avoided being sprayed.

Even though he was listening to Brentford, David's attention was focused on Emilie, as her father and the spitting woman helped her into the carriage where two other young women and the two massive dogs awaited. It seemed that the entire Hampton family were preparing to depart for the tournament field now, but Brickley was very concerned about keeping the young women from the prince's view. He was even trying to talk them into going back to their apartments but the two younger sisters put up such a fuss that Brickley backed down and Lyle simply gave in.

David, Edward, and Brentford therefore ended up climbing into the wagon to accompany the House of Hampton to the lists where knights were already taking their practice runs for the day's events. It was for protection, of course, but more than that, David simply wanted to ride next to Emilie.

He wasn't quite finished with her yet, this perplexing and magnificent creature that made him feel things he wasn't used to feeling. Brentford climbed up next to the driver whilst David and Edward sat back in the carriage itself, with Edward striking up a conversation with the spitting woman as the big black dogs seemed to make themselves right at home next to David. One beast put his big doggie head on David's lap while the other simply sat next to him and leaned against him. From the sheer dead weight, it was like having a building collapse against him. David grunted when the wagon would hit a bump and the dog's weight would crush against him.

As much as David wanted to speak to Emilie on the short ride to the tournament field, he ended up being the prized possession of two drooling dogs.

And Emilie laughed at him the entire ride there.

CHAPTER FOUR

T HE GRAND AURA of the games was much more than any of them
had bargained for.

It was a spectacle of pageantry and people. Seated in the lists to
the left of the prince's gaily decorated royal box, there were enough
spectators already at the field that Prince John, in all of his lascivious
glory, didn't notice three young women as they sat together in the
lists, slightly behind the prince's line of sight. Four Hampton soldiers
took up position towards the rear of the boxes to keep an eye on the
ladies, as the rest of them went to the field with Lyle and Brickley and
both the big dogs. Preparations and practice were underway and,
already, the excitement of the games was in the air.

The cool fall air grew brisk as the morning deepened and dark
clouds appeared, scattered around by the wind. Nathalie and Elise
and Lillibet conversed excitedly about the knights riding past, or the
general preparations, but Emilie's attention was elsewhere.

David, Edward, and Brentford had politely departed the carriage
when the group had arrived at the tournament field and Emilie had
watched, somewhat sadly, as David had walked away. But she had
some hope in her heart because he had turned around at least twice
to wave at her as he departed, and she had waved in return. It gave
her hope that, perhaps, she had made some impression in on him. At
least, she sincerely hoped so. It was still difficult to tell. She wanted to

ask him to carry her favor that that *would* have been extremely bold, and she wasn't willing to come across as too terribly forward, not just yet, so she hadn't asked. It was something she was now coming to regret.

So she sat in the lists next to Nathalie, watching the field anxiously for any sign of David de Lohr as more competitors took the field to practice. She saw when Brickley emerged into the arena and she saw her father standing down by the edge of the field, but still no David. It began to occur to her that she wasn't even entirely sure what a de Lohr banner looked like so she called one of her father's soldiers over to ask him, and he quickly pointed out at least two de Lohr tunics upon knights who were out in the arena. The big de Lohr lion against the sapphire blue backdrop was now emblazoned in her brain. There was a Latin inscription on the bottom of it, sewn in gold thread. *Deus et Honora.* It meant God and Honor. She would make sure to watch for more of those tunics, and for the de Lohr brother in particular.

But it was a long wait. She kept glancing over at the royal box to catch a glimpse of the terrible man who had ordered the attack against Richard's supporters the night before, the prince that even great knights like David de Lohr seemed fearful of. Fearful in the sense that John was the son of Henry I and the son of Eleanor of Aquitaine, and from that angle, he was royal to the bone on both sides.

The prince's mother had once been the queen to Philip, the king of France. She had been the queen of two countries and the mother of ten children, with John being her last, and Eleanor – more than any other woman in the history of England – held tremendous power over her sons and over the country in general. When Richard had left on crusade, he had left his mother ruling as Regent in his stead.

John, seemingly, didn't care about that and any man who so openly bucked his powerful mother was a man to be feared because he was reckless. Recklessness often came without conscience or common sense. That, more than anything, was to be feared. Even

Emilie understood that.

From the position of her seat, it was difficult to see everyone who was in the royal box. There were several people in it, including a beautiful woman with long blond hair and a dark haired man sitting next to her. She thought she caught a glimpse of the prince's head, once, because he was wearing something on his head from what she could see. She thought it might be a crown. As more and more people were filling the lists, including a man in the royal box who had a hugely swollen and battered face. He sat next to the prince and Emilie lost sight of him, but the excitement was building as more knights came onto the tournament field, warming up their horses. Her attention moved from the royal box and returned to the field.

Now, she saw four de Lohr tunics as men rode about the arena, trotting by the stands and waving to the crowd, eliciting screams of excitement from the women. Natalie was one of those who was shouting with excitement until Lillibet admonished her. Even then, Nathalie would still manage a wave or a shriek now and again. She was too excited about the influx of knights to keep still.

Emilie was full of excitement, too, but only for one man. The knights on the field were covered in mail and tunics, most of them wearing the bucket-like helms of protection on their head. Some of them had articulated face plates that would lift, allowing the knight better visibility, but advanced armor of that sort was only for the very wealthy. Most men had the helms that lifted off in one piece.

But the de Lohrs had the latest and best armor money could provide. The four knights that she could see wore coats of chain mail and tunics that went to their knees. Big leather belts cinched the tunics about the waist and while most knights wore leather shoes that only went to their ankle or mid-calf, the de Lohr knights wore heavy leather boots that went up to the knees to protect the entire shin area. It was most impressive and Emilie was riveted to the men in the lion tunics as they moved around the arena.

"Look at them!" Natalie gasped in awe. "I have never seen so many knights. This is so exciting! I am so glad we came!"

Emilie glanced at her sister, who was flushed with glee. She couldn't help but grin at the excited young woman. "Brick has passed by the lists a few times," she said. "You should go to the edge the next time he goes by and offer him your favor."

Nathalie nodded eagerly. "I shall," she said. "I hope he will carry it. Papa is down there at the edge of the field; mayhap he will force Brick to carry it."

Emilie put her hand on her sister's arm. "Do you truly want to force the man to carry your favor?" she asked. "He should want to carry it willingly. There is no romance in a man who is forced to carry your favor."

Nathalie shrugged; in theory, she understood but in practice, she very much wanted Brickley to carry her favor and was willing to have her father force the man if necessary. Either way, she wanted Brickley carrying the small piece of silk with the hummingbird embroidered on it that had once belonged to her mother. As she mulled over her reply to her sister, because she didn't have the same opinion about it that Emilie did, she heard Elise muttering.

In truth, it wasn't unusual for Elise to mutter. She was fourteen years of age but she was still, in many ways, a young girl. She was very smart, and a bit odd, and very clever with the pranks that she and Natalie would play on the men at Canterbury. With wispy blond hair that tumbled down her back and big brown eyes, like Emilie, she looked somewhat plain and innocent. But there was a fire that burned behind those brown eyes, something that Lyle thought was rather sinister. He thought his youngest daughter was a mad genius planning to rule the entire world someday. In that case, he wasn't entirely wrong. Elise *did* rule a world; a world of her very own.

It was a world of her own creation. With her, she carried her precious wooden box, a box that she'd had for many years. It was painted with flowers on it and had once belonged to her mother. While Lady Willow had used it to carry cosmetics and toiletries, Elise had another purpose for it – it carried an array of small figurines that Elise had made herself. They were little figures of wood, perhaps two or more inches tall, and Elise had painted faces upon them. There were men, women, and children, and she even dressed them. She would use small rocks for dogs or other animals. She would paint faces on the rocks that would soon rub off and when they did, she would kill them off and bury them. In fact, she would make her families fight and have the fathers dies, only to bury them and replace them with other fathers. It was Elise's world and she ran it as she saw fit.

It was part of Elise's personality, as odd as it was, and as she sat in the lists watching the knights in the arena beyond, she opened her box of people (for they went everywhere she did) and brought them out to sit with her on the bench beside her. The muttering that both Nathalie and Emilie had heard was Elise as she spoke of the games to her wooden families. Emilie was tolerant of Elise's quirk but Nathalie wasn't; she leaned into her younger sister, frowning.

"Put them away," she hissed. "Do you want the knights to see this? They will think you are a child!"

Lillibet heard her. She shushed Nathalie, shaking a finger at her. "Leave her be," she admonished. "She may do as she wishes."

Spit was flying fast and furious from Lillibet's lips as Nathalie, and even Emilie, dodged it. Nathalie frowned at her nurse. "But it is so childish," she insisted. "I care not what she does when we are at home, but here in public, it is silly for her to play with her families. What will people think?"

Lillibet simply held up a stern finger to silence her. "And it is unseemly for a young lady such to want to give her favor to a man old enough to be her father," she said, clearly referring to Brickley. "Mind who you call silly, Nathalie, and take care that your father does not hear of your interest in his commander."

Nathalie turned red in the face and looked away, catching Emilie's eye before lowering her head in shame. Emilie fought off a grin, rather sympathetic for Nathalie but also sympathetic for Elise and her odd eccentricities. Quickly, she sought to change the focus for both of her sisters' sakes.

"I am rather hungry," she said, looking around. "Mother, may we find a food vendor? I thought I saw a few near the end of the field when we first entered."

Lillibet was straining to see Lyle, down on the arena floor as he was. "We must ask your father," she said, spit flying out and hitting the woman seated in front of her in the back of the head. "I do not see him."

Now, all three girls were looking for him, too. He had been standing just below the level of the lists, along the edges of the field, but he'd moved position. Emilie sat up straight, then stood up, looking for her father, but as she did so, a de Lohr knight astride a fat dappled stallion came up to the edge of the royal box and lifted his visor.

The man was handsome, with a blond beard from what Emilie could see, and he was speaking to someone seated in the royal box. Emilie studied him, seeing a faint resemblance in the nose and eyes between the man and David. She was coming to think it was David's older brother, the great Christopher de Lohr. Eyes riveted to the de Lohr knight, she failed to notice when another knight in a de Lohr tunic pulled alongside the lists nearly directly in front of her.

Emilie had no idea how long David had been there, looking at her. He had flipped his visor up, looking into the stands, as several women were on their feet, calling to him. One or two threw a favor at him. Someone even threw a flower. Emilie, who really hadn't seen him because of the women standing up in front of her, finally pulled her attention away from the bearded de Lohr knight to catch sight of David as he lingered near the edge of the lists. As she watched, a favor of some kind, went sailing into his helmed head and he didn't even flinch. He didn't look at it. He was looking strictly at Emilie. When their eyes met, he smiled.

So did she.

Grinning, biting her lower lip, Emilie waved at him and he dipped his head in her direction, acknowledging her. There was warmth in the air between them and hawk-like focus, as if they were the only two people in the entire arena. Emilie's heart was fluttering wildly and she summoned the courage to ask him to carry her favor. So many had been thrown at him that she wasn't sure what would make hers any different. Mayhap he would simply refuse hers, too. So as she sat and smiled at him, struggling to gather her courage, Brickley pulled his big red steed alongside David.

Brickley pointed to the four women sitting at the bench. Nathalie, hoping he was pointing at her, stood up to go to him with joy in her heart but he shook his head and pointed to Emilie, who pointed to herself as if to confirm she was, in fact, the one he was summoning. He nodded and she stood up, making her way down the wooden steps until she reached the railing where the two knights w ere located. Her attention was mostly on David, still smiling at him, and thankful that Brickley had given her yet another excuse to speak with David. But what came out of Brickley's mouth was not what she had been expecting.

"I will carry your favor, my lady, as the eldest daughter of the House of Hampton," Brickley said. "Do you have something fine and sweet to give me?"

Shocked, and greatly dismayed, Emilie looked at the man. *Nay! I want David to carry my favor!* "I... aye, I do, but... but Papa will want to carry it, I am sure," she said, struggling not to offend him. "Where is he?"

Brickley nodded his head in the direction of the tents to the east. "His horse has come up lame," he said. "Your father will not be competing today. Therefore, you can give your favor to me."

Emilie was nearly beside herself with disappointment. She didn't want to upset Brickley but she did not want to give the man her favor. "I think you should carry Nathalie's," she said. "This is her first tournament, after all, and she would like for a competitor to carry her favor. She was hoping it would be you because… because she doubts Papa will allow anyone else to carry it. I… well, since Sir David came to my rescue last night, I was going to offer my favor to him in gratitude. I think that is most appropriate, Brick. Don't you?"

Brickley wasn't thrilled with any of it, but David, next to the man, extended a hand to Emilie without hesitation. "It is more than enough gratitude, my lady," he said, expecting her favor as Brickley frowned at him. "I would be greatly honored to carry your favor on this day. It will bring me great fortune."

Emilie smiled so broadly that her face threatened to split in two. She pulled a small kerchief out of the cuff on her left wrist and handed it over to David, who took it with a grin. He smelled it, a scent of sweet roses, before tucking it into his tunic. Meanwhile, Emilie turned for Nathalie and gestured to the girl furiously, which brought Nathalie shooting out of her seat and nearly tripping in her haste to make it down to Brickley. She handed her favor over to him and he took it politely, but it was clear he was most displeased by it. David gave Emilie a bold wink, which Brickley saw, before reining his horse away from the lists and thundered across the arena. Courteously thanking Nathalie again, Brickley followed.

As the women remained on the railing in the distance, watching their favored knights ride off, Brickley caught up to David just as the man was leaving the field.

"David," he called to him. "Wait a moment."

David paused just outside of the arena gate and waited for Brickley to catch up to him. As Brickley came alongside, he propped his helm up on top of his forehead so he could better see David. His expression was somewhat serious.

"David," he said. "About Emilie's favor…do not think it is an invitation from her. She is young and somewhat naïve, and her father already has someone in mind for her. I just thought you should know before you think that this favor means more than it does."

David regarded Brickley a moment, thinking that the mood between them had just turned oddly unpleasant. There was something in Brickley's tone that wasn't particularly friendly and David didn't appreciate that. Not only was it presumptuous, but it was rude.

"'Tis a mere favor, Brick," he said evenly. "It was not a proposal of marriage."

Brickley's gaze hardened though he tried to fight it. There was something happening in his expression that suggested great displeasure. "I know," he said. "But I am telling you that the favor means nothing. Emilie is not to be trifled with."

David sighed pensively, leaning forward on his saddle. "Come out with it, Brick," he said. "You are clearly warning me off of her. Is it you her father has in mind for her?"

Brickley faltered a moment but was trying to appear as if the question hadn't rattled him. He tried to be evasive about it, unsuccessfully. "She just wanted to thank you for coming to her aid last night."

"I know."

"I… I was not attempting to offend you, David."

David shook his head. "You did not," he said. "But you may as well be honest with me. Do you have interest in her? Is that why you asked for her favor?"

Brickley averted his gaze. It was a moment before he spoke. "Possibly," he said quietly. "I have spoken with her father but he does not seem to think she is old enough for marriage."

David lifted his eyebrows. "How old is she?"

"She saw eighteen years this summer."

David pondered that information. She was indeed old enough for marriage and if Lyle was trying to hold off Brickley, it was possible that he, in fact, didn't want Brickley for his daughter. Perhaps he told the man she wasn't old enough simply to keep from offending him. In any case, David was starting to understand more about the situation but it didn't deter his interest in the least. He was attracted to Emilie and the fact that Brickley wanted the woman didn't make any difference to him.

David always got what he wanted.

"Am I to assume Lady Emilie does not know any of this?" he asked.

Brickley shook his head. "Nay," he said. "It is between her father and me at this time. She needn't know any of it. Therefore, out of respect to me, will you please keep in mind that her favor means nothing to you? It means a great deal to me, however. Treat it well."

David could have become angry at that moment, or at the very least offended, and in truth, his irritation rose. He couldn't help it.

"I would treat it with nothing less than the greatest respect, which is more than I can say for the way you treat her, Brick," he said frankly. "Do you think she is too stupid or foolish to know of your interest in her? Why do you not ask her how she feels about it? Why assume she is simply there to do your bidding and her father's bidding? Mayhap she has a say in how her life will end up. Have you even considered that?"

Brickley's expression hardened. "It does not matter how she feels about it and I resent your implication," he said, tightening the reins on his horse and turning away. "Make sure you return her favor after the event."

David watched the man ride away, mulling over the conversation and realizing that whatever interest he had in Emilie would need to be explored. Brickley's threat had pushed him into that position. He didn't like to be threatened and he didn't like to be challenged, so it was really Brickley's fault to begin with. Brickley had made his decision for him. Or perhaps it was more that Brickley had simply made his decision for him.

Perhaps he felt nothing more than an infatuation, but David wasn't entire sure about that. He'd never felt this way before, about any woman, after having known her so briefly. Therefore, it would stand to reason that it was more than an infatuation and bordered on genuine interest. But interest to what regard? Was the fact that his brother had so recently married weighing heavily on his thoughts, so much so that he, too, was considering marriage?

From what David had seen with Christopher, marriage was an agreeable thing, indeed. At least, most of the time. It wasn't hard for David to admit that his brother's marriage had put marriage in general in a rather pleasant light. It had him thinking about it. Mayhap his infatuation with his brother's wife hadn't been infatuation so much in her as it had been in wanting to see himself in the same situation. Wanting to have a wife of his own.

Wanting someone like Emilie Hampton for his own.

... *wanting Emilie.*

Scratching his neck, David reined his horse around and headed for the de Lohr tents that had been set up just east of the field. One of his brother's knights, Leeton de Shera, had managed to set up an excellent encampment in an area that had a good view of the arena. As David headed back to the tents, knights were passing him, heading towards the arena with the word that the field marshals were preparing to draw lots.

With that information, David made haste back to the de Lohr tents to make sure that all of the de Lohr knights preparing to compete were aware – Edward de Wolfe, Leeton, a knight by the name of Sir Thomas Dudley were all preparing their horses. Squires were scurrying about, including Christopher's squire, Darren, helping the knights finish up their preparations, but David's information about the field marshals drawing lots prompted the knights to push the squires aside and quickly mount their horses, heading out to the field to see who they had drawn in the first round.

Now, the games were truly about to begin and each man was anxious to know his competition and realize his chances for survival to the next round.

It was time for the games to begin.

With Emilie's favor tucked next to his heart, David had never felt quite so invincible.

CHAPTER FIVE

T HE JOUST WAS brutal from the onset.

After the knights drew lots to see who they would be competing against, Emilie and her sisters and nurse watched the first bout with great anticipation. It was exciting and thrilling to watch thousands of pounds of man and horse flesh charging at one another, dirt flying in the air as spectators screamed. But that thrill turned to horror very quickly because in the very first round, a young knight nearly had his arm torn off when the limb took the full brunt of a joust pole. The knight was unseated, landing on the bad arm, and was quickly ushered off the field by men bearing a litter.

After that, the reality of the games hit home very quickly. It was thrilling, of course, but it was also quite dangerous. Elise put all of her wooden people back in their box so they wouldn't see such horror, as Emilie and Nathalie watched with mounting apprehension.

"There must be rules for this game," Nathalie said, distressed. "Surely the knight who hurt that man will be punished for it."

Emilie didn't know much more about the joust than her sister did and simply shrugged. "I do not know," she said. "It seems to me that there are not many rules to dictate how a man his hurt or not. Anything can happen when men run at each other with poles."

Nathalie frowned. "I do not think I like this very much," she said, looking off to the east end of the field where the next competitors were entering. "Look, Em! It is the knight you gave your favor to!"

Emilie's attention flew to the opposite side of the field where David and another knight were indeed entering. After giving David her favor, she hadn't really told her curious sister much about him other than he had been the man who had saved her the night before, and Nathalie hadn't asked much more than that because she was more focused on Brickley.

Emilie was glad Nathalie hadn't pestered her with a thousand questions; she rather wanted to keep David to herself for the moment, as if it was her delicious little secret. He was her little fantasy and she didn't particularly want to let Nathalie in on it, for Nathalie might even find David favorable as well. She might even harbor a secret affection for him simply because Emilie did. If that were the case, then Emilie was sure she would have to kill her sister and bury the body. Well, perhaps not kill her, but it might ruin whatever sweet dreams she had about him. Nathalie and her over-active lust would spoil it.

"That is him," she agreed, her heart beating with excitement at the sight of him.

Nathalie was looking at him, too. "I did not see his face," she said. "Is he handsome?"

Emilie could already hear the interest in her sister's voice and she did her best to keep her irritation down. "Aye," she said evenly. "But do not think of him for you might ruin any chance you have with Brick. He will not want a woman who is thinking of another man."

That was enough to straighten Nathalie out. Fearful that Brickley might be able to read her mind, she stopped asking questions about David, and even turned her attention to his opponent, a big knight bearing a red and black tunic with a big yellow cross emblazoned upon it.

"Look at that knight, Em," she said. "The tip of his pole is a spear."

Emilie could see the sharp blade at the end of the joust pole and the idea that something like that could penetrate David brought waves of anxiety. Her attention quickly moved to David to see what kind of joust-tipped pole he had and the end of his pole was shaped like a fist. A big, steel fist.

Her heart began to beat in fear.

"David does not have a spear on the end of his," she said. "Surely this is not fair. Surely the other knight must use another pole that does not have a dagger on the end of it."

Over on Nathalie's other side, Elise leaned forward to look at her eldest sister. "Em?" she asked. "Is it safe to let my families see the joust now? Can I bring them out?"

Emilie wasn't sure what to say. She didn't want to frighten her little sister but the truth was that she was feeling a great deal of uncertainty about the entire thing. Before she could answer, however, the field marshals dropped their flags and the competitors began to charge.

A roar went up from the crowd, filling the air with a blood-thirsty excitement. The masses liked victory and exhilaration, but they also liked gore, but not from their favorite competitors, of which David clearly seemed to be one, but from their unworthy opponents. They loved to see unworthy men trampled.

Heart in her throat, Emilie watched David charge full-force against the knight with the spear-tipped pole as the crowd around her shrieked. The ground shook with the very power radiating from the horses and the men upon them, a ground-trembling force that was difficult to describe. The knights drew closer and closer, the crowd screamed, and the competitors lowered their poles, aiming them straight for each other. Emilie resisted the urge to cover her eyes as the men drew together at great speed.

The moment was upon them.

It could be victory or defeat in a swift, bloody moment.

Crash!

A resounding jolt filled the air of the arena and suddenly, the knight in the black and red tunic was flying off his steed. The man hit the earth heavily as the crowd leapt to their feet and cheered. David, completely unharmed, lifted his pole and held it vertically as he made a sweeping circle astride his big white rouncey and ended up making a pass in front of the lists for his adoring public.

And no one was adoring him more than Emilie at the moment. Her hands were clasped against her chest, her eyes alight with relief and admiration as David passed before the stands. She wasn't even cheering; she just stood there and watched him, overcome with a pride she'd never before experienced. But her admiration of David was marred by a woman in the royal box screaming David's name at the top of her lungs.

Emilie had noticed the woman once before; she had long, thick blond hair to her knees and she sat with a dark-haired man who had his right hand and arm heavily bandaged. Now, the woman was standing on her seat, screaming at David as he passed by the royal box. David lifted a hand to acknowledge the woman before the dark-haired man pulled her back into her seat. But the woman wouldn't be deterred; she kept shouting David's name and cheering for him, and he acknowledged her again and again, finally pointing at her seat so she would sit and be still. It was a rather familiar gesture, as if he knew the woman well.

Knew the woman well....

After that, Emilie's blind adoration of David became somewhat confused.

Who was that woman? She wondered. Was it perhaps another adoring admirer, because the woman certainly seemed to admire David a great deal from the way she was yelling. She clearly knew him and David clearly knew her. Could it be perhaps another admirer? Certainly, David could have more than one, and Emilie was aware that she hardly knew the man. She didn't know if he had other admirers or perhaps he even had a wife. She remembered that a man bearing a de Lohr tunic, the man with the beard, had also stopped by the royal box to speak with the woman, but that didn't mean a thing. She could be a family friend or he could be a relative. A wife, even.

A lover.

Feeling bewildered and greatly disappointed, Emilie tried to tell herself that David would not have taken her favor had he been married, or even if he'd had another special woman, especially when the woman was seated within close proximity of her, but the truth is that she didn't know him. She didn't know the man's character. It was true that he was a gallant knight and had saved her from certain doom, but beyond that, David de Lohr was a man she knew nothing about. He was a great knight from a great family, so perhaps he was only toying with a naïve young woman to feed an overinflated ego.

Perhaps he'd only paid attention to her because she had all but thrown herself at him.

Lost in thought, she was aware when David passed by the lists where she was sitting. Women were screaming his name, throwing ribbons and flowers in his direction, but he ignored them all. He lifted his visor to seek out Emilie, who was gazing back at him with not much enthusiasm at all. He was smiling at her but she didn't smile back. In fact, in a rush of embarrassment and disappointment, she suddenly stood up and dashed from the lists before Lillibet could stop her.

Emilie raced down the stairs from the list, losing herself in the crowd as two of her father's soldiers went in pursuit. She didn't want to be caught. She wanted to go back to the apartments they had been staying in and wait for this terrible spectacle to be over. She wanted to go home and not think about the knight who had taken her favor when he'd clearly had another lady in the lists. She felt humiliated and sad and disappointed, ashamed that she had been duped by one of the great de Lohrs.

She felt like a fool.

The streets were dirty and busy, smeared with hundreds of people coming to and from the tournament field. There were also dozens of vendor stalls along the avenue selling food and drink and other things, and people were crowding up around them, making big obstacles for her to walk around. The problem, however, was that she wasn't walking – she was running, so on more than one occasion, she ran right through a group of people without stopping, knocking back one of the men. She never even apologized.

By the time she reached the eastern end of the arena, she was out of breath and verging on tears. A quick look over her shoulder showed her father's men close behind and she knew, in long run, that she wouldn't be able to stay ahead of them. They would catch her, eventually, if she tried to make it to the apartments and she didn't want to be caught, not now. She needed time alone, to think and recover her composure.

She needed time to breathe.

A glance at her surroundings showed that she was at the same intersection where she had been standing with David and the other knights when the prince had first made an appearance. She recognized the alleyway David had taken her into, the one that led to the small alcove with the vine and the stone bench. In a flash, she darted into the alleyway to shake her pursuers and, very quickly, she found herself along the walkway between stalls where the bench wait, cold and in the shade. It was partially hidden by the vine. Emilie sat down on the bench and huddled back against the wall, as far away as she could get from the walkway.

And she waited for her father's men to come upon her at any moment. Already, she was prepared for the disappointment that would bring, knowing they would be forced to escort her back to the lists. But the more seconds ticked away and no one came, the more she thought that she might have avoided capture. It was cool and shady in the little alcove, the little stone bench where she'd had her first real conversation with David. The first conversation with a man that had gone beyond simple flirtation. It had actually meant something to her.

Emilie wasn't the flighty type but she didn't like being made a fool of. She didn't want to sit in the arena and watch David wave to one woman and then try to warm to her in the next motion. She wouldn't be one of a crowd; if he wanted more than one woman, then he would have look elsewhere. She wasn't apt to be that kind of girl. So the best thing for her to do was leave so she didn't have to see David and his flirtation with the other woman. He could keep her favor for all she cared. She didn't want it back now. It clearly meant nothing to him.

She tried to tell herself that it meant nothing to her, either, but the truth was that it had. She was drawn to David as she had never been drawn to anyone in her life. Something about the man sucked her in and held her fast, refusing to let go. Perhaps it was her youth or her naïve nature that caused her to feel such attraction to the man, but she didn't think that was the case. She'd known attractive men before. A few had even pursued her. But David de Lohr… well, he was different.

Hanging her head, she fidgeted with her hands, trying to convince herself that David de Lohr wasn't worth fretting over. Surely there were other fine knights who were worthy of her attention, men who wouldn't ask for her favor yet flirt with another. She hadn't really notice any because she'd been so focused on David, but she was certain that there must be some. She supposed that she would need to find one or two, or maybe more to battle over her. Fighting suitors had always upset her father and annoyed Brickley. It was rather fun to watch them condemn men who were emotional enough to challenge each other over a woman. Thinking on the subject brought a smile to her lips.

"I had a feeling I might find you here."

A soft, deep voice startled her. Emilie's head snapped up to see David standing a few feet away, looking at her. He was still dressed in the mail and tunic she had seen him wear when competing. In fact, he was in full battle regalia except for his helm. It was a rather imposing and proud sight. His blond hair, close-cropped, was stiff with perspiration, and his eyes were both warm and concerned.

Emilie didn't want to see that look in his eye and she quickly looked away, her heart pounding with distress now that he was in her midst. "It... it is nice and quiet here," she said, lying to him in the hopes that he would believe whatever she said and simply go away. "The lists are so crowded and busy and dirty that I... I had to leave. I do not like crowds, anyway. I was hoping no one would find me."

David's gaze remained steady on her; he wasn't an idiot. He could see that something had upset her and he suspected what it was. He had from the moment she had fled the lists because he could read it in her expression. When she'd run, he'd immediate bolted for the arena gate, leaving his horse with one of the de Lohr squires as he went in pursuit of her. He'd hoped to impress her with his bout but he could see that he'd only upset her. Perhaps he'd even discouraged her. Odd how he cared what she thought, but the truth was that he did. He cared a great deal although he had no idea why he should.

"Then I am sorry to impose upon your solitude," he said. "As your father's men are running in circles, I thought I might find you here. Call it a hunch."

He was smiling when he said it, but Emilie didn't see his smile. She simply nodded, keeping her eyes averted.

"Now that you have found me, mayhap you will do me the honor of leaving me in peace," she said. "As I said, it is quiet here away from the crowds. I rather like it here."

David could see the change in her manner and he sought to reassure her on what he thought was her problem.

"You need not be embarrassed, Lady Emilie," he said. "The joust is a violent spectacle and is not for everyone. I do not blame you for not wanting to watch it but I am truly sorry that it upset you so. I am sorry if I had a part in that."

He sounded so sincere, so caring, but Emilie would not be fooled. Perhaps that was one of his tricks, a ploy to lull women into a false sense of security with him. "I am not upset," she said, though her manner was stiff. "I simply wish to be left alone."

David didn't know her well enough to know why she was suddenly so cold to him. From any other woman, he wouldn't have cared a lick, but from Emilie... aye, he cared. He cared more than he wanted to admit. But he wasn't going to give in to the gnawing urge to know why she was being so cold with him when not an hour earlier, there had been warmth and interest in her eyes. She had asked him to leave, so leave he would.

"Very well, my lady," he said. "I am sorry to have bothered you."

Emilie was still looking at the hands in her lap. "You did not."

David's gaze lingered on her. "Am I to understand you will not be returning to the games?"

She shook her head. "Nay, I will not."

He reached into his tunic and pulled forth her favor. "Would you like this returned, then?"

Emilie had to look at him in order to see what he meant and when she saw her pale kerchief, she reached out and took it from his grasp.

"Thank you," she murmured.

David didn't say another word. He simply turned on his heel and headed out of the secluded area but he hadn't taken five steps when his curiosity, and concern, got the better of him. He was truly at a loss at her turn in behavior and could only imagine it was because he had done something to offend her. He must have done it unknowingly because he truly couldn't figure out what it might be. Or, perhaps, someone had told her something about him, something frightening? He shouldn't have asked her but he couldn't help himself. He very much wanted to know if he'd done something to offend her if, for no other reason, to know what in the hell he'd done.

He didn't have a clue.

Women were mysterious creatures, indeed.

"My lady, may I ask one question before I go?" he said. "Purely out of courtesy, may I beg you to give me a truthful answer?"

Emilie was coming to feel quite emotional. Her guts were churning and she felt very much like weeping. The man was so strong and proud and beautiful, and to see him standing so near her was nearly more than she could bear. It was foolish, really; so ridiculous and foolish, the way she felt about a man she barely knew. Embarrassed he had sucked her in with his charm, embarrassed that she hadn't been smart enough to see behind the bright de Lohr façade.

"I will always give you a truthful answer," she said hoarsely. "I do not lie."

"I did not mean to imply that you did."

"What is your question?"

He sighed faintly. "Only an hour ago you were quite happy," he said softly. "You were not afraid to look at me and you very eagerly gave me your favor. What has happened in this sweet and brief hour that should see you unable to look me in the eye and taking your favor back?"

Emilie thought on the question. She had promised to be truthful but she didn't want to sound like an idiot in telling him the truth, so she turned the tables on him. Perhaps he was the one who needed to clarify things, not her.

"I will answer your question if you answer mine," she said. "Who was the woman in the royal box that was waving to you?"

"My brother's wife, Lady Dustin."

My brother's wife. Emilie lifted her head to look at him, seeing the utter truth in his sky-blue eyes. He had answered without hesitation and that was not the behavior of a man with something to hide. *My brother's wife...* Sweet Mary, had she really jumped to such conclusions about the man? Barely knowing him yet behaving as if he somehow belonged to her, as if he somehow owed her something? In her haste, she could see she'd made an ass out of herself. She wanted to find a hole to climb into, something very deep and dark, where David's beautiful eyes wouldn't see her.

Oh, the folly of it....

"Your brother's *wife*?" she repeated, as if she had to hear it out loud once more to confirm what an utter idiot she had been. "This is the same woman who was attacked last night?"

David nodded. "Aye," he said. "She sustained a sword wound to her leg but she will heal. She is here at the field and not resting as she is supposed to be because she bullied my brother into allowing her to come. She can be quite petulant some times. Now, will you answer my question? What has happened in the past hour that you would take your favor back? What have I done?"

Emilie was cornered. She had no choice but to tell him, now knowing for certain that he would walk away from her and only remember the memory of Emilie Hampton to be a disturbing and silly one. She swallowed hard before answering.

"You have done nothing," she said quietly, looking him in the eye but having difficulty doing it. "It is my fault. I am the one who has done something. You see, I saw you speak with the woman in the royal box, the familiarity you had with each other, and I thought that... suffice it to say that I thought dishonorable things about you. I thought you were using my favor in secret, mayhap to even make the lady in the royal box jealous. I did not know she was your brother's wife. To be truthful, it is not my place to think such things because I do not know you beyond the contact we have had today, so it is my grave mistake to have assumed such things. I do not expect forgiveness, my lord, and shan't ask for it. I have behaved abominably."

By the time she was finished, David was looking at her with a faint smirk on his face. After a moment, he chuckled, shaking his head.

"Is that what you thought?" he asked.

Emilie nodded firmly. "I did."

He chuckled again. "When I brought my horse up in front of the lists, there must have been thirty women throwing favors at me," he said. "But I only had eyes for you. Did that not tell you that, mayhap,

I am not the type to have multiple women, and most especially multiple women in the same place? That would be utter suicide."

Emilie wasn't sure just how angry he was. She expected that he would be quite angry and she knew she deserved it. "As I said, I have only really met you today," she said. "I do not know your true character but I should not have thought so poorly of you without knowing more about you. Again, you have my sincerest apologies."

David still had the same lazy smile on his face as he'd had when she'd first admitted her issue. Silently, he retraced his steps, closing the gap between them. Thoughtfully, he stroked his chin.

"Are you truly sorry?" he asked.

Emilie nodded without hesitation. "I am."

"Prove it. Give me back your favor."

The kerchief was still in Emilie's hand and she lifted it, extending it to him. David's eyes never left hers as he took it from her fingers, bringing it to his nose again. He inhaled deeply and tucked it back into his tunic, in a safe spot near his heart. Before she could lower her hand, however, he took it and held it, all the while gazing into the woman's eyes.

"Shall I tell you something about me now?" he asked. "You said that you hardly knew me, which is true, so mayhap I should tell you something about me so that you will know I do not make sport of women's feelings. Not to say that I am celibate, for that is not the case at all. Like any other man, I appreciate a beautiful woman, but not more than one at a time. I do not do well in group situations. If a woman has my attention, then it is all of my attention and not merely some of it."

Emilie was quivering as he gently held her fingers; she'd known a man or two to hold her hand, of course, but not like this. Never like this. It was as if something wild and fluid was tearing through David's veins and flowing into hers. His touch made her tremble.

"I believe you," she said. "Truly, you do not have to tell me your entire life story, my lord. Your life is your own and I suppose I shall learn more about you as time permits. You do not need to tell me everything now."

His face fell dramatically. "Then you do not wish to hear my great stories of valor?" he asked. "I spent three years in The Levant with Richard; I have many great stories from my adventures in that land. There was the time when my patrol was ambushed by Saracen madmen and I saved the entire patrol by diverting the ambush. Thank God my horse was faster than any of theirs, else I would not be here to tell the story. My horse and I had to hide out for three days while they chased us before I was able to make it back to my army."

Emilie was grinning. "How brave," she said, suspecting he wanted to hear praise. They seemed to be quickly heading back to the mood they'd established earlier in the day, in this precise spot, when she had flirted with him but he'd remained rather indifferent to it. Or at least pretended to be. Now, she could see that perhaps he hadn't been resistant in the least. "I am sure that was only one of many times when you were forced to show your courage beyond that of a normal man's."

He nodded. "That is true," he said without modesty. "The sands of The Levant were meant for men to prove their mettle. It is not for the weak of heart. There was both victory and heartache there."

He seemed to subdue a bit, as if remembering the heartache more than the victory. Something in his expression clouded over and she hastened to lighten the mood, for both their sakes.

"I hope that someday you will honor me with details of your adventures there," she said. "My father mentioned that you and your brother had only recently returned."

David nodded. "Last month," he said. "Strange; it seems as if we have been home for a very long time. It doesn't seem as if much has changed here since we were away."

Emilie lifted her eyebrows curiously. "Do you miss The Levant that much?"

He shook his head. "Nay," he replied. "But we were there for three long years... *long* years. Now that we are home, I will be truthful when I say that it is almost disorienting. Much since our return has been disorienting."

"Such as?"

He glanced at her, thinking the obvious. It was becoming easier to talk to her and he spoke before he could stop himself. "My brother was given his wife by King Richard," he said. "He married her almost as soon as we returned. That situation is still taking some getting used to."

Emilie could see that the idea distressed him. She had no idea why, but it was clear that he seemed somewhat emotional about it. She smiled at him, once again trying to lighten the mood that seemed to be taking a heady turn.

"And the king did not gift you with a bride?" she asked, feigning outrage. "I am shocked. I should think that your actions in diverting the ambush you spoke of would warrant a very rich bride."

David smiled weakly at her. "I will select my own bride, thank you very much," he said. "I do not need our king to consign one to me as one would consign unwanted baggage."

Emilie laughed softly. "Is that what you think of a wife? Unwanted baggage?"

David shrugged, somewhat coyly now that they were on to his least-favorite subject – a wife. "I am not the type of man to have a wife," he said. "There is too much to do for king and country, and it would be cruel to leave a wife alone as I completed my duty. My brother thought that way, too, until Richard forced his wife upon him. Nowadays, he must think of her at every turn. For so many years, it was just the two of us completing our duty and now... well, you do not wish to hear any of this, do you? My apologies for rambling on."

Emilie shook her head, evidently greatly interested in what he had to say. She was indeed learning a great deal about him, including his opinion on marriage, and she tried not to let that bother her.

Perhaps with the right woman....

"No need," she said. "But I can understand how the introduction of your brother's wife had upset the balance in returning home."

He looked at her, a light of warmth glimmering in his eyes. "That is a very good way of putting it," he said. "The balance has been upset but it will right itself again, I am sure. While I am waiting for that to happen, I am enjoying my return home and I am enjoying this tournament. Can I implore you to return with me now? I should like my good luck charm in the stands when I make my next bout."

Emilie grinned, smiling sheepishly as she did so. Enchanted, and thrilled that things were well between them again, he tucked her hand into the crook of his elbow and led her from the walkway, out into the alley, and then back out into the avenue beyond. It was busy in the street as he led her back in the direction of the lists, his heart feeling lighter and happier than it had in a very long time.

In spite of Emilie's apologies to the contrary, he was very flattered that she'd thought enough of him to be jealous over his interaction with his brother's wife. It was true that jealousy was not a particularly pleasant emotion, but in this case, he took it to mean that it was because Emilie was warming to him just as he was warming to her. He was very glad he had her attention because she certain had his, and he kept turning to glance at her as they walked down the avenue, grinning at her when she would smile, shyly, and look away. It really was rather sweet, the delicate orchestrations of flirtation that he was becoming more comfortable with. Once out of practice, he was quickly gaining his feet again. They were just nearing the lists when he heard someone call his name.

"David!"

David came to a halt and turned swiftly, seeing Edward de Wolfe running in his direction. De Wolfe was sporting a massive bruise on his forehead as he came upon David, who peered closely at his head.

"Jesus," he hissed. "What happened to you?"

Edward was pale. "I was unseated in my bout right after yours," he said. "Where have you been?"

David looked at Emilie. "Lady Emilie required an escort," he said simply, returning his focus to Edward. "Why? Was someone looking for me?"

Edward shook his head, grunting wearily as he did so. "Nay," he said. "But there is much to tell, much you should be aware of. You must come with me. Now."

David could hear the tension in Edward's tone but it also bordered on rude, at least as far as Emilie was concerned. He was brushing her off as if she was unimportant and David wasn't sure he liked that.

"I will after I have seated Lady Emilie," he said steadily. "Wait for me here."

Edward was clearly impatient. "Hurry, then."

David was about to take a step towards the lists but Edward's tone had him perplexed as well as moderately unhappy. It was as if the man was ordering him about, agitated, and clearly eager to be rid of Lady Emilie. He frowned.

"Edward, if you have something to say, tell me now," he said. "Otherwise, I will return in good time once I have seated Lady Emilie."

With that, he started to move towards the stairs leading up the lists once again but Edward's voice stopped him.

"Brentford is dead," he said.

David came to a halt and looked at him, eyes wide. "What's this you say?" he breathed, incredulous. "Brentford is *dead*?"

Edward nodded, his pale face even paler. "Remember what we were told about the men John had hired to compete against us as legitimate knights?" he asked, watching David bob his head. "Dennis le Londe was one of them. Dennis the Destroyer broke Brentford's neck in a completely illegal move not ten minutes ago. The marshals have disqualified him but John overrode their decision, saying it was an accident. We all know it was not, but John ruling stands. Now the man has advanced to the next round along with you, Christopher, Leeton, and Thomas Dudley. At some point, one of you may go against him and your brother wants to talk to you. Now, will you come with me?"

David was stunned by Brentford's death. His friend had been alive and well only minutes earlier; he'd spoken to the man right after they'd drawn lots and Brentford had said nothing about drawing Dennis le Londe as an opponent. *Dennis the Destroyer*. That was what the man was called, a French mercenary who had fought with Phillip Augustus in the Holy Land, now returned to England as a paid assassin. There was no other way to put it; Dennis went where the money was and killed whomever he was paid to kill. In this case, it had been Brentford le Bec.

Dennis being back in England, and at this tournament in particular, was very bad news indeed. But David thought it rather strange that no one had mentioned Dennis' name or had even seen him, up until now. Dennis was well known to the knighthood as wicked and immoral and, worse yet, a very skilled warrior. Still reeling from the news, David struggled against the sorrow over his friend's death, and nodded his head sharply.

"Give me a few moments," he said. "I will join you."

Edward simply stood there as David took Emilie up the steps leading to the lists. He didn't even stop to think that Emilie had heard everything Edward had said; he was lost to his own thoughts, of Brentford's death, and of Dennis le Londe's behavior, when he happened to look at Emilie. Her eyes were wide on him, her brow furrowed with concern. When she caught him looking at her, she tried to amend her expression but it was too late. He had seen it. When their eyes met, he forced a smile.

"Nothing to worry over," he told her with as much confidence as he could muster. "There are always unscrupulous knights at these events. We will weed them out, so you needn't worry."

Emilie forced a smile in return. "I can only imagine the type of men these competitions attract," she said. "The purse is rather large, is it not?"

David nodded. "It is," he agreed. "Therefore, every fool who can joust will enter hoping to win money, but they are eliminated in the end."

"They are?"

"Aye, they are; by me. I intend to win everything."

The arrogance was back in his tone and she laughed; she couldn't help it. The man had an immeasurable amount of price. But she also suspected he was trying to alleviate the very worrisome things she heard coming from de Wolfe, and she was touched that he should be so concerned for her feelings. In fact, she was touched by his actions in general, for he did not have to seek her out when she ran from the lists, nor did he have to explain himself. He could have very well walked away from her, but he didn't. To her, that showed the mark of a noble and compassionate man, and she felt very bad for the ills she'd thought of him. It was utterly her foolishness and she knew it, vowing to never thing poorly of the man again unless he earned it.

Nathalie, Elise, and Lillibet were open-mouthed when the mighty David de Lohr re-seated Emilie next to her sister and politely kissed her hand before he left the lists. Emilie sat there with a big fat smile on her face, realizing that not only were her sisters shocked at David's appearance, but so were half the young women in the lists. All of those women who had been tossing their favors at David gazed upon the one who actually managed to capture the knight's attention, and some of them were looking at Emilie rather hostilely. She stuck her tongue out at a pair of women who were shooting her particularly nasty expressions.

Victory was sweet, indeed.

When the nasty women looked away, incensed, Emilie went back to smiling. She simply couldn't help it. But she was unaware that spurned young women weren't the only people who had seen David de Lohr escort her back to her seat.

From the royal box, Ralph Fitz Walter had seen it, too.

He tucked the information away until it was the right time to act on it.

CHAPTER SIX

D AVID COULD HEAR the weeping even outside of the tent.
After leaving Emilie in the lists, he and Edward headed for
the Earl of Derby's encampment to see about Brentford, and the
sounds of sorrow reached him well before he even entered the tented
area. Derby's tents were undyed wool with yellow tips on the crests
where the poles held them up, and the entry to the largest tent had
the Derby stag embroidered on it in yellow silk.

As the bustle of the encampment went on around them, David
and Edward made their way into Derby's settlement and headed for
the largest tent. The weeping was drawing them towards it, like a
siren's call of sorrow, and it was a heady sound indeed. They saw a
few soldiers they recognized standing outside of the large tent, men
who knew them and gestured for them to enter. Edward had already
seen Brentford and wasn't apt to view him again, so David pushed
aside the flap and went inside.

It was dark in the tent, lit only by two oil lamps from what David
could see. It smelled of leather and damp, that moldy damp smell
that was so common to the tents because the wool would get wet
sitting upon the damp ground. David's eyes hadn't yet adjusted to the
darkness when a figure was suddenly in face.

"David," the man said, gladness in his voice. "Thank God you
have come."

David found himself looking at the young heir to the Earldom of Derby. He had fought with William de Ferrers in the Holy Land, as the young man was a great favorite of Richard, as his father was. The Earldom of Derby was technically just the estate of Derby, and not the title itself, as it had been stripped from the family some time ago, but everyone called the elder William 'earl' as a courtesy. The younger William, at twenty years and four, managed a good deal of his elderly father's business and had always handled himself responsibly. He was well-liked. But now, David found himself looking at the strained young lord, looking much different from the confident and happy man he had known.

"I just heard about Brentford, my lord," he said. "Edward told me it was Dennis le Londe."

William nodded his head; it was clear the young man was quite shaken. "It happened so fast," he said, hesitantly looking over to a corner of the tent, in the darkness, where a woman was weeping over a supine body. "I was only just speaking with him and now…."

He shook his head, unable to continue. David looked over at the pallet in the darkness, seeing Brentford's feet as the woman hovered over the body. He sighed heavily.

"I am so very sorry," he murmured. "Brentford was my dear friend. I was only just speaking with him, too. I simply cannot believe this has happened."

The young lord sniffed loudly, composing himself. "It has been a difficult year for us, David," he said. "Leeton de Shera left his position as captain of my father's army when his wife, my sister, died two years ago this winter. You know Leeton, do you not? Did you know his wife had died?"

David nodded. "I did," he said. "He came to see my brother last month and told him everything. He has come with us to Windsor, but surely you knew that. He told Chris that he could not stand the memories associated with Derby, memories of his dead Rachel, so Chris has allowed him to remain with us for now."

Young William wiped at his nose. "Leeton left his son with my parents," he said. "The child my sister died giving birth to. I swear to you that young Richard is the only thing that keeps my father going. He lives for the boy."

David lifted his eyebrows in understanding. "I am sure it does an old man good to have his heirs about him," he said. "Have you seen Leeton? He is here, competing with us."

William shook his head. "I have not seen him yet but even if I do, he will not speak to me," he said. "I suppose the memories are still too difficult for him to deal with. He was quite in love with my sister, you know. But when he departed, it left a hole in our command structure and Brentford assumed the post. He was supposed to marry my other sister, Rebecca. Did you know that?"

David sighed heavily, hanging his head with the horrible sorrow he was facing. "I did not," he replied. "Jesus, I did not. Am I to assume that is your sister weeping over his body?"

William nodded, looking at the corner of the tent and starting to tear up no matter how hard he tried not to. "Aye," he whispered tightly. "I… I do not know how to take her away from him. He… he must be prepared for the return home."

David put his hand on the young man's shoulder. "Leave her alone," he said. "Give her all the time she needs. Brentford does not need to be prepared for a little while yet. Allow your sister her grief. When the time comes to prepare him, I will help. Send for me."

William simply nodded his head before looking away, blinking the tears away. "First Rachel and now Brentford," he muttered. "My parents will be devastated. They liked Brentford a great deal."

David squeezed the young lord's shoulder before dropping his hand. "As did I," he said. "I will pay my respects, if I may. And I will say again how very sorry I am. If you need anything at all, please send word. My brother and I are at your service."

David started to move towards the corner of the tent but William reached out to grasp him before he could move away. "Before you go," he said, keeping his voice low, "it was le Londe who killed him. Did you even know he was here, David? I did not know until Brentford drew his name for the joust. What in the hell is he doing here?"

David paused, seeing by William's expression that the young lord had evidently not heard about John and his mercenary crew. Since William had been in the Holy Land with Richard, however, he too knew of Dennis le Londe. He knew of the French knight's wickedness. The man had a reputation that spanned continents.

"It seems that John has hired mercenaries to compete against Richard's supporters," he said softly. "These men will do anything to win, including kill. But trust me when I say that Dennis will pay. This offense against Brentford will not go unanswered, my lord. My brother and I will see to it."

That seemed to bring some relief to young William's features. "I knew you would," he said, his grip still on David. "Whatever you do... make sure it hurts. Make sure it hurts a great deal. Make him suffer, David. Please."

David nodded his head, feeling so much hatred and angst towards Dennis le Londe that it was difficult to control. But he steeled himself. Without another word, he moved to the pallet where Brentford was lying.

The woman weeping over Brentford didn't even look up as David stood there and gazed down at his dark haired friend. The man didn't have any visible signs of injury; he merely looked as if he was sleeping. There was dirt in his hair and on his tunic where he had hit the ground, but it was clear that Brentford had not suffered at all. He looked very peaceful.

That peaceful expression was like a stab to David's heart. It just wasn't fair, any of it. He went to his knees beside the man, riveted to his face, thinking of the horrible waste of it all. Brentford le Bec was an excellent knight, a good friend, and David was feeling his loss already. Bending over, he kissed the man on the forehead.

"This is not over, Brentford," he murmured. "Dennis will pay. With every damn bone in his body, I will ensure he pays. Every blow we deal him will have your name on it. You shall be avenged, my friend, I swear it."

With that, David reached out and clasped one of the hands that was resting on Brentford's chest, squeezing it. There was a promise in that squeeze, the affirmation of knightly bonds and brotherly affection. It was a painful farewell. As he released Brentford's hand, the woman next to him spoke.

"Thank you," she whispered. "For avenging him, I thank you."

David turned to look at her; she was pretty, dark haired and dark eyed, her nose red from weeping. "You are Lady Rebecca?" he asked.

She nodded. "I am," she said, sniffling. "Will you... will you make sure it hurts a great deal? Whatever you do to the man who killed my Brent, will you make sure it hurts terribly?"

It was a shocking request from a lady but in hindsight, perhaps not so shocking. William had made the same request, too. It seemed that both of them understood revenge in its purest form.

Make it hurt.

From the depths of the soul, Brentford's lady demanded satisfaction and she evidently wanted an eye for an eye. That was usually a man's point of view. But David respected her request and looked her straight in the eye as he spoke.

"He will feel agony such as no man has ever known," he swore softly. "I vow this, my lady. For Brentford, he will be punished."

David would swear, until the end of his days, that he had never seen a sinister or grateful smile as the lady thanked him. "You have my gratitude," she murmured.

"David!"

The hiss came from the tent entry, distracting David from that wicked gesture on Rebecca's lovely face. He turned to see young William, as well as Edward, standing in the darkness. Edward was gesturing to him so he quietly excused himself and made his way over to Edward.

"What is it?" he asked.

"The marshals are drawing lots for the next round," he said quietly. "We must go if we are to be given a slot."

David nodded reluctantly, turning once more to watch the lady as she bent over Brentford, now stroking the man's hair. As David and William and Edward watched, she began singing to Brentford. It was a soft lullaby. Sickened, and enraged, David turned for Edward.

"Let us go," he said. "Let us pray that I draw Dennis in this round, for I would sincerely like to punish the man. Did we bring the spear-tipped joust poles, Edward?"

Edward shook his head. "We did not, not this time."

"I have spear-tipped poles," William intervened in their conversation. "You may take them. Take all of them. Use them well."

David didn't have to be told twice. He and Edward left the tent to collect all of the spear-tipped poles that Derby had, which amounted to six total. Hastily, they carried them back to the de Lohr encampment where Christopher and the rest of the men were. When Christopher saw the spear-tipped poles, he understood why David had them but he personally refused to use them. He insisted that he didn't need a speared pole in order to bring down le Londe but wouldn't fault the others if they wanted to use them. As the elder de Lohr brother remained true to his crow's-foot tipped joust poles, David and Leeton were more than eager to use the spear tipped. David was more hot-headed than his much cooler brother; in this case, that difference was clearly showing.

David wanted vengeance any way he could get it.

David and Leeton and Edward were in the process of adjusting the tips when Christopher's wife, escorted by Burton, came out of the lists and joined them for a short while. David, however, spared the woman little time. He continued to work on tightening up the spear tips so they would not bend or break when meeting with the steel of chain mail or even the immovability of a shield. Between he and

Leeton, they managed to sharpen the spears into razor-sharp daggers, tips that could do Dennis le Londe a good deal of damage.

This time, there would be no mistakes or oversights. What they intended to do to Dennis, they intended for it to be permanent.

For Brentford.

THE JOUST COMPETITIONS continued on for the rest of the morning, the field of knights narrowing down little by little. There were two more substantial injuries, but for the most part, the majority of the combatants walked away unharmed. By midday, the list had been narrowed down to only two men and, as expected, Christopher was to face-off against Dennis the Destroyer.

Dustin had actually enjoyed the rest of the bouts and was even able to watch her husband dispose of his final three challengers with nary a twinge of apprehension, but when it became apparent that his final round would be against John's champion, her anxiety returned worse than before.

Sitting between Edward and Marcus, her stomach was twisting into painful knots. Christopher was at the opposite end of the field and she could see his spiral-decorated shaft pointing up to the sky as he adjusted his shield over his left side. Sir Dennis was closer to her, his horned helmet quite imposing as he sat stock still, watching Christopher settle himself.

Dustin found herself staring at the man, her eyes shooting daggers and every inch of her body conveying pain and hatred. She didn't even know him yet she hated him all the same; from what she had heard, he was a disgrace to the brotherhood of knights and for the simple fact he was competing against her husband, she hated him all the more.

Sir Dennis reined his steed over to the lists where John and Ralph were sitting. He raised his visor and Dustin was able to catch a glimpse of the despised face.

"Ten marks, did you say?" the knight said in a heavy French accent. "Seems like a small amount for a man's life. He is married, n'est-ce pas? Where is his wife?"

Ralph jerked his head leisurely in Dustin's direction. "The Lady Dustin de Lohr."

Dennis' bright, pale eyes immediately focused on Dustin and she went rigid under his naked scrutiny. He was probably as old as her husband, plain-faced, almost boyish-looking. She found it hard to believe that this man had the nickname of "Destroyer." He smiled and she quickly averted her gaze.

"I want her, as well," Dennis said to John. "Ten marks and the mademoiselle."

As he reined his horse away, Dustin's lovely face washed with shocked anger.

"What is he talking about?" she demanded hotly of John and Ralph, ignoring the titles completely.

The prince glanced casually over his shoulder at the sheriff, who shrugged lazily. "I wouldn't know," he replied. "Ralph? Do you know what he's talking about?"

"I have no knowledge, sire," Ralph lied. "We will have to ask him to clarify his statement when the joust is finished."

Dustin was shaking with fury and confusion so Marcus reached out to pat her arm. He and Edward exchanged disgusted glances, each man knowing exactly what the knight had meant. Had Christopher heard it, there would be French guts spilled out all over the ground.

The tournament marshal took the field, looking at both competitors to make sure they were ready. A hush settled over the crowd and Dustin's palms began to sweat terribly. She wanted to cover her eyes but could not seem to lift her hands. The stands grew quieter and quieter until it seemed that all she could hear was the scream of the hawk riding the drafts high above the arena, and she wondered vaguely if it were a bad omen.

Dustin closed her eyes a brief second, fighting off her lurching stomach. She swore at that moment that if Christopher survived, she would make him promise never to compete in a tourney again. She simply could not take the terror it provoked; excitement be damned.

The marshal dropped the flag and Dustin's heart surged into her throat as she watched her husband and Dennis charge at one another like rolling thunder, poles leveling out as they closed the gap. Dustin's fingers flew to her mouth and she bit hard to keep from screaming, seeing the two mailed and colored knights come together in a scream of wood and metal, horse and man. Yet a split second before their poles collided with one another, she saw her husband jerk sideways in the saddle and then came a thunderous, shattering crash.

Christopher's whole body snapped like a rag-doll from the force of the blow, but he remained seated as his destrier came to a halt at the end of the run. The crowd let up a collective groan and rose to their feet, concerned for their newly-returned hero. Dustin shrieked as Marcus and Edward shot angrily to stand.

"Damnation!" Marcus shouted. "He brought that pole to bear on Chris' head."

Edward furiously agreed. "Had he not ducked when he did, he would have had his head torn off."

"Jesus, his shoulder must be broken from that blow," Marcus raged. "How does he look, Edward?"

Edward was standing at the end of the platform, scrutinizing Christopher closely. His liege seemed to have righted himself adequately, but he could see that his left shoulder was bleeding through the mail.

"He shall live," Edward said reluctantly, turning back to his seat. "But that shoulder is going to need attention."

Dustin was still seated, her hands folded at her mouth and her huge gray eyes full of tears. Marcus gazed down at her, realizing they must have terrified her further with their shouting.

"He's fine, Dustin," he said softly, sitting beside her. "Another pass and he shall have the bastard on his arse."

She shook her head and closed her eyes, wiping at the tears as quickly as they fell and trying hard to be brave. "I know," she said with courage she did not feel.

The field marshal and a few other officials were conversing with Christopher and they could see his head nodding faintly. John turned to gaze at Dustin, his eyes grazing over her.

"I do hope your husband is well enough to continue," he said. "'Twould be a shame to lose de Lohr. The competition wouldn't be the same without him."

Dustin looked hard at the prince, sick and tired of his deceptions and games. "Why do you offer me such bold-faced lies? You hate my husband and would like nothing better than to see him dead."

Only Dustin and her forthright manner could get away with such blatant disrespect. John's eyes widened with feigned surprise.

"How untrue, Lady de Lohr," he insisted. "I greatly respect your husband and his skills. To lose him would be to lose the Defender of the Realm and leave us all vulnerable."

Dustin's face twitched with fury. "You are a liar, my lord, and a disgrace to the crown," she snapped. "I should have listened to my husband when he told me to stay away from you."

Ralph turned on her savagely. "Any more from your mouth, madam, and I throw you in the dungeons for blasphemy."

Marcus and Edward were up, preparing to rip Ralph joint from joint but John put up a quelling hand. "Sit down, everyone, or I shall have you all removed." His hand fell limply to the arm of the chair. "Emotions are high, especially with an injured comrade, which is why I forgive Lady de Lohr her words. Look, now; the marshal is moving to centerfield."

Dustin, her beautiful face dark, sunk back into her chair as Marcus and Edward regained their seats. The whole day had been draining on her and it wasn't even noon yet, she could not even fathom what the afternoon might hold.

Dustin wasn't mentally prepared when the marshal dropped his *flag. Christopher and Sir Dennis stormed toward each other with a deafening roar, shafts leveling out, and Dustin tried to close her eyes but could not manage the action. She could only stare, frozen in her seat, waiting for what would happen next.*

Two glancing blows and naught else occurred. With the next pass, Christopher broke his shaft and took his brother's as a replacement. As he handled the heavy pole, Marcus and Edward glanced at each other over Dustin's head, silent words acknowledging that their liege was definitely favoring his left shoulder.

The crowd's feelings were rising and falling like waves upon the shore, and Dustin's emotions with them. Every time Christopher made it through a pass unharmed, she whispered a prayer to God that his next one would be as successful. It was completely maddening and frustrating and she was so sick to her stomach that she thought she might vomit, but she didn't want to leave the lists. As much as she was terrified to watch, she knew there was no other place she would rather be.

At the other end of the field, Sir Dennis switched from his crow's foot shaft to a spear-tipped one. Marcus saw the exchange and his body went stiff with fury.

"Damnation," he spit, then turned to see if Edward had caught the switch. Indeed, Edward had and his golden eyes were wide with apprehension. In the midst of their anxiety, Dustin suddenly shot to her feet.

"He has got a dagger on the end of that shaft," she gasped with realization. "He is going to kill Christopher with it."

Marcus grabbed her arms and set her down as the combatants took up position. But Dustin would not be so easily sated.

"You must stop this!" she said frantically.

"I cannot," Marcus said quietly. "'Tis perfectly legal for Sir Dennis to joust with the spear-tipped shaft."

"Like hell!" Dustin shot out of her seat again, thrusting herself forward towards John and Ralph. "Sire, surely you will not allow your

champion to compete with a blade on the end of his pole?"

John looked amused with her terror. "My lady, 'tis painfully obvious that you have never been to a tournament before. Until a year or two ago, spear-tipped shafts were the only type used in a joust. The crow's foot tip is very new."

Dustin looked back at the prince in disbelief, her eyes trailing to the field helplessly as the competitors prepared for their run. The field marshal raised his flag and with the drop, the destriers sprang into a rumbling gallop.

Dustin could not move. It took all of her concentration to stand there and watch, her breath caught in her throat and her heart quivering in her chest, as her husband and the prince's champion raced toward each other at breakneck speed. Behind her, the crowd slowly rose to their feet in anticipation of what was to surely come.

When it happened, it happened too fast for the human eye to comprehend. The shafts came down and suddenly there was a deafening noise; Sir Dennis went flying from his destrier as if unseen hands had thrown him. Dustin's heart soared until she saw a split-second later that Christopher, his destrier gored by the 12-foot shaft, went down hard enough to shake the ground. Dust and chunks of earth spewed into the air, and before she could react Marcus and Edward flew from the lists and were racing across the arena.

Dustin was in shock. In fact, almost the entire lists were rushing onto the field. Even Ralph had jumped from the platform and was running toward the mass of people, all swarming around the two competitors. The arena turned into a boiling pot of knights and officials, and she completely lost sight of her husband and his horse.

The crowd in the lists was loud with their concerns, but Dustin could not hear them. It was as if she were locked in her own little world, her entire life hanging on what was happening out on the dirt in front of her. She tried to pick out her husband's knights, any familiar head, but there were so many men in armor that it was impossible to single out any one person. She could hear shouting and see all sorts of *movement surrounding her husband and his animal.*

"My, my." Prince John was standing beside her, shielding his eyes from the glare of the weak sun as he gazed out on the field. "Quite a finish to an exciting bout. I do hope everyone is alright."

Dustin could not even manage a retort. Her mind was like mud. Before she realized it, she descended the stairs and made her way across the field like a woman hypnotized. She saw nothing and heard nothing; her focus entirely on where she last saw her husband. The honor guard that Christopher had left in charge of her broke rank and began to follow, wondering if they should prevent her from going any further. Yet they did not, instead they acted as an escort and shoved people out of her way as she went. Dustin didn't even notice their assistance.

Sir Dennis' men managed to get him back on his feet. He was several feet to her right, quite shaken as he leaned on his comrades for support. Dustin snapped out of her trance long enough to stare him down with a look of completely loathing. He didn't see her as he was helped from the field.

She pushed into a crowd of knights and suddenly the legs of Christopher's horse became visible through the crowd. Seized with anguish, she tried to shove her way further but was grabbed with large, firm hands.

"Lady de Lohr." It was an older knight, his visor raised and his face coated with perspiration. "I am Lord Lyle Hampton, Earl of Canterbury. Certainly there are better places for you to be than out here on a dirty field. Please allow me to escort...."

Dustin jerked away from him roughly. "I would see my husband."

The earl eyed the sergeant of the escort as he grasped Dustin again, more firmly this time. "I understand completely, my lady," he said gently, "but it would be much better if you wait in the lists to see your husband."

"Nay!" she screamed. "Let me go or I shall scratch your eyes out."

Lord Hampton, fortunately, was a man of even temper, having three daughters of his own. He was a friend of Christopher's and also a friend of Christopher's uncle, Sir Philip de Lohr of Lohrham Forest. Christopher had pointed Dustin proudly out to the earl before the competition, which was how the earl knew who the lovely lady was on sight. And he also knew without a doubt that she should not be here.

"As you wish, my lady," he said, holding her with an iron grip. "But it will have to wait. We must get you out of this dirt. Sergeant, your help would be appreciated."

The sergeant-at-arms gripped Dustin's other arm and between he and the earl, were able to direct her back toward the stands. But Dustin would have no part of it and turned into a wild animal. She slugged the earl in the nose, drawing blood, before she turned like a banshee on the sergeant and kicked him in a weak point in the armor by his groin. Free for the moment, she grabbed her skirts and tore through the crowds of knights and men, knowing her greatest advantage was the fact that men in armor lack decent balance and are not quick on their feet. With enough shoving, she knew she could throw them off, enough to reach Christopher.

As she rounded a particularly tall bank of knights, she caught sight of Edward's head and she screamed his name loudly. At the sound of his name, Edward whirled around and rushed to her as she moved toward him. He snatched her firmly around the torso and she twisted and punched him.

"Let me go!" She fought Edward with every ounce of strength she possessed. "Where is Christopher?"

Edward was having a devil of a time holding onto her. "Come on, Dustin," he said, grunting when she elbowed him in the gut. "Let's get you back to the lists."

"I will not," she shrieked. "What happened to my husband? Is he dead?"

"Nay, he's not dead," he said, getting a better grip on her when she relaxed a bit. Mayhap if he was honest with her she would stop fighting so much. As it was, she had no idea what was transpiring with her husband and was understandably terrified. "He's trapped under his horse, Dustin. They are trying to free him now."

As he hoped, she stopped struggling and instead strained around Edward to get a better look at what was happening.

"Oh, Lord," she whispered, seeing only seas of mailed legs. "Is the horse dead?"

"Aye," he replied quietly. "The spear went right into his chest."

"Is Christopher alright?" She turned her brimming gray eyes up to him. "Please tell me, Edward."

Edward could see her anguish. He loosened his grip and put his arm around her waist. "Come with me," he said softly.

He led her around the crowd and soon Christopher and his horse came into view. Dustin's hands flew to her mouth to stop the sobs as she viewed the scene closely; the destrier, mortally wounded, fell sidelong into the dirt and trapped her husband's right leg underneath thousands of pounds of horseflesh and armor. Christopher, helmetless, was supported by David and Leeton as dozens of knights and soldiers and grooms tried to truss the horse up with rope, enough so they could lift him off Christopher.

Dud was near the animal's head and Marcus, his brow sweaty from exertion, was controlling the entire operation as he shouted orders loud enough for the king of Scotland to hear. Seeing her husband so helpless nearly drove Dustin over the edge.

She was standing yards away from Christopher, watching the urgent actions of the men working furiously to free her husband. Had Edward not been holding her firmly, she was sure she would have slipped to the ground from sheer grief. She found herself leaning against him, her head against his armored chest. As long as she could see Christopher and see that he was alive, she could keep herself calm.

"So this is where you went." The Earl of Canterbury strolled up casually, a handkerchief to his nose. "I thought as much."

Edward glanced over at the earl. "What happened to your nose, sire?"

The earl snickered. "Lady de Lohr and I were introduced," he said, studying her lovely profile as she watched the rescue effort on her husband.

Edward raised his eyebrows in horror but the earl waved him off, still chuckling. Together, the three of them watched the last of the rigging go around the destrier's body. The task had been difficult and time-consuming due to the angle the horse had landed and also for the fact that the men had to dig trenches underneath the animal to run the rope through.

Marcus tested the ropes himself and when he was satisfied, he ordered the men to be ready. Dustin tensed as the ropes were pulled taut, moving the beast inch by inch, while David and Leeton grasped Christopher's arms and tugged. In synchronization the men would pull at the horse as Christopher's men attempted to slide him out from underneath the animal.

It took several tries until finally, after a lifetime of torturous waiting, Christopher slipped free.

"I DO NOT like the joust," Elise said, tears in her eyes. "They frighten my families and they are violent and terrible. Two horses were killed! I want to go home!"

Emilie had her arm around her younger sister, trying to comfort the girl as the men on the field worked to clear up the mess created by one competitor ramming his spear-tipped joust pole into the chest of the other competitor's horse. One man had walked away but the other knight, a competitor who happened to be none other than David's brother, was still pinned on the ground beneath his dead destrier.

It had been a horrific accident that had sent many women fleeing the lists. Delicate female senses did not want to see that kind of carnage. But Emilie and her sisters and Lillibet had remained in their seats even as Christopher's wife had fled the royal box to see to her husband. The girls had watched her run off but they had lost sight of her in the crowd. They had lost sight of their father, down on the field, and of Brickley, too. Now, they simply sat and waited for the field to be cleared, but their thrill of seeing their first tournament had been summarily doused. There was nothing wonderful or exciting about it.

It was a blood sport.

"I am sorry, sweetheart," Emilie hugged her distraught sister. "Look, now; see Brick down on the field? He is helping rescue one of the men. It is not a bad thing to see our heroic knight in action, is it?"

Nathalie, who was glued to the activity on the field, never took her eyes off Brickley in the distance as he worked to shore up the horse that was lying on the elder de Lohr brother. "He is helping them remove one of the dead horses," she said. "The other horse fell on one of the knights. I can see that they are trying to remove the horse. Maybe they will cut its legs off so they can take it away in pieces!"

Elise squealed in horror and started to cry as Emilie swatted Nathalie on the shoulder. "Was that really necessary?" she hissed. "Stop being so dramatic."

Nathalie turned to her sister and frowned. "It could happen," she insisted. "You have never been to a tournament. You do not know how they remove dead horses. They are too heavy to carry all at once!"

Emilie sighed heavily and was preparing to verbally lash her sister but Lillibet intervened. "I think it would be a very good idea to take Elise back to our apartments," she said, spittle flying onto Nathalie's arm. "Shall we go, ladies? Your father's soldiers can escort us to the wagon to take us back."

Emilie and Nathalie immediately protested. "But the games are not over yet," Emilie insisted. "There is still the mass competition to see and I do not want to miss it."

Nathalie was also shaking her head, vigorously, as she wiped the spit off her arm. "I do not want to leave," she said. "It would be terrible if Brick were to win the coming mass competition and I was not here to see it. He carries my favor. It would be shameful if I left!"

Lillibet, seeing that she would have a struggle on her hands with Emilie and Nathalie, backed off somewhat. But Elise was still upset, still sniffling in Emilie's grasp. "I cannot leave you two alone," she said, wiping her mouth when she spit upon herself. "But Elise clearly is not enjoying the games. She is too young to have come. It would be unfair to force her to remain."

Emilie hugged Elise again. "Then you must return her to the apartments," she insisted. "Take a soldier with you and leave three for Nathalie and me. They will watch over us as we finish watching the games. Father is here, as is Brick. Nothing will happen to us, I promise."

Lillibet frowned. "It is not proper for me to leave you here without a chaperone."

Emilie sighed impatiently. "I am of age, Mother," she said. "Please do not worry over us. The soldiers will protect us from harm. Make sure one of them finds Father to tell him you have left us in the lists so that he knows. He will keep his eye on us."

Lillibet sighed heavily, looking at Elise, who was obviously unhappy. The youngest daughter's misery won over her dilemma about leaving the older girls without an escort.

"Very well," she said, unhappy. "I will return with Elise. But you will both promise me that neither of you will leave the lists without an escort. Will you swear this to me?"

Thrilled that they were going to have a bit of freedom with Lillibet gone, Emilie and Nathalie struggled to keep from appearing too excited about it.

"We swear," Emilie said seriously. "Take Elise, now. The poor child is quite upset."

Lillibet still wasn't sure about leaving the older girls but Elise's was weeping softly and she sought to comfort the girl. Taking a soldier with her to head for the wagon, she sent a second soldier hunting for Lyle in the gang of men on the field to inform him that his elder daughters were alone in the lists. That soldier soon returned after delivering his message, joining the remaining two soldiers who were charged with Lady Emilie and Lady Nathalie's safety. Considering how the games had gone so far, the men were on their guard. There seemed to be violence and death lurking about, as the joust had clearly proven.

Eventually, the field was cleared of dead horses, in one piece in spite of what Nathalie had predicted, and David's brother was slowly helped to his feet. The crowd, seeing the elder de Lohr brother stand, began to cheer loudly for the man. Being helped by two of his men, Christopher de Lohr labored towards the royal box where the prince and the man with the hugely swollen face were waiting.

But Emilie's focus was on David, who had been charged with escorting Lady de Lohr back to the royal box. Evidently, she was to award the prize to her husband for his victory in the joust and Emilie could see, even from the distance, that Lady de Lohr was a wreck. Given what she'd just seen her husband go through, Emilie didn't blame the woman, but her attention on Lady de Lohr was short-lived. Truth be told, she really only had eyes for David.

He was such a handsome man and her heart swelled at the sight of him. Grimy, sweaty, and dirty from having lost a hard-fought bout to his own brother that had sent Christopher to his round with Dennis le Londe, he had a firm grip on Lady de Lohr as he helped the woman back to the royal box.

David stood proud and tall, unmovable and unbreakable, as if he hadn't just seen his brother come within a hair's breadth of death. He was standing firm against the horror they'd all just witnessed, the cheating and death and tyranny, even if his stance was only for the benefit of Lady de Lohr, who was truly broken up about the circumstances. Still he stood next to her, holding her elbow until she pulled away to award her husband a ribbon of valor.

The prince had a few words to say before de Lohr was given his prize, a red brocaded ribbon held by his wife, and as Emilie listened to John speak to the crowd, she swore she could hear wickedness in his tone. His voice was medium-pitched and unspectacular, but his words were odd. He congratulated de Lohr on his victory against le Londe, but he did it in a way that did not seem sincere. It was almost condescending, as if the words masked a distaste that ran deep. Perhaps Emilie was reading something into it; perhaps not. But she was certain she heard scorn.

If David and the other de Lohr men heard it, they made no indication. It seemed that they were mostly concerned with getting the farce of an award ceremony over with and seeking treatment for Christopher's injuries. Lady de Lohr, weeping, handed her husband the ribbon, a seemingly small and unworthy thing to do considering what the man had gone through to win, but the elder de Lohr took it from his wife proudly.

The crowd cheered again when their champion collected his prize, and he was helped off the field; followed by his wife. David was with the group and he passed a look into the lists, as if to make sure Emilie was still there, to make sure she was safe with his own eyes. She was, on both accounts, and she waved at him discreetly. He smiled in return before he vanished from view, surrounded by de Lohr men.

But that sweet, lingering smile was enough to fill Emilie full with joy. He may have been out of her sight at this point but he clearly wasn't gone from her mind. She knew he would return at some point but until then, she had a great longing to see him again. She was concerned, however, that the unscrupulous knight who had killed Brentford and injured the elder de Lohr brother was still in the competition. If David remained in the competition as well, at some point, he would be facing the man. Emilie didn't like that thought at all. What happened to David's brother could very easily happen to him and she was greatly distressed at the thought. She didn't want to see him on the ground in agony as his brother had been.

Mulling over those torturous thoughts, Emilie was surprised to see her father suddenly appear. Clad in mail and the green and black colors of Canterbury, the man had come in from the rear of the lists, holding a bloodied kerchief to his nose as he sat down next to his daughters. Emilie's eyes widened at the sight of her father's bloody nose.

"What happened, Papa?" she demanded. "How did you hurt yourself?"

Lyle chuckled weakly. "Lady de Lohr and I came to know one another," he said, shaking his head when both daughters began to press him. "It does not matter what happened, truly. I received Lillibet's message – so she took Elise back to the apartments, did she? I am not surprised. This joust has been particularly bloody. There is very bad blood here on this day between Richard's supporters and John's forces. It makes me very curious to see what the mass competition will look like."

Emilie's brow furrowed. "Have you seen many of these mass competitions, Papa?" she asked. "What are we to expect?"

Lyle took the kerchief away from his nose, his gaze moving out over the field. "There will be two teams," he said. "Men will fight in combat against each other and they are allowed to do most anything except kill each other. They are permitted to disable and beat each other to a pulp, and once a man is down, he must stay down. He is unable to re-enter the battle. Men can also capture each other and demand ransom. It is quite chaotic, a melee of sorts, but it is great fun. I have always enjoyed it. Why, I was in one of these mass competition years ago that went on for two days. It will not stop until there is a decided victor."

Emilie and Natalie were listening intently. "So the two sides simply fight it out to the last man standing?" Emilie asked. "Will you be fighting, Papa?"

"I will indeed."

"And Brick?"

"He will fight by my side."

Emilie tried not to show too much distress. "But…," she began, stopped to glance at Nathalie, who was equally concerned, and started again. "But you are older than most of the men who are fighting, Papa. We do not want to see you hurt. Mayhap you should reconsider."

Lyle frowned at his daughter. "Why would I reconsider?" he asked, incensed. "Everything will be fine. I will capture a knight or two myself and ransom them. We will return home richer than when we left."

He sounded quite confident and neither girl was sure what to say to that. No one wanted to insult their father by suggesting he was too old to fight in the mass competition that was coming, but the truth was that they were worried for him.

"Please do not, Papa," Nathalie said, her young face serious. "So many terrible things have happened today. Men have been badly injured or have died. We do not wish to see you hurt."

Secretly, Lyle had been thinking the same thing. Men had been hurt and killed on this day, especially with Prince John and his hired band of mercenaries playing rough and dirty against honorable knights. With his wife gone, Lyle was the sole parent for his daughters. Were he to become injured, or worse, it could be very bad for them without adult guidance other than Lillibet. Although he trusted the woman, his girls were strong-willed, and he sometimes bowed to their wishes, whether or not they were sound. And Emilie…sweet, responsible Emilie would become the Canterbury heiress; a valuable woman indeed.

But Lyle didn't want to think negative thoughts like that. He was excited for the coming mass competition, to prove his mastery one more time. It was true that he was older than most of the competitors – or even all of them – but that didn't mean he couldn't compete on the same ground with them. He was a great knight. It would be good to prove himself one more time.

And that meant not listening to his daughters and their fears. Patting Emilie on the cheek, he stood up and quickly moved away from them.

"I appreciate your concern, ladies, but rest assured that I will not be injured," he said. "I am on de Lohr's team and we will triumph. Will you cheer for me?"

Both Emilie and Nathalie nodded, although there was still distress in their expressions. "We will, Papa," Emilie said with resignation. "Do be careful."

Lyle nodded as he turned and headed for the steps that led to the field level. "Do not leave the lists except with an escort," he told them. "Emilie, do you have coinage with you in case you or your sister are hungry?"

Emilie shook her head. "I do not, Papa."

Lyle pulled tight his gloves. "I will make sure your escort has money," he said. "If you wish to eat, now is the time, for you will not want to leave once the mass competition starts."

The girls simply nodded, watching him pass money to the escort before leaving the lists and disappearing down by the field. When he faded from view, Nathalie turned to Emilie.

"Should we find something to eat, then?" she asked. "I am a little hungry."

Emilie shrugged; there was nothing to see on the field at the moment and with David gone, she had lost some interest in all of the activity. Therefore, it would be a good time to find food before the games resumed. Standing up, she gathered her skirts and made her way out of the seating area.

"We saw vendors earlier," she said to her sister. "I did not see what they were selling but I am sure we can find something to eat."

Nathalie was right behind her sister, eager to see some of the sights, even if those sights were only food vendors. But still, she kept looking behind her, at the field, for signs of Brickley.

"I saw a man who was selling some kind of cream pie," she said. "He was near the lists when we disembarked the wagon. Where do you think Brick is right now? Do you think he will wish to eat with us?"

Emilie shook her head. "I am sure he is very busy right now, preparing for the mass competition," she said. "We shall see him later."

Disappointed, Nathalie followed her sister out into the avenue beyond with the three Hampton soldiers who comprised the escort.

The timing was perfect and unfortunate, for their sakes.

Their departure did not go unnoticed. Ralph Fitz Walter, who was still in the royal box, saw them leave. In fact, he had been watching them for quite some time. After Christopher de Lohr's departure, Ralph's focus had turned to the lovely young woman David de Lohr seemed to favor, a young lady who was apparently the daughter of the Earl of Canterbury because Ralph saw the earl join the young woman and he saw, clearly, when the earl had departed. Now, David's lady and another young woman were leaving the lists with only a few soldiers as escort.

An idea came to Ralph at that moment.

With Christopher de Lohr now out of the games, that left David to maintain the family honor. Christopher was a big, muscular knight, bigger than most men. But David, although shorter than his brother and of lesser weight, was pound for pound the best man in the entire tournament. No one moved as fast as David de Lohr did, or fought with such skill. The man was nearly unbeatable in hand-to-hand combat, which was what they were facing that afternoon in the mass competition. Ralph wasn't ready yet to see his mercenaries fall to David de Lohr. It would be an extreme waste of money, something Ralph wasn't ready to accept.

Therefore, he had to have a plan.

Two of Richard's most powerful supporters had been eliminated in this competition already. Brentford le Bec had been killed and Christopher de Lohr had nearly been killed. Others had fallen, too, but no one of the same significance that Christopher de Lohr had. David de Lohr was the only other man at the tournament with the same kind of stature, so it was clearly time to play dirty when it came to David. He knew he couldn't force the man out of the competition and he'd already tried, without success, to disable him, so Ralph Fitz Walter, John Lackland's most influential advisor, had something more in mind for David.

Something very distracting.

It started with the lovely woman who had given David her favor.

WITH A FEW whispered words to Prince John, Ralph slipped out after Emilie and Natalie as the girls went in search of food. He took ten soldiers with him, men loyal to the prince, and men who were unscrupulous without reason.

It was time for Ralph to make his move.

CHAPTER SEVEN

CHRISTOPHER ENDED UP with several broken ribs and a sore shoulder, which was extremely fortunate considering how heavily he had hit and how the majority of the horse's weight had come down on him. The good news was that he was declared the winner of the joust because he had unseated Dennis before Dennis had killed Christopher's horse, and once Christopher managed to get himself on his feet, he was awarded his prize and quickly taken away.

David had accompanied his brother from the field back to his apartments at Windsor so that the physic, a burly man with wild red hair known as Burwell, could tend the man's ribs. Burwell tended all of the king's troops so he was a well-trusted, crass, but knowledgeable man. It took them some time to get Christopher back to the castle and into the apartments so his injuries could be treated.

When the group entered the lavish, two-room apartment, practically carrying Christopher between them, they were met by Lady de Lohr's maids, two dogs, and a small monkey, all pets of Lady de Lohr. The group moved past the menagerie for the most part, ushering Christopher, David, Leeton, and Burwell into the bedchamber, which was dark with its oilcloths and wine-colored brocaded furnishings. As Christopher sat upon a sturdy chair, David and Leeton held on to man while Burwell tightly wrapped his ribs. Dustin, kept out of the chamber so she would not hear her husband's groans of agony, paced in the sitting room beyond with Marcus Burton, Edward de Wolfe, and Thomas Dudley for company.

It was an excruciating wait.

Wrapping a man's ribs was never an easy thing and it was especially painful for Christopher. Burwell presumed he had at least five broken, possibly more, so the man was in considerable pain by the time the physic had finished. Once the bindings were in place, tight and firm, Christopher was permitted to lay back on the big bed, pale and sweating, as Burwell fumbled around in his medicament bag.

"You must stay abed for a few days, baron," the gruff physic said. "Moving around too much will see those ribs pop out and you will puncture a lung. Do I make myself clear?"

Christopher exhaled slowly, feeling the pain as he did so. "Aye."

Burwell eyed the man. "I know you were recently married, but I will stress to you that you must not partake in marital activity, at least not for a week or two."

Christopher turned his head on the pillow to look at the man. "I am not exactly sure what you think I do when I partake of marital activity, but it is not as wild or strenuous as you seem to think it is," he said, watching David fight off laughter. "I told you I would stay in bed and I will."

The physic frowned. "Stay in bed and *rest*."

"I heard you the first time," Christopher said, becoming irritated. "What can you give me for the pain?"

Burwell dug around in his leather satchel and pulled forth a pouch. He peered in to it before handing it over to David. "Two spoonfuls of this in wine," he said. "It will ease the ache but it will also make you sleep. Take it now before I leave."

As the physic took another look at his handiwork on the wrappings, David put some powder into a cup of wine, swirled it, and handed it to his brother, who drank the entire thing. He smacked his lips, making a face at the bitterness of the brew. As Burwell took his medicament satchel to a nearby table and pulled out a few things to mix, more medicines for Christopher's injuries, David took the empty cup from his brother and set it back where he'd found it.

"What now?" David asked softly. "What would you have me do, Chris? The mass competition is next. Dennis will be my target."

Christopher gazed up at his younger brother; they were closer than most brothers, friends as well as siblings, warriors together. They had fought and killed for each other and there wasn't anything they wouldn't do for one another. Christopher knew they'd seen some rough times since he'd married his wife, not even two short months ago now, and it was the first time in their lives that he and David had ever been at odds. But that didn't diminish the love and respect they had for each other. The entire world could collapse around them and still, it would be Christopher and David, brothers until the end. Christopher reached out and grasped his brother's arm.

"And you will be his," he said softly. "Dennis killed Brentford and has tried to kill me. You will be his next target and he will be expecting your wrath, so you must be extremely careful in approaching him, David. He knows you will be out to kill him and he will try to kill you first."

David sighed faintly. "You know," he said casually, "I have come to believe that Dennis was part of the group that attacked your wife last night. I never saw him, for it was dark in the corridor when the attack occurred, but I have a feeling he was there. He has been trying to get to all of us; Dustin and you, and I fully expect him to come after me. I am prepared."

Christopher knew that; he believed him. David was an exceptionally intelligent warrior and he knew that the man would be one step ahead of Dennis. But that did not diminish the danger.

"I know," he said. "But you must understand that Dennis has failed to kill me, which means he will be trying very hard to kill you. He will not want to fail twice and especially not in John's eyes. You must be doubly on your guard, David. Make sure you are not caught alone in this mass competition. Make sure someone is always at your back because if you are not covered, Dennis will find that weakness. He will exploit it. And I will not lose you, do you hear? I could not bear it."

David smiled. "You grow sentimental and foolish in your old age."

Christopher grinned, big white teeth set within his trim blond beard. "Not foolish but practical," he said. "I would have to break in another knight and I have no patience for that."

David laughed softly. "It is good to know that I do not mean anything more than that to you."

Christopher squeezed his arm and let him go, sighing with pain and exhaustion. "Nay, you do not," he said. "Nonetheless, I will beg you to be wary of le Londe. With Marcus and I out of the competition, you must make sure to take Leeton, Edward, and Dud with you and keep them close. Will you do this?"

David cocked an eyebrow. "I am not a weakling who needs protection," he pointed out. "Certainly I will stay close to Leeton and Edward and Dud, but you seem to forget one thing, brother – it is not Dennis who will be hunting me. It is I who will be hunting *him*."

Christopher's gaze was steady on his brother. "Do as you must," he said quietly. "But take care. I would rather have my brother living than Dennis dead."

"Not to worry."

There wasn't much more to be said between them. The stakes were higher than they'd ever been and David was prepared, but it was difficult not to let his sense of vengeance and anger overwhelm him. The price this day had been far too high and now he was the last man standing, the last de Lohr able to exact revenge against their enemies.

He intended to come out on top.

Burwell opened the chamber door to allow Lady de Lohr to come in, which she did in a rush of blond hair and silk. David, having his conversation with his brother was cut short, quit the chamber. He and Leeton walked out as Christopher's wife came in, and Leeton closed the chamber door behind them as Burwell could be heard lecturing Dustin on the care of her injured husband.

Out in the common room, de Lohr knights were sitting about, looking anxiously at David for word on his brother. David held up a hand as if to calm their fears.

"He has at least five cracked ribs and a damage shoulder," he said. "But he will recover."

Marcus Burton, seated in a chair near David, sighed heavily. "Great thanks to God," he muttered. "I had my doubts."

David eyed Marcus. The tension was there between them even now, as there had been for weeks now. It seemed like forever.

In the Holy Land, David and Christopher and Marcus had been inseparable. They had spent their days and nights together, fighting for Christendom and for each other. They were brothers, the three of them, but the truth was that only two of them were really blood brothers. That wasn't so evident as it was when Lady Dustin was introduced. Now, David couldn't seem to remember when he hadn't been suspicious of Marcus and his motives. Even if Christopher was blind to the man and his lust for Dustin, David wasn't, which made Marcus' thanks for Christopher's safety sound hollow and trite.

It was insincere.

Big, muscular, and talented Marcus. He was excruciatingly handsome with his black hair and cobalt blue eyes, and he was as fine a knight as had ever lived. He was a man with an unparalleled reputation, who was spoiled and arrogant, and was used to getting what he wanted. What he had wanted for several weeks now was Dustin. He was evidently willing to see his relationship with the de Lohr brothers go to waste for it, and through it all, Christopher continued to trust him. Perhaps he was blind or perhaps he didn't want to think the worst of his best friend, but for whatever the reason, David had enough suspicion for the both of them.

Perhaps deep down, Marcus really was thankful that Christopher hadn't been irreparably injured, but David didn't believe him; not completely. As the man wanted Dustin, perhaps there was some small part of Marcus Burton that was hoping Christopher might be out of the way so that the path to Dustin was cleared. Knowing Marcus as well as he did, David was willing to believe that.

Therefore, he didn't comment on Marcus' praise for Christopher's recovery. He simply turned away, leaving Leeton to respond.

"It will take him time to recover," Leeton said. "I do not foresee the man competing in any tournaments for some time to come."

Edward, over near the lancet window that looked out into the upper ward, grunted. "Tournaments *or* battles," he said. Then, he looked out to the group of knights, his golden eyes serious. "You realize that his condition will be a serious issue if we are called to battle. John has been waging war against his brother's supporters for some time now, and with Richard declared missing, and given the events of last night, it is my sense that John will try harder than ever to gain control of the country. If Christopher cannot fight, that will pose a problem."

David, still standing near the bedroom door, crossed his big arms thoughtfully. "You have forgotten Eleanor," he said quietly. "She is ruling in Richard's stead. Up until now she has tolerated John's attempts to gain control of the country, but now that Richard is missing she will not let John take the country by force. John cannot defeat his mother, no matter how hard he tries. She has all of Aquitaine and most of England behind her, including us. Do not underestimate the Queen of the English and the Duchess of the Normans, Edward. It is her I would fear most of all; not John."

Edward nodded his head, as if forced to agree, while Marcus glanced over his shoulder at David. "Do we know where she is?" he asked. "Surely she has heard of Richard's absence by now."

David shook his head. "I am sure William Marshal has sent word to her about that, and also about John's activity since receiving word of his brother's disappearance," he said. "I am sure we will be hearing word from her soon enough, but until then we hold this castle and this country for Richard. John may have other plans, but he shall not succeed, not while there is breath left in my body."

He spoke passionately, as he always did when speaking of king and country. Marcus smiled weakly.

"Well said, Lion Cub," he said. "We shall hold the line until Eleanor tells us otherwise."

David gaze on Marcus was emotionless; the man had used the nickname that David had earned for himself in the Holy Land, as a minion of King Richard. Since the English king had been called the Lionheart, Christopher, as his champion, had been called the Lion's Claw; for a lion was only as deadly as his claws were sharp. David, as Christopher's younger and more hot-headed brother, had been called the Lion Cub; a name David detested. Marcus knew he detested it, but it was also used as a term of affection in Richard's inner circle. David wasn't sure if Marcus had used it affectionately or with malice. Given the contention between them at the moment, David couldn't be sure of anything.

"We shall hold the line until Richard returns," he said deliberately. His gaze lingered on Marcus a moment, bordering on hostile, before tearing his focus away and looking at the men in the room. "As for me, I intend to destroy le Londe once and for all. He has already cost us greatly this day. The mass competition is coming and I, for one, intend to make Dennis my target. Edward, Leeton, and Dud will accompany me to the field and prepare for the coming mass. Marcus, you remain here in case Christopher needs anything. I will leave a contingent of soldiers in the corridor for protection should you require it."

Orders were given and men were on the move; they couldn't linger over Christopher's injuries any longer. He would recover and the games, the contention between the prince and his brother's supporters, was still as antagonistic as ever. Worse, even. There were more important things at hand.

Marcus, ordered to remain behind while the other knights proceeded to the games, moved to the window Edward was now vacating. He was feeling left out with his broken hand, and his competitive spirit disappointed, but he was no good in a fight with his hand the way it was. He knew that. Moreover, he suspected that David didn't want him along, which was understandable. He and David weren't on the best of terms and hadn't been for a few weeks now. It was because of their differing views on Lady de Lohr, he knew, but he suspected more it was because David, too, lusted after the woman. David accused Marcus of lusting for her and he wasn't wrong, but the solid and close relationship they had shared over the years had been weakened by the introduction of the new Lady de Lohr.

Marcus did regret that sad state of affair between him and David and Christopher, but not enough to keep his distance from Dustin. He loved the woman, pure and simple, and thought he had been keeping his secret rather well. But David knew; he'd always known. Now, that brotherhood they shared was in danger of dissolving altogether.

But some women were worth such a cost.

Some women were worth dying for.

Marcus sincerely hoped it didn't come to that.

"MY LADY?"

Emilie was looking at a vendor on the busy street who had some kind of meat pie sitting out to entice customers. The pie was rather large, shaped like a half-moon, and broken in half so potential customers could see the contents. They could see browned meat of some kind and carrots, round orange discs set amid a good deal of thick gravy. Nathalie thought the pies looked rather good but Emilie wasn't too sure; she wanted to look around and see what else there was to offer, but the meat pies had Nathalie's attention. And then the voice came, a male voice from behind, and it spoke twice more before Emilie turned out of curiosity to see whom the man might be addressing.

It was her.

"My lady?" a soldier dressed in a dark tunic was speaking to her. He was older, with missing teeth, and when she turned to him, he smiled rather grotesquely. "My lady, will you please come with me? The Sheriff of Nottingham wishes to speak with you."

The Sheriff of Nottingham. Emilie was shocked to hear the name, instantly on her guard. She recognized the name as the man David had warned her about, a deviant who was associated with Prince John. She honestly didn't know of him, and hadn't even heard of him until David brought up the name, but she trusted David. She knew he would not have lied to her about such things. Now, the very man she had been told of was in her midst.

And he wanted to speak with her.

Emilie struggled to cool her shock and struggled to think straight. Only clear heads would prevail. She didn't want to run or be outride rude. She had a feeling that might not go well in her favor. Considering she was with only three Canterbury guards, she looked beyond the soldier who had been doing the inquiry to see several more guards standing behind him dressed similarly.

Sweet Jesus, she thought to herself. Now it was difficult to keep her fear at bay. If they wanted to overwhelm her guards, they easily could. Therefore, she did the only thing she could do – she put on the bravest face she could manage.

"I do not know the Sheriff of Nottingham," she said. "Why should he want to speak with me?"

The soldier simply bowed to her, making a sweeping motion with his hand as if indicating someone well behind him. Emilie wasn't sure what he was doing, or what he meant, until she caught sight of the man she'd seen in the royal box, the one with the hugely swollen face. Slender and rather tall, he had dark hair, shaggy, and was finely dressed. In fact he was quite richly dressed, which she hadn't notice before because of the crowd and the distance between them. Now, she could see him quite clearly and she didn't like what she saw.

"This is Ralph Fitz Walter, my lady," the soldier said, indicating the richly dressed man. "He would like to speak with you."

Fear threatened to overwhelm Emilie. She didn't want to go to the man, but she was fairly certain she had little choice. There were enough guards between her and the sheriff to force her to comply and she was starting to feel like a trapped animal. The hunters were staring her down and she needed help. Thinking quickly, she bent close to Nathalie, who had been standing next to her and watching the exchange.

"Get out of here," she whispered in her sister's ear. "Find Papa. Tell him the Sheriff of Nottingham has asked to speak with me. Tell him to bring help immediately."

Nathalie, who had no idea who Fitz Walter was, looked at her sister curious. "What do you...?"

Emilie grasped her sister by the arm, digging her fingers into her flesh. "By God, Nathalie, do what I say or you will probably never see me again," she hissed. "Run now and find Papa. *Hurry!*"

Wincing at her sister's grip on her arm, Nathalie did as she was told. Greatly confused, as evidenced by her expression, she quickly moved away from her sister and took off down the avenue, heading in the direction of the tournament field. The three Canterbury guards looked very confused, and very concerned, because the women were separating and they didn't know what to do. They had been charged with keeping watch over both of them. While one of them went after Nathalie, the senior man in charge leaned in to Emilie.

"What is amiss, my lady?" he asked.

Emilie's gaze was still on the sheriff and his guards. "Do you know who these men are?"

The soldier wasn't entire certain. "I have seen them, my lady, but I do not know them by name or by house."

Emilie hissed at him as well. "This is Nottingham," she said. "He evidently wishes to have a word with me. I have sent my sister for my father. You will go now, too, or I fear there will be trouble."

The soldier was a seasoned one. He shook his head. "I will not leave you, my lady," he said without fear. "You will not speak with Nottingham without an escort."

Emilie didn't argue with the man; truth be told, she was much more concerned with her own hide at the moment. The Nottingham soldier who had originally spoken to her was still smiling at her, rather sickeningly, and the sheriff himself was standing there rather expectantly. It was obvious that he was waiting on her, and Emilie could do nothing more but obey the summons. She was afraid of what would happen if she didn't.

Without another word, she walked towards the sheriff with the Canterbury soldier at her side, the both of them making their way through several Nottingham soldiers. Odd how there was activity all around them on the street; visitors and vendors, customers and entertainers, all of them milling about, going about their business, but Emilie had never felt more alone in her entire life. None of those people could help her and she was seriously concerned for the conversation that was about to take place.

God, help me….

The Sheriff of Nottingham dipped his head politely as Emilie came near. "My lady," he said. "Thank you for receiving me. I am Ralph Fitz Walter, Sheriff of Nottingham. I noticed you in the lists and realized I have never seen you before. The prince has also seen you and is quite taken with your beauty. He would like to meet you also."

Emilie's heart was pounding against her ribs, the fearful ripple of terror. "Mayhap when the games are finished, my lord," Emilie replied, hoping her voice didn't sound as fearful as she felt. "I am afraid my father is expecting to see my sister and I in the lists. I am sure he would be most honored to meet the prince when the games are over."

Ralph shook his head. "Not your father, my lady," he said. "*You.* The prince would be pleased if you would spare him a moment of your time."

Emilie could see that Ralph would not be put off. "When?" she asked.

Ralph's thin lips divided into a smile. "If you will come with me now, my lady, I would be grateful."

Emilie certainly didn't want to go with him and her resistance was obvious. "Where?"

Ralph's smile didn't waver. "Some place where the prince may speak with you privately?"

Emilie snorted, an impatient sound. "Privately?" she repeated. "I think not. That is highly improper, my lord. I am shocked that you would suggest such a thing. I would be more than happy to speak with the prince after the games are concluded, but for now, my father is expecting me back in the lists. Good day to you, my lord."

With that, she turned on her heel and marched over to the lone Canterbury soldier standing in a sea of Nottingham men. She continued to march along, pulling the soldier with her, hoping that if she presented a strong and unbreakable front, Nottingham wouldn't create a scene. There were people everywhere, in fact, enough witnesses if he tried something violent, or so she thought.

She was wrong.

She hadn't taken ten steps when she was set upon from behind. Her first clue that all was not well was when her escort grunted and fell to the muddy ground, unconscious from a blow to the head. Then someone grabbed her by the arm, roughly. Furious, and terrified, Emilie found herself looking into Ralph's black eyes.

"You will not deny your prince your company, my lady," he said through clenched teeth. "You will come with me peacefully now and your dignity will remain intact. Fight me and I will have my men carry you through the streets. Is this in any way unclear?"

Emilie was trying to pull her arm free. "Unhand me," she snarled. "You have no right to touch me. Let me go now and my father shall not hear of this."

Ralph's grip on her arm tightened to the point of causing her some pain. Emilie winced as he yanked on her, pulling her against his smelly torso in its rich garb. All politeness and propriety was gone at this point; Ralph's true self was revealed.

"Insolence will not be tolerated," he growled, his foul breath in her face. "Behave yourself and you may live through this yet."

Emilie's eyes flew open wide at what she considered a threat to her life. Panicked, she balled up a fist and swung as hard as she could, catching him in his bruised face. Ralph howled and released his grip, his hands flying to his damaged face as Emilie took off at a dead run.

She'd never run so fast in her life. For the first several feet, she had no idea where she was running to; all she knew was that she had to get away from the sheriff and his lascivious men. She was simply running blindly at that point. She needed help and protection, and the first name that popped to mind was David. He had gone off with his injured brother, to where she knew not, but she knew that de Lohr, and many other houses, were in the tent city to the east of the field.

The tent city quickly became her destination and she gathered her skirts around her knees, running as fast as she could for the vast sea of wool structures that crowded off to the east.

Ralph's men were in pursuit and Ralph was screaming at some of them to find their mounts and go after the lady. People in the streets were scattering, fearful of the shouting and soldiers. The men that were running after the lady were bogged down with mail and weapons, slowing them down, while Emilie had no such encumbrances. She was petite, and quite fast, and very soon she lost herself in the great city of tents, plunging deeper and deeper, trying to find a place to hide, as Ralph's men charged into the settlement and began demanding to know who had seen a small blond woman in a crimson gown.

Emilie could hear them as she tucked in behind a rather large oak tree nestled against a creek that dumped into the Thames. There was heavy foliage around the creek and she slipped into the greenery and eventually into the creek itself, hearing the angry shouts of Ralph's men and even hearing some of the inhabitants of the tent city shouting at them in return. No one seemed particularly helpful, thankfully, but Emilie was terrified and uncertain. The cluster of tents were full of people and animals, and it was not particularly difficult to lose oneself in the mass, but she was still fearful that she would be caught. If she was caught, they would kill her. Waist-deep in the creek, she hid in a thick bunch of reeds and grass and waited.

And waited. The minutes passed and she began to lose track of time, having no idea how long she had been in the water, waiting and watching. The creek was quite cold and she was beginning to tremble, soaked to the skin from the waist down. Once, she saw a pair of the sheriff's soldiers on horseback, recognizing their dark tunic, and she hunkered down even further into the creek to avoid being seen. When they began to move in her direction, she left the reeds and submerged herself, holding her breath as the creek took her downstream to a bridge that was at the far end of the tent city.

Unable to hold her breath any longer, she came up for air beneath the bridge and hid up underneath it, freezing cold and shivering, but well concealed beneath the stone structure. She could see the tent city from her position underneath the bridge but it was at a distance, and she knew that all she could do was wait it out until Nottingham's men gave up the search. Having no idea when that would be, she resolved to remain there until the tournament began again and the hunt for her inevitably died down. Then, perhaps, she would go in search of the de Lohr encampment and seek protection. She knew, without question, that David would protect her. She had to find him.

The prince has been known to take any woman he fancies for his own pleasure.

In her case, that unfortunately happenstance had almost come true.

In the cold and in fear, she waited.

CHAPTER EIGHT

T HE MASS COMPETITION was still about an hour off when David returned to the cluster of tents lodged within the tent city. Leeton, Edward, and Thomas Dudley, a knight known amongst friends as 'Dud,' were with him as they entered the tent, making note of the men preparing for the mass competition.

Several great houses had brought their smithies with them and the acrid smell of soft steel filled the air, as did the smoke from the anvil fires. Men were in groups fixing weapons, tightening up armor, or simply discussing strategy for the upcoming event. David and his men passed through these groups, stopping to speak with a knight on occasion, until they reached the de Lohr tents, manned by de Lohr soldiers.

As David entered the large tent and went for his array of weaponry, which had been carefully placed in a wooden rack by one of his men, the tent flap opened behind him and young Darren, Christopher's squire, entered. David had a morning star in his hand, inspecting it, as he turned around to see who had entered behind him. He smiled when he saw the anxious young man.

"He will be fine, Darren," he said. "Five broken ribs and a dislocated shoulder, but no further damage than that. Since he will not be competing in the rest of the games, you will pack up his possessions and take them back over to the apartments. Where did they take the remains of his horse?"

Darren threw a thumb back over his shoulder. "To the southern side of the encampment, my lord," he said. "I have already taken the tack off of the horse. It was truly unfortunate – Boron was an excellent steed."

David nodded. "He was," he said. "My brother will feel his loss. Since my brother will be out of action for some time, however, I would like for you to squire for me for the upcoming mass competition."

Darren's eyes widened at the honor. "It would be my pleasure, my lord," he said. "But Walter and Arthur de Edwin already squire for you. What of them?"

David put the morning star back into the rack. "You will simply work alongside them," he said. "They are very good, but they are also very young. You are nearly a knight yourself, Darren. This mass competition could prove to be vicious, so I would have you along with the de Edwin brothers on the outskirts of the field in case I need assistance. Will you do this?"

Darren nodded eagerly. "Aye, my lord," he said, turning swiftly for the tent opening. "I will return Sir Christopher's possessions to his apartment and quickly return."

David nodded, picking up a pole axe to inspect the shaft. "Please do," he said. "Meanwhile, send Walter and Arthur in here. I must start preparing."

Darren nodded quickly and moved to leave the tent but he ended up plowing into a big body who was just coming in. Darren was a large boy at seventeen years of age and he bounced off of the man, sending the man sideways into the tent wall. The squire reached out to grab him so he wouldn't fall all the way through.

"Forgive me, my lord," Darren said, mortified. "I did not see you until it was too late."

Brickley let the squire steady him. "Not to worry," he said. "No damage done."

Glad to hear he didn't injure the man, and eager to be gone, Darren bolted from the tent as David now looked curiously at Brickley. He wasn't exactly sure why the man had come to visit him but he suspected. A lovely blonde-haired reason. Quietly, he put the pole axe back in the wooden stand. He was prepared.

"The games are not over yet," he told Brickley, thinking he was giving him an answer before the man even asked the question. "I will give her back her favor when everything is over. It is still safe and undamaged. I told you I would take care of it and I have."

Brickley shook his head; he looked particularly strained, and not simply because a young man had plowed into him. He rubbed at his chest where Darren's shoulder had rammed him.

"That is not why I have come," he said. "Have you seen Lady Emilie?"

David's brow furrowed, puzzled by the question. "Not recently," he said. "I have just returned from tending to my brother. He was injured in the joust, you know."

Brickley nodded. "I know," he said. "I saw what happened. How does he fare?"

"Well enough. He will recover."

Again, Brickley nodded shortly. "That is good to know," he said. "But I have not come about the favor or your brother's health. Emilie is missing and Lord Lyle has sent me to ask you if you have seen her."

David's eyebrows flew up in surprise. "Missing?"

"Aye."

Now David scowled as if confused and dubious. "What do you mean by this?" he demanded. "Missing how? Has she simply wandered off or do you suspect worse?"

Brickley sighed heavily, obviously distressed. "After your brother was removed from the field, Lady Emilie and Lady Nathalie went to find food," he said. "Lady Nathalie returned to her father to say that Lady Emilie had been cornered by the Sheriff of Nottingham near the food vendors. She sent Nathalie away to find help. By the time we returned to the area where Nathalie last saw her sister, everything was in an uproar. Witnesses told us that Emilie had hit Fitz Walter in the face and took off running. The last anyone saw of her she was heading into the tent city. I thought she might have come to you."

Now David had the full picture and he was greatly concerned. "Nay, she did not," he said, already moving for the tent exit. "If she did, I have not seen her. Damnation… I cannot believe Ralph cornered her. I can only imagine what he said to force her into defending herself."

Brickley was following David as they emerged into the sunshine. "Fitz Walter has been hunting for her for the past half-hour," he said. "I have run into his men and so has Lord Lyle. In fact, they are gathered near our encampment, thinking she will make an appearance there. Lyle has sent me to you, David. He asks that you find her and keep her from the sheriff's wrath. Fitz Walter will want his vengeance against her blow."

David's jaw was ticking. "He'll get nothing but the steel of my sword if he tries," David growled. "Of all the young women in the lists, Ralph chose Emilie to contact? I do not know how… wait… Jesus, I think I know why. God in Heaven, I do. He must have seen her give me her favor. He has gone after my brother and my brother's wife, and I fully expected him to come after me. But he has gone after Emilie instead because he saw that I carry her favor."

Brickley could see that David was blaming himself for the circumstances. Truth be told, Brickley blamed David, too, but he wouldn't say that, at least not at the moment. He needed David's help and insulting him wouldn't make the man want to help in any way. Still, David was taking the situation very personally. Brickley could hear it in his tone. It was that tone, and that personal behavior, that had Brickley's jealousy rising. Now, he couldn't help what was coming out of his mouth.

"She should have carried my favor from the beginning so the prince would not single her out as a de Lohr follower," he said before he could stop himself. "If Ralph is out to hurt those associated with the House of de Lohr, why did you take her favor? You should have thought of her safety first and kept her far from politics she has nothing to do with."

David's jaw ticked, hearing a jealous rebuke in Brickley's voice. The problem was that the man was absolutely right. David could not refute him. He felt guilty enough about it and Brickley's envious posturing wasn't helping. It was, however, feeding a jealousy in David he never knew he had. It was quite surprisingly, actually. He'd never been jealous over a woman in his life, but now....

"It is done," he snapped quietly. "I cannot change it. But I *can* find her, which is something you have evidently been unable to accomplish. Where have you searched?"

Brickley didn't like the implication but, he supposed in hindsight, that he deserved it. He had made the first jab, after all. But he had more sense than to try to argue with the man again because more arguing would not find Emilie. Therefore, he swallowed his pride, as much as he could, and answered David's question.

"We have searched the main areas," he said, pointing to the tents that seemed to be more clustered around an open area near the center of the city. "Lyle took men to the south side and I was going to head into the town."

David looked around, seeing the creek and the trees that lined the northern part of the encampment. "You take the eastern end of the encampment and I will take the northern area and that northern section of the town," he said, gesturing towards the castle. "Mayhap she is hiding in the city somewhere. Have Ralph and his men combed the city yet?"

Brickley nodded. "From what I could see, they have swept in the direction of the castle."

David shielded his eyes from the sun as he looked town that bordered the field and the tent city. "Very well," he said. "I will mobilize my men. We shall meet back here shortly before the mass competition."

Brickley's gaze lingered on him. "You are fighting in the mass, are you not?"

David glanced at him. "I am," he said. "But I must find Lady Emilie before I do, so there is no time to waste. Tell Lord Lyle I will be back here in an hour or sooner if I happen to find the lady sooner."

With that, they parted. David went to find his squires and several soldiers, gathering about fifteen of them and instructing them to spread out and look for Lady Emilie Hampton. The men didn't really know what she looked like so they were instructed to be discreet in their search and only call her name when Fitz Walter men weren't about. That was a great sense of urgency imparted upon them by David, who was truly concerned for the woman. He knew he wasn't getting the whole story about Emilie's encounter with Fitz Walter but he did know Ralph and he knew, without question, that the man would not give up hunting for Emilie. Already, the man had a jump on him.

David had to find her first.

So the group spread out and began looking for a blond woman in a rich red surcoat; the last thing David remembered seeing her wear. Part of her hair had been styled upward, leaving curls cascading down her shoulders and back, and he had tried to describe Emilie's astounding beauty without sounding besotted. It was a tricky game. He thought he had succeeded because he didn't get any odd looks or smirks from his men. When the men disbursed, he headed for the north side of the encampment and the creek.

He wasn't sure what, exactly, drew him to the creek that flowed along the edge of the town and dumped out into the river, but there was a lot of growth surrounding it and it seemed to him like a logical place to hide if one was trying to avoid detection. There were growths of heavy reeds and grass lining the creek and as he approached, he could see where men had washed clothing or even themselves. The latrines for the encampment were set further downstream, thankfully, so the water at this point was relatively clean.

David walked along the creek, peering into the reeds, looking on the opposite side to see if there were any wet footprints or anything else that would indicate someone had come out of the creek. All the while, he kept abreast on what was going on around him, spying soldiers wearing John's dark tunics now and again, and he caught on fairly quickly to the fact that they were watching him. In fact, several of them were. Once he'd come out of his tent and headed to the creek, the eyes of John and Ralph's men were upon him. Where David went, so went they lady.

But David remained cool. They knew what he was looking for but he wouldn't acknowledge the fact that he was being watched. He began to wonder what would happen should he come across Emilie, wherever she might be, and he was sorely regretting not having brought his sword with him, for once he found her, he was going to have to fight off John and Ralph's men to keep her.

It would be a battle to the death.

The day was starting to cloud over a bit and he glanced up, noticing the increase of dark clouds in the sky. They were passing in front of the sun now and again, and he was coming to suspect there might be rain in the near future. The mass competition would go on rain or shine, and he didn't particularly mind fighting it out in the rain. But he wouldn't fight, *couldn't* fight, if Emilie wasn't found before he had to compete. He just wouldn't be able to concentrate. Time was passing quickly.

He had to find her.

There was a sturdy stone bridge towards several yards down from him, one that allowed a wide avenue to pass over. David continued down the side of the creek, studying the ground, trying to determine if he saw shoe prints that were small and dainty, as a woman's would be. As he drew near the bridge, he caught sight of three of Ralph's men about forty feet away, lingering over at an intersection of the wide bridge avenue and a smaller road. There were a few businesses there and they lingered, pretending to be enjoying a casual conversation when what they were really doing was watching every move David made, waiting to pounce. David eyed them but made it look as if he wasn't.

The game was on.

David came to a particularly heavy cluster of grass, one that could have very well hid a woman who was tucked down in the water. He didn't want to be obvious but he didn't have much choice in calling Emilie's name; if she was hiding in the grass, he couldn't see her and perhaps she couldn't even see him. He crossed his arms casually and began to whistle, all the while strolling casually by the grass.

"Emilie?" he hissed when he wasn't whistling. "Emilie, are you there?"

No answer. Still whistling, still strolling, he made his way to the water's edge and crouched down, pretending to wash his hands. He happened to look over at the stone bridge as he did so, catching sight of a scrap of red fabric and two feet coming from beneath the bridge. Startled, his heart beating with excitement and with some apprehension, he stood up and sauntered over to the bridge, going down to the water's edge again and crouching down to wash his hands all over again. As he splashed water on his face, he bent low, peering underneath the bridge.

"Emilie?" he hissed. "Emilie, 'tis David!"

The feet moved and so did the fabric. Suddenly, Emilie's pale and frightened face appeared, nearly upside down as she was bent over to look at him, and her big brown eyes gazed at him with a huge amount of surprise and relief.

"David!" she sobbed, her eyes filling with a lake of tears. "Oh, David…."

She broke down in tears and David continued splashing water on his face, simply to make some noise so big ears wouldn't hear her. "'Tis all right, lass," he assured her quietly. "I am here. Nothing terrible will happen to you now. But listen to me carefully – be quiet and remain there. It is critical that you obey me. Can you do this?"

Emilie was wiping at her eyes, struggling to compose herself. "Aye," she said, fear in her voice. "But why? Why can't I come out now? I am freezing and wet and I swear to you that my hands are blue. Can't I please come out?"

David shook off his hands and wiped off the water dripping from his face. "Not yet," he told her, his tone soft. "The prince's men are all around, watching me, waiting for me to find you. I will not pull you out of there until I have a contingent of men to protect you. Stay there, stay out of sight, and I will be back shortly."

Emilie nodded her head, utter trust in her expression. "As you say."

He winked at her. "Good lass," he murmured. "All will be well, I swear it. I will not let harm come to you. Do you believe me?"

"I do."

"Good."

With that, David watched her pull herself out of view, tucking herself well underneath the bridge, which surely must have been a very uncomfortable experience. He stood up, shaking the water off his hands, as he casually made his way away from the creek, glancing at the prince's soldiers over by the intersection to see that they were still watching him. He pretended not to notice as he headed back into the encampment, moving for the de Lohr tents.

There were a few soldiers still there, packing up Christopher's possessions under Darren's instruction, but everything came to a halt when David sent the remaining six soldiers out to find those who had gone in search of Emilie. David kept watching the stone bridge somewhat anxiously, watching for any sign that John's soldiers may have been too curious about it, but the bridge remained uninteresting as people continued to pass over it, going about their business.

All David could think about was getting to Emilie, but he was thankful that he at least knew where she was now. That helped his anxiety somewhat. Soon enough, the soldiers he had sent out returned with the men David had sent in search of Emilie and, with a quick explanation as to what David had discovered, he led sixteen heavily armed soldiers, including Edward and Leeton, over to the bridge where he got down into the water and pulled Emilie out from underneath the bridge himself.

Carrying the wet, freezing, and shivering woman up onto the shore, he kept her in his arms, surrounded by his armed men, all the way back to the de Lohr tents.

Ralph heard, very shortly, about David de Lohr extracting a wet young woman out from beneath a stone bridge, but he wisely made no move to go after her. He knew that David wouldn't turn her over to him, anyway. But it didn't matter much; soon enough, David de Lohr would be in the midst of a mass competition where anything could happen and, if Ralph had anything to say about it, anything *would*. David was his intended target all along; he had simply tried to use the woman to get at him. That hadn't really worked, for now David had her and she was protected by heavily armed men, but Ralph wasn't concerned, not in the least.

One de Lohr was down and there was one more to go. Ralph made sure that Dennis le Londe received that message as the two sides of the mass competition began to assemble a short time later. While Dennis would take ten marks and Lady de Lohr for the fall of Christopher de Lohr, the price for David was even higher. As good as Christopher was as a knight, and he was the best England had to offer, David held a slight edge over his brother in hand-to-hand combat, simply because he was so unpredictable. He would fight dirty when the situation called for it, and that made him particularly dangerous.

As the peal of the trumpets called the fans to the lists to watch the great mass competition, the two sides took to the field.

The bloodiest game of all was about to begin.

CHAPTER NINE

S HE WAS NUDE beneath the pile of heavy woolen blankets.

It was perhaps a bit awkward, embarrassing even, but it couldn't be helped. Emilie's clothes were all soaked through and even now, David had his soldiers waving them over a blazing fire outside of the tent, drying them for the lady, who was so cold that her teeth hadn't stopped chattering. As Emilie practically lay her body over the brass brazier in David's tent in an attempt to warm her icy flesh, David went about dressing for the coming competition. Now that she was found, and safe, the focus had shifted to the upcoming bout.

It was a bit surreal, actually. As Emilie sat precariously close to the red-hot brazier, she watched David as three squires moved around him, dressing him. It all started with the hose and a padded under tunic, followed by a series of mailed pieces that were fastened on with leather straps and buckles. One squire was charged with the legs, one with the torso, and the third, a very tall young man who seemed to be quite competent, with the head and shoulders and weaponry. They moved in an efficient bunch as David stood there and held his arms out, assisting the boys when required, but he mostly let them work. They seemed to know what they were doing.

Emilie had lived in castles her entire life, with military capabili- ties, but she'd never been this close to a knight who was dressing. It was very interesting to watch, and very intimate. Somehow, she felt closer to David than even when she'd given him her favor. She was seeing the man on an entirely different level now, in his natural state, preparing for war. In this case, even though it was a competition, she knew that it would be a battle.

This day had shown her that there was a fine line between an enemy and an ally, and even men under the guise of pleasantries were not to be trusted. She'd learned that all too quickly. All was not as it seemed in the upper hierarchy of the royal court. As David and his squires worked, a soldier came into the tent to bring her hot wine, which she accepted gratefully.

"I am sorry I do not have much more to offer by way of comfort," David said when he noticed the soldier hand her the hot wine. "I had to have my men hold that cup over the fire to warm the wine so it is likely to be quite hot."

Emilie grinned as she held the pewter cup with the blanket. "I have quickly learned that," she said. "I am very grateful for your hospitality, my lord."

David gave her a half-smile, his gaze lingering on her blonde head as she sipped at the liquid. He hadn't spoken to her much since he'd brought her back, mostly because he assumed she was too distraught to speak, but her state of mind seemed improved as she gingerly slurped the wine. He thought it might be a good time to find out what, exactly, had happened.

"It is my pleasure," he said. He hesitated a moment before continuing. "Do you feel strong enough to tell me what happened with the sheriff? I should probably know since I am risking my life to protect you from him. Tell me of the wonderfully terrible thing you did to him that made him chase you into hiding."

He was smiling as he said it and Emilie laughed softly. It wasn't as if there was really much to laugh about, but David's attempt at humor made her feel better about it, as if it wasn't as seriously and horrible as she thought it was. She knew the man would protect her until the death, and that thought alone made her feel braver.

It also made her like him even that much more, a feeling that had, long ago, passed from something simple into something that was far more of a deep infatuation. Coming to her aid as he had and carrying her off to safety had somewhat marked the man for life as a hero in her eyes.

A hero she was coming to very much long for.

"It all happened rather fast," she said, thinking back. "Nathalie and I went to the food vendors to find something to eat."

"Nathalie?"

"My sister."

"I see. Continue, please."

She did. "As we were standing in front of a vendor who sold some kind of meat pie, a soldier addressed me," she said. "When I turned around, there were several soldiers standing behind me and a man who introduced himself as the Sheriff of Nottingham. He told me that the prince wanted to meet with me privately and when I declined, he grabbed me and tried to force me to go with him. I panicked, hit him, and ran away. And that is really all there is to it."

David's features were grim by the time she was finished. He sighed heavily. "You are not the first young woman he has done that to," he said. "But I would wager to say you are one of the very few that had the sense to fight back. I applaud you, my lady. You show remarkable bravery."

Emilie lifted her eyebrows. "I am not sure I see it that way," she said. "All I know was that I was frightened and I remembered what you said about him. I could not let him take me, my lord. I could not make it that easy for him."

David was looking at her until the big squire had him bend over so he could put the hauberk on his head and shoulders. David's voice was muffled as the mail went over his face. "You did exactly what you were supposed to do," he said. "Fitz Walter does not like to be denied. His only issue with you is a damaged ego and nothing more. But from this point on, you must remain with me or your father or another trusted man who can bear arms and protect you. I fear that the sheriff might see the capture of you as a game now, one he intends to win. The hunter does not usually let his prey go so easily."

Emilie's pale face tightened in alarm. "He views me as prey now?"

David stood up as the big squire straightened out his mail hood. "More than likely," he said. "But have no fear; I will change his mind."

She smiled at him, something of a besotted gesture. "Thank you, my lord," she said. "Since you and I have met, you have gone out of your way to protect me. You will never know how grateful I am."

Something warm was in the air, something that made David's heart race. Emilie seemed to have that capability with him and he was both annoyed by it and thrilled by it. He didn't like it that a woman should make him feel as giddy as Emilie had made him feel, but the more time he spent with her, the more he was coming to not particularly mind that special power she had over him. If he was honest with himself, he really didn't mind it at all. All he knew was that something about the woman affected him and it was difficult to fight it. He wasn't sure he should try.

He wasn't sure he *wanted* to try.

Fully dressed, he sent the squires out to help the other men prepare and to gather the clubs they were intending to use in the mass competition. But he mostly sent the boys away to get them out of the tent so he could be alone with Emilie. It was true that she was without clothing under the bundle of blankets covering her and it was further true that, even if she had been dressed, being with a woman who wasn't properly escorted was scandalous, David didn't care about scandal at the moment. He simply wanted to steal a few moments with her before the mass competition.

"I can appreciate how grateful you are," he said as the boys fled the tent. "You must, of course, realize how grateful I am that you gave me your favor. It has brought me much luck. Since you are my favored lady, it is my duty to protect you but I would say that it is also the reason Ralph came after you. He must have seen you give me your favor in the lists. He sought to get to me through you."

Emilie was looking at him quite seriously. "But why should he do that?" she wanted to know. "It is not as if we are married or betrothed. It was simply a favor given to you. How could he think that meant that I somehow matter to you?"

Because you do. He stopped himself from saying it even though he was thinking it. Instead, he shrugged. "Fitz Walter would kidnap my horse if he thought he could get to me," he said. "As I told you before, he is a hunter. He has been hunting de Lohrs, along with the prince, for quite some time. I am sorry you became caught up in his pursuit. Had I known he would try and hurt you, I would have never accepted your favor. I would have never knowingly put you in harm's way."

Emilie pondered his words. "The moment you accepted my favor was the proudest moment of my life," she said, a warm glimmer in her eye. "You would have denied me such pride?"

David found himself sucked into those lovely brown eyes. "If it meant putting your life in danger, I would have," he said honestly. "But surely you would have known that, in my heart, you still would have been my favored lady."

It was such a sweet thing to say, exactly what she had been wanting to hear from him since nearly the moment they met. Her heart, that wildly fluttering thing, threatened to burst from her chest.

"Am I, my lord?" she whispered. "Am I truly?"

David could hardly answer; he was being drawn towards her, invisible fingers grasping hold of him and pulling him towards her as if he had no way of resisting. He had no strength against whatever magic she possessed and he found himself moving towards her. Her lips were in his line of sight; he wanted to kiss her, perhaps more badly than he'd ever wanted to do anything in his life. The world around him seemed to fade away as he drew closer and closer still.

"Aye," he finally muttered. "You are."

He was preparing to take a knee beside her with the intention of pulling her into his arms, blankets and all. All he could see or think or feel was her. But his focus was fractured when the tent flap flew back and men were entering his tent. He heard Lyle's booming voice.

"Did you know they are waving your clothes in the air outside for all to see?" he said to Emilie. "Men are waving your... your *under-things* as if to display them for the entire world!"

Emilie, who had been as upswept in David as he had been in her, was startled by her father's appearance and his loud tone. She held the blankets up around her neck to cover up whatever flesh may have been exposed.

"They are drying them, Papa," she insisted. "I was hiding in the creek until Sir David found me. He is having his men dry my clothing. And this is how you thank him? By barging into his tent, uninvited, and shouting? I am ashamed of you."

Lyle, who was fully prepared to berate both his daughter and David, faltered in his anger. Emilie's reasons behind her clothing being waved about like banners now made some sense. He turned to look at Brickley, who had entered the tent behind him, but Brickley was looking at Emilie, seated next to the brazier, swaddled in woolen blankets. He pointed.

"So you wear nothing beneath those coverlets?" he demanded, looking to David, horrified. "She is *without* clothing?"

Emilie could see where this was leading and she quickly intervened. "Must I repeat this for you, Brickley?" she said angrily. "I was forced to hide in the creek so the sheriff's men would not find me. Sir David found me and brought me back here to safety. I took off my wet clothing, in private, and Sir David's men are drying them so that I may have something to wear and not die from the damp. If you think Sir David has brought me back to his tent to... to take advantage of me in this state, then you have a filthy mind and an even worse opinion of me. Do you truly believe I would let him do such a thing?"

She was shouting by the time she was finished, which was something she never did. Emilie had a very cool manner about her most of the time. Lyle and Brickley were looking at her with some uncertainty, perhaps some chagrin. Brickley was the first one to surrender, and he did it quickly. He could see how upset she was.

"Nay, I do not believe you would let him do such a thing," he assured her. "Forgive me, my lady; it has been an upsetting day for us all. I did not mean to accuse you of anything but you must admit that it does not look... proper from my perspective."

Lyle, who was starting to feel quite foolish in his behavior, put up a hand to still any retort coming from his daughter because now they were all very close to appearing like ungrateful idiots in front of David. His focus moved to the man.

"Apologies, David," he said. "As you can see, we are all rattled by the events of the day. One of your men found us up by the castle, and we have run all the way from the northern end from the town to see that Emilie is alive and well. I know you would never do anything improper with her. Forgive us for suggesting it."

David was perfectly willing to let Lyle and Brickley make arses out of themselves in front of Emilie, mostly because he had indeed been about to kiss the woman, which would have been very improper. Both Lyle and Brickley weren't too terribly wrong on their assessment of what his intentions were but he would never admit it. Instead, he was content to let them look like fools. Better them look like fools than him looking like a rake. So he pretended to be very forgiving.

"No need for apologies," he said. "As you can see, she is well but she is very cold. I found her tucked up underneath the stone bridge to the south and she was quite wet. She has been sitting here by the brazier as my squires dressed me for the coming competition. Lady Emilie and I have been having a pleasant conversation."

Lyle, once again drawn to his found daughter, went to her and fell to his knees, drawing her into a snug embrace. "Em," he murmured, kissing the side of her head. "I am so sorry you have had to suffer through this. But what happened, my love? Why did you run away?"

Emilie hugged her father, trying to keep her blankets up around her neck as she did so to preserve her modesty. "As I told Sir David," she said, "the Sheriff of Nottingham found Nathalie and me near the food vendors. He tried to take me to the prince and when I refused, he tried to force me. I hit him and ran away."

Lyle glanced at David, his expression rather ominous. "Did he say *why* he would take you to the prince?" he asked. "Did he say anything at all?"

Emilie nodded. "He said that the prince wanted to meet me," she replied. "When I told him that I would wait for my father and we should both like to meet the prince, the sheriff made it very clear that you were not invited, Papa. He only wanted to see me. The way he said it… it was clear that he meant it improperly. It frightened me."

Lyle sighed faintly as he came to grips with what his daughter had been through. "You are certain of this?" he asked. "There can be no doubt?"

Emilie shook her head. "Nay," she said. "Ask the soldier who was with me if you do not believe me. They hit him on the head when they tried to take me. I believe the soldier was Henley."

Lyle was deeply unhappy, growing unhappier by the moment. "It was," he said. "He has already told us what happened, or at least what he remembered, and it is nearly what you have told me. A frightful, terrible event, I must say."

Emilie was watching her father's serious features as he mulled over a second attack on his eldest daughter in as many days. "It was just like last night, Papa, when those men who attacked us tried to take me away," she said. "This is twice that men have tried to take me to the prince and twice that Sir David has rescued me. We owe him all of the gratitude in the world for his selflessness."

Both Lyle and Brickley turned to look at David with various expressions on their faces; Lyle with thanks and Brickley with jealousy. The man was positively seething with it. David cleared his throat softly.

"As I told the lady, I am happy to be of service," he said, looking at Lyle and ignoring Brickley. "But it is very clear that she must not be out of my company. No offense to Canterbury, but it is clear the lady needs all of the protection the House of de Lohr can provide. We have more men with us and are better able to protect her. Moreover, John and Ralph will think twice before attacking her again if she is in my custody. I fear they would not think twice if she remained with you and Brick."

Brickley snorted. "You think me incapable of protecting her?" he demanded. "I find that extremely offensive, de Lohr."

So now the man was resorting to calling David by his last name. When they were friendly, he had called him David. Now that the situation was turning, and Emilie was becoming a bone of contention between them, Brickley was removing that shield of friendliness and resorting to a more impersonal form of address.

David could feel the tension between them but it didn't bother him in the least; in fact, he was comfortable with it. He had determined he was unhappy with Brickley's intentions towards Emilie so if Brickley wanted to draw that line between them now, a line in the form of Emilie Hampton, then David was more than ready to stand toe to toe with him on that line.

He wasn't about to back down.

"I never said you were incapable of protecting her," David said, facing Brickley as if daring the man to throw a punch. "I simply said that the House of de Lohr has more men and is therefore *more* capable of protecting her. Clean your ears out, de Dere, and hear what I am saying. If I was going to insult you, I would do it to your face. I do not hide behind sly comments."

Lyle was suddenly coming to realize that there was a good deal of hostility between David and Brickley. He'd spent the day with

Brickley and the man never gave any indication that there was any animosity between him and de Lohr, so to see the two big knights posturing aggressively towards each other was something of a shock.

But it didn't surprise him, to be truthful. He knew of Brickley's want for Emilie and it was understandable that the man should be hostile towards David, who carried Emilie's favor. Lyle felt foolish for not seeing the signs of that jealousy before now. Quickly, he released Emilie and stood up, putting himself between the two knights before a battle started.

"Brick, please," he hissed at his knight, turning to David. "We are all still upset, David. Brick has been running like a madman all about the town and is quite exhausted. He does not mean what he is saying."

Emilie, who was also seeing the hostility for the first time, rose to her feet, keeping the wool blankets tightly pulled around her. Shocked, she frowned at Brickley.

"By what right do you speak to Sir David like that?" she asked. "It was very unkind of you, Brick. You will apologize to him this instant."

Brickley's jaw ticked as he fixed on Emilie. He was struggling with his temper as he scratched his head. "I am sorry if I offended you, my lady," he said calmly. "That was not my intent."

Emilie's eyes widened and she pointed at David. "That was *not* an apology to Sir David," she said. "Apologize now or I shall never speak to you again."

Lyle was well aware that his daughter had no knowledge of Brickley's feelings for her. That had been Lyle's preference. He didn't want Emilie to suspect at this point for it would only complicate an already complex situation. He didn't want his daughter to be uncomfortable around Brickley, especially now that the Sheriff of Nottingham was evidently hunting for her, because there would be a time when Brickley would be in charge of her safety. Perhaps not here at Windsor, and perhaps only on the way home and when they were back at Canterbury, but he still didn't want the added complication of Emilie knowing Brickley was in love with her, feelings she clearly did not return. Therefore, Lyle intervened before too much was said.

"Emilie," he scolded softly. "This is between David and Brick. They do not need or want your interference. Sit down and behave yourself."

Emilie wasn't ready to be put off. "But…."

Lyle grasped her by the arm and turned her around, pointing to the brazier. "*Go*," he commanded softly. "Please, sit. Let the men handle this. This is not your business."

Emilie, still frowning at Brickley, wasn't happy with her father's directive but she obeyed him. With great reluctance, displaying the fact that she was quite unhappy with both Brickley and her father, she went back to the brazier and set down, huddling around it. When Lyle was certain she wasn't going to stand up and start arguing again, he turned to the knights.

"David, I am grateful for your offer to keep Emilie with you and protected by de Lohr soldiers," he said. "I fear that I have only Brick with me and about twenty Canterbury soldiers. I still have Nathalie and Elise to watch out for. If you can provide Emilie with greater protection until we leave Windsor, I will thank you for it. I fear my men do not have the experience with the sheriff's men, or the prince, as your men do. That puts them at a disadvantage. And that disadvantage puts Emilie's life at risk. Are you sure it will be no trouble?"

David shook his head. "None at all," he said. "In fact, I will put twenty men on her, as well as a knight, while I compete in the mass competition. As much as I hate to be down a knight in that event, Emilie's safety is of greater concern."

"I will guard her," Brickley said, looking at Lyle. "Truly, my lord, your daughter's safety is more important than winning a competition. Allow me to guard her."

Lyle shook his head. "I am competing in the mass competition alongside David and so are you," he said. "We are on the team of Richard's supporters. David, which knight will you place on her, then? One of your men will be very disappointed."

David smiled ironically. "Actually, I have a feeling Edward de Wolfe will not be so disappointed," he said. "Edward is an excellent knight and a fierce fighter, but the truth is that he does not have the aggressive drive that most knights do. Things like the mass competition do not excite him like most. He will be agreeable to watch over Lady Emilie whilst the competition takes place and I will make sure he understands the seriousness of it. But what of your other daughters? Will you permit them to sit in the lists and watch after what happened to Emilie?"

Lyle shook his head. "My other daughters have returned to our apartments for safekeeping," he said. "I know you have asked me not to leave Windsor, David, but the truth is that I must think about my family. I at least intend to remove them from the castle. My sister has a manor outside of London and it is my intention to move them there when this competition is over. They will be safer there."

David nodded. "I believe that is wise to move the woman," he said. "But we need you here, my lord. There is much happening with regard to Richard and John, and your counsel and strength may be required. I would suggest you not return to Canterbury Castle at least until we know something more about Richard's situation."

Lyle knew David was more than likely correct; with the circumstances of Richard's disappearance still fluid, it would be wiser for him to stay in London at least until more was known. Still, he had his children to think about. His daughters.

Emilie.

"We shall see," he said vaguely, not wanting to commit one way or the other at the moment. "My priority is taking my daughters to safety, David. If it is not safe for them in London, then we will return home. I must."

David knew that. "I understand," he said. "We shall see what the next week or two brings. I hope you will give the situation at least that long."

Lyle shrugged. Then, he nodded as if knowing, eventually, he would concede. David clapped the man on the shoulder in thanks for having his tentative agreement as Lyle ordered Brickley from the tent. He wanted the man out of there because he could still feel the tension, and jealousy, radiating off of him. He didn't like that tension, not when David was doing his best to help Emilie.

But there was more to it. Lyle had seen, from the brief confrontation between David and Brickley, that there was more than likely an ulterior motive behind David's altruism. And Emilie seemed quite defensive of David to Brickley's slander. Aye, there was probably more going on here than met the eye, but Lyle wasn't all that distressed about it. He would be rather proud to have David de Lohr as a son, but he knew that if that happened he would more than likely lose Brickley's service. He wouldn't expect the man to stay and serve the man who had stolen away the women he loved.

Love and marriage was a complicated thing, indeed. As Brickley headed out of the tent, Lyle turned to Emilie.

"I am leaving you in David's charge until I can remove you from Windsor and take you to Aunt Coraline's home," he said. "Until that time, you will behave yourself and do what David tells you to do. Am I clear? You will obey him as you would obey me."

Emilie nodded solemnly. She was secretly very glad that her father had left her in David's charge, thrilled to be with the man who made her heart skip beats and exceedingly glad to be away from Brickley, who was acting quite strangely. Almost as if he was being overly-protective over her, as if she was a possession, which she didn't like at all. She was glad her father had ordered the man away. One more insult against David from his mouth and she just might have to slap him.

Truthfully, it wasn't like Brickley to be so rude but she knew she didn't like it. She wondered what was wrong with him but only for a moment or two; the truth was that she didn't much care. She had a mass competition to look forward to and David de Lohr to cheer to victory. That was all she cared about at the moment. She was exactly where she wanted to be in the presence of a man she was growing increasingly enamored with.

After her father and Brickley left, David's squires returned bearing clubs and David's tunic. The yellow de Lohr lion against the dark blue with the words *Deus et Honora* embroidered on the bottom. *God and Honor*. It was that recognizable tunic that Emilie had kept her eye on all day. Once David finally donned the tunic, it seemed that to Emilie that he went through a transformation of sorts – no longer did she see just a powerful knight. Now, she saw something more surreal than that, something more glorious than any knight who had ever lived. She saw David de Lohr as he was meant to be.

A warrior without compare.

The horn peal sounded in the distance, calling the games to order.

CHAPTER TEN

T HE MASS COMPETITION was chaos from the beginning.

David and his men were banded together in a very powerful team that consisted of Richard's major supporters – Derby, Bath, de Lohr, Sedgewick, Canterbury, and a host of others. Generally speaking, there was an order to a mass competition – two sides assembled against each other, on horseback or on foot, and when the field marshal rang the bell or blew the horn (depending on the competition and what the marshal had at hand), the two sides rushed each other and the fight was on.

On this day, the fight was most definitely on.

Each side had twenty-four knights with clubs. Mass competitions in the past had used real swords and other sharp instruments, but too many men were badly injured in what was supposed to be mock-combat, so the past several years saw clubs used instead of actual weapons.

Furthermore, since they were conducting the competition in the rather small enclosed area of the tournament field, the field marshals had decided against using horses, so all of the men were on foot. The object of the mass competition was for the sides to charge one another, one side hoping the other would break rank; and clubs were swinging wildly very early on. A few men dropped right away and either limped off the field or were dragged.

The crowd in the lists cheered loudly for their favorite knights, for it was quite exciting to watch. It was also difficult to tell what, exactly, was happening because it was literally a giant mass of men slugging it out in the middle of the arena. Even though it appeared like an unorganized brawl, the truth was that there was skill and strategy involved.

That was where knights like David de Lohr found their strengths.

David was quite methodical, in truth. He would single men out, mostly men he knew he could overcome quickly, and with one blow to the head, he would have Darren and his squires drag the man off the field and keep watch over him, as he was now David's captive. David had made a deal right before the games began that he would give Darren a portion of any ransom received from the prisoners, so Darren was standing guard over the prisoners with a sword in hand, daring anyone to try and run.

But no one had, so far. It would be foolish to run because the mounted de Lohr soldiers on the outskirts of the arena would simply run them down. Usually, David and his brother would strategize in competitions like this and it never varied much from mass to mass. David and Christopher would charge into the group and single out the weaker but richer men competing, club them over the head, and have their men drag them off. They would usually try to work from the far ends of the ranks towards the middle where most men were clustered, because it was more difficult to move in the middle of the mass. The ends were far less choked and it made it easier to site prey.

Without Christopher on his flank, David pulled Leeton and Dud into that position. The two knights worked on one end while David worked on the other. But David was mostly trying to get to le Londe, who was in the center of the mass with several other of John's mercenary knights. Very early on David and the other allies realized that this mass was about to become very bad, indeed. John's mercenaries were bearing spiked clubs meant to seriously injure or even kill opponents. The field marshals declared them illegal but

John overrode the decision, and when that happened Richard's supporters went on the offensive.

David had the squires run back to their encampment and collect axes, swords, and other battlefield weapons. Clubs weren't doing any good against the spiked monstrosities that John's mercenaries were using, so the decision was made by William Marshal, no less, to play just as dirty as John's men were. It was either that or be killed. Once David traded his club in for a shield and a broadsword, he charged into the mass and went straight for le Londe.

The blood began to spill.

In fact, it turned into a literal bloodbath as John's mercenaries began to take as much as they were giving. Men began falling, bleeding and wounded, and the squires who skirted the edge of the field to take prisoners for ransom were now dragging bleeding men off the field so they could be tended. What had started out as an honorable mass competition, at least at first, now became a battle in the real sense. Everyone was out for blood.

David, of course, was out for Dennis in the most mortal sense. He couldn't get to Dennis at first, blocked by some serious fighting in the middle of the mass, so he began swinging his shield, which wouldn't normally have meant much except the edges of David's shield were razor-sharp blades, like the blades of an axe, so when he swung it, the very gesture was meant to maim or kill. He swung it at men he knew were hired by the prince, men who had already taken down several of Richard's supporters, and as he plowed into the heat of the battle in the center of the arena, he had already cut off one Frenchman's arm and had seriously sliced into the chest of another.

Men began backing away from David, who had been joined by Leeton, Dud, Brickley, and Lyle. Now, the battle was real and intense as men were being killed or badly hurt, as David and the rest of Richard's supporters went after John's mercenaries in earnest. Now, it was the contest between Richard and John in full color, right there on the tournament field for all to see.

It was mayhem.

It was so bad that women began leaving the lists in droves when they realized how gory the mass had become. Knights and noblemen who weren't competing were now crowded up around the fence, watching the fighting with awe and, in some cases, horror, as the mud of the arena field turned red with blood. Overhead, the gray clouds that had been gathering began to let loose, pouring down upon the fighters and very quickly turning the field into a swamp. Men were ankle-deep in red mud, slugging it out to the death.

The field marshals had lost control of the mass competition; that much was clear. There were five of them, men now gathered at the western end of the field and simply watching as best they could, unable to do much because every time they tried, the prince overrode their decision. They knew that Richard's supporters had brought out the weapons purely so they wouldn't get slaughtered, but even so, they were doing a great deal of damage to John's mercenaries. In fact, they clearly had the upper hand. John was losing mercenaries as fast as the squires could drag them off the field.

David and his blade-edged shield had done a massive amount of damage. He had been keeping his eye on le Londe but could never seem to get close enough to engage him. Other's would charge him and he'd find himself in a fight for his life, using his shield and broadsword to disable or kill. Already, he'd sliced four men, forcibly amputated three arms, used his broadsword against at least two, and now he was fighting a very tall Teutonic mercenary who had the biggest spiked club David had ever seen. It was a club that, when it came into contact with David's shield, sent him stumbling backwards.

But he didn't go down with the force of the blow. He managed to stay on his feet but it didn't really matter much, as all mass rules had been broken. Men who had fallen down were getting back up again and continuing the fight, so David thought nothing of it when he ran for the Teutonic warrior, fell to his knees and skidded through the mud, coming up under the man's enormous swing and goring him straight in the belly. The warrior fell over, bleeding out into the lake of mud the field had now become. It had been a brilliant tactical move on David's part.

But the fight wasn't over, not in the least. Leaping to his feet, David's attention was now back on tracking le Londe with the enormous Teutonic warrior out of the way. The mass of men had thinned out considerably now, with men like Lyle out of the competition and nursing a nasty wound to his arm. Brickley was still in it, as were Leeton and Dud, but as David watched, Dud took a heavy blow right to the back that put him down onto his face. In the mud, which was now at least a foot or more deep, not including the several inches of water on top of it, a man could quickly drown, so David raced in Dud's direction to pull the man out so he wouldn't suffocate.

He was nearly to the man when he also saw Darren running out onto the field, moving for the knight as well. David was nearly to Dud when his path was suddenly cut off by a warrior who swung a massive studded club right at his head. David was forced to throw himself to the ground and tumble out of the way to avoid having his head taken off. As he came up, covered with muddy water, he turned to see Dennis le Londe bearing down on him.

Now, the fight was real. Infuriated, David charged after Dennis, leaping up into the air and kicking him squarely in the chest before Dennis could get another swing of the club in. Dennis fell backwards, into the mud, and David jumped right onto the arm holding the club in an attempt to force him to release his grip. The broadsword David was holding also came up, bearing down on Dennis but Dennis saw the blade coming down upon him and he managed to roll to his side to avoid being speared. In the same movement, he hammered David behind the knees and the knight pitched backwards, stumbling off of Dennis' arm as he lost his balance.

Somehow, they had both lost their weapons in the process and

David had lost his helm. It was now upside-down in the mud. The battle turned into a fist fight as David and Dennis pummeled each other viciously. Dennis was taller than David, but David was stronger, faster, and a better fighter. David dropped several blows onto Dennis' face, dislodging the man's helm and sending it sailing into the wicked weather.

By now, most of the combatants were down or out of the competition with five left, including David and Dennis. The perimeter of the arena was lined with men, injured or not, watching David and Dennis battle to the death because that was most certainly what this was – a battle to the death. Brickley, Leeton, and one other mercenary remained and Brickley and Leeton made short work of him. Then, the two of them headed for David and Dennis with the intent of doing away with Dennis. It didn't even matter at this point if they won the competition or not; at the moment, it wasn't about winning. It was about exacting justice for Brentford and for Christopher. David, in the brutal beating he was giving Dennis, was doing just that.

He was dealing justice.

The lists, oddly enough, were mostly silent as the battle between Richard's Lion Cub and John's champion slugged it out. Although Dennis had taken a massive beating, David wasn't much better off – he had a cut over one eye and blood was pouring into the eye, making it difficult for him to see, but he kept track of Dennis with his one good eye, making sure the man felt every blow delivered. David kept punching him in the same place on his face, loosening teeth and causing the man extreme pain. He wanted him to feel every agony.

David wasn't aware that Leeton and Brickley were tracking him, and even if he did know he wouldn't have cared. He was more concerned with driving Dennis into the ground because, truth be told, he was becoming quite exhausted. He didn't want Dennis to exploit that exhaustion, although the mercenary was surely feeling exhaustion of his own. What David didn't realize was that their weariness was very apparent to everyone watching, as their movements had slowed and become sloppier. Still, Dennis was taking the worst of it.

Everyone in the lists and on the field sensed that the end was drawing near, made more apparent when David put a foot in behind Dennis and shoved the man to the ground. Then, he pounced on him, slugging him in the face as hard as he could.

"That," he grunted, "was for my brother. And this," he hit him again, "is for Brentford. You were unworthy to even fight the man much less kill him, you bastard. Now I'm going to flip you over on your belly and drown you in this mud. You're going to suck it up into your lungs and breathe it in, you filth, and with every painful last breath, I want you to think of my brother and Brentford. See their faces and know that your death is because of what you did to them."

Dennis was in a bad way because David had him at a tremendous disadvantage; in the position he was in, with his arms pinned beneath David's body weight, he simply couldn't get the range of motion to dislodge the man. Still, he kept calm. Panic would not help him at this moment for he knew that men seeking vengeance as David de Lohr was would only feed on his terror. If he wanted to live, he couldn't give the man any more strength or purpose than he already had.

"You cannot win," Dennis said, his French accent heavy and distorted by his swollen mouth and missing teeth. "This is something neither of us can win, David. This is between Richard and John."

David stopped punching him and wrapped his swollen, battered hands around the man's neck. He began to squeeze. "This is most definitely between us," he snarled. "I will kill you if it is the last thing I do."

Dennis knew that. He'd known that from the start of the mass competition it would come down to him and David. He knew the man was out for revenge after what happened to his brother. David's hands squeezed tighter and Dennis threw out his arms as much as he could, feeling around for a weapon, something to use against David before he lost consciousness. His fingers finally came across something but he didn't know what it was. He didn't care. Grasping it, he swung it up and managed to catch David in the head.

Without his helm, David fell like a stone. Gasping for air, Dennis struggled up from his back and rolled over onto David, shoving his face into the mud with the intention of drowning him, but Leeton and Brickley prevented it. They had been standing a few feet away, watching the battle, and now Leeton rushed forward with Brickley on his heels, grabbing Dennis by the hair and throwing him off of David. As Brickley dragged Dennis away, Leeton pulled David up out of the mud and quickly, clumsily, cleaned out his mouth and nose, slapping his face to force him to come around. There was panic on Leeton's fair face as he gazed down at David's mud-covered features.

"Breathe, David," he hissed. *"Breathe!"*

As David took a choking breath and struggled to come around, Dennis yanked himself away from Brickley and kicked the man in the groin, kicking him again when he doubled over in pain. With Brickley down, and Leeton on his knees trying to revive David, Dennis staggered over to the lists where John and Ralph sat, where an entire collection of shocked people sat, and threw his arms up in the air in a signal of victory.

Per the rules of the mass, a competition that had seen every single rule broken and then some, Dennis le Londe, by sheer definition of the rules, had come out on top.

Last man standing.

EMILIE WASN'T QUITE sure what to make of the mass competition at first.

It was a brutal affair from the onslaught, with two sides crashing into each other and men all twisted up with one another, limbs intertwined, hands flailing. It seemed to Emilie that no one was getting anything done, really, because they were in such tight quarters that they simply seemed to be shoving each other around. There wasn't room to do much else.

David had instructed de Wolfe to keep Emilie out of the lists for fear of what would happen if Ralph caught sight of her. Therefore, Edward, Emilie, and seventeen de Lohr soldiers were standing near the eastern gate of the arena, watching the roiling mass of men in the middle. For the first few minutes, there really wasn't much to see at all. It wasn't even all that exciting.

"So… they just push each other around, Sir Edward?" Emilie asked as she peered through the fencing. "I do not think I understand this game very well."

Edward grinned. Wearing most of his armor and the de Lohr tunic because up until several minutes ago he had been planning to compete, he leaned against the fence next to Emilie.

"The mass competition is truly exciting, my lady," he assured her. "Unfortunately, the restricted area of the field is making for very close quarters, but soon men will start to fall and the field should even out. We will be able to see much more when that happens."

Emilie cocked her head thoughtfully as she looked at the mass undulating about. "The goal is to capture men and ransom them?"

"Aye, my lady."

She shook her head. "It seems to me that all one would have to do is reach out and grab a man to capture him," she said. "I am sure there is more to it than that, however."

Edward laughed softly. "There is," he said. "You must look at the mass competition as you would look at a battle. There is strategy involved. Why, I attended at tournament in Rouen last year where the mass competition took place over a two-mile area. Men were running everywhere, fighting and capturing each other. In fact, the spectators had to ride horses or take wagons to follow the games about. It was quite spectacular, truly, so this mass is very small compared to that one. But they all differ to some degree."

Emilie found that a bit more interesting than what she was seeing now. "Fascinating," she said. Growing rather bored of the men on the field pushing each other around in a tight jam, her attention moved to the lists. They were full this day, crowded with people, and she could see the prince and Ralph in the distant royal box. Wary, she moved towards the fence post as if to hide herself from them.

"Do you think the sheriff has seen me?" she asked.

Edward's gaze moved to the royal box as well. "If he has, he will make no move against you," he said. "Not while the mass is going on. I would not worry, my lady. You are safe."

Emilie glanced at Edward. "I am safe at the expense of you being unable to compete in the mass," she said. "You are very kind to stand watch over me while Sir David is competing."

Edward smiled at her. "I am most happy to be here," he said, gesturing to the men on the field. "Look at them. Clubbing each other, falling in the mud, getting their fingers broken. I am in a much better place than they are so do not feel pity for me. I will not be battered and bruised come the end of the day."

Emilie returned his smile. He seemed rather pleasant and she was comfortable with him. "I will not pity you, then," she said. "Let us point fingers and laugh at those men who are dirty and broken when we are clean and whole."

Edward laughed softly. "Speaking of clean," he said, "are your garments sufficiently dry now?"

Emilie nodded, smoothing down her currant-colored wool. "Dry for the most part but I fear the garment is ruined," she said. "The color has run and the fabric is starting to smell. But it will do for now, thank you."

Edward simply nodded, smiling politely before returning his attention to the competition at hand. He had been watching David and the other men as they moved in and out of the crowd, clubs wielded, but the crowd was starting to thin out a bit now and he was noticing that some of the men were bearing clubs with great spike on them, instruments meant to injure or kill. The smile faded from his face as he realized John's mercenaries were using illegal weapons, weapons that the field marshals were allowing. Or, more than likely, weapons that John had declared they could use.

"Why do some men have clubs with spikes sticking out of them?" Emilie asked, interrupting his thoughts.

So she had noticed, too. Edward wasn't entirely sure he liked where this competition was heading. "I know," he said. "Those are illegal. It would seem that those loyal to John are carrying them."

Emilie frowned as she watched the mass between the fence slats. Men were falling more frequently now and most of them were bloodied. The game in general was starting to become more bloody. Concerned, she watched as men were dragged from the field, or limped from the field, and suddenly de Lohr squires were racing in their direction. Darren, the oldest squire, came straight to Edward.

"Sir David wants his weapons and his shield," he said quickly. "He says to tell you to bring forth all manner of killing instruments. His men need them."

Edward nodded swiftly. The squires could not leave the field so it was up to Edward and the de Lohr soldiers to collect what they needed. But they simply couldn't run off and leave Emilie standing there, so she would have to come with them. Edward reached out and grasped her elbow.

"Come along, my lady," he said quickly and quietly. "You can help."

Emilie was more than willing to help. Gathering her skirts, she ran back to the de Lohr encampment along with the rest of the de Lohr men, who began bringing forth axes and shields and swords once they reached the tents. Emilie stood just outside of the main tent, holding her arms out when Edward carefully laid an axe across them. It wasn't too heavy but it was razor sharp, and once the rest of the weaponry was collected, weaponry even for the squires, they made their way quickly back to the field.

It was worse now there than when they'd left. Rain was starting to fall heavily and the field, bloodied, was turning into a muddy red swamp. It was all quite distasteful and they could see women leaving the lists in droves. But Emilie didn't pay attention; she was concentrating on delivering the axe to the squires, who took it from her carefully and thanked her for bringing it. Emilie felt as if she had accomplished something, as if she was part of that legendary de Lohr war machine somehow. It was rather exciting to be part of the games, however peripherally. It made the event far more interesting in her eyes.

But not for too long. With the addition of the de Lohr weapons, and weapons from other great houses, the mock battle soon turned into the real thing and the mass became far more gory than interesting. Blood spurted and limbs fell, severed, but as she was about to turn away so she wouldn't become sick, she noticed David moving through the group with his razor-edged shield and his broadsword. Then, the games became interesting again and she watched, fascinated, as the man fought warrior after warrior, sometimes with his sword, sometimes with his shields, and even sometimes with his feet, but he fought with every piece of his body as he moved. No movement was wasted.

It was like watching a well-choreographed dance. David had so much talent, and moved so quickly, that his movements were fluid, one into the next. He moved as if he knew what would happen ten steps ahead of him – he never faltered and he never stopped. He simply kept on moving as if knowing once he stopped, he would be lost. The energy the man exhibited was impressive, and Emilie watched, enraptured, as he fought man after man.

He is the greatest warrior in all the land.

In spite of the bloody circumstances, she managed a smile as she watched David move, a man of such bravery that surely his heart was made of steel. There was no other way to explain the skills or courage of such a man. She knew the de Lohrs were legendary in their fighting ability, in their reputations, and now she was coming to understand the truth behind that legend.

Now, she was seeing the reality of the de Lohr war machine.

But her admiration soon turned to fear. The field of men were dwindling now, and it was clear who the allies were and who the enemy was, as told by the muddy tunics they wore. A man with a de Lohr tunic was hit by a club squarely in the back and went face-first into the mud. That brought David and Darren running, but as those outside of the arena watched, David was abruptly cut off by a man aiming a club at his head. David threw himself and rolled out of the way to avoid having his skull crushed, but from that point on, the fight became the most brutal thing Emilie could have possibly imagined.

The men on the field declined until there was all but three or four men left as David and a man bearing colors for the prince went at it. At first, it was weapon upon weapon, and that was a terrifying and thrilling thing to watch, but soon enough, the weapons fell aside and they went after each other with their hands in a barbaric fistfight in ankle-deep mud.

On and on it went. Punches flew, heads snapped back and helms fell to the mud, but overall David seemed to be winning. He was as fast with his fists, as he was with his sword, and his opponent was taking a serious beating. Emilie watched in horror as the men beat on each other; she'd never seen anything like it in her life.

Having spent her time in feminine pursuits, this was something so out of the realm of her experience that it was making her sick to her stomach. The only reason she watched it was because David was in the middle of it and she couldn't have taken her gaze away from him if she'd wanted to. She was riveted to him, terrified for him, and with good reason.

This was a battle to the death.

Both David and his opponent eventually grew exhausted. They

were throwing punches still, but with not nearly the ferocity as before. David's opponent even threw a punch and missed, and David got a foot in behind the man's foot and tripped him, shoving him over backwards. David fell atop the man and began pummeling his face.

"It is over," Edward hissed with satisfaction. "He will kill Dennis now for what the man did to his brother. What a stunning and impressive battle for David."

Gripping the fence post in terror as she watched, Emilie recognized the name. "Dennis the Destroyer?" she said to Edward. "I heard you mention that name once before. He is the same man who killed Brentford le Bec, is he not?"

Edward's gaze was riveted to David in the center of the bloodied field as he pounded Dennis' head. "Aye," he muttered. "David is seeking vengeance for Brentford as well. This is a reckoning, my lady. Make no mistake."

Emilie tore her eyes off of the scene long enough to look up at Edward, who seemed unable to take his eyes away from what he was seeing. She looked around to the other de Lohr soldiers and they, too, were all focused on the beating their liege was dealing the man who had injured Christopher. *A reckoning*, she thought. *Is that how men truly think*? As she pondered that mind set, the idea of vengeance that would see one man kill another to seek justice for a wrong doing, or to even the score of some imaginary tabulation, the entire lists let up a collective gasp and she saw Edward jump. Startled, she turned to see that David was now lying face-down in the mud as his enemy, Dennis, pushed his head down into the slop.

Panic filled her. Without thinking, Emilie started to crawl between the fence slats with the intention of running to David's aid. It was clear that Dennis was trying to kill him as well and she could not stand by and watch that happen. She would *not* stand by. But the moment she moved, Edward grabbed her and refused to let her go any further.

"Nay, my lady," he hissed. "Look! Look at Leeton and Brick!"

Emilie stopped fighting him as her gaze sought out what he was describing. She could see Brickley and one of the big de Lohr knights rushing to David's aid. Brickley took on Dennis while the other knight pulled David out of the slop. Brickley, however, was kicked by Dennis and he fell to the ground as the de Lohr knight held David, who was clearly not moving, and tried to bring him around. Dennis stumbled around, his arms raised in victory to a politely applauding crowd, leaving three downed knights in his wake.

After that, Emilie didn't see much of anything else. All she knew was that David was injured and must be tended to. She could think of nothing else.

"Bring David to me," she told Edward, throwing an arm in the direction of the field, pointing. "This foolish competition is over. Bring David to me so that I may tend his injuries, of which I am sure there are many. Do you have a physic with you?"

Edward realized he was being very firmly ordered about. He didn't contest her, though; after what they'd seen, he didn't blame her for being upset.

"The physic is with David's brother, I believe," he said. "I will have the soldiers take you back to David's tent and bring you what you need in order to tend him."

With that, he motioned to a few of the men to take the lady back to the encampment. Emilie was escorted back to the de Lohr tents by twelve de Lohr soldiers, but she kept turning around to see if David was moving under his own power, or if he were being carried off the field. From what she could see he was being carried off, but she soon lost sight of him by the time they entered the encampment. Then, her focus turned to what she needed in order to tend the man.

A man who had fought so bravely against men who were trying to kill him. A prince who was trying to kill him, who had very nearly killed his brother. David de Lohr and men like him were in a league of their own, fighting for good and justice in an England that was shrouded in greed and darkness. She didn't even care that he didn't win the mass competition, or that he didn't win any game in this tournament. To her, he was beyond such things. He was too great to be considered with the rabble.

It was this man she would tend and make well and, God willing, she would never leave his side.

This man with the heart of steel.

CHAPTER ELEVEN

D AVID WAS FIRST aware of someone very carefully swabbing his face. He came in and out of consciousness, and back in again, and now someone was literally picking out his nose. It was uncomfortable. He snorted. He began to grow more lucid, in a misty dreamland where he could hear voices as if they were at an end of a tunnel, but then his last memories began pouring into his mind and he was suddenly in the fight for his life again. He began swinging again, fighting, and he heard a female yelp as several strong hands held him down.

"Sir David?" a woman's urgent voice filled his ears, familiar. "Can you hear me? 'Tis all right. You are safe."

Pinned down, David recognized Emilie's voice. His mind was foggy but he instantly felt at peace. He knew he could not be in a terrible place if she were here. He tried to open his eyes but was only able to open one. Something was wrong with the other one, crusted over. The first thing he saw was Emilie's smiling face.

"Welcome back," she said, a bloodied and dirtied rag in her hand. "We were wondering when you were going to join us."

David blinked, barely able to see her through his clouded vision. "How... how long have I been out?" he rasped.

Emilie turned to wring out her rag in clean water. "Not long," she said, turning back to face him. "A half-hour or so. How do you feel?"

David closed his eye and shifted slightly, trying to get a feel for the pain in his body and the damage. He'd been through this kind of thing before, injured or beaten, so he knew how to test his body to see how badly he was feeling. From the pain he was experiencing, however, he imagined that he wasn't too terribly off. He was both surprised and relieved.

"Sore," he said after a moment. "But nothing seems to be out of place. What is my prognosis?"

Emilie grinned as she put the clean cloth gently to his nose. "First, blow in to this as hard as you can."

He did. It hurt his head, and face, tremendously to do it but he could feel all manner of blockage and debris coming out of his nose, into the cloth Emilie was holding. Afterwards, he could breathe much better.

"Excellent," Emilie said as she tossed that rag into a pile on the floor and took another clean one that was next to the pallet. She rinsed it in the water again and began to dab at his forehead. "You had half of the field in your nose. You should be breathing much easier now."

David blinked, now able to open his other eye a bit as Emilie gently dabbing over it. "I am, actually," he said. "But you have not told me what my prognosis is yet. What is the damage?"

Suddenly, Edward was leaning over him. "You will live," he said. "God only knows why or how, but you will. Dennis almost killed you at the end."

David looked up at Edward, the cobwebs of his mind clearing as he recalled the last part of the mass competition when he was beating Dennis to death. "What happened?" he asked. "I had my hands around his neck and then suddenly I am here. What did he do?"

Edward crouched down, next to the pallet that David was laying on near the brazier in the big de Lohr tent. Dud was there, as was Leeton, and several other de Lohr soldiers, all anxious to see if David would awaken from unconsciousness. Having nearly lost one brother earlier in the day, they were edgy about losing another. Therefore, the fact that David was awake and talking came of something of a relief to them.

"Dennis hit you over the head and then tried to drown you in the mud," Edward said as he settled on his haunches. "That is why there was so much debris in your nose. You must have tried to breathe some of it in. Had it not been for Leeton and Brick, you more than likely would not have survived."

David's mind was clearing rapidly now as the events of the mass competition began to come back to him. "Where are Leeton and Brick now?"

"Here," Leeton said, coming up from behind Edward. He gazed down at David, a weak smile on his lips. "At least, I am here. You may thank me with gold coins and copious amounts of wine."

"And you shall have it," David said, his eyes glimmering faintly. "Words of thanks are not enough, Lee, but I will speak them just the same. You have my gratitude."

Leeton waved him off modestly. "I will take the wine, but give the coins to Brick," he said. "He is worse off than I am. Dennis kicked him in the groin when he pulled the man off of you."

"Where is Brick?"

Leeton threw a thumb in the direction of the castle. "Lord Hampton took him back to the Hampton apartments," he said. "He left Lady Emilie here to tend you because so many of the physics are stretched thin after the mass. Nearly everyone who competed is wounded one way or the other. I have competed in a lot of tournaments, David, but I have to say that this one is one of the worst ones I have ever participated in."

"It was a disaster," Edward grunted in confirmation.

David's opinion was much the same. "No rules," he said, disgusted. "John would not allow it. Do we have the final tally on how many men Richard lost?"

Leeton nodded. "Fortunately, none," he said. "Several are seriously wounded but no one has died yet. John's forces, however, suffered four dead including the Teutonic warrior you killed. Do you know that man had mayhap the worst reputation of the bunch? They called him the Saxon Butcher."

David mulled the information over. "Then I did the world a service, I suppose," he said. "What about Dennis? Was he able to walk away?"

Edward glanced at Leeton, who sighed heavily. "He staggered away," Leeton said. "As I pulled you out of the mud, Dennis staggered about for a few minutes before collapsing completely. From what I've heard, he's not yet regained consciousness. You dealt him a terrible beating, David. He may never be the same."

David simply lay there, emotionless on the outside but feeling great angst on the inside. "It was my intention to kill him," he said quietly. "See how I have failed. For Brentford and for my brother, I failed. I allowed Dennis to live."

Emilie, who had been cleaning out the cut above David's left eye, could see his genuine distress. They all did. But her heart, a soft and caring thing, was often her guide in most situations, even more than her common sense. The knights understood David's lament while Emilie didn't. She saw something entirely different.

"You fought more truly and more bravely than any knight has ever fought, Sir David," she insisted softly. "I saw you; I have never seen a man with more courage. Every man who fought in that competition today should be ashamed because they did not fight as well as you did. You lasted until the end, something no one else did. I understand you wanted to seek a reckoning for what Dennis the Destroyer did to your brother and to Sir Brentford, but everything happens in the appropriate place and time. Mayhap this was just not the time. It had nothing to do with your failure."

The woman who knew virtually nothing about the hearts of men or the code of the knighthood still had some very valid points in her attempt to comfort David. She actually had his attention, which was a rarity with him. He always felt he knew best in most situations but in this one, perhaps what Emilie said had some truth to it. In any case, her words were soothing. There was some comfort in them. He smiled at her, his swollen lips twisted.

"You are kind, my lady," he said. "I suppose everything happens in God's time, but I have been known to want to rush God's timing. This was one of those times."

Emilie grinned at him, reaching over to pour something from a cup onto the rag in her hand, which she promptly put on the cut above David's eye. "That is understandable," she said. "But your haste has left you with a few wounds. I will do what I can for you."

David was quite pleased by her attention even though whatever she had put on the rag stung like mad. Still, it didn't matter. He was quite pleased by her observation of his knightly skills as well as her attention to his injuries. Perhaps it was almost worth being injured just to have her lovely attention on him, to bask in her beautiful warmth.

"And I am grateful," he said, "but whatever you are putting on the gash is stinging me more than the actual injury."

The knights snorted and Emilie shook her head reproachfully. "After what you went through today, I can hardly believe a small amount of wine will hurt you," she said. "I am doing to cleanse your wound, not torture you. But steel yourself; I will be cleaning your hands next and they are in terrible shape. I promise not to hurt you more than necessary."

David grinned at her, a rather besotted expression from the look on Edward's face when David eventually glanced at the man. Edward was smirking and Leeton was simply shaking his head, as if ashamed that David should fall victim to a lovely face. Seeing the expressions around him forced David into action; he had been caught in a weak moment and, as much as he had berated his brother for falling victim to his new wife's charms, David didn't want to look like a hypocrite for his sweet expression at Emilie. He moved quickly to divert their attention.

"I am well enough," he told his men, reaching up to lower Emilie's hand where she was cleaning another small cut on his scalp. He grunted as he pushed himself up into a sitting position, fighting some nausea that accompanied it. "Edward, make sure my brother knows I survived the mass competition but tell him what happened to Dennis. Tell him everything. Leeton, will you see to breakdown our encampment? I will leave it to you and Dud to make sure everything is disbanded. I also want an accounting of what weapons we lost and what needs to be prepared."

The soldiers began to move, as was usual when David gave an order, but Edward and Leeton remained.

"Lay down, for Christ's Sake," Edward hissed, trying to force David to lay back down again. "You had a serious blow to the head. You need to rest. Allow the lady to finish tending you for when she is done, I must send word to her father and he will come and escort her back to their apartments."

David pushed Edward away. "I am no weakling," he said. "Go now and do as I say. As soon as the lady is finished with me, I will send word to her father, I swear it."

Edward sighed with resignation; David was trying to pretend he was well enough when the truth was that he wasn't. He was pale and injured. Edward looked at Leeton, who was gazing at David with a critical eye. Leeton caught Edward's expression, silently asking for his support, and the man complied.

"We will go when you lay down again," Leeton said. "It was I who dragged you off the field, David, and you most certainly were not well. Let the lady tend you while we go about our duties. We will come back to you when all is complete."

David frowned. "Where is my sword?" he asked, looking around. "I am going to chase you both out of here if I have to."

"Sir David," Emilie, who had pulled back when David sat up and started arguing with his men, spoke softly but firmly. "Lay back down this instant. I am not finished tending your head or anything else. Please do this for me."

They were the magic words; David obeyed her soft plea without another word of protest. The truth was that he felt much better lying down. Grunting as his head throbbed, he caught sight of Edward and Leeton as they quietly quit the tent. They were smirking because David had acquiesced so easily to Emilie. He was smitten with the woman and the knights knew it.

But, strangely, David didn't care as much as he had only moments earlier.

He let them think what they wanted to think.

When the tent was emptied very quickly as Emilie collected her rag dipped in wine and went back to work on David's head. He lay there with his eyes closed, as still as stone. Outside of the tent, they could hear Edward and Leeton ordering men to begin breaking down the encampment. As the bustle went on around them outside of the tent walls, Emilie quietly and efficiently worked.

"Where did you get all of those medicines and supplies?" David asked, eyes still closed.

Emilie looked at the small table next to her. "I am not entirely sure, to be truthful," she said. "I told Sir Edward that I needed a few things to clean up your injuries and he had your men find these things and bring them back. There is a needle and silk thread, wine with herbs, bandages, and a compound that smells terribly of garlic but I was told to put it on your bleeding wounds and wrap it tightly to cure them."

David peeped an eye open to see what she was talking about; he could see that the small table next to her was cluttered with things. "Garlic has healing properties," he said. "We always carry that with us, especially in battle. I do not recognize some of those things. They do not belong to us."

Emilie lifted her eyebrows. "I think some of this was stolen," she whispered loudly. "Edward would not tell me where it came from."

David grinned and closed his eye. "It is of no matter," he said, changing the subject away from stolen medicines so she wouldn't think he was the leader of a gang of thieves. "Have you done much healing, then?"

Emilie was carefully threading the fine bone needle. "A little," she said. "It is something that has always interested me. I fostered at Rochester Castle and the lady of the house knew a good deal of healing. I learned from her. And Elise is sick a good deal and I tend her. Well, Lillibet and I tend her together, actually."

He opened an eye again to look at her. "Elise?"

"My youngest sisters."

"I see," he said. "And who is Lillibet?"

Emilie was focused on the needle. "My nurse."

David thought back to the group of women in the wagon earlier that day. "The older woman I saw with you this morning?"

"Aye."

"The one who spits?"

"Aye."

"And who do those terrible dogs belong to?"

Emilie laughed. "They liked you a great deal, my lord," she teased. "How can you call them terrible?"

He grunted in disapproval of dogs in general. "Although they have good taste in men, they are still smelly beasts," he said. "Do they belong to you?"

Emilie nodded. "They belong to all of us," she said. "They sleep with Nathalie and Elise. Sometimes they even sleep with Brick."

David clearly disapproved of the dogs sleeping with their masters, but the mention of Brickley reminded him of the contention he'd had with the man earlier in the day. Contention over Emilie. David was leaning heavily towards hating the man until Edward told him that it had been Brickley who had pulled Dennis off of him, quite possibly saving his life.

That had stopped David's hatred towards Brickley. Perhaps the man was jealous but at least he didn't wish David ill will. It hadn't stopped him from saving his life. That said a good deal for Brickley's character. David was thankful but that didn't make him feel any less hostile towards the man who lusted after Emilie.

Brickley had said that Emilie knew nothing of his feelings but David couldn't believe that. It was very difficult for a man to keep his feelings to himself where a woman was concerned. Surely Emilie suspected something. David decided to put his theory to the test.

Does she know?

"I would not have thought Brick the type to sleep with dogs," he said after a moment. "Doesn't he have a wife to sleep with?"

Emilie shook her head but her focus was on the needle, now threaded. "He does not," she said, moving to David. Her eyes met his, apologetic. "I must put a few stitches in your forehead now. I apologize for any pain I will cause."

David simply closed his eyes. "I am sure it will be nothing at all," he said, his thoughts returning to Brickley. He was being deliberate about it, and sly, mostly because he wanted to know what her feelings were about the man. If she was fond of him, as a lover would be fond of another, then at least he would know. It wouldn't lessen his determination to steal her away from Brickley, but at least he would know. Therefore he continued carefully. "Back to Brick. Before today I had not seen the man since before I left for the Levant. I cannot believe he has not married yet. He is amiable enough. Surely some woman would find him attractive enough to marry."

Emilie took the first small stab into his forehead, working quickly. "He is indeed amiable," she said. "I hope he finds a good wife someday. We look upon him as family and wish him only the best."

That gave David a little more clue as to what she might feel about Brickley. She didn't sound as if she longed for the man or as if she even knew of his feelings for her. "He would be family if he married you or your sisters," he said. "Has your father not considered such a thing?"

Emilie shrugged. "I do not know," she said. "My sister Nathalie is quite fond of Brick and hopes he will notice her, but so far he has not. He has known her most of her life and looks at her as a child still, much to Nathalie's distress. I do believe she wants to marry him."

Ah, so the *middle* sister had her sights set on Brickley. David was pleased to hear that. "And you?" he muttered as she put in the third and final stitch. "Do you want to marry him?"

She made a face, horrified. "Not in the least," she said. "I have known Brick so long that he is like an older brother. I could never think of him as a husband."

David felt a great deal of relief at that statement and struggled not to show it. "I see," he said. "So if not Brick, do you have anyone you hope will notice you?"

Emilie blushed furiously, turning away from him and going for a sharp dagger to cut the silk thread. She cut it quickly, putting the needle and dagger back onto the table. She was rattled by his question because, of course, he was the one she hoped would notice her but it would be horribly forward – and desperate – for her to say anything about it. Unless....

"*You* have already noticed me," she flirted cautiously, gauging his reaction. "You took my favor and have allowed me to tend your injury. In some countries, we would be considered betrothed."

David's eyes flew open, noticing the grin on her face. *So she is toying with me*, he thought. He was on to her flirtatious little game.

"Not in *this* country," he said firmly, "but I could send for a priest right now. Certainly we could be married before your father could stop us. I wonder if he would try to kill me if I married you without permission?"

She looked at him, noticing the smirk playing on his lips. He was teasing her just as she had been teasing him. But she realized she would have given anything for this to be a serious conversation and not a jesting one. Still, she played his game. It was fun to pretend, even if he wasn't serious.

"Undoubtedly, he would attempt to kill you," she said. "But I think summoning a priest is a fine idea. Why not marry without his permission? He would get over it soon enough, especially when presented with his first grandchild. And, as your wife, I would follow you everywhere you go like an adoring fool, hanging on your every word, and feeding you every meal out of my own hands."

He made a face. "Jesus, woman," he said. "I am no babe to be fed. Would you really do such a thing?"

"Of course I would, my master. I mean my lord."

He scowled, exaggerated. "Then the marriage is *off.*"

Emilie giggled. "I am destroyed," she said, feigning great distress. "You would do such a thing to me? After I scraped mud out of your nose?"

He started laughing although he was trying not to. "You have a point," he said. "You have done things to me that no woman ever has. I do not recall having anyone stick their fingers up my nose, ever."

"Romantic, is it not?"

His laughter broke through as he looked at her, seeing the impish twinkle in her eye and the big dimple in her cheek. God, she was an alluring creature and as he gazed at her, he realized one thing – whatever control he'd ever had over his emotions, especially when it came to women, was weakening. What had started out as a giddy infatuation with a beautiful young woman was becoming something much more. Even now, as he looked at her, all he could do was feel a pull towards her that came straight from his heart.

"Very," he said. "I suppose I shall reconsider marriage to you, after all."

Emilie's smile faded into something warm and hopeful. She sensed that he was being quite serious now simply by the expression on his face. It was as warm and hopeful as her own. Averting her gaze, she fought off a powerful flush.

"If you insist, my lord."

He was watching her as she began to tear up pieces of linen for bandages. "David," he said softly.

She looked at him, somewhat curiously. "My lord?"

He shook his head as much as he was able, reaching out to take one of her hands. "You will call me David," he murmured. "I give you permission. May I call you Emilie?"

She nodded, her heart beating wildly against her ribs as his rough, bloodied fingers touched hers. "You may," she whispered.

Pulling her hand to his bloodied lips, he kissed it gently. For a moment, their banter faded and they simply stared at one another. There was something heady in the air now, something that hadn't been there before, a miasma that bespoke of interest and warmth and even affection beyond what they were currently experiencing. Earlier in the day, before David had competed in the mass competition, they had been in a situation similar to this, close to one another, until Lyle and Brickley had ruined it. Now, there was no one to ruin it. Reaching up, David put a hand behind her neck and pulled her down to him, kissing her sweetly on the lips.

"Aagh," he suddenly grunted in obvious pain.

Startled, flushed, Emilie pulled back, looking at him with horror. "Did I hurt you?" she asked. "I… I did not mean to. I…."

He reached up and pulled her down to him again, his hand behind her neck, kissing her gently on the cheek. "You did nothing," he said, thinking her cheek was quite soft and smooth. "But my mouth seems to be paining me, and my lips in particular. But it was worth the pain to taste your lips."

Emilie had no idea how to react. His move to kiss her had been unexpected and she was giddy with the thrill of it. She'd been kissed before, of course, but not like this. Never like this. Her cheeks were hot with the excitement of it and she put a hand to her face, feeling the heat, giggling when David grinned at her. He felt the heat, too.

"Was it wicked of me to let you do it, then?" she asked.

He laughed softly. "Probably," he said. "But who cares? I have wanted to do that practically since I met you. I am glad I did it. I will do it again if given a chance, so be warned."

Emilie was moving to re-thread the needle for the gash on his scalp, anything to keep her hands busy because she was so rattled by his kiss that she was having difficulty thinking straight. It was a wonderful feeling.

"So long as you do not kiss me in front of my father," she said. "Unless, of course, you were serious about marrying me."

David lay there, his half-lidded gaze studying her for a moment. A smile played on his lips as he wondered just how serious she was about it. She seemed to be teasing him about marriage an awful lot and he wasn't sure if he liked it. He undoubtedly liked her, but marriage....

"I told you that I am not the marrying kind," he said.

"Then you cannot kiss me again."

"Is that so? I must marry you in order to kiss you?"

She cocked an eyebrow at him. "How would *you* feel if you married a woman who had been repeatedly kissed by another man who would not marry her? Would you want his leavings?"

He sighed heavily, scratching his chin with his bloodied hand. "Probably not," he said. "Let me be clear on this; if I want to kiss you again, I must offer for your hand?"

"That seems reasonable."

He frowned. "It is not reasonable at all if I never intend to marry."

Emilie wouldn't relent. Certainly, she had let men kiss her before, but only once. Never anything more. What David seemed to want to do was much, much more; she could tell simply by his tone and that warm, liquid expression when he looked at her. It made her want to succumb to his lusty wishes. Not that she didn't want him to kiss her again and again, but she didn't want to be something convenient to him. She wanted him to be serious about her, as she was about him.

She didn't want to be used and discarded.

"So I should simply let you kiss me as much as you want without any hint of commitment from you?" she asked. "You do not believe I am more respectable than that?"

His jaw ticked. "I will *not* promise to marry you just to kiss you once or twice."

"Then you shall never have another kiss from me."

"Mayhap I do not want one, then."

"That is a good thing because you shall not have one."

"I am content with that."

"So am I."

The mood had quickly turned from giddy and playful to something serious. Emilie's feelings were hurt and David, on unsteady ground with talk of marriage, was starting to feel cornered. *A marriage proposal for a kiss? Ridiculous!* He thought. Was it possible she was even serious, that he simply wanted kisses because he did not respect her?

But the truth was that he respected her a great deal. If he ever considered marriage, it would be to someone like Emilie. Actually, it would be *to* Emilie. The thought of her marrying another didn't sit well with him in the least. What if Brickley managed to marry her? That would upset David to no end and he knew, as he lived and breathed, that he could not let that happen. He didn't want to marry her but he didn't want anyone else to marry her, either.

David had a dilemma on his hands.

The safe thing to do was not to speak to her anymore, so he fell silent, closing his eyes and pretending to sleep as she stitched up the cut in his scalp. He thought that she might have stabbed his flesh a little harder than normal but he didn't say anything about it. He remained silent, feigning sleep.

But he couldn't hold out the ruse. Exhausted, and wounded, his pretend-sleep soon became the real thing.

WHEN DAVID AWOKE, the tent was dark except for a pair of lit tapers and the soft golden glow from the brazier. Startled to realize the sun had set, he shifted around on his pallet, thinking he should get up and see where everyone had gone. It seemed rather quiet to him, the encampment around him still and vacated for the most part, but the moment he moved, he heard a soft voice from the darkness.

"So you are awake," Emilie said. "How do you feel?"

David couldn't see her so he tried to sit up but suddenly, her hands were on his shoulders, pushing him back down again. "Stay," she commanded softly. "I will summon Sir Edward. He is waiting to take you back to your apartments."

David let her push him back down, blinking up at her in the darkness. She was wrapped in something; a cloak he thought, and she moved to collect one of the tapers that lit the tent. Her sweet face was illuminated by the golden light from the candle, but her expression was anything but warm. She appeared rather subdued as she made her way to the tent opening and pushed it back, sending the nearest soldier for Edward. When she let the flap fall back into place and turned back into the tent, David spoke.

"How long have I been asleep?" he asked.

She turned her serious expression on him and David was distressed to see that there was no light in her eyes for him at all. He thought back to the conversation they'd had before he'd fallen asleep and wasn't particularly surprised by the lack of warmth in her face, but he had hoped things would smooth over with time. She would forget, or so he hoped, but he could see that wasn't the case. He was coming to regret their unhappy exchange but not enough to make amends. Not enough to agree to marry her in exchange for a kiss.

"You have been asleep for several hours," Emilie said, interrupting his thoughts. "I waited here with you in case you needed something or were in distress, but you have slept heavily all that time. My father is here, waiting with Sir Edward, to escort me home. We have been all waiting for you to awaken so that you could be moved."

David scratched his head, gingerly feeling the stitches in his scalp. "You should have awoken me," he said. "You have been sitting here in the dark all of this time, waiting for me. That is not a particularly pleasant way for you to spend your evening."

She set the taper down on a small table. "You carried my favor today," she said. "It was my duty to tend you. You may return my favor, by the way. You shall not need it any longer."

David looked at her, feeling some sadness and guilt that she was still cross with him. He could see it in everything about her. He didn't like that feeling, not in the least.

"Emilie," he said quietly. "Would it be too much to ask to keep your favor?"

She shook her head almost immediately. "There is no need for you to keep it," she said. "It was simply a favor given to you to wish you luck for the games. The games are over now. In fact, my father has informed me that we are leaving Windsor on the morrow for my aunt's home in London. I am sure you and I will never see one another again, so there is no reason for you to keep my favor. I would like it returned."

David had been stripped of his outer tunic and mail when Emilie had tended him, but the padded tunic next to his skin remained. It was dirty and stained, and smelled horrifically of sweat, and Emilie's favor was tucked into that, pressed up against his chest. With a heavy heart, he reached into his tunic and fumbled for it.

"What makes you say we shall never see each other again?" he asked as he held it up to her, damp and smelly. "You will be in London and I may visit you, with your permission."

Emilie took the favor and avoided looking him in the eye. "Why?" she asked. "Why would you come and visit me? David, we enjoyed a day of festivities and excellent conversation. I even let you kiss me because I thought… well, it does not matter what I thought. What we shared today is ended and I enjoyed it a great deal. I wish you well in your life and pray you enjoy good health."

David pushed himself up on an elbow, eyeing her in the faint light. "Is this because I told you I was not the marrying kind?" he asked. "Is that why you do not want to see me again? Because I will not agree to marry you after knowing you only one day?"

Hugely embarrassed, Emilie blew out of the tent, crashing into Edward and her father as they entered. She wouldn't look at either of them as she headed for her father's horse, as he'd come to escort her home when the sun began to set, but she wouldn't leave David's side whilst he was sleeping. Lyle understood her attention to duty, and he and Edward had enjoyed a pleasant conversation for the past several hours.

Now, Lyle was concerned with his daughter's distressed behavior so he bid Edward a good evening and left the transport of David to Edward and his soldiers. Emilie's task was finished and he went to her as she stood next to his horse, seemingly wiping at her face.

"Em?" he asked, concerned. "What is the matter, sweetheart?"

Emilie shook her head; she wasn't about to tell her father that she'd made an utter fool of herself. *Is this because I will not agree to marry you after only knowing you one day?* He was right and Emilie knew it; he was utterly correct. But she had fallen for the man so swiftly that she would have gladly married him after knowing him only one day. What a fool she had been. A silly, besotted fool.

"Nothing is wrong, Papa," she said. "I am simply exhausted. It has been an eventful day."

Lyle accepted her excuse although he didn't really believe her; she was usually very good at keeping her emotions under control and he swore that she had been weeping, but he didn't press her. She was correct – it had been an eventful day for them all. He was willing to let Emilie deal with her emotions in private. Even if he knew what was bothering her, which he suspected he did, he couldn't help her. If she had her heart set on David and the feelings were perhaps not returned, there was perhaps nothing he could do at all.

He wondered if that was the case.

Lifting his daughter onto his heavy-boned warmblood, Lyle mounted the horse behind her and, in the darkness, headed towards Windsor Castle.

PART TWO
DEUS ET HONORA

"Gold and silver in countless tale,
Mules and chargers, and silks and mail,
The king himself may have spoil at call.
From hence to the East he will conquer all"
~ Song of Roland c. 1040 A.D.

CHAPTER TWELVE

December 1192

*T*HE JUSTICES MET *after the tournament and decided that until they had a body or confirmation of Richard's death, the man was still England's king and they would continue administering the country in his absence, or at least until Eleanor returned from France. Christopher, in full agreement with their conclusion, decided to delay his return to Lioncross until there was any change regarding Richard's well-being. It did not, however, sway his mind to send Dustin northward. He had yet to speak with Marcus about it, but knew the man would do as was asked of him.*

John and Ralph had kept a remarkably low profile after the tournament that saw Dennis le Londe emerge the victor. Even with Sir Dennis and his henchmen as the prince's constant companions, there were no confrontations, threats, or attempts on Christopher or David's life. In fact, it was almost too good to hope for and Christopher was increasingly concerned that John was merely attempting to lure him into a false sense of security. There was, however, one point of great distress in the midst of the calm – John's mercenary army was growing in strength and size and Christopher, as well as the justices, suspected that Philip Augustus was channeling funds into England somehow to pay for them. There was also the unmistakable fact that a great majority of the mercenaries were Frenchmen.

It was a few days before Christmas when John decided to have a mask. It was a season of celebration and prayer, but the prince took it to the next level. He wanted a mad party. The mood struck John to have a mask, and a mask all of Windsor would have.

Home of Lady Orford, sister to the Earl of Canterbury
London, England

SHE DIDN'T DO much more than lay there and spread her legs, but that was truthfully all Lyle needed. She didn't even take off her clothes, which he found rather erotic. All Lillibet would do was lift her skirts and either lay on the bed, as she was now, or bend over and hold on to the end of the bed or a table, whatever happened to be closest, as Lyle thrust into her. She may have spit like a cobra when she spoke, and didn't particularly have a handsome face, but she knew how to please a man from the waist down.

Even now, as the sun began to set over the western horizon and the sky turned shades of pink and dark blue, Lyle thrust into Lillibet as the woman held tight to the head of the bed, grunting every time Lyle rammed his big organ into her body. She would tighten up her muscles internally, squeezing him, and by God he loved that. Someone had taught her to do that, although he had never asked her who. All he knew was that she serviced him well, and had since his wife had died. She had managed to keep that part of him satisfied even though his heart still longed for something more. Not with her, but with someone worthy. Lillibet had simply been a means to an end until something better came along, even after all of these years.

But it had been foolish to sneak Lillibet into his bed this time of day while his girls were in the house. Still, the urge had struck him and Lillibet had answered the call. The time had been ripe; his daughters had been napping because of the big, formal mask that evening so with a quiet house, Lyle's thoughts had turned to satisfying his needs. He was just about to find his release, for he could feel it building, when he began to hear his daughters' voices, raised.

Someone was unhappy; he thought it might have been Elise, for she was always the most vocal. Mixed in with the girl's voice were more voices. It sounded as if there were some kind of argument going on, and Lyle had to quickly take his pleasure. Too much was going on for him to feel comfortable with Lillibet in his bed. He was a hypocrite and he knew it, but it had been going on so long this way that it was simply the way of things.

Once finished, he shooed Lillibet from his chamber by having her leave through a servant's door. His sister's home was quite large, with a maze of servant passages and stair cases, so Lillibet took the stairs to the bottom floor and came back up the main stairs, into the girls' suite of rooms. It had been her intention to soothe whatever argument was brewing but when she entered Nathalie and Elise's chamber, she came face to face with Lady Orford, who had been trying to calm the situation herself. Upon seeing Lyle's sister, Lillibet immediately left the chamber; there was no love lost between the lady of the house and her brother's lover.

The Lady Coraline Hampton Russell, Countess of Orford, had been a lovely woman with flaming red hair in her younger years. She had married very well, into a rich family that still held a great many properties in Sussex and Essex, but her husband had died when they were both still young and they had been without children. Coraline had inherited his wealth but had never remarried, instead, becoming the patroness of four poorhouses in southern England, including one near Canterbury Castle, and becoming a doting aunt to her three nieces. She didn't see them much but she always sent them gifts and messages. Having them in the house with her for the past two months while her brother engaged in London politics had been pure heaven and she most certainly didn't need the help of Lyle's servant to help raise them. That woman Lyle seemed to think no one knew he was fucking.

Aye, fucking. That's what Coraline called it and she didn't mince words. Lyle didn't have much to say about it when she berated him, but that was usual for him. They never had much to say about anything to each other, mostly because Coraline, the older sister, dominated, and Lyle didn't much like to engage her. So he stayed away from her as much as he could, especially since his wife had died, and he'd taken that spitting beast into his bed. At least, that was how Coraline looked at it. In her opinion, her brother could do much better.

Therefore, Coraline was relieved when her brother's courtesan left the room as quickly as she had entered it. She didn't want to see or speak to the women. Coraline was in the process of helping her nieces dress for the prince's mask on this cold winter's evening but there was a problem; at the moment, she was having a stand-off with Elise, who wanted to bring the dolls she took everywhere with her. Coraline was trying to be gentle about convincing the girl to leave them behind but, so far, Elise was having none of it.

"If my people cannot go, I will not attend!"

Elise was adamant. Coraline, dressed finely in a golden frock that had golden thread woven throughout it, was patient with her youngest, and strangest, niece.

"My darling girl," she said sweetly. "They would not be able to enjoy the mask. They would simply be in the way. What if someone stepped on them? What if some were lost? You would be devastated. Therefore, it is best for them if you leave them behind. They will be happier here."

Elise wouldn't do it. Pouting, and gripping her box tightly, she flounced off into an adjoining room with Coraline following her, leaving Emilie and Nathalie behind.

The older girls could hear their aunt pleading with Elise, but they didn't pay much attention to it. They even heard when Elise began crying for Lillibet, which made for an awkward situation with Aunt Coraline, but they were more concerned with how they looked and not with two contentious old maids. The mask this evening would be an opportunity to see and be seen by all of London and there was excitement in the air as they put the finishing touches on their wardrobe. This event was to be the thrill of their young lives.

Aunt Coraline had commissioned new gowns for the girls, just for this occasion, and the results were stunning. Nathalie wore a gown of the palest green, with gold embroidery around the neck and detailed down the long sleeves. Emilie wore a creation that was the most magnificent of all, with layers of sea colors, shades of blue, and a snug bodice that laced tightly with silver ribbon over her breasts. Her blond hair had been artfully arranged by Coraline's French maid, with pinned curls on her head culminating in her hair gathered on the right side of her head, tumbling over her shoulder in a cascade of more curls that went all the way to her waist.

The results were truly stunning. Emilie inspected herself in the mirror and noted the hint of lip rouge the French maid had put on her. It was enough to bring a smile to her lips, something rarely seen since leaving Windsor two months ago. Since the day of the terrible tournament that people were still talking about, Emilie had been quiet, and miserable, and nothing anyone did could seem to bring her out of her melancholy. She ate little, spoke little, and spent most of her time sewing. She'd made a few lovely things in that time with the help of Coraline's maids, shawls and even a find bodice for a surcoat that still needed to be put together. But still, nothing seemed to make her smile and Lyle knew it was because she was yearning for a certain young knight who was evidently yearning for her as well.

At least, that was what Christopher de Lohr had said one night, about three weeks after the tournament that nearly ended his life as well as his brother's. He had cornered Lyle at Windsor after a meeting with Richard's supporters, dancing around the subject of Lady Emilie and her health, the general health of his family, before casually mentioning that his brother, David, had recovered quickly from his injuries thanks to Lady Emilie but seemed to be perpetually foul of mood. Lyle had agreed that Emilie was the same way and with those leading statements out of the way, Christopher and Lyle came to the meat of the subject and realized, between the two of them, that something must have occurred between David and Emilie that had the two of them longing for one another.

Or hating one another, although neither Lyle or Christopher thought it was truly hatred, but neither man wanted to interfere in the situation. In fact, there wasn't anything they could do to pull David and Emilie together. Whatever happened would have to come from David, as the man in the equation. Emilie was helpless to make any sort of move, as the lady.

Christopher was clear in that he couldn't particularly guide David in this matter. As always, and especially when it came to women, David did what David wanted to do. He further commented that David had difficulty adjusting since returning from The Levant those months back. He suggested that Emilie may have just been a passing fancy to his confused brother.

If that were the case, then Lyle was saddened for Emilie's sake, for she had known her share of suitors and none of them had elicited this manner of reaction from her that David de Lohr had. And then there was the trouble with Brickley, who had seemed to be pushing his suit of Emilie very hard since that terrible tournament. Lyle had managed to hold him off for the past two months but he was fairly certain he wouldn't be able to hold him off much longer. In fact Brickley had asked to escort Emilie to the mask this night, and without a good reason to refuse him, Lyle had reluctantly agreed. He had no idea what Emilie was in for that night with Brickley, so he braced himself, expecting the worst. Worse still because David de Lohr would presumably be attending the same event.

It could be bad all around, in many ways.

Of course, Emilie knew none of it. All she knew was that she had been sad and lonely the past couple of months, mourning the loss of a man she never really had. She'd caught a brief glimpse of a perfect life with him but it wasn't meant to be. At least that's what she kept telling herself.

Even now, she gazed at herself in the polished bronze mirror, inspecting her appearance and wondering, as she had been for some time, if David would be at the mask. She hoped he was so he could see how beautiful she looked and then feel badly that he hadn't staked his claim when he'd had the chance.

Tonight, there would be many eligible men and Emilie intended to dance with every one of them who asked, and she would particularly make sure that they danced where David was seated. She wanted to make him very, very sorry he had treated her so callously. Wanting to kiss her, and Lord knew what else, without speaking of his permanent interest in her.

All he'd wanted was a toy to play with.

Emilie had been given two months to think over her last conversation with David. Two months of living it over and over in her mind, wondering where she had gone wrong. The truth was that she didn't believe she had gone wrong, anywhere. David had informed her that he intended to steal kisses whenever he wanted to and she told him that she would have none of it unless he wanted to court her. *Marry her.* She hadn't been wrong in the least.

Perhaps her demand of marital consideration had been a bit premature, as David had indicated, but she certainly wasn't going to let the man have his way with her without any commitment on his part. So she'd taken a stance, and so had he, and she hadn't seen him in two months because of it. *Two long months.* But the truth was that she missed him very much and she thought of him every hour of every day. She wondered how he had been and if he had recovered well from his injuries. She knew her father had seen him from time to time when he'd gone to Windsor Castle on business, simply because she knew all of Richard's supporters were there, and the de Lohrs were the greatest supporters of all. But she hadn't asked about David and her father hadn't offered anything. She was too proud to ask, too proud to admit that one man, out of all the suitors she'd ever had, finally left an impression on her.

A knock on the door distracted her from her thoughts. Nathalie, who was closer to the door, opened it to find Lyle standing there. He smiled at his girls, entering the room to admire their lovely new gowns.

"You look lovely, Nathalie," he said to his middle daughter, watching her beam. "You look just like your mother in that color."

Nathalie twirled around in the dress, displaying it for her father in full. "It is so beautiful, Papa," she said. "Do you think we can have a party when we return home so that I can wear it again?"

Lyle laughed softly. "I am sure we can, my lovely little flower," he said, looking to Emilie, who was exquisite in her shades of blue. "Ah, Emilie… you are positively radiant in that gown. You will outshine every woman at the mask tonight."

Emilie glanced at herself in the mirror again, fingering the silver and sapphire necklace her aunt had loaned her. It went perfectly with the dress, a luxurious piece of jewelry that hailed the wealth of the houses that ruled Canterbury and Orford. The dress was beautiful, the necklace was beautiful, but still she felt no real joy in any of it. She smiled weakly to her father's flattery.

"Thank you, Papa," she said without much enthusiasm. "Will we be leaving soon?"

Lyle nodded. "The escort is ready," he said. He eyed Emilie a moment before clearing his throat softly. "Since every young lady must have an escort, Brick will be yours, Em, and I will escort Nathalie and Elise. Brick is waiting downstairs if you are ready."

Emilie sighed with displeasure. "I would rather not go with him," she said. "Let him take Nathalie. She wants him to, anyway."

Lyle was careful in his reply even as Nathalie, who was crushed when she heard Brickley was escorting her sister, was now looking at her father with great hope as Emilie brushed the man aside.

"It would not be suitable for him to escort your sister," Lyle said.

"The eldest daughter of the house is entitled to any single male escort. It would not look right for him to escort your younger sister while you are escorted by your father."

Emilie rolled her eyes as she turned away from the mirror and went to collect the deep blue cloak that matched the dress. There was also a sheer blue scarf that went with it, meant to cover the head without mussing the elaborate hairstyle. It was truly an exquisite presentation but, at the moment, Emilie didn't much care. She snatched at the cloak unhappily.

"Papa, I really would rather *not* have Brick as my escort," she said. "I would be much happier if he escorted Nathalie."

"Why do you not want him as your escort?" Lyle asked. "Has he upset you somehow?"

Emilie was reluctant to say much, careful in her words. She didn't want to upset Nathalie, who was quite sensitive about Brickley and the fact that the man still wouldn't pay her any attention, at least the attention she wanted from him. But the truth was that the man had been hanging around Emilie for the past two months behaving very strangely. He was always around, wherever she was, hovering and asking her questions and trying to make conversation with her. It was most odd coming from a man she had known most of her life, a man who had never been so solicitous until the day of that terrible tournament. If Emilie hadn't known better, she would have sworn the man was trying to warm her to him or somehow ingratiate himself to her. Emilie didn't like it and she was becoming increasingly uncomfortable with it.

"Nay," she said after a moment. "He has not upset me, but he will not leave me in peace. He is constantly bothering me."

"How is he bothering you?"

Emilie shrugged. "He is always *around*."

"He has always been around."

Listening to the exchange, Nathalie didn't like the fact that Emilie seemed to be scorning a man she was very fond of. "He is just being kind, Em," she insisted. "Brick is constantly around me as well and it does not bother me in the least."

She said it rather cheerfully and Lyle eyed the girl, thinking that Brickley was only around her because she was, most of the time, around Emilie. Lyle could see that the situation was going to grow very uncomfortable unless he did something about it, so he put a hand on Nathalie's shoulder and pointed to the connecting door, the one that led to the chamber where Elise and Coraline had gone.

"See if your sister and aunt are ready to depart," he instructed her. "And gather your cloak. It is very cold outside. And where are the dogs? Make sure they are adequately tended before we leave."

Obediently, Nathalie slipped off and when she was gone, Lyle made his way over to Emilie, who was struggling with her heavy cloak. Lyle went to the rescue. He had a few things he wanted to say to her and hoped that Nathalie would stay away long enough so he could do it. With time against him, he spoke quickly.

"Em, I must tell you something about Brick," he said as he helped settle the cloak on her shoulders. "I cannot let you go on thinking he is bothersome and hovering. 'Tis more than that and it is time you know. I have refrained from saying anything because I had hoped Brick would forget about you and move on, but it seems that is not the case. He has not forgotten about you in the least. Surely you must know by now that Brick is very fond of you."

Emilie didn't understand Lyle's tactful statement, at least in the way he meant it. In hindsight she should have, but she simply wasn't thinking along those lines. "I am fond of him as well," she said. "But he is making a nuisance of himself, Papa. He will not leave me alone. It is all I can do to keep from screaming at him sometimes!"

Lyle could see that she didn't understand him. "Emilie, listen to me," he said, forcing her to look at him. "Brick has watched you grow from a young girl into a lovely young woman and with his wife's passing those years ago, it is only natural that he views you... well, *fondly*. A lonely man without a wife... do you see what I am saying, lass?"

Emilie still didn't understand what her father was telling her until the last few words. It was the way Lyle had said it that made her suddenly realize what, exactly, he was saying. Her eyes widened with shock and her red-tinted mouth popped open.

"Nay!" he gasped. "Not that. He…he could *not!*"

Lyle could see the dismay in her expression, the reaction he had expected. "I am afraid he could," he said softly. "Do you truly understand what I am saying, Em? Brick came to me months ago and asked permission to court you. I denied him at the time and told him you were too young, but the truth is that you are not too young. You are of marriageable age and he has taken a fancy to you. I have asked him not to tell you of his intentions and I see that he has not."

Emilie shook her head, her shock turning into revulsion. "He has not said a word," she said. "Is that why he has been hanging about and trying to speak with me at every turn?"

Lyle nodded, almost sadly. "It is," he said. "And you had no idea of his intentions?"

Emilie was truly at a loss, reeling with the news. "I did not," she said. But then, she cocked her head as if an idea occurred to her. "Except when I think back to the tournament at Windsor and how rude he was to Sir David, I remember that moment because it was so very odd for him to behave that way. Was it possible he had these… these *feelings* for me even back then?"

"He did."

"I thought the man had lost his mind!"

Lyle shook his head. "Not his mind," he said softly. "His heart. To you. And he was so jealous that de Lohr carried your favor that he could hardly stand it."

Emilie was genuinely astonished. Her hands flew to her mouth, covering the gaping lips, as the revelation of Brickley's secret feelings for her ran deep. Then, she turned away from her father, struggling to comprehend what he had told her. Struggling to understand that a man she'd known most of her life had suddenly grown romantic for her.

"I cannot believe this," she said. "Brick has always been with us, a shadow, a protector, but now... Papa, I feel so very uncomfortable knowing he has romantic intentions towards me."

Lyle watched her as she fussed with her cloak, absently, lost in thought. "Is it so terrible, then?" he asked softly. "Brick is an excellent knight from a fine house. I have no doubt he would make you an excellent husband. He would be kind and considerate and think only of you."

Emilie turned to look at him. "You cannot possibly wish for me to marry him, do you?"

Lyle shook his head. "Nay," he replied. "It is not my wish for you to marry him but I would not oppose you if that was your desire. You are young and beautiful and will have many opportunities for suitors who will make fine husbands. But my thoughts are of Brick... he will watch you as you accept suitors or find young men to be fond of. It will eat him alive to see it, but he will keep it to himself as he has for so long. It will be cruel to force him to watch."

Emilie thought on the situation from that perspective and she could see her father's point. "I do not know what to do about it," she said. "I cannot accept his suit simply to spare his feelings. It would not be fair to me."

Lyle went to her, putting his hands on her shoulders. "I know," he said. "But Brick has meant a great deal to us over the years. He is a good man. If you could mayhap be kind to him, Em... be kind but firm that you are not interested in his suit... mayhap that will be enough to ease him."

Emilie shook her head. "A polite rejection may not be enough," she said. "If he truly has feelings for me, I am afraid being polite or too terribly kind might have the opposite effect – it might give him hope. I fear the only cure for his damaged heart will be for him to find a woman who will respond to him, who will be a good wife, someone to take his mind off of me. A distraction."

Lyle lifted his eyebrows. "Nathalie?"

Emilie looked at her father, at the twinkle in his eye, and bit her lip. "Why would you say that?"

"Because she yearns for him."

"You are not supposed to know about that."

Lyle laughed softly. "How can I not know about it?" he asked. "Your sister makes it frightfully obvious that she is smitten with Brick, and he responds to Nathalie much as you respond to him; with aversion."

Emilie knew that; she had seen it from Brickley, the way he went in the other direction when Nathalie came near. "She is young," she said. "She is trying very much to mature, however. Mayhap with a little encouragement from you, Brick would look to Nathalie instead of me."

Lyle removed his hands from her shoulders. "I will *not*," he said. "He is far too old for your sister. His son is her age, in fact. Nay, I will not coerce Brick into finding interest with your sister when he clearly has none. Could I coerce you into feeling something for him? I think not."

Emilie understood. "So what do I do?" she asked. "I feel very strangely about him now, Papa. I do not want him to escort me to the mask. Everyone will believe we are a pair and I do not want to give Brick that false hope."

Lyle was silent for a moment. He was thinking something quite devious and hesitated to speak of it to his daughter, but he surmised he may as well. He remembered being young once, too, and pursuing Emilie's mother. He remembered a particular instance when Willow had attempted to make him quite jealous with another man. In reflecting upon his conversation with Christopher about his brother, Lyle couldn't help but think that Emilie might use Brick to her advantage when it came to David de Lohr. But, then again, he wasn't supposed to know about that. He scratched at his chin, pretending to be thoughtful, when he was really being quite calculated.

"Em," he said slowly. "I… I was thinking. Mayhap you should allow Brick to escort you to the mask because other young men will see you with him and, of course, nothing intrigues a single man like a woman who is already spoken for. In fact, you being seen with Brick might bring forth any number of suitors based on jealousy alone. David de Lohr, for example. He will be there tonight, you know. You have not seen him in two months."

Emilie's head snapped to her father, her eyes widening in surprise and outrage. "David?" she repeated. "Who said anything about David de Lohr? Who had told you such lies?"

Lyle was trying very hard not to laugh at her reaction; she very much wanted to deny anything about the man but he could see in her expression that she could not.

"No one has told me anything about him," he said, "except, possibly, his brother. I have seen Christopher many times over the past few weeks and we were speaking once, in a casual conversation of course, and he mentioned that David might be missing you."

Emilie's eyes were still wide with astonishment. "He is not!"

"It is possible that he is."

Her lips twisted with rage. "How can he miss me when there is nothing between us?"

"Can you not be honest with me, Em? It is clear that you wish there was."

Emilie was greatly struggling now. She didn't want to lie to her father but the subject of David was a very difficult one for her. She refused to look at him, walking the fine line between admitting such a thing and denying it altogether.

"If such a thing were true and he really was yearning for me, he has an odd way of showing it," she said. "He has not come to see me in all of these two months and he could very well find out where I am. It is no great secret we are staying with Aunt Coraline."

Lyle couldn't help the grin now. "It is my suspicion that David is nearly as stubborn as you are in showing his emotions," he said, watching Emilie flush furiously. "My darling, I have no intention of asking you what you feel for David, if anything, because certainly that is your affair. But if you do feel something for him and had any inclination of making the man jealous enough to swallow his pride and mayhap speak of his feelings for you, then allowing Brick to escort you to the mask might be a good way to do it. You saw how the two of them nearly came to blows over you at the tournament those months ago. If David were to see you with Brick at the mask, it might very well drive him over the edge."

Emilie was no longer shocked or outraged by the mere mention of David de Lohr, but actually intrigued by what her father was saying. She knew very well how David and Brickley had behaved towards one another, which she was now coming to understand was because Brickley was jealous. But David... he responded the same way Brickley had. Did that mean he had felt something for her, too, only he'd been too shy or stubborn, or both, to speak of it?

For the first time in two months, Emilie had some hope. Hope that perhaps she could draw David to her by making him jealous. Was it foolish? Of course it was. But it wouldn't be too terribly foolish if it worked.

"But what of Brick?" she asked. "Won't he feel terrible if he realizes I am using him to make David jealous?"

Lyle shrugged. "I am sure he will," he said. "But if it is between my daughter's happiness and my knight's, then you know the choice I am going to make. But have no fear; I will make amends to Brick if you end up married to David and not to him. Besides, your mother did this once to me and you see what happened to us. The same tactic might work well for you, too."

Emilie grinned; she could hardly believe her father was being so devious, to help her bright forth the man of her dreams, no less, but she loved him for it.

"Oh, Papa," she sighed. Her guard with him was down completely now. "How did you know about my feelings? Who told you about... about David? I never told anyone, not even Nathalie."

Lyle smiled and collected the sheer blue scarf from the bed. He toyed with it a moment, perhaps remembering when he was her age and all of the hopes and loves he had at that time in his life. "No one told me," he said. "But I am not so old that I do not remember what it was like to feel for someone. I put the pieces of the puzzle together and figured it out for myself. I like David a great deal, Em. He is a fine young man."

Emilie wasn't sure what to feel; embarrassment that her secret was out, or relief that her father was willing to help her. She settled for a little of both.

"He is," she agreed, taking the scarf and moving to the bronze mirror to put it on her head. "But I feel terrible that I am about to take advantage of Brick in order to get to David."

"Badly enough that you will not do it?"

Emilie shook her head. "Nay," she said quietly. "Not that badly. I suppose Brick will just have to understand that in the end. It is a terribly cruel thing to do, but given the choice between gaining David or hurting Brick... I am wicked to say that I want to gain David."

Lyle nodded. "All is fair in love and war, my darling," he said. "Brick will simply have to be a casualty in the quest for your true love. Now, he is waiting downstairs to take you. I suggest you go. I will bring your sisters soon enough."

Emilie finished with the scarf; along with the matching cloak she looked absolutely stunning. Going to her father, she kissed the man on the cheek before quitting the chamber and heading down to the entry of her aunt's massive home where Brickley awaited, finely dressed in leather and wool. His face lit up when he saw her, and in that instant Emilie could see that everything her father said was the truth. The man did have feelings for her.

But it was of no matter. If the choice was between Brickleys' feelings and her own, she was prepared to be selfish. She had baited the trap; now, all she had to do was wait for the prey.

Tonight, she became the hunter.

Chapter Thirteen

Windsor Castle

DAVID HAD BEEN to a lot of parties and celebrations, but never anything like this.

The prince, in his earnest to have the most spectacular party England had ever seen, had provided a feast on a colossal scale. Forty cows had been killed and cooked, the smells of which lay heavily over the grounds of the castle and wafted upon the wind for miles. He'd also killed thirty sheep, about the same number of goats, rabbits, swans, peacocks, pigeons, wild boar, and any number of smaller birds. Everything was being roasted or boiled, sauced and salted, and several of the cooked birds sat upon the cluttered tables in the great hall with their feathers replaced so that they resembled living creatures.

It was grand decadence, and the House of de Lohr was dressed for the occasion. Christopher's wife wore a rich, red brocade that was a gorgeous piece of work; while the only other lady in the group, Christopher and David's younger sister, Deborah, wore a lovely blue silk. Lady Deborah de Lohr had fostered with the Earl of Bath for many years and was reunited with her brothers when the earl had come to Windsor for the great tournament, as so many other households had come.

Having not seen their sister in many years, David and Christopher welcomed her into their group, and when the Earl of Bath had taken his household back home after the tournament, Deborah had remained with her brothers. After having been apart so long, the de Lohr siblings were together once again.

Tall, slender, and blond, Deborah fit in well with her brothers and with Christopher's new wife. In fact Dustin and Deborah had become fast friends, and even now, having arrived in hall on the arms of Christopher and David, the women were chatting like magpies. At least, that's the way David would have described them. Deborah was truly a gentle and sweet girl, but she could talk God off of his mighty throne. And Dustin, of course, being surrounded by men day in and day out, was happy for the female company. They made a cozy pair, seated at one of the long feasting tables in the hall, chatting about everything from the food to the dresses other women were wearing.

David stood away from the table, watching the women gossip and thinking that the hall was entirely too warm for his taste. And it smelled like smoke and urine beneath the heady scent of roasted meat, not exactly an appetizing combination. His brother was conversing with his men, including Marcus, who no longer had his right hand wrapped and was working daily to strength the damaged hand. Burton was still a fixture in Christopher's ranks but David still didn't have much to do with Marcus these days. He kept to himself mostly, wandering behind the pillars, looking to see who was in attendance. Much like the tournament those months ago, the mask this night promised to be a well-attended event.

Although David paced the room with the excuse of seeing who had come from John's stable of supporters, the truth was that he was looking for the House of Hampton to arrive. Certainly, he'd played it cool these past two months, pretending that nothing was amiss with him, going through the daily motions and duties alongside his brother, as if everything was normal in his world. But the truth was that nothing was normal since the day of the great and terrible tournament. Ever since Emilie had fled from his life, things hadn't been normal in the least.

He'd cursed himself daily for his thoughts of her. He should have forgotten her the moment she'd left his sight, but he couldn't seem to manage it. He'd even tried to distract himself by pursuing the attention of other ladies at Windsor; one being the daughter of Baron Audley, Lady Lucinda Bartley, and the other had been the daughter of the House of de Bohun, a Lady Maryann. And those were the two he could readily remember, but the truth was that there had been many more, simply to pass the time.

Lady Lucinda and Lady Maryann were pretty women, but shallow and catty, and even as he'd chatted with them over supper in the great hall, or walked through the upper ward with them on an escorted walk, he found himself comparing them to Emilie again and again. Try as he might, he couldn't shake the woman. As the days advanced, so did his longing for her. By the time December had rolled around, he was willing to forget their argument and go and beg her forgiveness, but he couldn't seem to summon the courage to do it. He was afraid she might laugh in his face, or worse. He was afraid she might have forgotten about him altogether.

But he knew she hadn't left London. He had seen her father at several meetings for Richard's supporters and he had come to depend on seeing Lyle, as if seeing him somehow meant seeing his daughter. Lately, he'd wanted to inquire about Emilie's health whenever he saw Lyle, but he refused to look like a fool by showing interest in a woman who wouldn't let him kiss her without making some kind of marital commitment to her. It had been foolish and premature of her to do that, in his opinion, but if he were totally honest with himself, perhaps it wasn't so foolish. He would have thought much less of a woman who would have simply let him kiss her at his whim, as if there was no value attached to the gesture.

As if she didn't mean anything to him.

But she meant a good deal. More and more, she meant everything to him. So he slugged through the days without much humor, trying not to think on the angelic lass with the big brown eyes who had stood up to him. He'd wanted to kiss her and she wasn't going to let him. She'd called him brave when the truth was that she was braver than he was; no one stood up to David de Lohr without consequences. But she hadn't cared about the consequences; she'd been more than willing to walk away from him.

Therefore, this night was important to him. He'd known about it for weeks and had assumed, and hoped, that Emilie would be here with her father. He had even bathed that day and had Edward cut his hair, because Edward was good at that sort of thing. Most knights didn't keep their hair so short, and some even let their hair hang as if they'd put a bowl on their hair and cut around it, but David didn't like his hair in his eyes so he always cut it very short. It was thick, however, thick enough to stand on end when it became dirty or wet, but this evening saw his hair neatly combed. In his finest leather breeches, linen tunic, and a heavy leather sleeveless coat that was lined with fur and went all the way to his ankles, he made a fine presentation. Quite plainly, he was the best-looking man at the feast.

Finely dressed or not, he was still a warrior and kept an assortment of daggers on his person; that was simply prudent in these times. As Christopher and the others lingered near one of the feasting tables, David positioned himself next to one of the supporting pillars so he could see all who entered the hall. It was very cold outside on this night, but was without snow or clouds of any kind, so the weather was good as the guests began arriving in droves.

Thousands of fat tapers lit the massive hall and along the fireplace that was taller than a man. Guests wandered into the hall, dressed in their finery, and went to find a seat. It was an unspoken rule that John's supporters claim one side of the room whilst Richard's supporters claimed the other. Feasting tables that seated anywhere from eight to ten people were put end-to-end, flanking the sides of the room, while the center was left open to dancing. The two sides began accumulating great houses, each of them facing their rivals across the hall. In what was supposed to be a festive gathering, it was an oddly confrontational seating arrangement.

A minstrel gallery was overhead and the musicians began to play for the crowd, which was unfortunate because smoke from the malfunctioning hearth was gathering up in the minstrel gallery and David could hear the musicians coughing. There was a table off to his right that had all manner of food and drink on it, and he made his way over to pour himself a cup of sweet red wine. He found he needed the fortification to help his courage. He had nearly drained the cup, all the while keeping his eye on the entry, when his sister approached.

"David, will you please dance with me?" she begged. "The music is so lovely and I have no one to dance with."

David held up his hands, trying to beg off. "Edward likes to dance," he said. "Have him dance with you."

Deborah pouted, although it was good-natured. "I have not seen you in twelve years and you want me to dance with someone else?" she said. "That is a terrible thing to do to me. Besides, you are my escort. It is *your* duty to dance with me."

David made a face at her, knowing he had little choice now. "I do not like to dance."

Deborah would not be refused. Grinning impishly in a gesture that looked much like her eldest brother, she held out her hands to him. "Please?"

David rolled his eyes, set his cup down, and took her hand, tucking it into the crook of his arm. He led her to the dance floor where a few couples were going through the ritual of a *carol*, or a circle dance, but there weren't very many male dancers on the floor to really make it a grand carol. Giggling, Deborah led David into one of the circles and they joined in, holding hands and essentially dancing in a big circle with several other people.

David knew how to dance but it bored him to tears. He kept trying to watch the door to see if Emilie had arrived, but as of yet, she hadn't made an appearance. The hall was filling up and becoming stuffy with the stench of bodies as David and Deborah finished the *carol* and then launched into a *rondelet,* which was more of a choreographed dance for two people. The more David danced with his smiling sister, the more he wished he wasn't. He wanted to be standing back by the table that held the alcohol, having more than his share of wine. He didn't want to be out here on the dance floor when Emilie arrived, dancing with his sister. *How embarrassing!*

More guests arrived during the *rondelet* before the song was mercifully over. Quickly, David pulled his sister back to their table while she begged to dance again, but he refused her. He left the table before she or Dustin could press him, because he really didn't want to be bullied into dancing any more foolish dances, so he scooted off towards the table with the wine as Leeton volunteered to be Deborah's dance partner. Back to the floor they went, which David noted with relief.

Moving between guests, and around a pillar, he thought he was being quite clever at avoiding Deborah or Dustin, until he suddenly spied Lady Lucinda and Lady Maryann heading in his direction. Unfortunately, they saw him before he could hide himself, but that didn't stop him from seeking refuge behind a group of knights from Derby. He made no secret of running from the women. But he ran so fast that he ran headlong into young William, the Earl of Derby's son.

"David," William said happily, clapping him on the shoulder as they bumped into one another. "How are you faring on this fine evening? I, for one, am ready to eat and drink and not think about the fate of the country. As much as I love William Marshal, if I have to sit through another one of his meetings where half the men are sleeping and the other half are arguing, I will go out of my bloody mind."

David grinned. "And I thought I was the only one who felt that way."

William, who was slightly drunk, shook his head exaggeratedly.

"You are not!" he said. "I do believe I will head home before the New Year to see my father. I already sent my sister and most of my retainers home long ago. Had to, you know. We had to bury Brentford."

David sobered. "I know," he said. "I plan to visit his grave when we return to Lioncross."

"When will that be?"

David shrugged. "It is up to Chris," he said, looking around to make sure Lady Lucinda and Lady Maryann weren't sneaking up on him. "He will be sending his wife home but I do not think we will be accompanying her. In truth, everything is so uncertain right now. I believe Chris wants to remain in London a while longer to await news about Richard."

William sobered a bit. "I understand," he said. "When Richard is found, will you ride to his aid?"

David suddenly caught sight of Lady Lucinda; she was fairly close, on the other side of the group of Derby knights, and he spoke quickly to the young lord.

"It is my guess that will we ride to Aquitaine to seek Eleanor and her money at some point," he said. "Chris thinks that the king might even be ransomed, so the Marshal has intimated that we may be traveling to France soon. But I will speak to you about it later. I must go."

With that, he dashed away, ducking behind a pillar to hide himself before slipping into the shadows at the edge of the room. He was heading in the direction of the entry, making sure he was not seen by Lady Lucinda or Lady Maryann, for he surely didn't want to dance with either of them this night and he was positive that dancing and feasting with him, while gazing dreamily into his eyes, was on their agenda.

He spied the pair, still behind the group of Derby knights, for it seemed that they hadn't seen him yet. Relieved, he continued to make his way towards the entry, staying in the shadowed edges of the room beneath the lancet windows. He was nearly to the door when he caught sight of a familiar figure.

As if heaven had opened up and spit out an angel, Emilie entered the hall and David's breath caught in his throat. She was bedecked in resplendent shades of blue, looking like a queen as she entered. David was out of her line of sight, back against the wall as he was, so he took a moment to simply watch her as she entered. She moved with the grace of a goddess, and when she turned slightly he could see her profile. *Exquisite,* he thought. Two months of stubborn confusion gave way to a pounding in his heart that he could hardly contain.

But his lovely vision was cut short as another familiar figure came up behind Emilie. Brickley was splendidly dressed as well, an evidently escorting Emilie, much to David's dismay. The big knight stuck close to Emilie, pointing out the tables where Christopher was sitting, and they headed in that direction.

As David watched, Emilie and Brickley approached Christopher, who greeted Emilie gallantly and introduced her to Dustin and Deborah. David watched as Emilie removed her scarf and cloak, handing them over to Brickley, who politely took them from her and headed to a cloak room, where the women's possessions were being guarded. With Brickley out of the way, David made his move. He knew he had to do it quickly before Brickley returned.

As he came upon the table, he could hear Dustin and Deborah and Emilie chatting. He was behind her, watching her, not realizing that Christopher had spied him. Christopher, too, was watching his brother's expression as he gazed at Emilie. A smile came to his lips and he elbowed Edward, pointing to David and muttering something to the man, causing Edward to grin as well. It was Edward who then spoke loudly.

Startled by Edward's loud voice, which was undoubtedly meant to capture Emilie's attention, David abruptly found himself gazing into that angelic face that haunted his dreams.

Emilie....

"AH, DAVID," EDWARD said loudly. "So you have decided to join us finally. Have you had enough of wandering the room? Anything interesting out there?"

Seated next to Deborah, Emilie jumped at the sound of David's name. In truth, she had been nervous well before entering the hall, a condition that only worsened once they entered the warm, smoky structure.

Sitting at the de Lohr table had been Brickley's idea, fortunately, and even as she sat with Christopher's wife and sister, she was still as jumpy as a cat. She hadn't seen David yet, but she knew he was here, somewhere. At least she hoped he was in the hall, hoping she wouldn't have to hear that he'd ridden out of London some time ago and his whereabouts were unknown. But hearing his name made her heart lurch and she whirled around to see that he was standing a few feet behind her.

Their eyes met and Emilie felt a bolt of lightning run through her. She didn't think her heart could pound any harder than it was, but she was wrong. For lack of a better response, she simply smiled at the man although she was trying desperately not to. She didn't want him to think that all was forgiven between them, that she would be the one to surrender her pride first. Or maybe she really didn't care about her pride at all, and that was the truth. Gazing into that handsome, shaved face, a face she had dreamed about for sixty-four days, she couldn't help the smile. She simply couldn't.

"I have found nothing interesting," David said to Edward's question, although his focus was on Emilie. With a look of utter adulation on his face, he spoke to her. "Good evening, my lady. I hope this day finds you in good health and spirits."

That voice. God, she'd missed that soft, deep voice. It filled her with liquid fire, running through her veins, causing her entire body to flush with delight as she nodded to his statement.

"It does, my lord," she said. "It is agreeable to see you this eve. I pray you recovered well from your injuries."

David nodded as Deborah spoke. "Injuries?" she repeated, looking at David. "What injuries?"

David, so far, hadn't taken his eyes off of Emilie. He was moving towards her now, drawn to her by those silent siren calls that were only meant for his ears. "The injuries from John's tournament back in October," he explained to his sister. "Lady Emilie tended me, if you recall. Had it not been for her, I am sure I would not have recovered nearly so well."

"Sit, David," Dustin said, indicating the seat on Emilie's right. "I have heard of your Lady Emilie but have only just now met her. Sit and thank the woman for what she did for you."

David was already sitting as Dustin had instructed. All of the hesitation, the frustration and confusion he'd felt over the past two months was draining away. The more he looked into that magnificent and beautiful face, the more he could feel himself succumbing to the wild attraction between them. It was stronger than it had ever been.

"Thank you," he said as he sat next to her, his eyes boring into hers. "Thank you for what you did for me. I am in your debt."

Emilie's cheeks turned a sweet shade of pink as she smiled at him. "It was my honor, my lord," she said. "You look to be in very good health."

"I am, thanks to you."

"Have… have you been well these past months, then? No more tournaments and no more injuries?"

He shook his head, giving her a half-grin. "No more tournaments," he said. Then, he took his eyes off of her long enough to look down to his tunic, digging into the pocket at his chest and pulling for a slip of white fabric. He held it up to Emilie. "I have carried your favor daily. It seems to ward off any evil that threatens to befall me."

Emilie looked at her white silk kerchief and her heart melted away on a flood of flattery and sweetness. The man had carried it all of these months and she was deeply touched. Had he been angry with her once, accusing her of being foolish in demanding a marriage betrothal simply to kiss her? She couldn't even remember that anger. She couldn't even remember the hurt. Looking into his face, she couldn't remember anything but the joy he brought her.

"It is yours," she said softly. "It belongs to you more than it belongs to me. I would be honored if you would keep it."

David smiled faintly as he tucked it back into his pocket. "I was not going to give it back even if you asked for it," he said. Then, he sobered, his expression very serious. The words, when they came, all came out in a rush. "Forgive me, Emilie. Forgive me for being brash and demanding and inappropriate. You were quite right in your refusal to allow me to… well, to allow me to impress myself upon you. I became angry at you and I should not have. I hope… I hope we can be friends again."

Emilie sighed, deeply, relief and happiness such as she had never known filling her. "There is nothing to forgive," she said. "I was foolish and stubborn. I should never have expected so much from you after only having known you a short amount of time. You were absolutely right, in everything you said. If anyone should ask for forgiveness, it should be me."

David was so overjoyed that he was nearly lightheaded with it. "As you said, there is nothing to forgive," he said. "We will not speak of it any longer. In fact, I would like to ask you if I may come to call on you. You are staying at your aunt's home in London, are you not? I would be greatly honored if you would allow me to visit you."

Emilie was nodding her head before he even got the words out of his mouth. "Yes," she said. "Oh, yes. I have been hoping you would come and see me."

David chuckled. "I would have come sooner but I did not think I would be welcome."

"You will always be welcome, wherever I am."

"Lady Emilie?"

A deep voice came from behind and they both turned to see Brickley standing there. The big knight had made a reappearance and he looked decidedly displeased as his gaze moved between Emilie and David. Emilie could see that, already, the hostilities were there between the two men. The old jealousies had never died. After what her father told her, she could most definitely see it in Brickley's expression and she hastened to take control of the situation before it veered out of hand.

"Greet Sir David, Brick," she instructed. "We have been speaking about his injuries from the tournament in October. See how healthy he looks now."

Brickley couldn't have cared less about David's health. He had seen the man in passing over the past couple of months but they hadn't said more than a two words to one another. He knew David was fine after the tournament, but he didn't care. He just wanted the man out of his seat.

"I have seen David since that time," he told Emilie, eyeing David. "I have escorted the lady to the mask tonight. You will forgive me for asking you to vacate my seat next to her."

So the situation was clearly established. Brickley was Emilie's escort and David was not. But before David could move, as he had been asked, Emilie put her hand on his arm.

"Nay, Brick," she said. "I have seen you much for the past two months but I have not seen David at all. He will leave when I am finished speaking with him. Go and sit elsewhere for now."

Brickley's jaw ticked with great displeasure and David gave him an expression bordering on triumphant. *The lady wants me to sit with her and not you, you old bear.* It was the silent message from David's expression. That fueled Brickley's jealous rage to no end to the point where the man was clenching and unclenching his fists. Before he could throw a punch, which he was very close to doing, Christopher intervened.

The elder de Lohr brother had been carefully watching the exchange. Although no one had ever mentioned that Brickley de Dere was fond of Lady Emilie Hampton, Christopher could see, in just those brief few words exchanged, that there was a definitely rivalry between David and Brickley for the lady's attention. Like two dogs fighting over the same bone, but in this case, it was a woman, which was even worse. Men tended to do odd things where a woman was concerned. Not wanting a brawl on his hands, and especially not in front of his wife, Christopher stepped in when Emilie essentially brushed Brickley off.

"Brick," he said, stepping in to put himself between Brickley and David. "Come and meet my wife. I do not believe you have met her yet."

Edward, who had been watching the exchanges as well, moved beside Christopher and together, the two of them escorted the enraged Brickley over to Dustin, where Christopher introduced the man to his new wife. As Dustin engaged the man in small talk, Emilie turned to David.

"Brick is still very protective," she said, smiling weakly. "He thinks that every man is out to ravage me."

David grunted, scratching at his neck. "Brick is a very smart man," he said. "He wants you for himself and he does not want any competition. For the last few months I would wager to say he hasn't had any…has he?"

Emilie smiled coyly, shaking her head. "He has not."

David was relieved. "I did not mean that as an I insult, you understand," he said. "If any woman warranted gangs of suitors, it would be you. I simply meant… I meant that I have not been around the past couple of months."

Emilie laughed softly. "I did not take it as an insult," she said, sobering. "Are you telling me that you intend to come around often?"

"Every day if you will let me."

"I will."

David was thrilled. Reaching out, he took her hand and lifted it to his lips for a gentle kiss. Unfortunately, Brickley saw the kiss and nearly came apart. He growled menacingly and Christopher, having no idea what had the man so upset, and noticed that David was holding Emilie's hand. A bit miffed at his younger brother for doing it so openly in front of de Dere, as if to provoke the man, Christopher handed Brickley off to Edward, who shuffled the man away from the situation and towards the table with all of the wine on it. Leeton, who had been standing by watching the entire exchange, went with Edward for good measure. No one wanted a massive fight right before dinner, with David provoking Brickley. Therefore as Edward and Leeton plied Brickley with wine, Christopher forced his brother, with a mere expression to drop Emilie's hand, which David did.

David had seen Edward and Leeton escort Brickley to the wine table and he was glad to have the man out of the way, but he also knew he was being a bit amorous in public with a woman he was not formally betrothed to. *Damn marriage!* It ruined everything, a man's ability to move spontaneously and show affection towards an unattached woman. David still wasn't sure he wanted to marry, but he didn't want Emilie to marry anyone else – least of all Brickley – so his quandary was still very real. He had to admit, however, that being this close to Emilie was causing him to rethink his opinion of marriage. Gazing into her lovely face, there was no way he could help but imagine being married to this exquisite creature.

So he indulged in a lengthy discussion with her as if to make up for lost time. As they lost themselves in quiet conversation, mostly about Lady Orford's opulent home in London where Emilie had been staying, more people joined their table.

The new guests were Baron Sedgewick and his wife, Lady Anne. Lady Anne was a vivacious, petite woman who already knew Dustin and Deborah, and the three of them struck up a comfortable conversation. Sedgewick was one of Richard's supporters and he had a good deal to say as David, now distracted from him conversation with Emilie, was lulled into a political conversation. As David was pulled in with the men, Emilie became introduced to Anne Sedgewick. Reluctantly separated, David and Emilie went with their respective sexes. As the men conversed, the women chattered, and Lyle and Nathalie entered the hall.

It was clear that Lyle was flustered, for his weathered face was tense. He didn't like being late to any event but after the events with Elise and her wooden people back at Coraline's home, he found himself running late to the mask. The horses had galloped to Windsor all the way. In the crowded, smoky hall, he spied the de Lohr table, and Emilie, and made his way to his eldest daughter with Nathalie on his arm. It was such a crowded room that Emilie only noticed the pair when Nathalie took a seat beside her.

"Where is Elise?" she asked, looking between her sister and father. "Why did she not come?"

Nathalie sighed impatiently. "She would not leave her families behind," she said. "Aunt Coraline volunteered to stay with her."

Emilie understood; Elise never went anywhere without those little wooden people. "And Mother?" she said, looking around. "She did not come either?"

Lyle, his annoyance evident, shook his head. "Why should she come?" he demanded. "Lillibet is a servant, not a family member. Ah, Lord Christopher!"

Lyle was off, grouping with the men in their conversation, leaving Emilie to introduce Nathalie to Dustin, Deborah, and Anne. Soon the five of them were having a very pleasant conversation, but during the entire time Emilie kept glancing over at David, who was standing with his brother, her father, and with the rest of the men. She was trying not to be too obvious about looking at him but she simply couldn't help herself. Wine flowed, music played, and Emilie ignored all of it as she stole glimpses of David.

But David knew Emilie was watching him. In fact, he was watching her, too, and had positioned himself so that all he had to do was flick his eyes over to his right and see her full on. Several times she turned to look at him and smile coyly, and each time he would wink boldly at her. It was a game they played, just the two of them in the midst of all of these people, until Dustin caught on and began to tease Emilie about it.

It was sweet teasing, nothing terribly nasty, and David grinned as Emilie flushed. As he watched Dustin and Emilie giggle, suddenly he could see them all at Lioncross Abbey, sitting around the feasting table on a cold winter's night, laughing and teasing one another as a family would. And then they would all retire for the evening, David taking Emilie to their bedchamber where he would ravage her until dawn, as his wife.

Was it possible he could find satisfaction in such a thing? His thinking was starting to change. He was coming to think he could be very satisfied with Emilie as his wife. Clearly, he couldn't stomach the alternative.

Brickley's wife....

As DAVID FOUGHT off dreams of marriage, Emilie laughed as Dustin and Deborah teased. Nathalie was embroiled in her own situation.

The middle Hampton sister was only interested in one thing; Brickley. He had escorted her sister to the mask and now the man was nowhere to be found, which disappointed her greatly. In her lovely green garment with her hair artfully arranged, she felt old, wise and beautiful at sixteen years of age. There were many couples dancing and she wanted very much to dance with Brickley. She certainly didn't want the embarrassment of dancing with her father, who was laughing and conversing with the de Lohr men. There was quite a party going on around her, but Nathalie only had Brickley on her mind.

She had to find him.

She couldn't imagine that he'd gone too far off. As the hum of conversation went on around her, Nathalie searched the room for any sign of Brickley. She finally spied him over near a table that was crowded with pitchers of wine and men drinking from them. He was standing with two of de Lohr's knights, seemingly in deep conversation with them. Nathalie sighed with satisfaction at the sight of Brickley; he was perhaps not as handsome as some, but he had a quality about him that was difficult to resist. At least, she thought it was difficult to resist. And tonight, she intended to do something about it. Brickley had avoided her long enough.

Excusing herself from the table with the fabricated explanation of seeking the garderobe, she headed in the direction that Dustin had indicated for such a thing, but quickly changed her path when no one was looking. She ducked in behind a group of people, winding her way to the table where Brickley was standing. By the time she got there, the men were drinking steadily and Brickley seemed to mostly be listening rather than talking. Summoning her courage, she walked up to the three men.

"Good evening, Brick," she said, smiling sweetly at him. She looked to the other two men, whom she had seen, but didn't really know, except for the dark-haired man. She remembered him from the day of the tournament. She curtsied to them. "Good evening, my lords."

Brickley took one look at Nathalie, sighed heavily, and downed what was left in his cup. "You and your sister look quite lovely this evening," he said, although it was forced. He wasn't about to compliment her singularly, given that the girl was far smitten with him. He didn't want to encourage her. Aye, he knew about it; he had since her infatuation with him started months ago and he found his patience with her had been dwindling as of late. "Edward and Leeton, this is Lady Nathalie Hampton, Lady Emilie's younger sister."

Edward and Leeton politely greeted Nathalie as Brickley set his cup down and pointed to the table where Emilie sat. "You should be with the women," he said. "Your father will not be pleased to find you standing with three knights and a table filled with wine."

He said it somewhat humorously, trying to joke about it, and therefore Nathalie didn't take him seriously. "He will not mind that I am standing with you," she said. "Brick, will you please dance with me? I wish to dance but I do not want to do it with Papa. That would be too embarrassing."

Brickley, with alcohol in his veins, didn't have as much control as he usually had. He made a face, rolled his eyes, and made it very clear he did not want to dance. "Please permit me to decline," he said. "I am in no mood for dancing. I am sure there are any number of young men here who would be happy to be your partner. If you point one out, I will approach him for you."

Nathalie's face clouded. "But I do not want to dance with anyone else," she said, giving him a rather pathetic expression. "Please, Brick? Just one dance?"

Her hands were on him now, pleading, and he peeled them off of his forearm and turned her for the table where her sister sat. "Nay," he said firmly. "Go sit with Emilie and leave me in peace."

He hadn't meant to say the last part. It just came out. When he realized what he had said and saw the expression on her face, he hastened to make amends but Nathalie was already too hurt to let him. Her mouth flew open in outrage.

"Leave you in peace?" she repeated, shocked and hurt. "I... I... fine, then! I shall never speak to you again!"

She stomped off before Brickley could say a word. He watched her go, shaking his head and not being particularly careful about hiding his annoyance.

"That one is a problem," he said. "She follows me everywhere, looks at me with the most sickening besotted expressions you have ever seen, and simply will not give me a moment's peace. But now she will tell her father what I said and *he* will not give me a moment's peace for insulting her."

Edward and Leeton were watching Nathalie stomp away, heading for the de Lohr table. Both knights had various expressions of amusements on their faces. "She is not an unattractive girl, Brick," Edward said. "How old is she?"

Brickley rolled his eyes and poured himself another cup of wine. "She has seen sixteen summers," he said. "But do not let her blonde looks fool you; she is the devil."

He hissed the word *devil* as if describing a terrible and hideous creature, causing Leeton and Edward to laugh. "Why should you say such things?" Leeton asked. "She seems sweet enough."

Brickley was swallowing his wine. "That is where she fools people," he said. "Ever since I have known that girl, she and her younger sister have been up to tricks. Honey in my pillow, eggs in my helm, bees in my pockets. They have made my life miserable for ten years and now she is smitten with me? She should have thought of that before she put charcoal all over my gloves and allowed me to wipe my face with them. The black mixed with the sweat on my skin and I had a black-shadowed face for a week before it would all come off. Nay, I shall not be lulled into a false sense of security by that one. I'd sooner take her over my knee and spank her than dance with her, the little demon."

Edward and Leeton were still laughing about the tricks Nathalie had allegedly played on Brickley. As Brickley launched into a tale about more tricks from the mind of Nathalie and Elise, Nathalie had managed to reach her sister and plopped back down in her seat. She kept glancing over at Brickley, who was speaking quite animatedly as Edward and Leeton laughed uproariously.

Embarrassed, and thinking that Brickley was telling terrible tales about her, she faced the women at the table, not wanting to see the man who had spurned her. She involved herself in the ladies' conversation simply to show Brickley that he couldn't hurt her, that his rejection didn't matter in the least. But the truth was that it did.

Unhappy, she pretended to be involved in the conversation with

Dustin and Emilie, but in truth she was pondering her next step in the quest to win Brickley's heart.

JOHN AND RALPH *and their group of shady characters arrived late, as usual, and the prince made a grand occasion out of his first dance. He acted as a child in a sweet shop, pretending to be very selective with the women he would dance with. His faze fell on Dustin and he smiled, but one glimpse of Christopher's face sent him on his way. Christopher watched the man like a hawk as he made a move for a lovely brunette on the opposite side of the room. When the carol was over, John returned the woman to her friends and retreated to the dais with his collection of liars and murderers.*

There was tension in the room, undeniably now that John and Richard's supporters were all collected in the same hall, but a pretty ballad started, distracting the crowd from the angst surrounding the presence of prince, and the women all bound to their feet, all except Dustin. She looked confused as the ladies around her insisted she rise and dance with them.

"Dance?" Dustin sputtered. "But....but I haven't danced in ages. I do not remember how."

"This is a woman's dance, Dustin," Anne said, taking her arm. "Just follow what we do and I promise you shall love it."

Christopher stood up, the first time all evening, and eyed the women sternly as they attempted to persuade his wife to retreat with them to the dance floor.

"I have forbidden her to dance, ladies," he said firmly.

Deborah looked up at him. "But why, Chris? There is no harm in dancing."

He sighed, looking his wife in the eye. Not all of the women knew of Dustin's condition. They would all know eventually, anyway, and he saw no harm in revealing their joyous news. "Because she is with child and I do not want her to exhaust herself."

That bit of information sent the women into cries of congratulation and happy kisses, but it did not deter their determination that Dustin should dance. They tugged her free of the table only to run headlong into Christopher's huge body as he blocked their way.

"Surely, sire, your wife must dance this dance," Nathalie Hampton said. "'Tis an ancient fertility dance."

The women giggled and Christopher crossed his arms sternly, yet there was a faint smirk on his face. "I know what the dance is, my lady, I have seen it many a time. I simply do not want my wife to tire."

"This dance will not tire her, my lord," Anne Sedgewick said. "'Tis slow and beautiful. Surely you do not intend to forbid Dustin from any sort of activity until the child is born. She will not break."

He raised a disapproving eyebrow and looked at Dustin's smiling face. He could see that she wanted to go with them. "Very well, then. But no jumping or cavorting about."

"Cavorting about?" Dustin repeated. "Why do you always say that as if I jump from table to table? I have never cavorted about."

He grunted at her and moved out of the way, allowing the women to pass. His knights stood about, watching the ladies and grinning. Especially David. He smiled broadly at Emilie as she brushed past him.

"Can't I dance, too?" he asked her.

She turned her pert nose up in the air. "Nay, sire, 'tis a woman's dance."

"But I want to dance with a woman," he persisted.

She shot him a blatantly flirtatious look. "Then you should have asked sooner."

The knights laughed at David's expense as the women took to the huge parquet floor.

THE TRUTH WAS that David was grinning, too, even though the joke had been on him. He didn't mind in the least. He had rather liked watching Emilie move out to the dance floor holding Dustin's hand, laughing and chatting with his sister-in-law, as if she'd known the woman her entire life. But, much like his brother, he was keeping a very close eye on the women with John and Ralph about, especially considering the confrontation between Emilie and Ralph during the tournament those months ago.

Therefore, David stood right on the edge of the dance floor, watching Ralph as Ralph watched the dancing. One wrong move from the sheriff and David would be forced to act.

But Ralph didn't make a move, wisely remaining with John and seemingly detached from the dancing women. But David, as well as every other man in the room, knew that wasn't the case. Ralph and John were always watching women, as everyone well knew, and fathers and husbands were determined to protect the women they loved. David was, too. He thought he was being quite vigilant. But one thing he hadn't counted on was Dennis le Londe.

Dennis was now a permanent fixture in John's entourage. David had seen the man several times since the October tournament, and each time Dennis smiled and waved at him, as if he were a long lost friend. David ignored him, as did Christopher, but all the while they watched him, because they knew that men like Dennis would not remain idle for long. He was a guard dog waiting to carry out orders for his deviant liege.

Even though John and Ralph had kept a low profile for the past two months, nearly everyone was under the impression that it was simply a ruse. Something was going on with them, as it usually was, but being the clever men that they were, they were simply biding their time. Neither Christopher nor David nor the men who ruled England, including William Marshal and William Longchamp, Richard's Chancellor, believed that John had the intention of behaving himself. They knew, at some point, he would move again.

It was simply a matter of when.

Therefore David and Christopher were so intently focused on John and Ralph that they failed to keep an eye on Dennis, who had been on the periphery of the room nearly since his arrival. Dennis wasn't unhandsome; he was fair-haired and not unattractive, so he never had any difficulty finding a partner to dance with. But this was a woman's dance, so as the floor filled with lovely women he made his way over to the west side of the hall, opposite the de Lohr contingent, and watched the lovely blond-haired woman that had David de Lohr so captivated.

He had heard about Ralph's attempt to abduct the woman those months ago at the tournament and he had also heard how the man had failed. John had not been pleased. Since it was virtually impossible to get anywhere near Lady de Lohr, Christopher's wife, the focus that evening had turned back to the lovely young woman that David had his eye on. Not to hurt her or abduct her, because that would simply make a volatile situation even worse, but Dennis thought that if he could get to the girl, talk to her, and perhaps convince her that the de Lohrs were not as noble and righteous as they pretended to be, that he could plant a seed of doubt in her mind that would disrupt David. A disrupted David would be a weakened David, and that was the kind of prey Dennis liked. He'd failed to kill the man in the tournament arena.

Perhaps he could get to him another way.

So he lurked on the edge of the dance floor, watching as the women danced the ancient fertility dance. There were quite a few women on the dance floor, enough so that it was difficult to single out one for any length of time, so he positioned himself near the edge of the floor, wedging himself into the de Breaute party as he watched the dancing before him. Women were laughing, swinging each other about in some cases, and going arm through arm at the edge of the room. He spied David's young lady early on and his eyes never left her. When she came by him, swinging arm through arm with other women, he was able to reach out and snatch her.

Emilie's yelps of fear were drowned out by the music and the crowds, and Dennis was able to sweep her from the floor before anyone took notice. Quickly, he took her to the darkened edges of the hall, holding her fast by the wrist. They were back behind the crowds here, in the darkness, and largely unnoticed. Terrified, and furious, Emilie twisted against him.

"Let me go," she demanded, pounding on his hand. "How dare you lay your hand on me! By what right do you do such a thing?"

Dennis held her tightly, hardly feeling her fist against his hand. "All apologies, demoiselle," he said with his heavy French accent. "I thought to have a word with you and I am not a fine or mannerly man. Moreover, if I approached the de Lohr table, they would simply kill me."

Emilie recognized the voice; God help her, she did. She was sharp of mind, and remembered things clearly, and she had heard this voice at the tournament field those months ago.

As if in a living nightmare, it began to occur to her that this was the man called Dennis the Destroyer. She remembered very distinctly seeing David fight the man, only she hadn't recognized him tonight because of his fine clothes. Now, she recognized him completely and this murderer of men had a hold of her. Frantically, she continued banging on his hand, trying to force him to release her.

"They will kill you now for touching me," she said. "Let me go!"

"Please," Dennis said softly, begging. "Please allow me a moment of your time, demoiselle. I must warn you of David and his brother. They are killers of innocents. Now they are trying to bring you into their web of lies."

Emilie scowled at him. "What are you talking about?" she demanded, trying to yank her hand free to no avail. "I will not speak to you about them. Let me *go!*"

She was struggling to free herself but Dennis yanked on her, hard enough to cause her head to snap back. Startled, Emilie found herself gazing into pale green eyes. His breath, smelling like putrid alcohol, blew up her nostrils as he spoke.

"Ask your David what he did in the Holy Land with Richard," he hissed at her. "Ask him how he killed innocent women and children who were captives of him and his brother. Ask him how he slayed hundreds of them, hating them because they were against his precious king. He lied to Saladin and his men, and he killed innocents. Ask him about Ayyadieh!"

Confused, and terrified, Emilie began to kick and shove, trying to break his hold on her. "I will *not* ask him," she said. "I do not know what you are speaking of!"

Dennis let her pull partially away from him, mostly because he was trying to get a point across and not hurt her in the process. She was fighting him fiercely.

"Of course you would not," he said. "I was there, demoiselle. I saw Richard order knights such as Christopher and David to murder unarmed men as well as their wives and children. This is only an example of the horrors the de Lohrs have accomplished. And you believe him to be a virtuous and noble knight? Do not think such things, lady. He is an evil man"

Emilie had one arm free and was trying to pull the other one free. "What is it to you?" she shot back. "I am not your concern and neither is David. Leave me alone!"

She managed to yank her arm free just as a figure appeared behind her. It reached out, grabbing her by the arm, and pulled her back away from Dennis, as she gasped with fright. But Emilie's fright quickly dissolved when she saw that it was David.

Thank you, God! her heart cried. Like an avenging angel David had swooped down to rescue her in her hour of need, in all of his magnificent glory. And he had the biggest dagger in his hand that she had ever seen.

Angels did indeed bear weapons, and she was glad.

"For putting your hands on her, I will kill you," David said to Dennis. He had been watching Emilie from across the room and had seen the exact moment when Dennis grabbed her. He run straight across the floor, dodging women in his attempt to reach the spot where she had vanished. Finding her in the shadows, with Dennis le Londe no less, had his blood boiling. "I hope you are right with God for this shall be your last moments on earth."

Dennis smiled thinly and opened the heavy robe he was wearing to display his broadsword strapped to his right leg. "Is this truly where you want to fight, David?" he asked. "This is a celebration. If you and I engage in a fight, it will ruin the entire party and it will surely upset your lady. Is that what you truly wish to do?"

David's jaw ticked as Emilie, sensing great and terrible things were about to happen, grasped David by the arm.

"Please," she whispered. "Let us go, David. He did not hurt me."

David didn't look at her but he did push her behind him, gently, to shield her from anything Dennis might do. "You should never have touched her," he said, low and threatening. "You know better than that."

Dennis cocked an eyebrow. "Do I?" he said. "Tell me, David; does she only see you has a noble and chivalrous knight? Does she know about the terrible atrocities you committed at Richard's command? If you are going to court the lady, she really should know all about you. Why don't you tell her about Ayyadieh? I remember quite distinctly what you did there. Tell her, David."

The ticking in David's jaw grew worse. "You remember Ayyadieh because you were there, too," he said. "You followed the same orders that I did. What I was unhappily forced to do as my duty, you did with great glee. You were happy to spill the blood of three-year-old children, dancing over their bodies while I dug their graves. Did you tell her *that*?"

Dennis only seemed to find humor in that. "I am not the one courting her," he said. "Why should I tell her anything about me?"

Emilie, standing behind David and clutching the man by the waist, was growing increasingly confused with the conversation.

"Three-year-old children?" she repeated, somewhat appalled. "David, what is he speaking of? What is Ayyadieh?"

Keeping his eyes on Dennis, David spoke to her. "Something that happened when we were in The Levant," he said. "I will tell you later. At the moment, I think it is more important to return you to your seat."

Emilie didn't argue with him but she clung to him, feeling his warm and muscular body beneath her hands. She realized she was holding on to him because she didn't want him to get away from her, as if he would charge Dennis. But as they turned to go, Dennis lifted his voice over the noise of the room.

"He is not the man you think he is, demoiselle," he said to Emilie. "He murders children. Ask him!"

David didn't say a word; he put an arm around Emilie's shoulders and moved her away from Dennis and around the perimeter of the hall until they reached the de Lohr table on the other side. About the time they reached the table, the women, including Dustin and Anne and Deborah and Nathalie, were coming off of the dance floor as the fertility dance concluded.

Dustin went to Christopher and Anne went to her husband, and Deborah and Nathalie settled down to drink and giggle. But David helped the stricken Emilie into a chair and took the one next to her, pouring her a cup of wine himself from the pitcher on the table. He put it into her hands, forcing her to drink.

She did, choking down a few swallows, coughing as she wiped her mouth with the back of her hand. She smiled weakly as she looked into David's concerned face.

"Are you truly well?" he asked gently. "Did he try to hurt you?"

Emilie shook her head. "He did not hurt me," she said. "But he took me right off of the floor, right in the middle of the dance. I never saw him coming."

David nodded. "I know," he said. "I was watching you and saw him when he grabbed for you."

Emilie's expression was both confused and imploring. "But why?" she asked. "Why did he do that?"

David sighed heavily. *Because John is once again attempting to get to me through you*, he thought. Jesus, could he really put her through this? Could he continue to allow the woman to be a target of the prince? The next time she might not be so fortunate. There had already been three previous attempts; four if he counted the one when he had taken her into hiding when the prince appeared on the street on the day of the tournament. *Four attempts to get to her because of me.*

Reaching out, he took hold of her hands again, small warm appendages in his big, calloused mitts.

"I think," he said, "that I must have a discussion with your father. I believe the time has come."

Emilie cocked her head curiously. "Time for what?"

David sighed faintly, rubbing her hands, caressing them. "Time for your father to know what is happening," he said. "I do not believe he truly grasps it."

Emilie lifted her eyebrows. "*I* do not truly grasp it," she said. "Why would Dennis the Destroyer pull me away and try to tell me such things about you? I do not understand."

David could see that she meant it. She wasn't used to a world with intrigue, but he was. He was used to watching his back, and his brother's back, all day, every day, for fear that an assassin would jump out of the walls and try to kill them. It was the way he lived.

But it wasn't the way she lived.

Whether or not he wanted to marry her, she was tied to him now. John and Ralph had seen them together and they knew that David's attention was on her. That made her a target and it wasn't something he could walk away from in the hope that John and Ralph would see she no longer mattered to him. In the hope that they would leave her alone.

Whatever was to come, David knew he was tied to Emilie now,

irrevocably, and he was responsible for her.

He would protect her to the death. *His.*

"Come," he said, standing up and pulling her to her feet. "We must find my brother and your father. They must know what happened."

Emilie went along with him, holding fast to his elbow, but Christopher was nowhere to be found. David inquired about his brother to the man's wife, but Dustin mentioned that Christopher had told her he had some business to attend to. So David went in search of Lyle, who had wandered away, finding more allies to chat with. He could just see the man several feet away, speaking with Derby.

In fact, he was so focused on Lyle that he didn't see Brickley come out of the shadows. Drunk, and enraged by David's attention to Emilie that he had been watching all night, Brickley charged David before anyone could stop him.

A fist to David's jaw from Brickley sent David to the ground.

CHAPTER FOURTEEN

Later that night
Christopher's apartments

T HE FIRE BURNED low in the lush antechamber that belonged to
Christopher and Dustin. Comfortably decorated, with leather
sling-seated chairs near the fire, David sat in one of them as Dustin's
two dogs snored happily before the warmth of the hearth. She had a
little monkey, too, as a pet, a little creature she'd found on the streets
of London, and the little beast had a bed high on top of wardrobe,
away from the dogs that terrified it. Usually the monkey would come
and sit with David, but not tonight. Tonight the room was still and
quiet.

So David sat alone, staring into the low burning hearth, thinking
on the events of the evening. Not that it had been a disaster, but it
had certainly been momentous. Brickley's sock to the jaw had been
the least of his worries. He was more concerned with Lyle, who had
gone into a panic when David explained what had happened with
Emilie and le Londe. The man had packed up his disappointed
daughters faster than the blink of an eye, herding them out to the
carriage and whisking them home in the darkness before either lady
had been given much chance to enjoy the mask.

But David understood the man's fear. He had a good deal fear
himself, fear of what he'd brought down on Emilie, so in a sense, he

was glad Lyle had taken the ladies home. He was afraid that the next time Dennis or Ralph grabbed Emilie, he wouldn't be so timely in saving her. It was difficult enough to deal with a new attraction… someone he was deeply interested in… without the fear of John and Ralph, and now Dennis, trying to abduct her or somehow get to her.

It was all his fault, what was happening to Emilie, and he felt extremely guilty for it. But his guilt didn't stop it from happening or somehow make it all better. He was going to have to do something about it.

So he sat and brooded as Christopher remained in the bedchamber adjoining the sitting chamber. Dustin had become ill at the feast from too much food and wine, and Christopher was settling her in for the night. After the incident with Emilie, and then Brickley, the House of de Lohr and the House of Hampton had parted ways to retire for the night. But in David's case he was to come to a conclusion about the situation.

He had to do something about it.

The door to the bedchamber creaked open softly before closing softly. The dogs, sleeping by the fire, sat up at the sound, their gaze tracking the person who had entered the chamber in the darkness. David heard some liquid being poured and then a cup was presented to him, filled with wine. He took it as his brother sat down in the chair next to him.

"So," Christopher said, the orange glow from the hearth illuminating his rugged features, "it seems that we had quite an eventful evening, little brother."

David snorted before drinking deeply of his wine. "I would say so," he replied. "How is Dustin, by the way?"

Christopher nodded, drinking his own wine. "She is well," he said. "Simply tired. Pregnancy and too much activity do not mix, as I tried to tell her."

David smiled weakly. "I suppose she will learn."

"I suppose."

They fell silent, drinking their wine, contemplating the events of the evening. Christopher eyed his brother, wanting to speak, but hoping David wouldn't become too irate with him on the subject matter. It had to do with women, Emilie to be exact, and women were always a volatile subject where David was concerned, especially in light of Christopher's marriage to Dustin.

Christopher wasn't completely convinced that David was still comfortable with the addition of Dustin to their lives, but in the long run, it didn't matter. He would have to become accustomed to it. Moreover, Christopher had a feeling that David was already thinking about Emilie, given what had happened. It was probably occupying every corner of his mind. Christopher took another drink of wine before continuing.

"We must speak on what happened tonight with Lady Emilie," he said. Then, he looked at David. "Is it true that Brick punched you in the jaw?"

David lifted his eyebrows drolly, nodding as he continued to gaze into the fire. "He was drunk," he said. "That is the only reason I did not take his head off. Men often do foolish things when they are drunk."

Christopher watched his brother carefully. "But why should he attack you like that?" he asked, although he already knew the answer. He simply wanted to hear it from David. "What did you do?"

David looked at him, then. "Surely you can figure it out."

"Figure out what?"

David sighed heavily. "Emilie," he said flatly. "He hit me because of Emilie."

Christopher pretended to be confused. "Why should he do that?"

David gave his brother an impatient expression. "You know why," he said. "I am sure that by now, everybody knows why. He and I want the same lady."

"Emilie?"

"Aye."

Christopher fought off a grin, masked by the cup he lifted to his lips. "Shocking, David," he said. "I never knew you to truly want a woman."

David knew his brother was toying with him, but somehow, it made his confession easier. He knew that Christopher understood the value of a woman these days.

"She is different," he muttered. "I think... I think that I have wanted her since the first time I met her. She is sweet and beautiful, and she is exceedingly brave. She is not afraid to stand up for what she believes in. I like that."

Christopher scratched at his neck. "But you have not seen her for two months until tonight," he said. "Unless I am mistaken, before this evening, the last time you saw her was at the tournament back in October."

David nodded. "That is correct."

"So... if you are attracted to her, why did you not call upon her in that time?"

David frowned, now feeling rather embarrassed. "Because I was an idiot."

"What happened?"

David drained his cup. "I wanted to kiss her, anytime the mood struck me, and she would not let me," he said. "She said that it was not proper if we were not betrothed. Can you believe that? She would not let me kiss her unless I agreed to marry her!"

Christopher couldn't fight off the grin now. It blossomed. "Astonishing," he said, feigning the fact that he was agreeing with him. "What kind of woman would let a man take advantage of her and then demand marriage?"

He was teasing his brother, helping him see the foolishness of his opinion on the matter. But David scowled at Christopher, who started laughing. "Oh, shut thy nasty little face," he said irritably, listening to his brother snort. "So I wanted to kiss her and not commit to marrying her. Is that so terrible?"

Christopher shook his head. "It is not," he replied. "But you know as well as I do that you cannot toy with some women. It seems that Emilie Hampton is one of them."

David nodded in resignation. "She is," he said. "And... and I never wanted to toy with her. It is simply that she has attracted me as no other woman ever has. I cannot get her out of my mind, Chris. These past two months, not seeing her, have been torture. Seeing her tonight... well, it confirmed what I already knew. I am smitten with her."

Christopher was still grinning as he put a big hand on his brother's shoulder. "I am thrilled for you, truly," he said. "Smitten enough to offer for her hand?"

David didn't reply right away. When he did, his voice was low. "I do not know," he said. hesitantly "All I know is that I cannot stand the thought of her with another. And then there is de Dere; he has her in his sights and he has much more opportunity to be near her than I do. That is why he punched me tonight; he does not want the competition I bring."

Christopher nodded. "I see," he replied. "So what do you want to do about it? There would be no competition if you offered for Emilie's hand, David. The issue with Brick would be ended. Are you ready to take that step?"

David sighed heavily and stood up, moving through the darkened chamber to the table where the wine pitcher sat. He poured himself another cup.

"I am not sure," he said honestly. "I think so. But marriage... I am still not sure I am ready for it, with anyone."

"Are you prepared to see Lady Emilie married to Brick?"

David turned to look at him. "I am *not*," he said flatly. "That being the case, I suppose I should offer for her hand because I cannot stomach the alternative."

Christopher smiled at his younger brother. "I am deeply pleased to hear this, David," he said. "I am proud that you would realize you have found one woman above all others. Trust me when I tell you that it will fill your life like nothing else ever has. You will not be able to remember a time when she was not the center of your world."

David was both thrilled and frightened by his admission. It was a very big step for him to take. "Mayhap," he said, unwilling to commit more than that. It had never been easy for him to admit his feelings, to anyone. "I would like to go to Lyle and Emilie tomorrow. We have much to speak on now that John and Ralph has made Emilie a target. We must offer our protection to Emilie and to the House of Hampton."

Christopher was in full agreement. "Aye," he said. "It seems we have brought this down upon them. John and Ralph would have never targeted Emilie had they not known of her relationship to you. David... you do not consider marriage with her because you feel guilty about that, do you?"

David shook his head. "Nay," he said. "I consider marriage with her because she has managed to capture my heart, Chris. For that, and no other reason."

"Do you love her?"

David didn't say anything for a moment. "I do not know," he finally said. "I have never been in love so I do not know what it feels like."

Christopher, the older and wiser brother, smiled faintly to David's slightly confused response. "Trust me," he said quietly. "When the time comes, you will know. There will be no doubt."

David suspected his brother was correct. He wondered if it hadn't already happened and he was just too stubborn to admit it.

Lady Orford's manor
The next day

"ALTHOUGH I APPRECIATE your offer of protection, David, you must understand my position as a parent."

Lyle, standing by the hearth in his sister's lavish solar, was speaking to David mostly, but several de Lohr men were standing nearby, including his brother Christopher. It was a very serious matter and the mood of the room was somber as a result.

"Emilie is a target of the prince because of you," Lyle continued. "After what happened to her last night, I am terrified for her safety. I must take her home and away from this madness that you and the House of de Lohr seem to perpetuate. She is not safe here and you know it."

David did indeed know it and he felt a huge amount of guilt as a result. After last night's debacle with Dennis grabbing Emilie and the subsequent beating that Brickley had tried to give David, this morning saw the situation not much better where Lyle was concerned. As the sun rose over the eastern horizon, the Earl of Canterbury was still quite upset about the circumstances, and rightfully so.

David and Christopher had departed Windsor early in the morning and headed to Lady Orford's manor near London where the Hamptons were lodging. They went to offer their support to the protection of Lady Emilie, and to discuss the situation in general, but Lyle seemed convinced the only thing to do was to go home immediately. He didn't seem to want to speak about anything else. Not that anyone could blame him.

"I understand your fear for her," David said. "But you must understand that removing her from London may not solve the issue. John will send men to Canterbury. If they think they can get to me through Emilie, then they will do it."

Lyle sighed heavily. "Canterbury Castle is well fortified," he said. "I will bottle it up and we will stay there until this situation calms."

"When will that be?"

"When they are no longer after my daughter!"

"Then you may be in for a very long wait."

David was looking at Lyle as he spoke and not at Brickley, who was standing behind Lyle and posturing threateningly. After smashing David in the jaw last night, he'd been hauled away by Leeton and Edward, and then sent home in disgrace by Lyle. But this morning, the rage was still there, as was a nasty hangover. Everyone, including David, could see the anger in Brickley's expression. The man didn't have to say a word; his scowl said it all.

"Then what do you suggest, David?" Lyle asked, struggling not to become irate at Brickley's angry behavior. The last thing he needed was for the man to go after David again. "That I turn her over to the House of de Lohr for protection? Is that what you have really come to tell me?"

David was trying to remain calm, which was difficult for him in cases like this. He was usually the hot-headed and passionate one. "We have come to tell you that we will do all we can to protect Emilie," he said. "It may be that you will have to allow us to take her back to Lioncross and put her under our protection. She will remain with Lady de Lohr, properly tended of course, but the fact of the matter is that we have more resources and a far larger army than you do. We can offer her better protection."

Lyle waved him off. "Pah," he said. "That will only make things worse. If I take her home and keep her under my protection, then John and his cohorts will eventually forget about her. But they will not forget about her if she remains tied to the House of de Lohr."

David sensed something permanent and ominous in that statement, as if there was a veiled threat somewhere in those words… *IF she remains tied to the House of de Lohr.* David looked at Christopher, a silent plea for help, and Christopher took the hint. He knew that David was too embarrassed, and too uncertain, to discuss the situation on a personal level so Christopher sought to help his brother. Things needed to be said that a room full of knights didn't need to hear, and in particular, Brickley. The first thing he did was turn to Edward, Leeton, and Dud, standing behind him.

"Give us some privacy, please," he said. Then, he looked directly at Brickley. "This conversation is not for your ears. You will leave this room."

No one disobeyed an order from Richard's champion. Brickley, who had so far only been focused on David, seemed mildly surprised by the order.

"I am under Canterbury's command," he said to Christopher. "If he wants me to leave, he will tell me."

Christopher's eyes narrowed. "You struck my brother last night with no punishment from me," he said. "Unless you want me to change my mind, you will vacate my presence. I am still not entirely pleased with your behavior, de Dere. Get out of my sight."

Brickley seemed more apt to obey after that. Even Lyle turned to him and gave him permission to leave, both of them sensing that it was perhaps the smart thing to do. Enraged de Lohr brothers were never a particularly healthy thing, so Brickley left the room without a hind glance. Edward, Leeton, and Dud followed him. When the door of the soar closed quietly, Lyle looked at Christopher.

"You will never again order one of my men about in my home," he said quietly. "Is that clear?"

Christopher cocked an eyebrow. "My lord," he said, establishing that he meant no disrespect with what he was about to say. "You allowed your man to strike my brother last night. That is not what allies do to one another. I will not demand that he is turned over to me for punishment so be grateful for my mercy. I believe I am being most fair in this."

Lyle eyed Christopher before sighing heavily with regret, with sorrow at the entire situation. What Brickley did could very well alienate the House of de Lohr from the House of Hampton, and that wasn't something he wanted.

"I am sorry for that," he said, looking to David. "I apologized to you last night, David, and I will apologize to you again now. I am sorry for Brick's behavior. He was not himself."

David simply nodded in silence, eyeing his brother again. He didn't want to go back to last night; he only wanted to speak on the future. Now, it was time for Christopher to get to the real reason behind their visit.

"My lord," Christopher began, his manner cooler than it had been moments earlier. "David and I have come to be truthful and plain with you. We are very concerned for Emilie's safety and it is true that David feels responsible for what has happened, but I believe there is a solution to the situation."

Lyle lifted his eyebrows expectantly. "I am listening."

As Christopher moved towards Lyle, David shifted positions and went to set his helm onto a nearby table. The gloves came off as well, and he set them next to the helm. He didn't want to look like he was ready to go to war, especially in light of what Christopher was about to say. He wanted to appear as respectful and non-threatening as possible. He wanted to look like good and kind husbandly material for Emilie. He could only pray that Lyle would be receptive to his brother's proposal because it had taken Christopher all night to convince David it was the right thing to do. Now, David was completely convinced it was the right thing, too.

He had never wanted anything more in his life. His attention was riveted to his brother as the man began to speak.

"Do you remember the conversation you and I had about a month ago regarding the attraction between my brother and your daughter?" Christopher asked. "It was after one of the meetings of Richard's cabinet. We discussed Emilie and David and their respective... moods, shall we say. Do you recall?"

Lyle did indeed remember. A bit surprised by the question, he glanced hesitantly at David, over by the table, before replying. "I thought that conversation was to remain between us," he said.

Christopher smiled faintly. "You will forgive me for letting David in on it," he said, "because it seems that my brother feels very strongly about your daughter. Although the situation with John has pushed our hand a bit, it is true that my brother has been planning to ask your permission to court your daughter with the purpose of marrying her. As the head of our family, I would like to make that formal proposal to you now with the assurance that my brother is quite fond of your daughter and she would want for nothing. As you know, our mother was the sister of a former Earl of East Anglia and even now we are related to the current earl. He is our cousin. Through our parents, both David and I will inherit some wealth, but David has accumulated a good deal of wealth of his own over the years. As the Lord of Lioncross Abbey, I inherited the small barony of Kington when I married my wife. It is a lesser title, and one that I do not particularly use, but the point is that I have another title that I also inherited upon my marriage to my wife, one of Lord Broxwood. I was going to bestow it upon my firstborn son but I have decided to grant my brother the title when he marries. My brother is a fine and noble man, my lord, and would make a fine husband for Lady Emilie. I would be grateful if you would consider it."

It was the offer Lyle had been hoping for. It had all come down quite properly, as it should have, through David's older brother and head of the family, and he was terribly thrilled. More thrilled than he thought he would be. But the mess with John and Ralph weighed heavily in his mind and heart as well; these men wanted to hurt Emilie because of David. Could he knowingly marry the woman to a man who had a target on his back? A man who was associated with King Richard so strongly that even Richard's brother was out to kill him?

In good conscience, Lyle wasn't sure he could do that to Emilie. It was true that he didn't want her to marry Brickley, but at least with Brickley, she would be safe and anonymous.

But it would also mean that the earldom of Canterbury would pass to Brickley upon Lyle's death because Emilie was the heiress. In that respect, Lyle was faced with a very serious question – who would he rather see inherit the earldom? Brickley or David? Of course, it was David. A young knight who had made a name for himself, who was a fighter among fighters, related to perhaps one of the greatest houses in England. David and his brother Christopher had built an empire, and a marriage between Canterbury and de Lohr would seal that alliance forever.

But it also might bring John down over their heads. The truth was that with Richard missing, John was the next in line for the throne. Was Lyle willing to risk the wrath of the next king of England by marrying his daughter into the House of de Lohr?

Lyle wasn't sure. But Christopher and David were waiting for an answer, so he cleared his throat softly.

"I am deeply honored, of course," he said, looking between Christopher and David. "David, are you sure about this? You have only known my daughter a short amount of time and there was a period there where you stayed away from her for a couple of months. It seems to me that your relationship with my daughter, so far, has not been a completely trouble-free one."

David spoke. "It was my own stubborn stupidity," he said. "It had nothing to do with an argument between us. It was a simple misunderstanding that I let get out of control. Emilie has forgiven me, for which I am grateful."

Lyle thought on that. Pensively, he turned away, heading for one of the fat-stuffed leather chairs that faced the hearth. He sat heavily in one, contemplating what had been asked of him.

"I am sure it was not all your fault," he said. "Emilie can be stubborn herself at times. Adverse, even. When she gets something in her mind, it is very difficult to change it. You should know that about her."

David gave him a half-grin. "I am not concerned about it," he said. "She seems to be willing to discuss what ails her, which is an admirable quality. It should lessen the chance of misunderstandings in the future."

Lyle nodded, thinking on his beauteous eldest daughter. "You must also know that you are not the only bee humming about her hive," he said, turning to look at David. "Brick has already asked for her hand in marriage, six months ago. What do I tell him if I pledge her to you?"

It was a sore subject with David and he struggled not to become snappish about it, but that self-control was too much to hope for given the emotions of the situation.

"That is not my concern," he said. "You can tell him to go to hell. From me."

Christopher cleared his throat softly, intervening before he insulted Lyle and ruined his chances for a betrothal. "Heads are still heated since last night," he said to Lyle. "You will have to forgive my brother. Being caught off-guard by a punch to the jaw has naturally soured him against Brick."

Lyle lifted his eyebrows, putting up a hand as if to soothe David's irritation. "Do not hold too much against Brick," he said. "He has loved Emilie far longer than you have. You are the usurper in his eyes. But I never wanted him for her, you should know that. I would much rather have a de Lohr for my daughter."

David went from rage against Brickley to overwhelming thrill at Lyle's words. "Thank you, my lord," he said. "May I accept that as your decision to my request to court your daughter?"

Lyle's good humor faded. "I must be honest with you," he said. "I am torn. As the House of de Lohr, you lads seem to attract all kinds of trouble, trouble that bleeds over into those you associate with. My daughter is now caught up in that trouble and I do not know, in good conscience, if I can knowing allow her to marry into so much danger. I am greatly torn by this, David. I must have time to consider all sides of this situation."

David's thrill turned cold and he looked at Christopher, silently beseeching the man to come to his aid. Christopher understood the expression of disappointment on his brother's face.

"We understand, my lord," he said. "It is a very big decision. We do not want to rush you as you decide your daughter's future. That being the case, however, we are back to the original purpose for our visit to you – to offer Emilie protection from Ralph and John. I still believe it would be better to let her remain with us than for you to take her back to Canterbury. John could summon a mighty army if he really wanted to take her."

Lyle looked at Christopher, his expression serious. "Are you attempting to frighten me into giving my daughter over to you?" he asked. "Because if you are, it is most certainly not working. In fact, now that I know of David's formal interest in her, I am resolute in the fact that she will be returning with me to Canterbury. I would not send her with you to Lioncross now. That would be foolish on my part."

David suspected that his honor was being slandered. "Why?" he asked. "Do you think I would do anything improper in that case, playing patty-fingers with your daughter because she is under my brother's roof?"

Lyle shook his head; he could see that he had offended the man. "Nay," he said firmly. "But you must admit that it would not be the best and brightest decision, David. You have feelings for Emilie and, as I told your brother once before, it is my belief that she has feelings for you. In fact, I know she has. Now, just how much restraint would you two have if I were to send you off together, sequestered against John's reach?"

As David sighed heavily and hung his head, afraid he might say something rude, Christopher stepped in. "Am I to assume, then, that you are refusing our protection for her?"

Lyle looked at the big knight. "I am taking her home, with me," he said quietly but firmly. "Your brother may send her missives and he may even come to visit. But she goes home to Canterbury and I will think on your brother's proposal of marriage to her. It is a big decision I must make and I want to make the right one by my daughter."

"And Brick?" David said, his jaw ticking faintly as it often did when he was frustrated. "He will go with you to Canterbury."

"He will."

"And he wants to marry Emilie as I do," he said. "You worry about me playing patty-fingers with her? What about him?"

Lyle stood up from his chair. "He would never do that under my roof, David," he said. "He would not compromise Emilie so."

"And I would? You would trust me less than him?"

Lyle shook his head as he made his way over to David. In an act of reassurance, and to calm the man down, he put his hands on the young knight's shoulders. "The fact is that I trust you as much as I trust him," he stressed. "But Emilie does not have feelings for Brick as she has for you. He can try to play patty-fingers all he wants with her and she will only refuse him. But you… she would not refuse you, and our will-power is only so strong against women, is it not?"

David understood what he was saying. He wasn't particularly happy with it, but he understood. "Mayhap," he said vaguely. "But you will consider my offer of marriage, will you not?"

"I will."

"May I inquire on your decision in the next few months?"

Lyle shrugged and dropped his hands from David. "You may," he said. "I will think very hard on it. I like you, David; I truly do. You must understand how difficult this is for me."

"What of Emilie? Will you tell her?"

Lyle nodded. "Eventually," he said. "If I tell her now, she will pester me into an early grave. So you will permit me to tell her at my discretion, please."

David didn't have much choice. He simply nodded as Christopher spoke. "Will you at least let me send an escort of de Lohr troops back with you to Canterbury?" he asked. "How many men did you bring with you?"

Lyle turned to him. "This was supposed to be a tournament, not a battle," he said. "I left the majority at Canterbury and only brought fifty men with me."

Christopher pondered that rather low margin of men. "Then I will send another one hundred home with you to ensure you make it back to Canterbury with no issue," he said. "I would also like to send a knight."

Lyle cast a long glance at David. "Not your brother," he said. "I would be pulling him and Brick apart at every turn."

Christopher was forced to agree. "I will send Dud with you," he said. "Sir Thomas Dudley. A big man with short brown hair. You have seen him in my entourage. He is an excellent knight who will not get caught up in anything... emotional."

Truthfully, Lyle was grateful for the additional escort. "You have my thanks," he said. "We shall be leaving before dawn. David, if you wish to tell Emilie farewell before we depart, I am agreeable to that. But you will not tell her about your proposal of marriage. Are we clear?"

David nodded. "We are, my lord."

Lyle was satisfied. He began to move towards the solar entry, motioning to Christopher as he went. "Come along, Chris," he said. "Let's you and I do some damage to boiled beef and fresh bread as we break our fast together. I would guess, due to your early arrival, that you've not yet eaten this morning."

Christopher passed a glance at David as he followed Lyle. "Nay, we have not," he said. "I am quite famished."

Christopher was looking at David but David wasn't looking at his brother; he was beginning to brood, upset that Lyle hadn't given his instant consent. Christopher knew that. He hoped to speak to Lyle more about it when they were eating, leaving David to say his farewells to Emilie. Given Lyle's reluctance, and the fact that Brickley would be by Emilie's side all the way back to Canterbury and beyond, Christopher hoped that it wouldn't be David's last glimpse of the lady who had stolen his heart.

SHE KNEW HE had come because she could see the de Lohr horses in the courtyard of Aunt Coraline's home. *Men,* she thought with disgust. She hated them all.

After Brickley's rejection the evening before, Nathalie had reverted to her old and nasty ways. She didn't like men and they didn't like her. And she didn't like pompous knights in particular, knights like David de Lohr. Why Emilie should be so fortunate to have men falling all over themselves simply for the opportunity to speak with her, Nathalie didn't know. But she did know this – if she couldn't have a suitor, then neither could Emilie.

She would see to it.

But she needed help. Elise, still smarting from not attending the mask the night before, was a willing accomplish. She always was. She would line her people up on the floor near her bed and tell them of her wicked plans or deeds, and giggle. She was sure her people were giggling, too. But this plan was the best one of all because it would chase David de Lohr away from Emilie. No one needed him around, anyway. When Lyle sent a servant up to tell Emilie that David was down in the solar to see her, Nathalie and Elise slinked off without their sister noticing as she hurriedly dressed.

They had a plan.

A plan that involved the dogs. Cid and Roland were good for many things; they were excellent companions and guard dogs. They also had very large piles of excrement, which usually ended up in the hearth and burned. They would shite in the rooms and the servants would scoop it away even though the dogs were supposed to shite out in the garden. But Nathalie and Elise thought it was rather sad that the dogs had to shite out in the elements while they themselves were able to use a garderobe or chamber pot, so they didn't take the dogs out as much as they should. That being the case, their room was starting to smell strongly of dog urine and feces, much to Coraline's displeasure.

But the girls didn't particularly care. Big dogs were good for many things, but they were particularly good for fuel for the kinds of jokes Nathalie and Elise liked to play. In this case, the dogs had laid a big pile of shite near the hearth this morning and using the small shovel meant to scoop out ashes from the hearth, Nathalie scooped up the dog leavings. With Elise acting as a look-out, the girls fled the room.

And so their covert mission began. Aunt Coraline's house had been built with two big floors, eight rooms each, and four narrow servant staircases that led between floors at opposite sides of the house. At the end of the hallway on the south side of the house was a stairwell that led to the solar where David de Lohr was waiting for Emilie. As Nathalie headed down the dark staircase with the shovel of dog shite in her hands, she sent Elise down the main stair case so that she could call David to the solar door while Nathalie slipped in through the concealed servant's entrance.

Elise was nervous at first, as she did not know David, but Nathalie convinced her that the man wouldn't bite her, so Elise reluctantly agreed. Besides, it was rather thrilling for her and Nathalie to be back to their old tricks. As Elise went to the solar door, knocking before entering, Nathalie carefully and quietly opened the concealed servant's entrance into the room just as David turned to a young girl with blond hair who looked a good deal like Emilie. David smiled at the child as Nathalie slipped in at the far end of the room, unseen.

"Greetings," David said. "I heard a rumor that there was a third Hampton sister named Elise. Would that be you?"

Elise nodded, nervous in the big knight's presence. More than that, Nathalie was coming across the room behind him with a shovel full of dog shite. She was afraid the knight would hear Nathalie so she spoke quickly.

"Aye," she said. "I... I am Elise. I... I was not able to attend the mask last night."

Grinning, David crossed his arms and casually made his way over to the nervous girl. "You did not miss much," he told her. "It was hot and smelly and the food was terrible. I am sure you had a much better time remaining at home."

Elise bit her lip, awkward. She wasn't used to interacting with men and especially men she didn't know. Back behind David, she could see Nathalie moving swiftly to the chair the man had been sitting in but she quickly detoured when she saw his helm on the nearby table. In her haste, she tripped on a hide on the floor and Elise, terrified that David would hear Nathalie, coughed loudly to cover up her sister's scuffle.

"I… I remained home with my Aunt Coraline," she said. "She is Lady Orford. She has a great castle but she likes it here at her manor home better. Her castle is old and big and has phantoms in it. I like it here better, too."

David hadn't heard Nathalie's trip several feet behind him and he certainly didn't hear it when she dumped the shovel of dog shite into his helm. He was focused on the young girl who seemed to be growing more nervous by the moment.

"Ah," he said, trying to be kind to her because she seemed so frightened. "I do not like phantoms, either, although I cannot say I have actually seen one. Have you?"

Elise could see Nathalie dashing back to the concealed servant's door from the corner of her eye. She didn't dare take her focus off of David lest he see what she was looking at, so she kept her focus on him even as she backed away. When Nathalie slipped through the servant's door and disappeared, Elise dashed to the solar entry.

"I have not," she said, breathlessly. "Good day to you, sir."

And with that, she was gone. David stood there a moment, wondering what on earth he said to scare the child so. Shaking his head, baffled at the nature of skittish little girls, he turned around and headed back to the hearth to continue his wait for Emilie.

David quickly forgot about the nervous young sister as his thoughts returned to Emilie. He was thinking of her as his wife, of her strength and of her beauty. He thought of the sons he would have with her, sons with his strength and her good looks. Or perhaps his strength *and* good looks. The daughters they had, if any, could look like her. Oh, what daughters they would be.

Grinning at the thought of daughters with Emilie's blond hair, he leaned against the hearth, gazing into the fire, and losing himself in daydreams, which was not something he normally did. He wasn't the dreaming sort. In fact, he was staring into the fire quite distractedly when the solar door opened again and he turned, casually, to see Emilie enter the room.

Jolted from his daydreams, he came away from the hearth, his heart pounding at the sight of her. Dressed in a simple but flattering gown the color of violets, she looked absolutely beautiful. She smiled, he smiled, and all was right in the world.

"What a lovely surprise for you to come and visit me this morning," she said. "How do you feel after last night?"

He was confused by the question. "Last night?"

She brushed at her jaw, the exact spot on his face that Brickley had hit him, and he chuckled softly as she laughed, relieved he understood her sign language. "I am perfect," he told her. "Brick cannot hurt me. You should not worry."

She looked at him rather apologetically. "I am so sorry that he did that," she said. "I made it very clear to him how angry I was. I have not spoken to him at all this morning. He will be lucky if I ever speak to him again, truthfully."

David grinned and reached out, taking her hand in his. It was a rather bold gesture but the truth was that he didn't care. It might be his last chance to touch her for quite some time. Emilie grasped his hand with both of hers, holding on to him tightly.

"Come and sit with me," he said softly. "We must speak."

Emilie followed him gladly to the opposite side of the room

where there was a cushioned bench positioned by a window that overlooked the yard outside. David had Emilie sit first before he settled in next to her. He let go of her hand but his knee was touching hers. It was rather scandalous and daring, and Emilie folded her hands in her lap politely, waiting for him to speak. He would, after he'd finished staring at her, drinking in his fill of her. He very much liked to look at her.

"It is good to see you," he said, his voice soft. "I find that the world is a colorless place when I do not have you to look at."

Emilie smiled, blushing appropriately. "You are very kind."

"I am honest."

"What did you wish to speak on?"

David cocked his head thoughtfully. "I have been speaking with your father this morning," he said, noting her look of surprise. "That is why I am here, Emilie. I came to see your father about what happened last night and about… other things. My brother and I have offered our protection to keep you safe from John but your father seems to think that it would be best to return you to Canterbury immediately. Did he tell you any of this?"

The smile was gone from Emilie's face. "Nay," she said, shaking her head. "He was distressed last night, of course, but he said nothing about returning home. He really said that you?"

David nodded. "He is very concerned over your safety," he said. "I do not blame him. I am concerned for your safety, too."

Emilie was quickly becoming distressed. "But I do not want to leave London," he said. "It would mean leaving… that is to say, I like it here. We have not seen Aunt Coraline in so long and I would be sad to leave her."

His sky blue eyes twinkled. "Is that the only person you would be sad to leave?"

She could see the mirth in his eyes and she fought off a smile. "I cannot think of anyone else."

He frowned. "Is that so?"

Her laughter broke through. "Well," she said casually. "It is possible that I might miss someone else. Just a little, you understand. Not too much."

He looked away, pretending to be miffed. "And it is equally possible that when I leave London, I might miss someone else as well," he said. "Not too much, mind you. Just a very small amount."

Emilie was still grinning at him. "I hope you mean me."

He shook his head. "I do not mean you unless you are going to miss me as well."

"Of course I am."

He looked at her again, seeing the humor in her eyes. "Then I am pleased," he said. "But I do not want you to be too terribly distressed over this. When you return to Canterbury, I shall come and visit you. Your father has given me permission."

Her face lit up. "He has?" she said. "That is wonderful to hear. Will you really come all the way to Canterbury to visit me?"

He nodded. "All the way."

She was thrilled. "When will you come?"

He shrugged. "As soon as my duties allow," he said. "There is still much happening here in London that I must be a part of, but as soon as I am able, I will come and see you."

"Promise?"

"I do," he said firmly. "Now, tell me what you will plan for us to do when I visit."

Emilie was beside herself with glee. "Let me think," she said, trying very hard to gather her scattered thoughts. Her excitement had them all over the place. "Canterbury has a lake. My father would take my sisters and me fishing from time to time. Do you like to hunt for fish?"

"I do."

Emilie clasped her hands joyfully, holding them against her breast. "I also have a very fast mare that Papa gave to me," she said. "We can go riding into the town. There is a lovely church there and on the street of bakers, there is a woman who makes pies and fills them with almond paste and honey and fruit. They are delicious. Once, Elise ate so many that she became terribly ill."

David chuckled. "Speaking of Elise, I met her a few moments before you came in," he said. "She is a nervous lass."

Emilie's smile vanished. "She came in here?"

"Aye."

Emilie suddenly looked quite suspicious. "What did she do?"

He shrugged. "Nothing," he said. "She introduced herself, we exchanged a few words, and then she ran off."

Emilie didn't seem satisfied by that. "But she did not *do* anything?"

"What do you mean?"

"Did she touch anything?" Emilie asked. "Was she ever out of your sight, even for a moment?"

David had no idea why she was asking such questions. "She was never out of my sight," he said. "She walked in, introduced herself, mentioned that she was not at the mask last night, and then she fled. That was it. Why do you ask?"

Emilie looked around the room as if looking for anything tell-tale or out of place. "Did you see Nathalie?" she asked.

David shook his head. "I did not," he said. "Tell me why you ask these questions?"

Emilie turned to him, rather guiltily. "Because my sisters thrive on tricks they like to play on unsuspecting people," she said. "Brick lives in fear of them, or at least he used to. They have done terrible things to him in the past."

David was fighting off a grin now; he very much wanted to hear what Emilie's sisters had done to his nemesis. "Like what?"

Emilie sighed thoughtfully. "Once they put charcoal on his gloves so that when he wiped his face, it left black streaks," she said. "It took an entire week to wash them clean. They have strung small bits of twine across thresholds, tripping men, or worse, they've held them higher and nearly garroted people. There is a whole list of things they have done – eggs in beds, honey on pillows, dog droppings in boots… many, many things."

David was trying not to laugh. "But Elise looked so innocent," he said. "I cannot believe she would be party to such things."

Emilie nodded firmly. "She is evil and she is very smart," she said. "You must be very careful of Elise."

His laugh broke through. "Very well," he said. "But I promise you that she did nothing when she came into the room. It was all quite innocent."

Emilie wasn't so sure but with nothing more to go on, she let the subject go. Her focus returned to the prospect of leaving London. Of leaving David behind. The more she thought on it, the sadder she became.

"As you say," she said. But then she changed the focus away from her sisters and their wicked ways. "I wonder if I can change Papa's mind about leaving London. I truly do not wish to leave."

David sobered because she was. "Shall I tell you something?"

"Of course."

"I do not wish for you to leave, either, but your father seemed determined," he said. "But he not only said that I could visit you at Canterbury, but that I could send you missives as well. Do you know how to read?"

She nodded eagerly. "I can read Latin and French," she said. "Mother taught us all how to read."

"Your mother taught you?"

Emilie shook her head. "My nurse," she reminded him. "You will remember that we call her Mother. She has also been our teacher. Will you write to me often, then?"

"As often as I can."

Her smile was returning. "I will look forward to it," she said. "Do you know how long you be remaining in London?"

He cocked his head thoughtfully. Somehow, his hand found her knee, as inappropriate as it was, and caressed it through the fabric of her skirt. It was thrilling and indecent, but he didn't care as long as she allowed him to do it. He could only imagine what her naked skin would feel like against his hand. The mere thought had his lust rising.

"I am not entirely certain," he said, distracted with the feel of her knee beneath his palm. "We are all waiting to hear word about Richard so I suppose we shall be here until we do."

Emilie was relishing the feel of his hand on her leg, his gentle touch. His hands were big and calloused, and the gentle strength of them thrilled her. *He* thrilled her.

"But what will happen if you do not hear of Richard for months and months?" she asked. "You must return home sometime."

He shrugged. "I will go to Canterbury before I go home," he said. "Moreover, it is my brother's home. It is not mine. I do not really have a home, a place of my own."

Emilie reached out, gently taking the hand that was caressing her knee. She held it tightly. "That is so sad," she said. "Do you have nowhere that you belong? Where did you live as a child?"

David thought back to his childhood; his growing years. "My parents were older when my brother and I were born, older still when Deborah was born," he said. "My mother was a sweet and wonderful woman, but because she had her children late in life, she kept us close to her, well past the age when we should have left to foster. We lived at the ancestral de Lohr home of Lohrham Forest, in Derbyshire. Christopher went to Kenilworth when he was nine and I followed him two years later. Then, Deborah was born while Chris and I were both away and our parents passed away when she was about two. After that, Chris and I remained at Kenilworth and Deborah went to Derby. I suppose that means Kenilworth is my home."

Emilie was listening to him with interest. "I am sorry that you did not grow up knowing your parents," she said. "I am sure they would have been very proud of you. I am sure your father was a great knight."

David's eyes glimmered. "Both of my parents were great knights," he said. "My mother was the sister of the Earl of East Anglia and he permitted her to fight like a knight. She was quite good. In fact, my father said he had to best her in order to marry her."

Emilie laughed. "That's not true!"

"It is, I swear."

She continued to laugh a moment but the laughter soon cooled. "Then it is no wonder you and your brother are such great knights," she said, admiration in her expression. "You come from excellent stock on both sides."

He nodded. "That is true," he said. "I suppose my one regret in life is that my parents did not live to see Chris and I become the knights we are today. I think that would have made both of my parents very proud."

Emilie sensed some sadness in that statement. She squeezed his hand reassuringly. "They most certainly would have," she said. "But since they cannot be here, would you permit me to be proud of you? You carry my favor, after all. It is my right."

He smiled at her. In fact, he couldn't seem to stop smiling at her. With his free hand, he reached up, cupped her sweet face, and planted a gentle kiss on her cheek. "Thank you," he murmured against her flesh. "I am honored."

Emilie closed his eyes to his kiss, bathing in its glory, before turning her head and capturing his lips with her own. He wanted to kiss her cheek but she wanted more. Letting go of his hand, she threw her arms around his neck and squeezed him tightly as his big arms wrapped around her slender body. She was overwhelming him, holding him so tightly that she was nearly strangling him, when the door to the solar suddenly opened.

"Emilie!"

It was Lyle. Emilie let David go, jumping back, and falling onto her arse in the process. David, also startled by Lyle's swift appearance, reached down to help her to her feet but Lyle wasn't alone;

Christopher was with him and, behind Christopher, was Brickley. Brickley, seeing Emilie wrapped up in David's arms, began to charge into the room but Christopher threw a block into the man that sent him staggering into the wall. Meanwhile, Emilie was on her feet, rushing for her father.

"It was my fault," she said. "I kissed him! He did not kiss me; I kissed *him*. I threw myself at him shamelessly! You will not blame him, Papa!"

Lyle reached out and grasped his daughter, pulling her back and away from the knights. He wasn't sure what was going to happen with Brickley charging and Christopher shoving, so he pulled her away, towards the hearth and clear of the scuffle.

But Brickley stopped charging, instead, standing where Christopher had smashed him against the wall, holding onto the shoulder that had rammed into the stone. He'd injured it. Christopher stood between Brickley and David, his focus on Brickley.

"Just what did you intend to do?" Christopher growled at him. "Were you going to try and thrash my brother? Did you not think I would stop you?"

Brickley, far from the amiable man they all knew, was glaring at Christopher and David. "Of all the low things to do," he snarled at David. "You were trusted with Lady Emilie, unescorted, and this is what you do?"

David had enough. He marched up behind his brother, avoiding the big hand that came out to grab him, and charged Brickley. Brickley tried to tuck in low to take the brunt of David's rush, but instead of throwing his body weight behind the charge, David leapt into the air and came down right on top of Brickley as the man ducked low. He clobbered him right over the head with an elbow and Brickley collapsed, half-conscious, on the floor.

That was all David intended to do, especially in front of Emilie. He wasn't going to let the man get the better of him twice; there was a measure of pride at stake now. He circled Brickley for a moment before Christopher pulled him away.

"That is for the blow you dealt me last night," David said, his tone deadly as his brother grabbed him and pulled him back. "If you think to try and attack me again without consequences, think again."

Emilie gasped with shock, hands to her mouth, as Lyle put his arms around her. They were both watching the exchange with a good deal of fear and surprise. "David," Lyle said, softly but firmly. "No more. It is best that you leave now."

Emilie, still startled at the sight of Brickley wallowing on the floor, turned to her father. "It was *not* David's fault, Papa," she said. "He was defending himself from Brickley. Brickley tried to hurt him again!"

Lyle knew that; he had seen what had happened as well. He knew the score. His main purpose at the moment was restoring some order to the house and that meant removing David de Lohr.

"I know," he said, trying to ease her. He looked at David and Christopher. "David, if you please."

Christopher was pulling his brother to the door, who still had Brickley in his sites. David was waiting for the man to rise up, at which point he would kick him straight in the face. He was finished being tolerant of Brickley's wild jealousy. In fact, David had some jealousy of his own and he wasn't about to let Brickley antagonize him. But he let Christopher pull him away, towards the door. His focus, for a moment, turned to Lyle and Emilie.

"I apologize, my lord," he said to Lyle. "But I am not going to let the man beat on me and not respond. I know you understand that."

Lyle sighed heavily, distressed at the entire situation. "I do," he said. "But it would be best for you to leave now."

David's focus turned to Emilie. "My lady," he said. "My apologies for upsetting you."

Emilie was looking at David, her face aglow with warmth. "You did not," she said. "It was good of you to come and see me today."

"It was my pleasure, my lady."

Emilie's features turned to sorrow now, the realization that he was leaving. "You... you are always welcome to visit me, David. Remember that you promised."

He managed to smile weakly at her. "It is a promise I intend to keep."

Emilie returned his smile, both hopeful and sad in her reaction. Already, she missed him. David could see it in her face. His gaze lingered on her a moment before turning away, but not before he realized that he had left his helm on the table over near the hearth. He pointed to it, indicating he intended to collect it, and moved to retrieve it. His gaze was still on Emilie when he picked it up and plopped it on his head.

And that's when he felt it....

Cold, mushy something. He had no idea what it was but he wasn't about to pull it off his head and look. He had been instructed to leave and leave he would. Moreover, he was rather afraid to know what was in his helm, now squished into his hair. The first thing that popped into his mind was Emilie's admonition about Elise – *you must be very careful of Elise.* The girl must have been a sorceress to sabotage his helm because she never left his sight upon entering the solar. Yet there was unquestionably something in his helm.

Damnation....

But he hid his concern well. He remained calm as he and Christopher quit the solar and headed out into the yard beyond where their horses and knights await.

Edward and Leeton were there when Christopher and David approached, and they watched with great curiosity when David suddenly stopped, bent over at the waist, and pulled his helm off. There was something brown all mashed into his hair and when he lifted up the helm to look into it, he groaned with disgust. They could all smell the stench. Christopher, Edward, and Leeton wanted to know what it was and when David explained what he thought had happened, there was a brief minute of shocked silence.

That silence was followed by laughter so loud and sincere that Edward nearly choked.

CHAPTER FIFTEEN

March 1193
Windsor

CHRISTOPHER PACED THE FLOOR *of John's audience chamber calmly enough, but inside he was as cagey as a cat. He was almost frantic to know why John had called an audience of Richard's loyalists, and with him, the justices, and a few close advisors of the absent king. Yet even as he wondered, he knew the reason and his stomach tightened in response. Word must have come about Richard. He didn't know why his instincts told him that, but he knew it just the same. All of the justices sat or stood in relative silence, waiting in the chill of the ornate audience hall, their minds riveted to the same thought, they knew why they were here, too.*

William Marshal watched Christopher pace, his aged face creased with fatigue and worry this night. Whatever the reason they had been summoned, it could not be a good one, but he would not let his concern show.

"Would you sit down, Chris? You are going to wear a hole in the damn floor," he said quietly.

Christopher eyed William, slowing his movement but not sitting. William raised an eyebrow at him.

"I realize that you believe sitting in John's presence is a sign of submission, but force yourself," he said with suppressed sarcasm, trying

to lighten the mood a bit. "You are making me nervous."

Christopher continued to eye him doubtfully but did as the elder man asked and took a seat next to him. William relaxed back into his chair, eyeing Christopher's stiff body with faint amusement. He shook his head and smiled; Christopher hated John more than any of them, and for good reason, and was preparing to shoot to his feet the moment the prince entered the room. He might as well still be standing for all of the relaxing he was doing on his arse.

"Tell me, how is your wife?" William asked.

"Well, sire," Christopher replied. "Her appetite and vigor have returned, thankfully."

William nodded. "Well and good," he eyed Christopher. "Any thoughts on returning her to Lioncross?"

Christopher shrugged vaguely. "Thoughts, of course, but no action."

William nudged the big man with an elbow. "You'd miss her too much, wouldn't you?"

Christopher lifted his shoulders again, not meeting William's knowing gaze. "I'd rather have her here with me."

William laughed softly; Christopher was not a man to admit attachment to anything or anyone other than Richard, even though it was painfully obvious his wife had usurped their king in the Defender's heart. Yet before William could goad him further, a small door behind the throne swung open and Ralph marched through. He hadn't taken two steps when Christopher was on his feet, his huge body coiled with anticipation.

Everyone rose out of pure protocol when John entered the room, waving benevolently at the group of men and followed by his closest advisors. Christopher eyed the small group of seedy, shady characters, even if they were some of England's most noble blood. Bringing up the rear was none other than Sir Dennis le Londe.

He spied Christopher and gave him a wolfish sort of smile. Christopher met the expression with an unreadable face, wishing he could get the man alone just long enough to snap his neck like kindling. They never had gotten along, merely tolerated one another because they were fighting for a common cause. Dennis was a devotee of Philip Augustus, as passionate about his king as Christopher was for Richard. Since Richard and Philip Augustus despised each other, it was only natural for Christopher and Dennis to feel the same way. What had happened in the tournament had not increased Christopher's loathing, but simply reinforced it.

John took his seat, adjusting his robes as a woman would fuss over her surcoat. The justices sat and waited patiently while John deliberately stalled, conferring with various men around him before finally clearing his throat and facing the expectant throng.

"Loyal vassals of Richard," he began. "I am afraid 'tis bad news I must give you. I received word from the continent today regarding Richard's whereabouts and well-being and, I am sorry to say, the information is most disturbing."

Christopher braced himself mentally, not daring to glance at William Marshal but so wanting to. John continued.

"On December 12, Richard was captured by forces of Duke Leopold. He and Emperor Henry are holding our king hostage, and the inclination seems to be that they will demand a ransom for him; a ransom I am sure we as a country cannot meet." He was relishing the open reaction of some of the justices. "As Richard's heir, 'twould seem that England would be mine in that case."

William rose beside Christopher, eyeing John with disbelief. "Is Richard well?"

"He is healthy and whole, as far as we are told," John replied without a hint of distress.

"Then ransom or not, sire, Richard is King of England until his demise," William said evenly.

"But England needs a king who is not being held prisoner," John said, trying to control the temper that threatened to flare.

"Richard cannot rule from a cell."

"*Richard is king,*" *William repeated.* "*The throne of England is his. And it is quite possible that we may deliver the requested ransom; has any amount been discussed yet?*"

John's jaw ticked. "*Nay, not yet,*" *he replied quietly.* "*But surely it will be overwhelming and the royal coffers are already near to bone dry. There will be no way to pay it.*"

"*Begging you pardon, sire, but how do you know?*" *William said.* "*Richard has many loyal, wealthy vassals and it is quite possible that the booty will be raised. Mayhap we should wait and see what Leopold and Henry demand before we draw any conclusions.*"

John was thoroughly agitated. Already the meeting was not favorable in his behalf, as he had hoped. William Longchamp, Richard's chancellor, suddenly bolted from his seat, wringing his hands behind his back.

"*How dare they take Richard prisoner, as if he were a common thief!*" *he raged.* "*By what right do they possess the power to take our sovereign hostage?*"

"*They consider Richard a criminal, my lord, as you well know,*" *William said steadily, hoping Longchamp would calm down and realize now was not the place for dissension amongst Richard's ranks.* "*We have known that for a long while now, yet it changes nothing. Leopold and Henry the Lion hold Richard and we must deal with them.*"

Christopher was surprisingly collected. He crossed his massive arms over his chest, listening to Marshal's voice of reason.

"*Would an armed incursion be possible, my lord, were we to find out where they are holding him?*" *he asked William quietly.*

"*I will not allow it.*" *John shot out of his chair, shaking his fist at Christopher.* "*You will not take an army into the empire to free my brother. Such acts could be deemed provocative and before we would realize it, we would be at war with the entire empire.*"

Christopher's gaze was cool on John. "*We are already at war with Henry, so to speak,*" *he said.* "*He has captured our king. Would you not consider that act the least bit provocative?"*

John's mouth worked furiously. "No armed excursion, de Lohr. I forbid it."

"You cannot," Christopher responded flatly. "You have not the power. Only the justices can deny me."

The veins on John's neck bulged. "But I am the bloody prince and heir to the throne. 'Tis well within my royal right to approve or deny the use of crown monies and power."

"The troops are mine, as pursuant to Richard's decree," Christopher reminded him, wondering how long it was going to be before John was having seizures on the floor. "Your use of them is limited."

"They are crown property and I am the crown," John shot back.

"But you are not king." How Christopher loved to say that. "They are Richard's troops and he has given the responsibility to me in his absence. Why must we go over this, sire? You read the missive and know full well the royal appointment. 'Tis not up for discussion, and certainly not with me. I am simply following Richard's orders."

John was bordering on another fit and Ralph leaned closed to his liege, whispering in his ear until John visibly relaxed. All in the room watched as he regained his seat with mounting control over himself. He seemed to calm with amazing speed and Christopher wondered what in the hell Ralph said to him, but not really wanting to know.

"My brother will never leave captivity alive, you know," he said finally. "Philip is akin to this kidnapping, and he and Henry want him dead almost as badly as they want money. Mayhap they will decide that his death is more important to the good of the free world after all. 'Twill be interesting to see if there is a ransom demand at all."

A rapid change of attitude, no doubt to throw the justices off-guard. Christopher raised an eyebrow at the prince, but William remained impassive.

"Mayhap, sire," he replied. "I suppose we will find out in due time. Was that all you wished to speak with us about?"

John stared back at William, mulling over the question, before letting out an ironic snort. "I should think it would be enough, yet you do not seem overly concerned. It is possible you care not what happens to your king or that you have become accustomed to running the country in his absence?"

William smiled wryly. "I both care what happens to our king and look forward to his return, sire. As do you."

They all knew the final three words to be a flat out lie. John merely turned away, this meeting had not gone favorably in the least and he was eager to be done with it. He had expected outrage, pleading and cursing at the very least, but the seams of Richard's governing body were strong and showed no signs of deficiency. Informed of their lord's fate, they were now sure of his whereabouts, and were grimly determined to resolve it. John was not at all pleased with the show of strength, yet it did not mar his plans. He had an army waiting for him in Nottingham, he had hoped Richard's captivity would allow him a fairly bloodless route to the throne, but he could see that it was not going to happen.

So be it, then. He would take what was rightfully his by force.

There would be no better opportunity.

Canterbury Castle
Early May

"JOHN'S MERCENARY ARMY has moved to the heart of England," Lyle said, his tone somewhat subdued. "I have received a request from William Marshal to send men and material northward. It seems that John has embedded his mercenary army at Nottingham Castle and we must do all we can to stop him from taking England by force."

Brickley was listening without much enthusiasm. He had been the one to bring this missive to Lyle from an exhausted messenger bearing Marshal colors, so he knew the contents of the missive would be important. That concerned him. Now, with the contents revealed, he knew without question that he would be the one to lead the troops northward and he simply didn't want to go.

"With Richard presumed dead, I am not entirely sure why John needs to form an army to take with is rightfully his," he said. "I do not understand why we must fight him if the throne belongs to him."

In the small solar at Canterbury Castle where Lyle administered his business, the man stood near the hearth for the light it provides as he read a rather large piece of vellum. It was a square room, with massively thick walls and small lancet windows, and it was a rather lush chamber with fur rugs on the floor and two big tapestries against the walls to keep the iciness of the old red stones out of the room. It even had a precious glass window with colored pieces of glass in it, overlooking the bailey. The hearth that Lyle stood next to was taller than he was.

"According to this missive, Richard is the captive of Duke Leopold and Emperor Henry," Lyle replied to Brickley's statement. "William Marshal asks me to provide him what coinage I can for Richard's ransom, whilst also asking me to provide men and material to fight off John. Richard is still very much king, Brick. We must do as we are asked so that lazy-eyed bastard who covets the throne of his brother shall not have it."

Brickley sighed faintly, deeply unhappy. He was too old to fight in the field; at least, that was the way he looked at it. Not only did he not want to leave Canterbury, but he didn't want to die fighting a band of mercenaries who would probably disband in a few months when John's revenue dried up. He thought the whole thing to be rather ridiculous but he couldn't, and wouldn't, disobey or even question Lyle. Not when he wanted something from the man.

He wanted Emilie.

Brick had spent the past four months trying to woo a woman who wouldn't even look at him. She was still smitten with David de Lohr and nothing Brickley could do or say would bring her around. Even Lyle spoke to her about being so deliberately rude to Brickley, but it was to no avail. She still wanted nothing to do with him. The harder Brickley had tried to entice her, the more resistant she was. It had been a difficult task.

And then the missives began coming.

The task to attract Emilie became more difficult then. Brickley was in command of the soldiers and that included the sentries and those who manned the ancient gatehouse. It was a rather large gatehouse with two guard rooms built into the lower level. One of the rooms used to be for Brickley's personal use, but the room didn't drain well and in big rains the entire dirt floor became flooded. So Brickley turned it over to the soldiers and took another room on the second floor of the gatehouse, a room where he spent a good deal of his time. It was also a room where no one saw him burn the missives that had been coming to Emilie from David de Lohr.

There had been at least one a month because he had burned four to date. A messenger would come from London, wearing de Lohr colors and bearing the missive, and every time the messenger would ask to wait for reply, which Brickley always denied him. He would then take the missive meant for Emilie and go up to his room to read it. The first three had been generally sweet, speaking of daily events and inquiring about her health, while the fourth missives had politely wondered why she had not written him back. Brickley had burned that missive with particular glee. It was his hope that, eventually, David would just stop sending them and Emilie would think that the man had forgotten about her. That was his plan, anyway.

He didn't feel particularly guilty about it, in fact. He was doing what was necessary in his opinion. But the fact remained that Emilie wouldn't even acknowledge him, which was increasingly difficult for him to bear. Moreover, he was worried that if he went north with the troops, a de Lohr missive might slip through and make it to Emilie. He wouldn't there to intercept it. That perhaps the most predominant reason he didn't want to go north to fight John's army.

He had a battle of his own going on, one that he intended to win.

"Brick?" Lyle said. "Did you hear me?"

Brickley realized he had been daydreaming on thoughts of David de Lohr's missives as Lyle had expected an answer from him. "I did," he said. "Sorry. I was thinking of what the future might bring now with news of Richard's captivity."

It was a lie but Lyle believed him. "It means that you will take eight hundred men north to Nottingham," he said. "Mayhap you should stop and see your son on your way north. Isn't he fostering at Barnwell Castle?"

Brickley nodded. "He is," he replied. "I have not seen him in almost a year. Hux is nearly sixteen years of age now and the commander at Barnwell says that he already fights as well as any knight."

Lyle looked up from the vellum, grinning at the pride in Brickley's voice. His son, Huxley de Dere, had lived at Canterbury up until six years ago when his father sent him to Barnwell to foster. Huxley was a big lad, bright, with his father's big blue eyes. He had also been a cohort in crime with Nathalie and Elise, the one who had usually taken the blame for their tricks and pranks.

"I hope the lad has learned to speak up for himself these days," Lyle said. "Many was the time when Nathalie and Elise would wreak havoc and Hux would take the fall for them simply because he would not speak up."

Brickley grinned. "I hope he has learned to speak up for himself as well," he said. "I often chided him on the account, but he simply chose to take the blame rather than see the girls suffer. He is a truly chivalrous, I suppose."

Lyle shrugged. "You are more than likely correct," he said, looking back to the vellum. "In any case, you may visit your martyr son on the way north."

Brickley laughed softly but his humor quickly faded, once again reminded of the unsavory task ahead. He sighed, somewhat disgruntled. He hoped Lyle hadn't heard him.

"When do we leave?" he asked.

Lyle moved away from the hearth, to the big oak table that held things like map rolls, quills, a stack of vellum, and other things used to administer his lands and household. He set the vellum down on the tabletop.

"The Marshal asks for such things right away," he said. "I suppose you will leave as soon as you can assemble eight hundred men. But I do not want to be left wanting while you are away, Brick. If you take eight hundred men, that only leaves four hundred with me. Go out through my lands and see if you can find one hundred more farm boys or other men who would be willing to swear fealty to me on the field of battle in exchange for food and clothing. There should be at least a few we can convince. I would have the new men reinforce the existing troops."

Brickley nodded. "That will take me at least a week."

"Then get on with it."

Brickley was prepared to head out of the solar when something stopped him. Actually, it wasn't a random thought; it was the same thought he'd been having for nearly the past year, but now that he was to be sent off to war, thoughts of Emilie were heavy in his mind even as he knew he had duties to attend to.

He didn't want to leave the room without speaking on something that had become so important to him, something that would even cause him to behave in ways that weren't normally his character. Burning de Lohr's missives was one of those behaviors. Now that war was on the horizon, he couldn't leave without pressing his suit.

When he returned, he wanted it to be to Emilie.

"My lord," he said, pausing by the door. "May... may I speak with you about a personal matter before I go?"

Lyle didn't even have to be told what it was. He already knew. He'd been watching Brickley for the past few months now, ever since they had departed London, trying to warm Emilie to him, and he had further seen when Emilie had flatly ignored him. Unless her life depended on it, or unless she had no other choice, she would not speak with or acknowledge Brickley.

Aye, Lyle knew what Brickley was going to say before he even said it and he braced himself. It wasn't as if he could avoid this conversation. Lyle was sure the Marshal's missive had something to do with Brickley's willingness to once again speak on the subject of Emilie.

In Lyle's view, however, it was like beating a dead horse.

But so be it.

"What is it?" he asked, wondering if the dread he was feeling reflected in his tone.

Brickley quietly closed the door to the solar. When he looked at Lyle, it was with hesitation. Finally, he simply lowered his gaze and shook his head.

"It is about Emilie, my lord," he said. "I am sure you have de-duced that. I... I would like to ask if you have made any decision regarding my offer of marriage for her. If you recall, I made the offer last summer and with my leaving for war as it is now, there is a chance... that is to say, I would like to know I have something worthy to return home to. It will help me in my darkest hours of battle knowing that I will return to Emilie when I come home."

Lyle felt a good deal of pity for Brickley. He really did. The man simply didn't have a clue that none of this was going to come about. Still, he kept hoping beyond hope. Lyle sighed heavily, thoughtfully, as he sat down in the chair next to his table. He scratched his head before answering.

"Brick," he said, "you know I am fond of you. Quite fond. You and I have seen a good deal of life and death together, have we not?"

Brickley nodded. "I consider you my family, my lord," he said. "Other than Hux, I have no family."

Lyle averted his gaze. "I know," he said. "We are all fond of you and we consider you part of the family, too. But I must be honest when I tell you that David de Lohr has made an offer for Emilie as well."

Brickley's features tightened. "I assumed as much," he said. "I did not ask you because it is frankly none of my affair."

Lyle shrugged. "In a way, it is," he said. "I cannot help but notice how Emilie has ignored you since we left London. She will not speak with you and she will not talk to you. I am assuming you have noticed the same thing."

Brickley cleared his throat softly and lowered his gaze. "I have," he said. "But I am not discouraged. I am certain I can warm her to me, eventually."

Lyle sat back in his chair, studying the man. "Are you?" he asked. "Because I am not so certain. She has an aversion to you right now and I cannot, in good conscience, agree to your marriage proposal when your relationship with her is so sour. That would make her miserable, and you miserable, and me miserable. She would hate us both. Do you understand that, Brick?"

Brickley's jaw ticked furiously. "So you intend to betroth her to de Lohr?"

Lyle shook his head. "I did not say that," he said. "All I know is that I will make no decision now, and I certainly will not grant you permission to court her, given how she feels about you. It would only make matters worse. You will go and do what needs to be done against the prince and then we will revisit the matter when you return. But I cannot promise you more than that."

Brickley was grossly unhappy. "What if I do not return, my lord."

Lyle looked at him, his eyebrows lifting. "So you think that I would betroth you to her now and make her a widow?" he asked. "That is selfish, Brick. Terribly selfish."

Brickley knew it was but he didn't care. "I would be a good husband, my lord," he pleaded. "You have said that I am family – I would truly like to *become* family. Please do not deny me."

Lyle put up his hands to ease the man, who was close to begging. "Brick, I must do what I feel is right," he said. "This is no reflection against you or favoritism towards David. I love my daughter and want her to be happy, and right now, she would not be happy with you. Would you agree with that statement?"

Brickley persisted. "But if I *could* make her happy?"

Lyle shook his head. "You will not pester her," he said. "That will only make matters worse. The more you push her, lad, the more you will push her away. Mayhap a separation would be a good thing right now. Mayhap it will ease her stance against you, putting distance between the two of you. I fear that it may be the only solution right now."

Brickley was in denial. He didn't want a separation from Emilie and he was trying not to bully Lyle about it. As he and Lyle continued to discuss his suit of Emilie, the very object of their conversation was outside in the bailey, walking the dogs beneath the crystal blue spring sky.

OF COURSE, EMILIE had no idea that Brickley and her father were discussing her. Even if she had known, she wouldn't have cared. There was nothing about Brickley that interested her these days. The man could be a ghost for all she cared. The only man she was interested in was evidently not so interested in her and she was genuinely crushed by the thought.

He had promised. That was all Emilie could think of, what kept her rising every morning with hope in her heart – that David had promised to contact her, to either visit her or send missives, so four months with no contact whatsoever had her nerves on edge.

She knew he wouldn't lie to her so she began to fear that perhaps something had happened to her, something terrible. Had he become sick or injured in the past four months? She knew he was to remain in London, so it was possible that something had happened in London with Dennis le Londe or the Sheriff of Nottingham, men that had been trying to kill him since nearly the day she met him?

Fear filled her heart at that thought.

But she didn't voice her fear. There seemed to be an increasing divide between her and her sisters as of late and she didn't feel comfortable confiding anything to them, especially to Nathalie. Ever since the prince's mask in London, Nathalie had been quite withdrawn from her and had even reverted back to the nasty tricks she used to play with Elise. The two of them terrorized the soldiers, and Brickley in particular, and Emilie had been increasingly withdrawn from them, isolating herself from everyone but her father and Lillibet. But even Lillibet was distanced at times because she spent so much time with Nathalie and Elise. Either they were all pulling away from Emilie or Emilie was pulling away from them. She couldn't quite decide which was actually happening.

But one thing she did know was that Brickley's attention towards her had gotten more intense. She wanted nothing to do with the man and had made the repeatedly clear... *repeatedly*. But Brickley didn't let that stop him; he was at her door in the morning to escort her on a walk that she always refused. It got to the point where she was afraid to open her chamber door any longer, afraid that Brickley would be standing there. She didn't want to see him. Finally, about a month ago, Emilie asked her father to speak with Brickley so that the man wasn't so cloying, and it seemed to have helped, but Brickley hadn't stayed away from her entirely.

She wished he would go away and leave her alone.

On this spring day in early May, Brickley was, fortunately, nowhere to be found and Emilie was enjoying a walk in the bailey with Cid and Roland. The big dogs knew the soldiers at Canterbury, so they would run around chasing feathers, or anything else that happened to be blowing on the ground. Then they would run up to the soldiers who happened to be near them and jump on them. Men would push the dogs away, or they would pet them, and Cid and Roland would move on to the next men they saw. They were, in truth, good-natured dogs and were well-liked around the castle.

They found curiosity in everything. Emilie was trailing behind them as they neared the gatehouse, watching them sniff the ground determinedly and occasionally lift a leg to piss. Sometimes they even lifted a leg on unsuspecting soldiers. Emilie's thoughts were on the weather when they weren't on David, and even now she was looking up into the sky, thinking that the weather was pleasant enough to go for a ride on her swift mare. She had mentioned the horse to David, a little mare who was faster than any other horse in their stables. Emilie grinned when she imagined that the mare could even beat David's big rouncey. She hoped the little mare would have the chance someday.

As she was nearing the old gatehouse, a structure with Roman origins, she heard the sentries above as they called out the approach of a rider. Emilie didn't think anything of it but she did want to capture the dogs before the portcullis lifted and they were giving the opportunity to escape to wide open spaces.

She picked up the pace and ran after Cid, catching him first, and turned him over to the nearest soldier. Then, she went on the hunt for Roland, who had entered the gatehouse and was sniffing furiously nearly the iron-fanged portcullis. She quickly moved to the dog, grasping him by the collar, but as she did so, she happened to glance up and see the approaching rider.

The sun was glaring a bit but she could see him for the most part. As he drew closer, the man had her interest because he was wearing a tunic that had been ingrained into her memory.

De Lohr blue.

Dear God, is it really possible? Finally, after all of this time!

Heart in her throat, Emilie clutched Roland by the collar as the portcullis lifted and the rider drew near. Without thinking, she found herself walking outside of the gatehouse, passing beneath the portcullis, and making her way to the rider. It was if her feet had a mind of their own because surely she couldn't stop them. She didn't want to stop them. Four months without any word from David and now a de Lohr rider was on her doorstep.

She was ready to eat the man alive.

"You, there!" she called. "You are bearing de Lohr colors!"

The rider pulled his frothing, sweaty horse to a halt. "Aye, my lady," he said. "I have come bearing a missive for Lady Emilie Hampton."

Emilie was so excited that she let go of the dog. "I am Lady Emilie," she said, rushing the rider as Hampton soldiers came out of the gatehouse, following her. "Is the missive from Sir David?"

The rider nodded. "Aye, my lady," he said. "I have been asked to wait for a reply."

Emilie was beside herself with glee as Roland ran off in to the meadow to the east, followed by two soldiers who were whistling and trying to coerce the dog into coming back with them. She didn't even pay attention to the dog, for her thoughts were only of the missive the rider bore.

"Of course I will reply," she said, breathless, as she took the missive from the man. It was neatly folded and sealed with a wax stamp with wax the color of a sapphire. "Is David still in London?"

"Aye, my lady."

With shaking fingers, she broke the beautiful de Lohr seal. She was so excited she could hardly stand it. "He must have been quite busy if this is the first missive he has sent," she said. "What is happening in London these days? Have things been very busy?"

The messenger cocked his head curiously. "This is not his first missive, my lady," he said. "I have brought four others before this one."

Shocked, Emilie looked at him. The vellum was open in her hand but she wasn't looking at the words. All she was focused on was the messenger's stunning revelation.

"*Four* messages?" she repeated. "And you brought them here, to Canterbury?"

"Aye, my lady."

"Are… are you certain?"

"Aye, my lady."

"But I have not seen any of them!"

The messenger looked around at the soldiers, who were both standing in the gatehouse and wandering out onto the road. He even turned to look at the two soldiers who were chasing the frolicking dog in the distance.

"I gave them to a knight, my lady," he said. "And older man, big. But I do not see him here. I have been instructed by Sir David to wait for a reply with each message I deliver but the man told me you were indisposed and not inclined to provide an immediate answer."

Emilie stared at him. It began to occur to her who the messenger was speaking of and the excitement in her chest turned to something else, something dark and furious as the devil. *Four missives she had not received.* Any hint of happiness that she might have had in her expression vanished.

"A big knight?" she repeated, just to be clear. "He has big blue eyes that droop slightly?"

"I believe so, my lady."

"Did he give a name?"

"If he did, I do not recall it, my lady."

"And you said that you have delivered four missives here prior to this one?"

"Aye, my lady."

"And he took every one of them?"

"Aye, my lady."

Emilie's blood was beginning to boil. She was starting to realize that David had indeed been delivering missives to her, missives that she had never received. The only person at Canterbury who would have kept them from her was, in fact, Brickley.

Brickley!

Struggling to keep her temper under control, she motioned for the messenger to follow her. "Come with me," she said. "You will rest and eat, and I shall provide you with a returned missive."

"Thank you, my lady."

Emilie began to walk, passing into the gatehouse. The first thing she did was find the sergeant on duty, the man who was usually in charge of the gatehouse on any given day. He had been with the House of Hampton for years. She addressed the sergeant, pointing to the messenger as she spoke.

"Have you seen this man before?" she asked.

The sergeant was a tall, thin man with wild red hair. He nodded. "I have, my lady."

Emilie's jaw tightened. "He says that he has been here before," she said. "He has been here four times and every time he has delivered a missive. Do you recall Brick taking the missive from him?"

The sergeant, who truly had no idea what was brewing, or that Brickley had done anything wrong, nodded. "I do, my lady."

Emilie sighed heavily, something that sounded suspiciously like a growl. Turning away, she continued into the ward beyond. Behind her Roland had been corralled and was being brought back to the castle, and the de Lohr rider was being shown a place where he could rest. Everything was happening as it should, casual, conducting usual business on a usual day. But to Emilie, everything was far from usual. There was about to be a battle and it was one she fully intended to win.

Brickley was about to pay for his lies.

Aye, they were lies. Withholding information meant for her, missives that he knew she had been waiting for, meant he had been lying to her. It was deceit. She could only imagine that the man sought to erase David from her heart and mind, but it was not going to work. David was embedded into her more firmly than Brickley could ever comprehend. With the vellum still in hand, a message she had not even read yet, she marched into the keep.

It was cool and dark in the keep, smelling of moist earth, a scent that wafted up from the store room below the entry level. Lyle's solar was immediately to the right of the entry and Emilie went to it, knocking on the door. She heard her father's voice, telling her to enter, and she did.

But Lyle was not alone. The very man who had been foremost in her thoughts for the past few minutes was there, too, his eyes seeking her out and that sickening expression of hopefulness on his features. The sight of Brickley was enough to throw more fuel on Emilie's rage. Without looking at her father, she spoke directly to the knight.

"Brickley," she said. "I have just discovered that David de Lohr has sent four missives to me, four missives that I never received. The gatehouse sergeant confirmed that you received them. Since you are the only person in Canterbury who would not want me to read such things, I can only assume that kept them. Where are they? You will give them to me immediately."

The expression of hope vanished from Brickley's face and his brow furrowed. Shocked, his first reaction was one of denial. "Missives?" he said. "We... we receive many messengers, my lady."

Infuriated, Emilie shouted in reply. "Damnation, Brickley de Dere!" she said, throwing a finger in the direction of the gatehouse. "The de Lohr messenger is here. He has brought me what he has told me is the fifth missive from David. You are the only one who would keep such information from me, so I am ordering you now to give me my messages. They are mine and I want them. How dare you keep them from me!"

By this time, Lyle was coming around the side of his table, an expression of shock on his face. He looked at Brickley. "Brick?" he said. "Is this true? Did Emilie receive missives from David de Lohr?"

Brickley was caught; he knew he was caught. He was willing to dance all the way around Emilie's query without providing her with an answer but he couldn't lie to Lyle. Their relationship was built solely on trust, and if he lied to the man, he would be ruining years of service. Heart sinking, he was coming to feel sickened. Sickened that Emilie had discovered the truth. He wasn't sorry he'd done it but he was sorry they'd discovered what he'd done. Therefore, he did the only thing he could do – he looked Lyle in the eye and nodded his head.

"Aye, my lord," he said quietly.

He said no more than that and Lyle lifted his eyebrows as Emilie growled in frustration. Lyle held out a hand to his daughter, stilling her, as he focused on his knight. The situation was serious, indeed.

"She received missives from de Lohr but you never gave them to her?" Lyle asked.

Brickley shook his head, briefly. "I did not, my lord."

"But why?"

Brickley's jaw flexed but he continued to look Lyle in the eye. "Because I did not want her to have them, my lord."

Emilie shrieked, clearly overwhelmed with fury. "It is not your choice to make!" she cried. "How dare you do this, Brickley! I cannot believe you would do such a terrible and despicable thing!"

Lyle was still holding out a hand to Emilie, struggling to keep her moderately quiet as he dealt with the situation. "Emilie, please," he begged. His focus returned to Brickley. "Brick, I must say that I am having a difficult time believing this. You have never been the deceitful kind. Where are these missives that you have kept from Emilie?"

Brickley sighed heavily; this time, he hung his head, no longer able to look Lyle in the face. "I burned them," he said quietly. "I burned them because... because I wanted her to think that de Lohr had lied to her, that he had forgotten about her. My lord, you know how I feel about Emilie. You know that I want to marry her. Therefore, I did not want her to have de Lohr's messages."

Emilie was so angry that she was red in the face. "Listen to me and listen well, de Dere," she snarled. "I do not care how you feel about me. You have always been my friend through the years but now… now I cannot even stand the sight of you. What you have done to try and manipulate me is beyond contempt. It is vile and low. I do not want to marry you and I never shall. Even if there was no David de Lohr, there would be no chance for you. I will never trust you again and I will hate you until I die!"

Her fury was so great that tears came to her eyes and after the last few words, a sob sprang to her lips. In a fit, she ran from the room, leaving her father and Brickley in awkward silence.

When she was gone, Brickley simply stood there, looking at his feet. He refused to believe that Emilie meant any of that but something told him that he'd just ruined everything he'd tried to accomplish. If she really did hate him forever, it was his own fault. More than that, he had behaved in a way that had shamed Lyle, his liege. Having never met his father, Brickley had always looked to Lyle as a father-figure. He was trying very hard not to feel ashamed of his actions. He cleared his throat softly.

"A man said once that all is fair in love and war," he said to Lyle. "David de Lohr already has an advantage over me. I sought to take away that advantage and I would do it again given the chance. I will apologize if that is shameful to you, my lord, but it is the way I feel."

Lyle didn't know what to say. He was still a bit shocked at what had happened and he was starting not to like this entire situation. Brickley's attraction to Emilie was causing him to do strange things. After a moment, he shook his head and turned away, heading back to his table.

"Go now and find more recruits to remain here at Canterbury when you take the bulk of the army north," he said. When Brickley started to move, he stopped the man. "And, Brick… stay away from Emilie. That is a command. Leave her alone and stay clear of her. If she tells me you have done otherwise, I will release you from my service and send you away. Is this clear?"

Brickley was standing by the door. "It is, my lord."

"Then go about your duties."

With a heavy heart, Brickley did.

UPON LEAVING HER FATHER'S solar, Emilie had run up to her chamber with David's missive still in her hand. She had a table in her chamber where she would often sit and draw, and sheets of used vellum and paints and ink. She fully intended to write an immediate reply to David and send the de Lohr messenger back to him this very day.

She wiped any remaining tears from her eyes as she reached her chamber on the third and top level of Canterbury's red stoned keep. She wasn't going to weep anymore over the burned missives; she would make sure to focus on the one she had actually received and reply to David in kind. It was what she had been praying for, communication from the man. Finally, she had it.

Entering the chamber, she immediately bumped into the end of her bed. The chamber was rather small, and cramped, because the entire structure of Canterbury had Roman origins, including the keep, which meant chambers were small but efficiently arranged, and instead of windows in the chambers, there were long, rectangular openings at the top of the room meant to let in air and light whilst keeping the elements out.

That meant that on bright days, the chambers were well lit and the cross-ventilation between the rooms helped keep the temperature very pleasant. But Emilie wasn't paying attention to any of that; she was focused on the table that held her vellum and inks. Now that the shock of Brickley's behavior had worn thin, she was thinking of David's missive and was most eager to read it. She hoped it wasn't a missive telling her that he'd grown tired of being ignored.

So she plopped down on the wooden stool beside her table and eagerly read the contents of the missive. David was very polite, speaking of the fact that he had left London and his brother's army had seen a few skirmishes against John's mercenary army in the north, but he spoke of war, his health, and little else. He concluded the missive by stating he hoped she would find time to respond to him this time, which she most certainly would. She read the missive four times before setting it aside, collecting a piece of vellum that she hadn't painted on, and picked up her quill. Dipping it in the ink, she began to very carefully write.

The first sentence she composed was an apology for not replying to his earlier missives. She debated about what to tell him, perhaps something to gloss over and not really explain why she hadn't, but she didn't want David to think she hadn't replied to him because she hadn't been interested. That was the furthest thing from the truth. Therefore, she decided to briefly explain that Brickley had never given the missives to her, and had subsequently burned them, so she had never even seen them. She asked for David's forgiveness in the matter of not even knowing he had sent them. And with that, she went on to tell him everything that had happened in the months they had been separated.

It was a rather fulfilling experience writing to David. It was almost as if she was speaking to him, telling him of things that had happened, telling her of the jokes her sisters had played since they'd been home. The pranks were rather humorous, providing that they weren't being played against her, so she hoped he would laugh at them. She wished she could be there to tell him in person. She had missed him every day of their separation and she wanted to tell him that, but she thought it might sound too foolish and gushing, considering he had not said anything of the same measure in his missive. So she ended her message by telling him that she hoped he was well and she hoped she would see him again very soon. She was just signing her name when Nathalie happened to wander in from an adjoining door.

Emilie glanced up when her sister entered, eyeing the girl as she moved to her bed. Emilie and Nathalie shared a chamber, whilst Elise and Lillibet shared another. Emilie went back to her missive, sanding it as Nathalie opened a big square oak trunk against the wall that held her possessions and began rummaging through it.

"Em, have you seen my sewing kit?" she asked. "I cannot seem to find it."

Emilie shook the sand off of the vellum, blowing on it for good measure. "Nay, I have not," she said. "But mine is in the wardrobe. You may use it if you need to."

Nathalie finished searching the corners of her disorganized trunk, shut the lid, and stood up. She glanced at her sister and noticed what she was doing. "What are you writing?" she asked.

Emilie held the missive up before her, reading through it once more to make sure it was perfect. "I am answering David," she said, rather dreamily. "He sent me a missive."

Nathalie looked moderately interested. Considering the joke she and Elise had played on David the last time she had seen him, she was rather surprised to discover the knight had written her sister. She had rather hoped she had chased the man away completely. Now, she wondered if his missive said anything about the nasty prank that had been played on him back at Lady Orford's home.

"Oh?" she asked, innocent. "What did he say?"

Emilie shook the last of the sand from the vellum. "That he has been at war these past few months," she said. "There are wars in the north now, according to him. The Prince is trying to take the country from his brother and David is fighting him."

Nathalie wandered near the table, peering at the missive from David. "The de Lohrs fight a lot," she said. "Haven't they just returned from fighting with Richard in the Holy Land?"

Emilie nodded. "Indeed they have."

"So they are back to fighting again?"

Again, Emilie nodded. "For Richard's cause," she said. "They support the king."

"So do we."

Emilie lifted her eyebrows at her sister for emphasis. "I know, but they de Lohrs actually show their support," she said. "They do not sit at home and let others do the fighting for them, like we have done."

Nathalie lowered herself onto another stool, watching her sister carefully fold the missive. "Why did Papa not send his army to the Holy Land?" she asked before making a statement to her own question. "But... but I am glad he did not. Something might have happened to Brick had he been forced to fight the savages. Maybe he would not return home to Canterbury at all."

Emilie tensed at the mention of Brickley's name. "I do not care," she said flatly. "I wish he had gone and stayed there."

Nathalie frowned. "Why do you say that?" she demanded. "That is a mean thing to say!"

Emilie's focus flew to her sister. "Mean?" she repeated, outraged. "Do you want to hear what your sweet and wonderful Brickley did? I will tell you and then you may not think so kindly of him. David has sent me four missives – this missive that you see is the fifth. But I would not have known about any of them if it were up to Brickley; he took the first four missives and burned them. He did not even tell me that I had received them. He did not want me to know!"

Nathalie was shocked. It was true that she had been an enemy of Brickley ever since the John's mask those months ago, but the truth was that she still secretly yearned for him. He still had her heart. Now, hearing of this terrible thing from her sister, she was shocked and appalled. But she also refused to believe it.

"Why should he not want you to know?" she asked. "He has no reason to keep the missives from you. How can you blame him?"

Emilie was angry enough so that she wasn't considerate of her sister's feelings when it came to Brickley. Considering the pranks that Nathalie had played on the man as of late, she naturally assumed her sister had no feelings for the man.

She was wrong.

"Because he admitted it," she said angrily as she finished folding

David's missive. "He told Papa and I that he had intercepted messages from David and burned them. He is a terrible man and I hope I never see him again!"

Nathalie was becoming more and more appalled by what she was hearing. "But why should he do it?"

Emilie picked up the wax stick and held it over the flame of taper to soften the wax so she could seal the missive. "Because he does not want any competition for my hand," she said. "Brickley wants to marry he. He has told Papa that. So he is trying to keep David away from me, but I discovered his wicked plan. Thank God I discovered it. Brickley is terrible and evil, and I hate him. I will hate him for always!"

Nathalie sat there with her eyes wide and her mouth hanging open at what she was hearing. Her heart, a confused and fragile thing, had just been smashed into a thousand little pieces.

"He… he wants to marry you?" she asked in disbelief.

Emilie nodded firmly. "As if I would ever let him!"

Nathalie closed her mouth, staring at her sister as she digested the situation. She had known that David had been interested in her sister and, as of late, she had known that Brickley seemed to be paying a good deal of attention to Emilie as well, but marriage… he wanted to *marry* her? That had never entered her mind. It simply wasn't true! Nathalie went from stunned to wildly jealous all in one breath.

"It is not true!" she gasped.

Emilie didn't catch the inflection of resentment in her sister's tone. "I am afraid it is."

Nathalie was beside herself. "I… I think you are mean and hateful and terrible!" she raged, jumping off the stool and knocking it over. "I cannot believe Brick would want to marry you! Why would he? You are nothing special, Emilie. You are not special at all!"

Emilie's head came up, astonished at her sister's rage, and it was in that instant that she realized she may have said too much. In that moment, she could see that months of her sister's pranks against Brickley were all for show. The old feelings were still there. Concerned, she put the wax stick aside.

"Nathalie?" she said, going after her sister, who was rushing across the room and throwing herself onto her bed. "Nathalie, wait... I did not mean... do you still have feelings for him? But I did not know! I thought that was long over with!"

Nathalie's face was pressed into her pillows, angry tears coming from her eyes. "Leave me alone!"

Emilie felt terrible. She didn't know what more to say or do. All she knew was that she had hurt her sister deeply, something she'd never meant to do. Gently, she put a hand on her sister's shoulder.

"Nathalie, truly," she said softly and sincerely. "I did not know you still had feelings for Brick. I would have never... I would not have said such things had I known. I am sorry, sweetheart. I did not know."

Nathalie wouldn't speak to her sister; she lay there with her face in the pillow and wept. Filled with sorrow, Emilie simply sat there with her hand on her sister's shoulder. *Mayhap that is why she has been so distant from me as of late,* she thought. *She was masking her feelings for Brickley, trying to pretend she no longer felt anything for him.* As Nathalie lay there and wept, Emilie felt progressively worse. She could only imagine how she would feel if David didn't return her feelings or, worse, had feelings for someone else.

Saddened, Emilie sat with her sister until the young woman's tears quieted. It was odd, but she felt closer to Nathalie now than she had for months. Both of them drawn together over Brickley. As Emilie sat there, she began to wonder if she couldn't put in a good word with Brickley on Nathalie's behalf. She had vowed to hate him, and never speak to him again, but she would break that vow if only to help Nathalie. Perhaps Brickley needed help in focusing his attention elsewhere.

For her sister, she was willing to speak with a man she very much hated.

She was willing to do what she could.

CHAPTER SIXTEEN

One week later

BRICKLEY WAS BENT over the leg of his rouncey, a big leggy horse, who still had a good deal of his winter coat on him. The grooms at Canterbury had tried to shed the animal of it but he still looked shaggy in patches, like he was losing the hair some place and not others. He looked like he had a disease, patchy and rough as he was.

Out in the stable yard on a blustery day, Brickley was trying to figure out why the horse seemed to be walking gingerly. He thought that he might have a split in his hoof but he couldn't seem to find it. The stable master couldn't find it, either, so now Brickley stood on a patch of dry ground trying to make sure his horse was sound enough for the trip ahead. They had hundreds of miles to travel and he didn't want to do it with a horse who would go lame on him.

It had been a quiet few days at Canterbury since Emilie had discovered what he had done with de Lohr's missives. As Lyle had requested, Brickley had stayed clear of Emilie. He'd gone about his duties, going into the countryside and into the nearby towns to recruit men for Lyle's forces, and he'd been fortunate enough to come away with one hundred and thirteen men between the ages of fourteen and forty.

There had been one young man, living with an elderly farming couple near the edge of a village, that Lyle had asked him to recruit because he knew the parents. He'd even recruited one man and his three sons who had just lost their mother, men who had been looking for a purpose in life. They had come with him willingly. It was those men and the rest, who were on the eastern side of Canterbury, in a section of bailey that was fairly spacious. They were encamped there, learning the rules of the Canterbury army from the seasoned sergeants.

Brickley had been schooling the men for days but he had broken away to see to his own personal needs before they departed, one of which was the horse he was currently inspecting. As he continued to study the hoof, he heard a soft voice come from behind.

"Brickley?"

The sound startled him, mostly because he knew the voice. His heart began to race. He dropped the hoof and turned around to see Emilie standing in the stable entry. She was dressed in a simple gown of soft woolen fabric, yellow in color, and her blond hair was braided and draped over one shoulder. She looked beautiful. He couldn't stop staring. But he knew he should answer her.

"My lady?" he said politely.

Emilie just stood there, looking at him. Her features were fairly unemotional, at least for her. The last time he had seen her, she had been shouting at him, so he supposed the emotionless expression was better than the alternative.

"We must speak," Emilie said.

Brickley brushed off his hands, trying not to feel too much hope at her words. "I am your servant, my lady," he said. "What did you wish to speak on?"

Emilie clasped her hands in front of her; she hadn't moved from the entry and her manner was very formal. "I just wanted you to know that I have been doing a good deal of thinking since I discovered you burned David's missives," she said, "but I had to wait until I had calmed sufficiently before speaking to you about it."

Brickley tried not to appear too wary about the subject matter at hand; he was coming to wonder if she was going to start screaming at him again. "How may I be of service, my lady?"

Emilie thought a moment. "I wanted to ask you if you had read them before you burned them."

He nodded without hesitation. "I did, my lady."

"What did they say?"

She really didn't react to the fact that he'd read her private missive, which he found somewhat surprising. He'd expected the screaming to start right about then. But there was no screaming and her question had been civil. He answered.

"He spoke of your beauty, which is understandable," he said. "He spoke of being in London. He mentioned that his brother's wife had lost the child she was carrying. He said that he would look forward to your replies."

Emilie digested the information. Hearing what David had written about really wasn't why she had come but she had been curious and thought to ask him. Now, they would come to the real reason behind her appearance.

"I see," she said. Then, she paused. "You know that you are very wrong to have done what you did."

Brickley shrugged, a faint gesture. "I suppose that depends on how you look at it, my lady."

"It is wrong any way you look at it."

He tilted his head thoughtfully. "Let us turn the situation around," he said. "If you were interested in de Lohr but he kept sending messages to Nathalie, messages of romance, how would you feel? If you had the chance to keep those messages from her, would you?"

Emilie frowned. "I would not hurt my sister," she pointed out. "In fact, that is why I am here. If you wish for me to forgive you for what you did to my missives, then you will do something for me."

Brickley was interested in her forgiveness more than he was in what he had to do to obtain it. "Anything, my lady."

Emilie lifted an eyebrow. "Anything?"

"That is what I said, my lady."

Emilie considered what she might say next. "Nathalie has feelings for you," she finally said. "She has for quite some time now. I want you to make my sister happy any way you can. That is the only way I will forgive you, Brickley de Dere. That will mean you are seriously remorseful for the horrible thing you did to me. Will you do this?"

Brickley frowned. "Make your sister happy?" he repeated. "How am I to do that?"

Emilie shrugged. "Speak to her," she said. "She is very fond of you. Say kind things to her and make her smile. Show her that you are interested in her."

Brickley's frown turned into an expression of disbelief. "My lady, you know I am always willing to do as you ask, but in this case, surely you do not realize what you are asking," he said. "You know that Lady Nathalie and Lady Elise have had a campaign of terror against me ever since we returned to Canterbury. I have had dog shite in my boots, and the ropes on the bottom of my bed cut so that the bed collapsed when I laid down, and any number of small things that have been outrageous at best. I have no recourse against them because your father forbids it. And now you expect me to say kind things to your sister and make her smile?"

Emilie looked at him knowingly. "Why do you think she has been doing those things?" she asked. "It is because you have broken her heart. If you are kind to her, she will stop."

Brickley sighed heavily and turned back for the horse. He was quickly growing disinterested in the conversation.

"My lady, I should like for you and I to be on speaking terms again," he said. "I miss being able to even speak casually with you. I do not like having to spend my days avoiding you because your father has ordered me to. But if the only way to gain your forgiveness is to whisper sweet words in Lady Nathalie's ear, then I tell you now that I will not do it. I am sorry, but I cannot. I am old enough to be her father and I will not show romantic inclinations towards a sixteen-year-old girl."

Emilie regarded him. "But you want to show romantic inclinations to me, and I am only two years older than Nathalie is."

Brickley lifted up the horse's hoof, not looking at her as he spoke. "You are different," he said. "You have always been graceful and mature. Lady Nathalie is not."

Emilie watched the man pick at his horse's hoof. "Then you will not even try?"

Brickley shook his head. "As much as I would like your forgiveness, I cannot do as you ask, my lady," he said. "I am sorry that we find ourselves in this position. Even if you go through your entire life hating me, please know that I am sorry for that. I am sorry for everything."

He sounded quite sincere in his apology and Emilie, who had been stiff and formal with him in manner since the start of the conversation, could feel herself relenting just a bit. Although she still wasn't sure if she could ever forgive him for being so deceitful, she supposed that in some small way, she understood his point of view. He had been doing what he needed to do in order to keep de Lohr away because he felt so strongly for her.

Emilie understood well what it was like to feel strongly for someone. But she still wasn't sure she could forgive him for his actions and she felt rather badly about it, badly that their relationship had soured so. She thought about him going off to war now and it was possible he would not return. Would she feel guilty for having not forgiven him if he was killed in battle? She wondered. She watched him pick at his horse's hoof for a few moments, pondering what the future might bring.

"My father says the army is leaving tomorrow," she said. "Where are you going?"

"North," Brickley said. "We received a missive two days ago that said armies were gathering around Tickhill Castle, which is north of

Nottingham Castle, our original destination. Tickhill is an important stronghold and one that William Marshal evidently wants to purge, so that is where we shall go."

Emilie relaxed her stiff stance, leaning against the doorjamb of the entry. "David's last missive said that he had been fighting most of the spring," she said. "Has there been a lot of fighting going on since we left London, then?"

Brickley nodded and dropped the hoof, feeling up the horse's leg to feel for anything out of the ordinary. "Aye," he replied. "It seems that John intends to take this country by force and your father is joining forces with the rest of Richard's allies to stop it."

She was silent a moment. "That means the House of de Lohr."

He glanced at her. "Aye," he said. "They have been in the thick of it."

"At some point, you are going to see David."

"That is very likely, my lady."

Emilie came away from the door, moving towards him. "Brickley, I know you have made it your personal mission to separate me from David, but I will tell you now, as we were once friends, that you must stop this behavior," she said. "David knows you intercepted the missives he sent that were meant for me. It is quite possible he will seek you out to punish you. If he does, remember this – there is no hope for anything between you and I, ever, and even if David is somehow no longer part of my life, there is still no hope for anything between you and me. Challenging David or trying to kill him will not change that. Am I clear on this point?"

Brickley's movements as he stroked the horse slowed. "You are."

Emilie wondered if that was really the truth. "I do not want to hear any stories of you and David fighting one another because of me. I am not only telling you this, I am begging you as well. Please, Brick. No more."

Brickley simply stood there for a moment before faintly nodding his head. It was enough for Emilie. She turned and left the stable, leaving the man standing there with his horse, fighting off the feeling of devastation their conversation has brought down upon him.

More and more, he was coming to see that, perhaps, there really was no hope for anything between them. It was something he would have to reconcile himself to. But he foolish also hoped that separation might cause Emilie to see things differently. Maybe upon his return, the situation will have changed. It was something to hope for.

He would cling to that hope.

CHRISTOPHER AND HIS *mighty army were not in time to save Tickhill Castle from being consumed by John and his forces. Led by Sir Dennis and his band of mercenary generals, they were a surprisingly strong and disciplined army, and the crown troops laid siege to Tickhill for nearly two weeks before retreating. John was anchored in deeply at Tickhill and Christopher reluctantly decided to pull back to a safe distance to anticipate John's next move. Tickhill was lost for the moment and it was difficult for him to admit it.*

As Christopher knew, the army was not to stay at Tickhill. After establishing jail-like security in and around the fortress, the army banded together once again and moved northwest toward York. Christopher found himself chasing after the army as a mother after an unruly child. The mercenary army would attack every fortress in their path and the crown troops would be there to defend and repel, losing a few castles but saving more than they lost.

It was frustrating and exhausting work, for John was grimly determined to seize England castle by castle, hoping to shut off the north from the rest of the country and conquer it keep by keep.

Christopher knew the tactical planning to be Sir Dennis'. The man was a cunning soldier, if not a bit reckless. He had a huge army with voracious fighters that he used handily, moving from one castle to the next with incredible speed. Christopher had a devil of a time keeping up with them.

February moved into March, and March into April. His thirty-sixth birthday came and went on the battle field, the same day that Edward suffered a nearly mortal wound to the groin. The knight hovered one step above death for nearly a week before showing any improvement, and Christopher sent him back to Lioncross as soon as he was able to travel. Edward carried with him a special written message for Lady de Lohr from her husband, and Christopher had slept the night before with the message clutched to him, knowing it would soon be touching Dustin's own hands. He missed her more than words could express.

Spring came and went, moving into summer and Christopher found himself in East Anglia outside of Norwich. He had relatives here but did not stop to visit. The justices had been sending him regular communication regarding Richard's situation; a circumstance still unimproved. Richard was well, still being held captive, and the justices were in the process of raising the ransom demand. All they asked of Christopher was to control John as best he could. More and more of Richard's troops were coming home from the Holy Land every day and soon Christopher would have another army larger than the one presently under his command waiting at Windsor. With over four thousand men, he would surely destroy John and regain the seven keeps he had been unsuccessful in defending.

With the heated summer months, the battles seemed to wane and eventually there was a strained stand-off. John still held seven castles but he had made no more advances and the majority of his field army, including Sir Dennis, had retreated to Nottingham. The situation was at a stalemate, a state Christopher guessed would remain for a length of time while John rethought his strategy. At the beginning of August, he saw his opportunity to return to Lioncross for the first time in almost a year.

David saw it as an opportunity to go to Canterbury, albeit briefly. Brief or not, that was where he was headed.

CHAPTER SEVENTEEN

August Year of our Lord 1193
Canterbury

IT WASN'T THE HEAT but the moisture in the air, turning everything into a steam bath.

As David moved along the road out of Rochester, heading east, he was sweating rivers beneath his tunic and mail, and he was quite certain that the slightly-rotten smell in the air was coming from him. The Thames was to his north, bleeding its mixture of salt and fresh water scent in to the air because at this point, it was more sea than river. Sea gulls cried over his head, searching for food.

David was close to Canterbury. He knew this because he was starting to come across more traffic the more he traveled; people were heading into the town, or coming from it, and he passed the small castle of Denstroude off to the north, which he could see on a rise in the distance. Denstroude was a holding of Canterbury, an outpost of sorts between Canterbury and the sea, so he knew he was coming nearer to the town. Up and over the next rise, he could see it in the distance.

The sun was directly overhead as he spurred his fat white rouncey into a gentle canter, loping towards the town. He was hot as Hades beneath his clothing, wanting to strip out of what he was wearing and possibly even take a swim. He remembered that Emilie had mentioned something about a lake where they might go fishing. He was looking forward to that lake and spending time with her, even though their time together would be very brief.

There as a great deal happening in the politics of England these days. John was on the move and Christopher, as well as William Marshal and several others, were trying to stay one step ahead of him. Seasons full of skirmishes had been David's life for the past several months, months of fighting, of dealing with the politics that England had become, and of dreaming of a certain brown-eyed lady that he was becoming increasingly enamored with. In his case, it was very true that distance and separation had made the heart grow fonder.

His heart was fonder of her still.

For the first four months, he'd written to Emilie but had received nothing in return. It hadn't really concerned him until the fifth month, when he was coming to think that she had either decided not to ever write to him or that she was somehow being prevented from doing so. There was no way of knowing. But after he'd written the fifth missive to her, he decided that he would only write one more to her if he didn't receive a response. The sixth missive would be his last because he didn't want to make a nuisance of himself if he wasn't wanted. He was greatly disappointed at the thought, but there was no use crying over it.

Fortunately for him, Emilie wrote to him after his fifth missive. She had explained that Brickley had intercepted David's missives and went on to say many wonderful things, things that almost made him forget about the punishment he was going to deal Brickley de Dere when he saw the man again. But not quite; David was determined to punish Brickley in any way he could, any time or any place, and he wondered if he was about to see Brickley when he arrived at Canterbury. That being the case, he would be torn with what to do first – punch Brickley in the face or greet Lady Emilie. He figured she would frown upon him beating Brickley to a pulp before even acknowledging her, so he settled on greeting her first off. But if

Brickley was in his line of sight, he hoped the man had sense enough to run.

Canterbury was a very old town built atop of an ancient Roman town, and it had a spectacular cathedral that could be seen for miles. The castle was in the center of town, near the River Stour, and he made his way across the bridge towards the castle, passing by the inhabitants of the town as he headed towards the castle.

Canterbury Castle wasn't particularly large but it had an enormous curtain wall around it, protecting the four-storied keep, if one included the sub level, a hall, stables, and outbuildings. It also had a large gatehouse and David announced himself as he approached. Confused sentries, who evidently didn't recognize his name, made him wait outside of the gatehouse on the road, while seeking approval for him to enter. Fortunately, it wasn't long in coming.

Passing beneath the gatehouse, he emerged into a fairly large ward, noting the great all to his right and the big, square keep to the left. He couldn't see the entry to the keep so he assumed the stairs were on the opposite side. Slowly, he dismounted his weary animal, collecting his saddle bags as he turned the beast over to a pair of young stable boys who had come running to collect the animal. He grinned when his horse rubbed his foamy lips into the hair of one of the boys as they led him away. He could hear the child groan as the other one laughed.

"David!"

A shout caught his attention over near the keep and he turned to see Lyle briskly heading in his direction. He smiled, slinging his saddlebags over one broad shoulder.

"Greetings, my lord," he said.

Lyle seemed quite happy to see him. "Welcome," he said. "I did not know you were coming. Why did you not send word?"

David shrugged. "I could make it here just as fast as a messenger," he said. "My brother and I were in London and I thought to come visit Emilie before following him back to Lioncross."

Lyle put a hand on his shoulder, pulling him out of the bright sunshine and towards the keep. "London, you say?" he repeated. "We have had word that there has been a good deal of fighting up north, near Nottingham. I assumed you were in the middle of it. In fact, I sent Brick and eight hundred men north to reinforce Richard's ranks, as requested by William Marshal. Something about a battle brewing at Tickhill Castle. Have you seen Brick and my army?"

David nodded. "I saw him at a distance, a handful of times, but I did not speak with him," he said. "Has he not returned to Canterbury yet?"

Lyle shook his head. "He has not," he said. "I told him he could visit his son at Barnwell Castle, so I would assume that is where he has gone. I am sure he will return soon."

David shifted the load on his shoulders. "More than likely," he said. "The situation has quieted for now."

Lyle's brow furrowed. "Quiet?" he said. "There is no more fighting?"

David shrugged. "Tickhill fell," he said. "It was a nasty battle. There has been scattered fighting all throughout the midlands, and only last month my brother and I ended up in Norfolk for a skirmish, but it seems that John and his mercenary army has pulled back to regroup. We know they are bottled up in Nottingham, but for now the situation is quiet. That is why Chris is heading home and I thought to visit Canterbury before I followed him."

Lyle listened to the news with great interest. "What of Richard?" he asked. "What do we know of him?"

David shook his head. "Still a captive, my lord," he said. "The ransom for his release is still being gathered."

Lyle sighed faintly, thinking of what that meant for the country. He was certain he wasn't the only lord thinking such things. He looked at David and started to say something but it suddenly struck him just how exhausted and hot David appeared. He was sure the man didn't want to discuss politics anymore, considering how he had lived and breathed them for the past several months.

"We will not discuss such things today," Lyle said, pulling David towards the keep. "Come and refresh yourself; Emilie and her sisters are at the lake, which is right outside of these walls to the south. They go there nearly every day in this heat. She will be quite happy to see you."

David smiled weakly. "I can only stay the night and then I must be gone by morning," he said. "As much as I would like to linger here at Canterbury, unfortunately, I cannot. Duty calls."

Lyle ushered David up the stairs to the second floor entry of the keep. "I understand completely," he said. "Come in and refresh yourself, lad. I will have the servants bring you water to wash the heat from your body. This year has been quite warm and I am sure it has made your travel somewhat miserable."

David didn't say much after entering the keep; Lyle seemed to do most of the talking at that point. David simply listened, speaking out once in a while. Lyle took him to a small chamber next to his solar, a chamber that was probably meant as a servant's alcove, but it had a sturdy bed and that was all David really cared about. Lyle sent the house servants running in all directions, bringing cool water and linen rags to wash with, and they even brought Lyle's personal soap, which smelled of pine.

David was grateful for the hospitality and as Lyle stood in the doorway and chatted, David stripped down to his linen breeches and washed every part of his body that wasn't covered with fabric. If he was going to see Emilie after having not seen the woman for months, then he didn't want to smell like a sty.

All the time he soaped and rinsed, including his hair, Lyle spoke to him quite amiably, but as David dried the water off his face, the mood in Lyle's tone changed.

"I assume that Emilie told you what happened with the missives you had sent her," he said quietly. "About Brick, I mean."

David paused, looking at the man as he realized the subject, and then continued drying his face. "She said he had intercepted most of the missives I sent to her," he said, wiping off his neck. "She said that he burned them."

Lyle nodded, trying not to appear too contrite at the behavior of his captain. In truth, he felt as if he should apologize to David about it but he wasn't sure that was entirely appropriate. It wasn't his fault, after all. But he still felt somehow responsible.

"I appreciate that words regarding Brick's behavior were not the first words out of your mouth when you arrived," he said. "If Emilie has already explained it all to you, I will not go into detail, but suffice it to say that I told Brick that he was to stay away from Emilie. He is not permitted to go near her after his lapse in judgement when it came to your missives."

David thought on that moment as he set the linen towel aside. "I received her missive weeks before Brick and your army made an appearance up north," he said. "I had told my brother what Emilie's missive had said and he made sure to keep Brick away from me and with the other commanders. I never really saw him at all."

Lyle nodded. "That is good," he said. "But to be truthful, David, I have been thinking on the situation quite a bit and it seems to me that this is something that will not mend itself. Brick is a stubborn man and used to getting his way in all things. In fact, if you marry Emilie, the situation will only grow worse. Brick will be subjugated to you and that will only cause problems."

David was about to turn for his saddlebags to collect a clean tunic but he froze when Lyle mentioned marriage. He looked at the man, fighting down the hope that bloomed in his chest at the mention of marriage to Emilie.

"*If* I marry Emilie?" he repeated. "Does that mean you have made a decision?"

Lyle fought off a grin. "I have," he said. "I have thought about this a great deal. You are all that Emilie can speak of. I hope you are as enamored with her as she is with you."

David didn't want to admit just how enamored he was. He didn't like to speak of his feelings so. But the mere fact that he had ridden all the way from London to see Emilie certainly said something about his feelings for her.

"She is in my thoughts constantly," he said.

Lyle laughed softly at the restraint of the knight. "Is that so?" he said. "Every day, in fact?"

"Every day."

"Then you have not changed your mind about her? You offered for her hand once."

"I remember. And I have not changed my mind."

That was what Lyle wanted to hear. "It is my sense that you and Emilie will be good for one another," he said. "Besides, she needs a husband who can handle her stubborn nature and I believe you are just such a man. Moreover, when I pass away, she will be the Canterbury heiress and the earldom will pass to her husband. I want it to pass to you, David. You are a worthy man."

David stared at the man a moment longer before breaking into a massive grin that threatened to split his face in two. "The earldom does not matter to me, although I am deeply honored for the consideration," he said. "All that matters to me is your daughter. That is all I have ever cared about. As her husband, I swear to you that I will not fail her, in any way."

Lyle put a hand on David's bare shoulder. "I know you will not," he said. "May I offer my congratulations on your betrothal, David. I will be proud to call you my son."

David was nearly giddy with joy. Of course, his offer for Emilie had weighed heavily on his mind on the trip to Canterbury but he wasn't going to bring it up within the first ten minutes of his arrival. He didn't want to seem crass or overbearing. He was, therefore, delighted that Lyle had brought it up and it was the best news he could possibly hope for. Now, he was officially betrothed.

Betrothed. It was a word that, in the past, he'd had an aversion to.

There was no secret about that and it was something he'd even told Emilie. Now, hearing the word didn't give him the shakes like it had in the past, and he attributed that to the fact that this was a welcome betrothal, as opposed to one that might have been forced on him. In any case, he didn't react to it as he thought he would. He was genuinely thrilled at the prospect.

"Thank you, my lord," he said. "I hope to live up to the pride you have in me."

Lyle could see that the man was nearly bursting with joy, but he restrained himself, perhaps out of embarrassment or perhaps because he simply didn't know how to express himself. Either way, it was rather humorous to watch the man fidget and grin. Lyle laughed softly and clapped him on the bare shoulder again.

"Get dressed," he said. "Let us go and find Emilie and tell her the good news."

He turned for the chamber door to leave but David stopped him. "She does not know?"

Lyle paused in the doorway, shaking his head. "I thought to tell you first," he said. "I knew you would come to Canterbury at some point whereupon I could render my decision. You should be the one to know first, shouldn't you?"

David snorted. "How did you guess that I was coming here?" he said, digging into his saddlebags and pulling forth a pale linen tunic. "Was it the eight missives I have sent your daughter?"

"That was an excellent indication," Lyle said wryly. "Finish dressing. I will wait for you in my solar."

He stepped through the door, shutting it softly. When he was gone and David was alone, he shook his fists in the air in a great gesture of victory, so very excited that Emilie now officially belonged to him. He was happy; nay, *beyond* happy. He'd never been so overjoyed in his life. He felt as if he was living a dream, a surreal confection of happiness and excitement that he'd never thought he'd experience. It was something that usurped nearly every profound or proud moment in his life.

The joy of a new wife. The joy in being granted the woman he loved.

Quickly, he finished dressing, extremely eager to see his future bride.

THE HEAT WAS sticky. Even the grass was sticky, although it was moderately cool beneath the great willow trees that flanked the castle's lake. On this lazy summer day, with the blue sky above and birds singing in the trees, Emilie lay beneath the canopy of the tree upon the cool but sticky grass, watching Nathalie and Elise splash about in the lake.

It was a rather large lake that was deep in the middle, and Elise wouldn't venture too far in because the fish weren't much afraid of people, and would swim up to her and nibble on her legs and toes. Twenty men-at-arms from the castle had escorted the three sisters and Lillibet to the lake, but one piercing scream from Elise would bring them all running, arms brandished. When they saw that it was simply Elise being afraid of the fish, they'd go back to their posts, sweating and grumbling. That had happened four times today alone.

Emilie didn't mind the fish. She could swim very well and would often swim out to the middle of the lake while Nathalie and Elise begged her to come back. She could stay in the water for hours, or at least it seemed like hours, and she had already been swimming a good deal today, which is why she was now laying on the grass, dozing in the heat. In her damp linen dress, a very simple dress that she used to swim in, and her hair braided and piled, in a big mess, atop her head, she was barefoot and content. Beside her, Lillibet was knotting with three balls of colored silk thread, creating some kind of creation for the hands or neck. Lillibet liked to knot, or knit as some called it, and she produced beautiful things that most often ended up in Emilie's wardrobe.

Emilie yawned as she watched Nathalie splash around in the water, while Elise, with her box of wooden people, now sat on the shore of the lake and played with them. Emilie yawned again, thinking seriously on taking a nap as the heat lulled her towards sleep.

"Your father is coming, Emilie," Lillibet said, spit flying onto Emilie's leg. "There is someone with him, although I cannot see who it is."

Lillibet's eyes were quite bad at a distance so it was difficult to see things that were far away, like approaching people. But Lillibet knew Lyle by form; she knew his form very well. Emilie, however, simply yawned again. She didn't really care about her father and some unknown man.

"Mother, did you see the apricot grove as of late?" she asked sleepily. "I have been dreaming of apricots all day. The last I saw, it was heavy with fruit. Did the servants harvest it?"

Lillibet was still knitting, but her focus was on Lyle and the man at his side as they drew closer. She thought she remembered seeing the man with Lyle, once, at Windsor. In fact, the closer they came, the more she realized that it was Emilie's Sir David. She peered closer to confirm that it was who she was seeing, before gently thumping Emilie on the leg.

"Emilie!" she hissed. "The man with your father...!"

"I do not care who it is," Emilie mumbled sleepily. "What about the fruit? Will you please get me some? I have a yearning for apricots."

"Emilie, it is Sir David!"

Emilie's eyes flew open and she bolted upright, turning to see that her father and David were only about twenty feet away. They had come very close before Lillibet and her bad eyesight could identify them. Horrified at her appearance, Emilie's gaze fell upon David and suddenly, she could hardly breathe.

David. He was smiling at her, that handsome face that had haunted her dreams, and she couldn't think of one coherent thing to say to him. He had promised to come and visit her, but that had been eight months ago. Eight long months. And now, here he was, looking like a blonde god from the high reaches of heaven. He looked magnificent and whole and healthy.

And she looked like a disheveled pauper.

"Emilie, look who has come to see you," Lyle said, as Emilie sat there in speechless shock. "Sir David has come all the way from London to visit with you, but he cannot stay long. Greet the man before I die of shame, Emilie. Say something."

Emilie, her cheeks pink with embarrassment, managed to emit a noise that sounded somewhat like a gasp. "My lord," she breathed as she stood up, trying to smooth out her damp dress. "I... I am surprised to see you. Welcome... welcome to Canterbury."

David simply grinned; she he'd caught sight of the woman, he hadn't stopped grinning. In her loose fitting dress, red cheeks, and mussed hair, he'd never seen anything so lovely in his entire life. Sweet and silky tones.

The voice of an angel.

Jesus, he'd missed it!

"Thank you," he said. "I see that my visit finds you frolicking by the lake you once spoke of."

Emilie simply nodded. Lyle, seeing how stunned and off guard she was, thought it might be better to leave her alone with David. It was often difficult to express one's glee in the unexpected appearance of a lover with an audience, and most especially with her father watching. Lyle waved a hand at Lillibet.

"Come away from there," he told her. "Let the two of them alone. I am sure they have much to say to each other than we need not hear."

Dutifully, Lillibet followed Lyle away, leaving Emilie standing in stunned silence as David smiled at her. As Lillibet and Lyle walked away, moving towards the lake where Natalie and Elise frolicked, David moved closer to Emilie, drinking in that lovely, flushed face.

"You are more beautiful that I had remembered," he said. "It is very agreeable to see you again."

Emilie let out a harsh gasp. "I did not know you were coming," she lamented. "I was not at the keep to properly greet you, properly dressed. Instead you find me looking unkempt and slovenly. I pray you can forgive me. This is not how I would usually greet you."

His smile broadened. "You are the most beautiful woman I have ever seen, in any state of dress," he said. "You could be covered with mud and I would still say the same thing. You needn't worry about how you appear to me."

Emilie grinned, embarrassed, chuckling because he was starting to. "So you sought to come and see me after all of these months?" she asked. "I was wondering if you ever would. I thought we would just be writing missives back and forth for the rest of our lives."

He snorted. "Nay, lady," he said. "I told you I would come and visit you. I came as soon as I could."

Her smile faded as she looked at him, rather adoringly. Now that the shock of his unexpected appearance had worn off, she was incredibly glad to see him.

"I know," she said softly. "I know you have been very busy as of late. Your missives said so. If you will allow me to return to the keep and change into something more pleasing, I would love to have a long and detailed conversation with you. I am so pleased that you have finally come."

He shook his head and went to her, reaching out to gently grasp her arm. "Sit down," he said. "There is no need to change your clothing. Let us sit right here and speak. I do not want to waste one moment returning you to the keep. I would be greedy and soak up every second I can with you."

It was such a sweet thing to say. Giddy, Emilie permitted him to help her sit back down in the grass while he stretched out beside her.

He positioned himself very close to her while she sat, cross-legged. All the while, they couldn't seem to take their eyes off of one another.

"So you have come," she murmured.

"I have."

"Did you receive my missives?" she asked. "I was only able to reply to the last three, you know. I told you about it in the first missive I sent to you."

He nodded. "I know," he said. "You told me about Brick."

"Are you angry?"

He lifted his eyebrows. "At you?" he asked. "Of course not. But the next time I see Brickley de Dere, he shall hear of my displeasure. He shall feel it, too."

Emilie couldn't argue with him. "He heard enough from me," she said. "I am sure hearing from you would not make much difference."

David's gaze lingered on her. "What did you tell him?"

She pulled a blade of grass, toying with it. "I told him that I would never trust him again," she said. "I told him that even if I had never met you, there would still never be any chance for him and I. I simply do not look at him that way and there is nothing he can do to change my mind."

David pondered that a moment. "It is difficult for a man to accept when a woman wants nothing to do with him," he said. "I can only imagine how I would feel if you had ignored me."

Emilie grinned, still fidgeting with the blade of grass. "I would never ignore you," she said firmly. "In fact, I have thought about you a great deal since we last saw one another. How have you been these past several months? What can you tell me about your life and travels that you did not tell me in your missives?"

He stretched out on his back, folding his arms casually behind his head and gazing up at her. "Not much more than the usual nonsense," he said. "You know that I have seen battle fairly steadily since January. This is the first break we have seen in that time so Chris has gone back to Lioncross to see his wife, and I told him I would visit with you briefly before following. The fate of England rests with me, you know. My brother cannot make a move without me."

Emilie giggled. "Well can I understand that," she said. "I would not make a move without you, either."

David grinned because she was. "You flatter me, my lady."

She shook her head. "It is not flattery," she said. "It is the truth. You are the greatest knight in the realm, are you not?"

He shrugged. "One of them."

She laughed. "Thy modesty is astounding."

She was so lovely when she laughed. David was enchanted by it. "I will tell you a secret."

"What?"

"I have no modesty."

She simply shook her head, her laughter fading. "You have every right to be proud and boastful," she said. "You have earned that right. You have done many great things in your life, I am sure."

He shrugged. "Great," he said. "And not so great. I am no different from any man."

As Emilie looked at him, she recalled those months back when Dennis le Londe had cornered her at the prince's great mask. *He is not the man he says he is, demoiselle*, Dennis had said. *He murders women and children.* Oddly enough, she really hadn't thought much about that until now, until David spoke of great deeds and not so great deeds. Now, she was curious about it. When Dennis had mentioned that odd sounding name, *Ayyadieh*, David hadn't denied knowing about it. He hadn't denied anything.

Perhaps she wanted to know about it. Perhaps she wanted to truly see the man's character.

"May I ask you a question?" she asked.

David nodded. "You may always ask me any question," he said. "I will always tell you what I can."

"Truthfully?"

"I do not lie."

She shook her head, quickly, as if to ease him. "I did not mean to suggest that you would," she said. "I know you will always be truthful with me. But you just mentioned that you had committed great deeds and some that are not so great. Did you mean Ayyadieh?"

David's warm expression faded. "Aye."

Emilie could see that the subject was not a welcome one but she felt compelled to ask. "I only heard of it when Dennis the Destroyer mentioned it," she said. "Was he lying when he said you and your brother murdered women and children?"

David thought about just how much to tell her. It was a complex situation, one that warranted more than a cursory explanation. Had he and Christopher killed women and children? The answer was not so simple. Much happened in war, the planned and the unplanned. Although he really didn't want to confide in her, he couldn't avoid the question. She would think he was hiding something. Still, he was afraid that she would not want to be married to him if she knew the truth of it.

Jesus, he hoped that wasn't the case.

"The situation was much more complex that Dennis made it out to be," he said quietly, rolling on to his side and propping his head up on his hand. "War is a bitter and ugly thing, Emilie. It spares no one. Three years in the Holy Land was truly hell in many a sense. One out of every two Christian soldiers died of disease. Hunger was common. Richard, although he is my king as well as my friend, fought some battles that were not particularly ethical, and Ayyadieh was one of them. But ethics in warfare are often put aside when one is attempting to win a battle."

Emilie was listening carefully. "So what happened at Ayyadieh?"

David reached out a hand, his big index finger brushing against the tender skin of her right wrist. It was a sweet, affectionate gesture. It was also a gesture meant to soften the blow of what he was about to say.

"Something I am not particularly proud of," he said. "Dennis was there. He participated, as well as many other knights. After the fall of Acre, the Christian armies had a great many Saracen prisoners. But the commander of the enemy armies, Saladin, held one of the great treasures of Christendom – the cross upon which Jesus Christ was crucified. Richard offered to exchange Saracen prisoners for the cross, but Saladin delayed his response. We found out it was because another Saracen army was approaching and Saladin hoped to use that army to recapture Acre from the Christians. That is one of the many things Saladin did to stall us, and Richard became enraged and ordered the killing of the Saracen captives in full view of Saladin and his armies. This also meant executing the retainers of the prisoners, which were often their wives and children."

By this time, Emilie was looking at him with horror. "Did you actually do it?"

David could see her fear and perhaps even revulsion. He was careful in his answer. "Richard was enraged, which was not an usual state with him," he said quietly. "Although I take no issue in executing prisoners of war, men who would just as easily kill me were the situation reversed, I refused what I considered a dishonorable order from Richard to kill the retainers. Christopher refused as well, as did several other English knights. But the French knights, Dennis le Londe included, did not refuse and in fact too particular glee in killing men, women, and children."

Emilie had such sadness in her eyes. "How many people were killed?"

David thought back to that horrific and particularly bloody event. "Around three thousand total," he said quietly. "Emilie, I know that you do not understand warfare. You have lived a pleasant life and for that, I am glad. You have lived a life that most of us would love to live. But I have not lived that life; I have seen the worse that mankind has to offer. I have seen death and destruction and the pure hell of man's determination to murder in the name of religion. I cannot say I am particularly pious after what I have seen acomplished in the name of God. It is a guilt I carry, I suppose. Guilt that I, too, have killed in the name of God. Somehow, I am not particularly certain God really wanted us to do that."

Emilie could see that he was baring his soul to her and she was surprised. It was a very introspective view of what had been touted in England as a great holy quest to the land of Christ, held by the barbarians. Through David's eyes, it was much more than that. There was blood and death and terror there, the terrible things he had done and witnessed. She was deeply touched by his honesty, raw as it had been. Somehow, the admission made her feel much closer to him, honored that he would confide in her.

"You did what you had to do," she said softly. "You did what you were ordered to do and what you had to do in order to survive. I do not believe God will fault you for that."

David's thoughts lingered on Ayyadieh a moment longer before forcing himself away from those hellish recollections. He forced a smile at her.

"Mayhap not," he said. "And then I come back to England and straight into a tournament were some fool tried to kill me in front of my favored lady. Battle and death follows me wherever I go, it seems."

Emilie reached out, clasping the big fingers that were by her wrist. "But it has not followed you here," she reassured him. "Did I hear Papa correctly when he said that you could not remain with us very long?"

He nodded, holding her fingers gently, caressing them. "I must leave on the morrow," he said. "I must return to Lioncross, which is near Hereford. My brother will be expecting me."

Emilie held to his fingers tightly now. "And when shall I see you again after that?"

David shook his head. "I do not know," he said softly. "It could be weeks or months. Much depends on what John is up to and when Richard shall be returning from captivity. But know that I will come for you as soon as I can. I will not stay away from you any longer than I have to."

Emilie smiled, that delighted and warm gesture that was one step away from shouting to the heavens for the happiness in one's heart.

"Then let us spend all of this time together," she said. "I will send one of the soldiers back to the castle for our fishing lines. Would you like to fish now? It is a peaceful thing to do. We can speak more on your adventures in the Holy Land, at least the ones you are fond of. I would like to see the world through your eyes, David. They are wise eyes."

More flattery and he soaked it up. She had a way of making him feel as if he was the most important man in the world. Perhaps that was what he liked so much about her. Or was it that he loved that about her? *Love.* Such a strong word. It was a word that, once given, could not be taken back. As much as he adored Emilie, he wasn't sure he could speak that word to her. At least, not now.

Yet, as he gazed into her eyes, he could feel it on the tip of his tongue.

It was a great dilemma, indeed, in a relationship that had been full of them.

SUPPER THAT EVENING was a festive affair.

An enormous knuckle of beef was the main dish but it was accompanied by the five fish that David and Emilie had caught in their afternoon of fishing, and the cook had prepared the fish by roasting them over an open flame so the entire hall smelled of cooked fish. Canterbury actually had two halls; a giant separate building in a corner of the bailey for more formal feasts and a smaller one inside the keep that the family used. The smaller hall was the biggest room in the keep with big stone columns, now warmly lit as the food was arranged upon the big feasting table that was heavier than ten men.

Lyle's grandfather had actually commissioned the table and local craftsmen built it inside the room. It was a permanent fixture, for it could never leave the hall except in pieces.

David and Emilie sat together as Lyle, seated next to David, ordered the servants to place the food where David could get at it. He was their guest and it was clear that Lyle was giving him first selection of everything. Along with the beef and fish, the cook had exercised her culinary talents – there were meat pies, called "graves," that hid a delightful array of beef and vegetables in gravy inside once one burst through the hard crust at the top of the "grave." There were also little cakes called *"bryndons,"* that had fruit and nuts in them; surrounded by a sweet wine sauce. There also was a cheese pie called a *"sambocade,"* that was a mixture of cheese, eggs, and dried elderflowers, baked in a crust.

David particularly liked the sambocade and ate the entire pie before anyone really had a chance to have any of it. Nathalie and Elise frowned as their sweet treat had been eaten out from under them, but Lyle shook his head at them, silently admonishing them not to complain before they could say anything. Elise, seated at the end of the table with her wooden people on the table around her, had placed all of them facing her trencher, and she was particularly unhappy about it. It was her wooden people's favorite thing to eat, so she whispered to Nathalie.

Elise fed her people the bryndons instead, but Nathalie wasn't so apt to keep her mouth shut. She kept frowning at David, who met her gaze coolly over the top of the table. They had mostly stayed clear of one another since his arrival, but now they were thrown together. There was a battle brewing between them; Nathalie could feel it in the air. Her father and older sister were quite happy to have David de Lohr as a guest, but she wasn't. She found him arrogant. She'd hoped that dog shite in his helm those months ago might have scared him off, but here he was, back again and making a nuisance of himself, as Emilie hung on his every word.

"I will have to ask if there are any more sweet pies in the kitchen," Nathalie said boldly, making a point of looking at David as she spoke. "Someone seems to have eaten this one."

Lyle hissed at his middle daughter. "Be still," he told her. "David is our guest. If he wants to eat this entire table, then he is welcome to it."

David gave Nathalie a droll expression, as if to taunt her that he had Lyle's support and she did not. Moreover, he was planning his vengeance; there was the little matter of revenge for the dog shite in his helm, and revenge on this night was particularly sweet as he plowed through the treats on the table that Nathalie and her sister seemed to very much want. He'd figured that out early on, which is why he'd eaten everything. He wasn't going to leave a scrap for those two little brats.

Enraged, Nathalie turned red in the face and grabbed a piece of beef on her plate, shoving it in her mouth and chewing, all the while glaring at David. He simply lifted his cup to her as if to toast a lovely meal. Then he confiscated the bowl containing the bryndons and ate every last one. Elise wailed.

"Quiet!" Lyle said to his youngest daughter as she pointed to the empty bowl where the bryndons used to be. "If you cannot behave politely, then you will go to your chamber and take your meal there. Nathalie, that goes for you as well. Am I clear?"

Emilie, not oblivious to what was going on between her sisters and David, was quickly growing mortified at their behavior. It had been such a lovely day with him, a day of conversation and fishing, of coming to know one another better, and to have it ruined by her two foolish sisters was more than she was willing to bear. Frowning at Nathalie and Elise, she apologized to David.

"We do not have many visitors," she said. "They do not know how to properly behave."

David's focus was still on the younger sisters. "It is no wonder you have few visitors if they are putting dog shite in helms or pulling any number of other nasty tricks," he said, listening to Emilie gasp. His next words were focused on Nathalie and Emilie. "Mayhap they have not yet met with someone who will do to them what they do to others. Tyranny such as theirs cannot go unanswered."

Now, Nathalie didn't look so enraged. She was looking rather fearful, and Elise beside her appeared equally as fearful. Lyle cleared his throat softly.

"They are young and spirited," he said. "Do not pay any attention to them. Since Emilie has monopolized all of your time this afternoon, I am eager to hear of your exploits since we last saw you. I know there has been skirmishes against John all spring and into the summer, but I am curious to know the details. I am also eager to hear of Richard's situation."

He was changing the subject away from his naughty younger daughters. "Of course," David replied, but when Lyle looked away to hold his cup to a servant for more wine, David looked at Nathalie and Elise and drew an index finger across his throat in a slashing gesture, signaling that the war between them was on. As Nathalie's eyes flew open wide in shock and Elise yelped, David reached for his cup of wine and pretended not to know the reason behind their troubles. He continued with the conversation as if nothing was amiss. "You were wise to leave London when you did, my lord. Shortly thereafter was when John began unleashing his mercenary army. My brother and I have been all over Nottinghamshire, Norfolk, and into Yorkshire trying to prevent John from gaining properties."

Lyle, oblivious to his terrified younger daughters, listened intently. "But he *has* gained property."

David popped a piece of bread into his mouth. "He has."

The mood of the conversation turned serious, veering away from the naughty daughters. Lyle took a long gulp of his wine. "Is he gaining the edge, David?" he asked. "Will Richard lose his kingdom?"

David shook his head. "John's army is full of mercenaries," he said. "French, Teutonic, and the like. John's allies are feeding money into his coffers but the source of money is not endless. It will dry up and when it does, the mercenaries will leave. John knows this, which is why he has been granting properties to some of the wealthier mercenaries, but they are crown properties that belong to his brother. We have spent a good deal of time purging these mercenaries from property that does not belong to them. Will John win this battle? I do not believe he will. Support for Richard is still overwhelmingly strong."

"But meanwhile, you still go and risk your life for a king whose fate is not certain," Emilie said softly. She had been listening intently to the conversation. "What will happen if Richard does not return and John becomes king? Will you then become an enemy of the crown because you supported Richard?"

David looked at her, a smile on his lips. He couldn't stop smiling when it came to her. "Nay," he said. "The House of de Lohr has always supported the crown. If John is the rightful king, then we will swear allegiance to him. Right now, he is not and that is why we fight against him."

Emilie smiled timidly, reaching out to take his hand but realizing she would be doing it with an audience. It was not proper. She quickly pulled her hand away but Lyle, who had seen the action, spoke.

"You may take his hand, Emilie," he said. "After all, he is your betrothed. You are permitted to touch him."

Emilie's eyes widened and her jaw dropped as the subject switched from battles to betrothals. She was not prepared for what her father said and it sent her head spinning.

"*Betrothed*?" she repeated in shock, looking between her father and David. "When… how….?

She was sputtering, bringing laugher from both David and Lyle. It was David who spoke. "Your father graciously agreed to my offer of marriage," he said. "I was wondering when he was going to tell you because I have had a difficult time keep the secret all afternoon. Do you have any idea how many times I wanted to tell you while we were sitting by the lake? I have bitten my tongue so much that it is surely in shreds by now."

Thrilled, Emilie let out a shriek and bolted up from her chair, rushing to her father and throwing her arms around his neck. She was laughing happily, something that almost sounded maniacal, as Lyle permitted her to nearly strangle him in her joy. It was good to see her so happy, something rarely envisioned when it came to Emilie. She'd had her share of disappointments and sorrow over the past several months, particularly when it came to Brickley, so to see her so truly joyful did Lyle's heart good. In seeing her reaction, he knew he'd made the correct decision.

He laughed softly as Emilie peppered his face with kisses, still gripping him around the neck. "Thank you, Papa!" she said in between kisses. "You have made me so happy!"

Before Lyle could reply, she released him and he nearly fell from his chair from the force of her happy grip. Then she turned her joy on David and threw her arms around his neck, too, laughing and jumping at the same time. David lost his balance from the momentum of her hug, tipping sideways in the chair and coming close to falling off of it as she embraced him. He managed to get one arm down, bracing himself against the floor, as the other arm held Emilie.

"I cannot tell," he said as she squeezed. "Are you pleased or not?"

Emilie laughed loudly, but quickly realized she had nearly pushed the man off of his chair. She let go of his neck, pulling on his arm to right him in his seat. David was grinning from ear to ear.

"I am pleased," Emilie assured him. "Can you not tell?"

He chuckled. "I can," he said. "Then you believe you will like spending your life as Lady de Lohr?"

Emilie's joy turned from exuberance into something much deeper and warmer as she gazed at him. Her hands were clasped against her chest, her expression one of utter delight and adoration.

"Aye," she whispered fervently. "I will love every moment of my life just as I will love my husband for every moment of it as well."

David stared at her. *I will love my husband.* Was she already declaring her love for him? Was it even possible she would feel that way about him? Her statement left him speechless, struggling to say something. He immediately thought of his brother, of Christopher, and of his wife, Dustin.

It seemed as if Christopher and Dustin had married so long ago but in truth, it was not that long ago at all. A year and no more. David had wrestled with the union since the beginning because he could see that Christopher had developed feelings for his wife, and David had been embittered about it. That was no secret. He had even criticized his brother for it. And now, here he was, betrothed to a woman that he dreamt about day and night. She was declaring her love for him. Suddenly, he was coming to understand what his brother had been feeling all of these months; being with a wife whom he adored.

Now, things were becoming clearer.

But David still couldn't bring himself to say it, even if it was true. *I will love my wife....*

"I am pleased, then," was all David could say to her glowing face. "For I never thought I would find a woman who could put up with me. It is too late to decline now. We are committed for life."

Emilie was still smiling, still gazing into his handsome face, but the truth was that she felt a bit disappointed. She had dared to speak of her love for him and he had not responded to her. She didn't even know why she said it, only that it had come out before she had realized what she was saying. She thought she might have seen a flicker of shock in David's eyes, but to his credit, at least he didn't pull away from her completely. He was still smiling at her, still enjoying the moment.

Still, she wished he could have said something sweet to her, something that would sing to her in her dreams of the love they could look forward to.

"You have me forever," she said. "I would not decline something I have been praying so earnestly for."

David appreciated her response. She didn't mention anything about him refusing to speak of his love for her. There was still joy in her expression, as if it really didn't matter all that much. It was enough to make him feel bad that he hadn't spoken of his love for her.

... did he, in fact, love her?

More and more, he was certain that he did.

"As have I," David said. "But that brings up a serious point. I do not know when we can be married. I am duty-bound to my brother and to Richard, so until things are settled I may not see you very much for the next few months. But mayhap that does not matter after all. Mayhap you would appreciate the time to build your trousseau and plan an elaborate wedding with many guests. I will leave that to you."

Emilie was delighted, of course, but she simply shrugged. "I have not thought of when we can be wed," she said, looking to her father. "Have you, Papa?"

Lyle shook his head. "I have no preference," he said. "It is your decision. I will leave it to you and David to decide."

"Papa!" Nathalie, who had been silent during the entire betrothal conversation, spoke up. "Elise and I would like to be excused. We want to go to bed."

Lyle looked at her. "Have you no congratulations to give your sister?" he asked. "She is to be married. Surely you can wish her great happiness."

Nathalie looked between David and Emilie, nervously. "I wish you great happiness," she said, mostly to Emilie, before returning her focus to her father. "May we leave?"

Lyle waved them off, glad to be rid of the troublemakers. "Find Lillibet," he said. "She will see you to sleep."

The girls quickly left the table, departing the hall and followed by

Cid and Roland, who had been sitting beneath the table, hoping for scraps. As the girls and dogs faded out into the darkness beyond the hall, Lyle lifted a cup to David and Emilie.

"I will expand on Nathalie's wish for happiness and give you a wish of my own," he said. "May you know more happiness than sorrow, more smiles than tears, and may you both be true and faithful to one another until the death. That is the best blessing I can possibly give you. May you both know happiness with each other, in this life and beyond."

David silently thanked the man for his good wishes and lifted his cup to him before drinking deeply. Emilie claimed her cup as well, smiling at David as she sipped of her wine. With the younger girls out of the hall now, there was more of a festive atmosphere with just the three of them celebrating the betrothal. In truth, that was all they needed – just the three of them celebrating something that had been several months in the making.

Lyle, for one, was glad that David had survived John's skirmishes. He was looking forward to having David as a son. He even wondered if David would swear fealty to him and remain in Canterbury, as opposed to returning to Lioncross with his brother. There were all details to be determined when the time came, but Lyle was selfish – he didn't want his daughter going to the Welsh borders so her husband could serve his mighty brother. Therefore, he wanted David here at Canterbury.

But then there was the matter of Brickley. That old, familiar subject of the conflict between Brickley and David. Lyle knew, as he'd speculated before, that Brickley would more than likely not remain at Canterbury with David as his liege. But that was Brickley's choice, something Lyle would not interfere in. The path was now set and David de Lohr would marry Emilie and become the next Earl of Canterbury. Lyle felt tremendous relief in that knowledge; even though the title would pass from the House of Hampton, it would be passing into one of the most prominent families in England. He couldn't hope for better.

As Lyle thought on the future for his earldom, Emilie was thinking on her future in general. She had dreamed of this day and now it was here. David was her husband for all intents and purposes, and all of the ups and downs she had experienced since knowing the man suddenly seemed hardly worth the effort. The tournament, escaping the Sheriff of Nottingham, the misunderstanding that separated them for two months, the prince's masque, and then Brickley burning David's missives. All of it seemed so far away, simply things she'd had to endure before David finally became hers. She had no idea that such happiness was possible.

"Thank you, Papa," she said to his toast, draining her cup of the sweet, tart wine. "Your blessing means everything."

Lyle set his cup down, looking at his daughter as she gazed into the face of the man she loved. He remembered an expression like that on Willow's face long ago, when they had been betrothed. He had felt like the most fortunate man in the world at that time and he still cursed God for bringing about the cancer that killed his wife. It had been so long ago and he missed her so. Looking at Emilie and David, he couldn't help but feel some envy. But he also couldn't help feeling the joy.

"Then I will leave you two to discuss what must be discussed before David leaves on the morrow," he said. "I will bid you both a good evening."

Emilie kissed her father good-night and David shook the man's hand. When Lyle finally wandered out of the hall, David turned to Emilie to see that she was looking at him expectantly. He lifted his eyebrows at her.

"You have something on your mind," he said. "What is it?"

Emilie shook her head, reaching out to take his big hand. He clutched her fingers, lifting them to his lips for a gentle kiss. "Did you truly believe we would ever see this moment?" she asked. "I will admit that I wondered."

He tugged on her arm, pulling her out of his seat and onto his lap. He wrapped his big arms around her as she snuggled close. "I hope your father cannot see this," he said. "I should not be holding you so improperly."

Emilie giggled. "Let him see," she said boldly. "We are to be married, are we not? You may do whatever you wish with me."

He cast her a long, doubtful look before breaking down into soft laughter. "If that were true, I might consider very inappropriate things with you."

Emilie was both intrigued and willing. "You entice me, my lord."

He looked at her rather strangely. "What do you know about inappropriate actions?" he asked, a hint of suspicion in his tone. "You should be fighting me off at the very least. Are you so willing to be ravaged?"

Emilie giggled, her arms around his neck. Her face was very close to his and she had the privilege of studying his face at close range, his long and straight nose with a dusting of faded freckles. His skin was somewhat weathered by the years in harsh climates, but it only seemed to make him more handsome.

"I am willing to be ravaged by *you*," she clarified. "You have behaved like a proper gentleman all afternoon. I am afraid I am starting to feel offended by your restraint."

David fought off a grin. "Is that so?"

"It is."

"I was trying to behave myself."

"And so you did. Now, my father is gone, my sisters are in bed, and we are alone. Will you still show such restraint?"

He cocked an eyebrow. "Are you sure you know what you are saying?"

"I am not sure. Why don't you show me what I think I meant?"

He looked at her, puzzled by her nonsensical answer, and then he started laughing. "I have never seen a lady so eager to be overwhelmed by a man," he said. "I thought you were a demure, sweet child."

She gave him a rather naughty look. "You were wrong."

His smile vanished. "I am?" he said. "Pray, tell me how I am wrong and careful your answer lest I be forced to spank you."

She giggled and tightened up her arms around his neck. "Come, now," she said, rather seductively. "Do you think I have been living in a convent for the past few years? Of course I have not. I have had suitors, many of them, in fact. Much as you find women attractive, I find men attractive, but none so attractive as you. I have a healthy appetite for men and I am not ashamed of it."

He looked at her, astonished. "A healthy appetite for men?"

Her fingers toyed with the hair at the base his skull as her hands lingered at the back of his neck. "A healthy appetite for *you*," she whispered. "Kiss me."

He didn't have the chance to do it, for she was descending upon his lips before he could speak. They had kissed before and it had been a spark of a kiss that had quickly grown into a raging blaze. This kiss was no different; something about the feel of Emilie in his hands and the taste of her upon his lips sent a flush of liquid heat through his veins. It had been so long since he'd held her and even in those times, the contact had been brief. Someone had always interrupted them. But tonight, there would be no interruptions.

He intended to experience this woman he was pledged to marry.

The situation quickly grew amorous, nearly out of control. Seated on his lap, Emilie was trapped against him as his mouth ravaged her. He moved from her lips to her chin to her cheeks, tasting every bit of flesh he could get his hands and mouth on, but it still wasn't enough. He could feel her rounded buttocks on his lap and his erection was already straining against his breeches. She was his, after all.

And he wanted all of her.

The hall was on the same level as Lyle's solar and the small room where David would be sleeping. He picked Emilie up and carried her through the solar and into the small chamber, kicking the door shut behind him. When he set Emilie to her feet, she threw the bolt to lock the door and David looked at her with some surprise, but she simply gave him a devilish smile that made his heart beat wildly. Before he could say a word, she threw herself at him, arms around his neck, and kissed him passionately.

David was as caught up in her heat as she was in his. The flames of desire were raging wildly. His arms went around her, his lips on hers, his tongue invading the sweet recesses of her mouth. Rather than respond timidly, or not at all, Emilie was a bundle of heated flesh that matched him in his aggression. In fact, she seemed to be more aggressive than he was, her sweet body pressed up against him as close as she could go. She wasn't timid in the least, which both surprised and pleased him. When she began suckling on his earlobe, David lost his balance and tumbled back onto his bed, which quickly collapsed.

With a big boom, they were both suddenly on the floor, looking at each other in surprise. David turned his head slightly to see the bedframe around them and realized that the bottom of the rope bed had been cut. He reached up, fingering a frayed edge.

"Someone has cut the ropes," he said deliberately, looking at Emilie. "I wonder who that could have been?"

Emilie was biting her lips to keep from laughing. "I am sure you know the answer to that," she said. "I should not find any of this humorous, but…"

She began to giggle and David's lips twitched. "No wonder those two ran out of the hall so quickly."

Emilie nodded, her laughter increasing. "They have done the same thing to Brickley," she said. "He told father about it."

David grunted faintly, rolling his eyes as he lay there on his collapsed bed with Emilie splayed out on top of him. "It is war," he muttered. "I will destroy them. I will destroy everything about them. They have not heard the last of me, those little devils."

Emilie was laughing so hard she could barely breathe. David

looked at her, seeing her laughter, and it only reminded him how sweet she tasted upon his lips. He wanted all of her, this very moment, but the collapsing bed had given him pause. He cupped her face with a big hand.

"I suppose this was for the best," he said. "If we do not stop now, we will not stop until I have bedded you as a husband beds a wife. Mayhap you should return to your chamber now. I will see you on the morrow before I leave."

Emilie shook her head. "I will *not* leave," she whispered. "I do not know when I will see you again. Do you think I will surrender this precious time with you to something as mundane as sleep?"

He stroked her soft cheek. "I understand," he said. "I do not want to waste time, either, but if you stay…."

Her answer was to kiss him, softly. "I want to stay," she said. "I belong to you, David. You are to be my husband. I am not afraid of ashamed of what will come if I do not leave."

He cupped her head between both hands and kissed her. "I will ravage you."

"I know."

"You will not be able to breathe."

"I am willing to face that."

"You will no longer be virgin by morning."

"I hope not."

He just looked at her. Then, he started laughing. "You certainly are a bold lass," he said. "Most maidens are quite fearful when it comes to something like this."

She lifted an eyebrow. "How would you know?"

He cleared his throat softly. "I have been told."

She could see that he wasn't being entirely truthful and she grinned. "I will accept the fact that you have had other women before me," she said. Then, she grew serious. "But swear to me that I will be the last."

He nodded, dragging a finger down her cheek. "The last and the best," he whispered. "I swear it with all my heart. And you will swear that you will find no other men attractive but me."

"I swear."

With nothing more to say, he latched on to her lips, suckling them gently. But he grew in power and force, putting his arms around her and shifting so that she was soon underneath him on the collapsed bed. Fortunately, the bed had fallen straight down and there was still quite a bit of padding beneath them, certainly enough for the two of them. In the dim light of a banked hearth, David went to work.

Emilie was wearing a simple gown, one that fastened up the back, and he deftly loosened it. He was wearing a linen tunic and linen breeches, and he quite ably pulled them off his body. Nude, he sat back on his heels and pulled her dress over her head, tossing it onto the pile of his own clothing. She had a shift on underneath, a very thin piece of goods that he could see through, and he could see her nipples through the sheer fabric. Bending over to kiss her, he slipped his hands beneath the shift and lifted it right over her head.

They were nude now, facing one another in the dim light. Emilie was on her back, looking up at him, and David could see that her focus was on his chest, his waist, and finally to his aroused manhood. He was quite well endowed. She simply lay there, looking at him for a moment, before lifting her gaze to his face.

David met her eyes, a warm glimmer in his gaze. "Please," he said. "Look all you wish. I will not stop you."

She smiled faintly. "I like the look of you," she said. "Let me feel you now."

He obeyed her request, laying atop her and wedging his big body in between her legs. Emilie was more curious than she was apprehensive, although the feel of his weight on her body made it all seem so very real and close. It was true she had been bold with him, insisting she was ready for such intimacy, but the truth was that she was still apprehensive about it, naturally. Perhaps she shouldn't be doing this, but she really didn't care. She couldn't remember when she hadn't loved him and it was her destiny to be the man's wife. She belonged to him. As she thought on what they were about to do, David rubbed his nose against hers, gently, breaking her from her train of thought.

"Do not be afraid," he said. "You will like this, I promise."

Emilie lifted her hands, her palms on his cheeks. "I am eager for you to show me."

He did. Kissing the tip of her nose, he slanted his mouth over hers, pulling her close with one arm while the other hand began to roam. Her skin was like silk, warm and lovely, and he touched her shoulder, her arm, dragging his hand over her belly. Her breasts were full, not too large, but certainly enough for him and he enclosed one in a big, calloused hand, caressing gently, feeling the nipple harden against his palm. All the while, he rubbed the inside of her right thigh with his erection, moving it ever closer to that elusive and delectable target.

His mouth moved away from hers, down her neck, to capture a hard nipple. He suckled on her and Emilie's body trembled with delight, with her first experience of a man making love to her. But not any man; it was David, her husband to be, the man only man she had ever wanted, and this moment was particularly poignant for her. Her hands were on his shoulder, in his hair, memorizing the feel and smell of him. Soon he would be gone but he would leave her with the greatest thing to remember him by – himself.

He was about to give her himself.

His son. Emilie secretly yearned for a child, a de Lohr son in the image of his father. They were not even married, and they had never made love before, but it didn't matter to her. She wanted the man to fill her with his seed and give her his son. That way, she would always have something of him.

I do not know when I will see you again. Perhaps he would never return, for the wars between Richard and John were vicious and the House of de Lohr was always in the middle of it. There was always the chance that this would be the last time she ever saw him. But if she had his son, at least she would have something of him.

Part of him.

The erection against her thigh moved higher and now the tip of his phallus was against the dark fluff of curls. Emily could feel it. Instinctively, she opened her legs wide to him, feeling his manhood rub against her, feeling impossibly large, so large that she wondered if he would even fit inside of her. David tightened his embrace around her, his mouth on her ear, his tongue on her earlobe, and suddenly he coiled his buttocks and thrust into her, filling her full of his desire.

Emilie gasped as the stinging sensation, his manhood feeling enormous within the confines of her tight body. But rather than fight it, her legs opened wider and she moved her hips forward, trying to capture more of him, and David coiled his buttocks again and drove into her, more powerfully this time, driving himself all the way to the hilt as she groaned and clawed at his buttocks.

It was too much for him to take; David withdrew completely and thrust into her again, listening to her groan again, feeling her young and nubile body conform to him. She was deliciously tight and slick; a gasp escaped his lips as he began to thrust into her, slowly at first, allowing her to become acquainted with the sensual intrusion, but then his thrusts gained speed. Emilie's legs were flung wide-open and he shifted himself so that he was on his knees, grasping her legs and holding them on either side of his body as he pounded into her. Beneath him, Emilie squirmed and groaned.

He had lifted himself off of her for a reason; he wanted to watch her as he made love to her, the jarring of her breasts every time his body came into contact with hers, and the sight of her flat stomach and parted legs, her body welcoming his deep inside. Jesus, it was too beautiful to describe, arousal beyond anything he had ever experienced. He looked down, watching his manhood as it entered her body, seeing the faint stain of blood from her breeched maidenhood. It was the sign of his possession, the evidence that she truly and fully belonged to him now. It was a sight that excited him beyond reason.

His thrusts increased. He could feel his release coming and he wanted her to join him, to experience the pleasure he was, so he released her right leg and reached down between their bodies, rubbing her swollen bud of pleasure as he continued to thrust. It was more than she could take; as highly aroused as she was, David's expert fingers brought Emilie to her first release rather quickly.

She started to gasp as he felt her tremors begin and he thrust hard, one final time, releasing himself within her. Still moving, still throbbing, he collapsed atop her again, his mouth finding hers, kissing her and stroking her gently with his fingers as he brought her off her first powerful release. Even then, he continued to move within her long after it was over. He simply didn't want it to end.

But end it did. The two of them lay upon the collapsed bed, wound in each other's arms, as bodies cooled and breathing calmed. David, half-asleep from perhaps one of the most significant emotional experiences of his life, finally forced himself to awaken enough to look at Emilie in the face. She, too, was dozing but she opened her eyes when he moved and when their eyes met, she smiled sleepily.

"Well?" he asked, grinning. "I would assume you found it pleasant?"

She nodded, wrapping her arms around his neck and pulling him back down to her. "I found it wholly wonderful," she murmured. "You are wonderful, my love. I thank God that he brought you back to me today. Truly, David, I think we were always meant to be together. I think I felt it from the first. I think... I think I have loved you before time began and I shall love you until well after it ends. I cannot describe my feelings for you any other way."

David's smile faded as she spoke of her love for him yet again. This time, it would be more difficult to dodge it. He was feeling uncomfortable now, crushing the afterglow from their love making. He withdrew himself from her body, kissing her forehead as he did.

"I am glad you feel that way," he said, having no idea what to truly say to her. He couldn't tell her that he loved her... even if he did. He simply couldn't bring the words to his lips because he had never told anyone he'd loved them, ever. "You are mine and I am yours. It shall be that way until death."

Emilie noticed that, yet again, he would not speak of his feelings for her. It was twice that she told him she loved him and he had yet to tell her that he loved her in return. "It is true," she said, eyeing him. "David, do you love me? I have told you that I love you but you have yet to speak those words."

He couldn't look at her now. "What is love, Emilie?" he asked. "Is it a man who will ride across England to see you, a man who will fight for you and protect you? Is it in his actions or is it simply in empty words?"

Now he was speaking in riddles, which upset her. She moved out from underneath him, grabbing at the shift he had pulled off her body. "I did not speak empty words," she said, clutching the shift to her breast to protect her modesty. "I told you the truth. My love is in my actions *and* in my words. Why can you not tell me what is in your heart?"

He shrugged, seeing that she was growing increasingly agitated. "Because I do not know how to verbalize it," he said. "You are much more comfortable with that kind of thing than I am. This situation is much like the one we faced back at Windsor at the tournament, when you wanted me to pledge marriage to you simply to kiss you. Why must you rush everything so? You are always in such a hurry to make this relationship what it will naturally become if you will only have patience."

She was becoming hurt now. She yanked the shift over her head and grabbed for her dress. "You speak in riddles," she said. "It is a simple thing to speak from the heart. All you say is 'Emilie, I love you'. It is not difficult unless you do not feel that way about me. If that is the case, then I am very sorry I made you uncomfortable by telling you my feelings. That was not my intention."

He sighed heavily, reaching up to grab her wrist before she could get away. "Wait, Emilie," he said softly. "Do not go away angry."

She yanked her hand from his grasp and pulled the dress over her head, reaching her hands around to her back to fasten it. "I am not going away angry," she said. "But at least I now know where I stand with you. I am sorry you will marry a woman you do not love. I thought you were at least fond of me."

"I am," he insisted, looking up at her and feeling more and more corner and ashamed that he couldn't speak what was in his heart. "I am very fond of you. I adore you, you know that."

"But you do not love me?"

He sighed harshly. "Did I not just say that?"

She frowned terribly. "You said you adored me," she said. "That is *not* the same."

Her gown was only halfway fastened up the back as she slid her feet into her shoes. David stood up, still nude, and grasped her arm.

"Wait," he commanded softly. "Please do not leave. I do not want our last moments together to be spent in anger. If I hurt your feelings, I am sorry. I never meant to."

Emilie was taut with emotion, her entire body strained. She was deeply hurt by his inability to speak his emotions and she pulled her arm away from him a second time. "Then tell me you love me."

He sighed again, heavily. "Why is that so important to you?" he asked. "I told you that I adored you. I will be your husband. Isn't that enough for you?"

She looked at him and he could see the tears forming in the big brown eyes. "If you do not love me, I will not hold you to this marriage contract," she whispered tightly as the tears began to fall. "Go in the morning. Go back to your brother and fight your wars. But at least send me a missive telling me you are not coming back so that I know that I was only worth the price of my virginity and nothing more. It would be the polite thing to do."

With that, she unbolted the door and flew out of the room before he could stop her. David tried to follow her but she ran up the stairs and into a chamber over his head, somewhere he didn't want to go. Her family was up there and he didn't want Lyle to question what had happened because he didn't want the man to know that he had just taken his daughter's innocence. It just wasn't something he wanted made public knowledge.

So he retreated to his borrowed room, wrought with angst and sorrow, hating himself for being too timid or shy or embarrassed to tell Emilie he loved her. *Love.* He didn't know why that word was so difficult for him to spit out, but it was. And his inability to say it had hurt someone who was very dear to him. Someone he did indeed love. Perhaps he was afraid that, somehow, speaking the word would make him weak. He'd accused his brother of being weak because he loved his new wife, so perhaps that was his problem – he didn't want to be perceived as weak and he didn't want to look like a hypocrite.

So he tossed and turned all night, buried in his dilemma. Then, in the early hours of the morning, he departed Canterbury in the darkness, heading out of the castle and off towards the Welsh marches where his brother waited. He'd sent a servant to wake Emilie before he left, but the servant returned to tell him that Lady Emilie was ill and could not see him off. And with that David left Emilie behind, his heart hugely heavy and his soul in tatters, as much for himself as for her. He knew he would be back for her; without question, he would. He simply didn't know when. He prayed, for both of their sakes, that it wasn't overlong.

As David rode off into the distance, eyes were on him from Canterbury. High in the keep in the midst of that warm and purple dawn, Emilie was watching him ride away, convinced it would be the last time she ever saw him.

After that day, Lyle swore she was never the same.

CHAPTER EIGHTEEN

December Year of our Lord 1193
Lioncross Abbey Castle

T WO DAYS AFTER CHRISTMAS, Dustin went out to the rabbit hutches to make sure the peasant boy had given the animals enough warm bedding and food. Christopher had the babe, as usual, in the great hall and Alexander had followed her out into the hellish cold, dancing around her feet to keep warm. As she was poking into one of the cages, a figure came up beside her.

"It is awfully cold to be out here," David said, his nose red with the ice. "What are you doing?"

"Making sure they do not freeze to death," she said, slamming a little door closed and securing it. "I thought you were tending to the new men-at-arms?"

"I was," David said. "But Edward and Leeton are drilling them in battle rules and I want no part of it. Where's Chris?"

"Inside with Christin, where else?" she snorted. "Sometimes I think he loves her more than me."

There was something in David's eyes that set her strangely. "I doubt it," he replied evenly, then paused a moment. His gaze was intense on her as he spoke. "I know, Dustin."

She blinked at him, tilting her head. "Know? Know what?"

He let out a hissing sigh, all of the friendliness gone from his face.

"Jesus, do not lie to me," he snapped. "You can lie to Chris because he loves you and he will believe anything you tell him, but for God's sake, do not lie to me. I know."

She honestly had no idea what he was talking about and her irritation grew. "Know what, David? What are you talking about?"

He suddenly grabbed her arm, his fingers biting into her flesh and she gasped. "You slept with Marcus, did not you?" he hissed. "Christin isn't Chris' child at all – she is Marcus'."

Dustin's mouth went agape. His words had hit her in the face like a slap and left her reeling, but she had the presence of mind to calm herself before she tore into him like a hurricane. Roughly, she tore her arm from his grasp and glared daggers at him.

"How dare you accuse me of infidelity," she seethed. "Christin is Chris' daughter, David, in spite of your wild imaginings. I cannot believe you would think so lowly of me."

He grabbed her again, this time with both hands, and she struggled angrily with him.

"You are a liar and a whore," David snarled. "Christin looks just like Marcus; admit it! She bears his dark hair. Explain how two blond people such as you and my brother can bear a dark-haired child!"

Dustin yanked free and slapped him hard across the face. David responded by slapping her just as hard and sending her reeling. She slammed into the rabbit hutch, grasping the first thing that came into her hand and swung it back at David with all her might. The short piece of wood caught David in the neck and he grunted, a mighty gash in his flesh. He put his hand to his skin, drawing it away sticky with blood.

"You bitch!" he hissed.

"I was defending myself!" she fired back at him, wielding the wood like a club. "How dare you accuse me of such terrible atrocities. I cannot believe you would think such despicable things about me when I have never done anything to deserve such distrust. And who are you to confront me with such things? You are not my husband!"

He reached out and disarmed her, but not without a struggle. The log went sailing and Dustin backed away from him, preparing for the next barrage.

"Somebody has to confront you," he growled. "Admit it – Christin is Marcus' child. I knew it from the very moment I laid eyes on her that she was not of Chris' loins."

"You did not, because it is not true!" Dustin shrieked. "I swear to God I shall kill you for such lies, David."

He charged at her, grabbing her by the shoulders and slamming her against the rabbit hutch. Dustin grunted and gasped, struggling in David's grip, but it was like fighting iron.

"They are not lies," he rumbled, his face close to hers. "So help me, Dustin, I shall kill you before I allow you to hurt Chris. He is the mightiest knight since Galahad and you have already turned him into a soft, simpering fool who cares only for the comforts of his home and family. He used to be the toughest, mightiest warrior in all the world and I have watched him turn into a tender family man right before my eyes. Jesus, he was right all along. You will destroy him."

Dustin's fear-filled eyes gazed back at her brother-in-law, his words overwhelming her. The hatred, the hostility, frightened her and after a moment, she could only shake her head slowly.

"I will not, David," she said, pain in her eyes. "I would never do such a thing."

"You already have," he spit with contempt, releasing her and stepping back, his big hands clenching nervously.

Dustin's fear was overshadowed by her anger. "Christin is his daughter, and I am his wife," she said, trying to figure out what the motivation was behind his fury. It was very unlike David. "If a family makes a man weak, then I suppose he is weak. Weak of his own choosing, David. I did not force it on him. If you want to be angry with someone, then be angry with him. I did nothing but love him and he chose to respond. I did not shove my affections down his throat like a stuffed goose."

346

He turned away from her but she refused to let him go that easily. She was starting to make headway with him.

"What do you want from me, David?" she wanted to know. "To swear to you that Christin is his daughter? Then I will. On the Holy Bible, I swear to you that she is his own daughter, and I furthermore swear to you that I never touched Marcus Burton!"

The latter was only a half-truth, yet, it could be the full truth. After all, she had once thought her encounter in her dark bedchamber to be a dream. Mayhap it was after all. Mayhap if she told herself enough it really would only be a dream again and not the reality of Marcus in the flesh.

David's jaw was ticking and he refused to answer. Dustin could see that there was so much more to his outburst but she still wasn't sure what it was. "This isn't just about Christin, is it?" she said, her tone considerably softer. "There is more to this than you are telling me. Why have you decided you suddenly hate me so, David?"

He wouldn't look at her, nor answer. He pulled free of her grasp and paced a few feet away, trying to collect himself. Dustin stood there, watching him, wondering if he was ever going to answer her when Christopher came out into the small courtyard, his face grim.

Dustin's eyes widened and she covered her cheek where David had struck her. David, however, had a bloody gash on his neck that was impossible to cover up as Christopher's eyes bore into him.

"I heard a nasty rumor that you struck my wife," he said calmly to his brother. "Is this true?"

David knew what he had done and fully realized the consequences. "I did."

Christopher's jaw flexed dangerously. "Might I ask why?"

David looked away. "Ask her."

Dustin watched the two of them apprehensively, knowing a servant must have heard the struggle and had run straight to Christopher. She feared for David's life.

"I am asking you," Christopher said. "Answer me and I may be

merciful."

David turned to face him, then, and his face was glazed with scorn. "Do you truly wish to know, brother? I struck her because she's been playing you for a fool. Look at Christin; does she look like you? She does not and do you know why? Because she isn't your daughter, she's Marcus'!" He gestured wildly toward Dustin. "She has been Burton's whore all along and God only knows why you haven't done something about it. Why do you think Marcus left? Because he was in love with her and he could not stand to see her with you. Goddammit, you are both in love with her and she has been playing both of you for idiots. I struck her because I will not allow her to damaged you any further; she's already brought the mightiest knight in the realm to his knees and now she threatens to drive a dagger into your heart!"

Christopher was astonished at his brother's tirade. He always thought David had adored Dustin, and he was honestly at a loss to understand his breakdown. But the fact remained that he had deeply insulted Dustin, as well as injured her, and he would pay the price.

"David," his voice was calm, controlled. "Christin is my daughter, my flesh and blood. She has her mother's gray eyes, her grandmother's dark hair, and my nose. Never think for one moment that Marcus had anything to do with that child. My wife was not his whore, merely his friend, and it is his misfortune to fall in love with a woman he could not have. You, little brother, have no right to accuse her of such a heinous crime, and you furthermore have no right whatsoever to strike her. And as far as weakening me, she has done the opposite and has made me the strongest man in all the world. Mayhap if you ever fall in love, you will understand. But I am afraid you will not have the chance; get yourself armed and stand ready to pay for your actions."

Dustin gasped, knowing that Christopher intended to kill his brother. "Nay, Chris," she begged. "Do not!"

He ignored her as David brushed past both of them and he waited until his brother was out of sight. Then, he took a few slow steps to his wife.

"Let me see what he did." He took her hand from her cheek and examined the bleeding welt. "He cuffed you good. Does it hurt?"

"Not much," she grasped his hand pleadingly. "Oh, Chris, you are not really going to kill him, are you? He was only trying to protect you."

"I do not need protecting," Christopher replied, caressing her fingers. "And I cannot allow him to be a threat to you or to Christin."

Dustin could not believe her ears. "You cannot kill your only brother. Chris, what are you thinking?"

"I am thinking that my brother has crossed the line," he answered. "He has injured you and insulted you grievously, and I will treat him as I would treat anyone who would damage you. I will defend your honor."

She was appalled and scared. "I do not want you to kill him."

"And I do not want to, but I must do what is necessary," he said more calmly than he felt. "Dustin, what would have happened had I not come out here to stop my brother from further harming you? As difficult as it is for me to believe, the proof of his brutality is standing out on your face and I cannot allow that. Brother or no, he will pay."

Dustin's eyes welled with tears. "But I am only your wife," she whispered. "He is your brother."

He grasped her face between his hands, swallowing up her head. His gaze was hard and soft at the same time.

"You are my life, Dustin," he whispered. "Everything else in this life, including my own brother, pales in comparison. He knows what he did was wrong, but he did it anyway."

She blinked and fat tears fell onto her cheeks. "Please do not kill him."

He kissed her and took her hand, leading her back toward the kitchen door. "Christin is sleeping. Go and relieve Griselda the sitting duties."

"Chris, I...." she started to protest, but he stopped abruptly at the entrance to the kitchens.

"Not a word, Dustin," he said hoarsely and she suddenly saw the pain in his eyes. "Please, sweetheart, not another word. Just do as you are told."

"But Chris," she tried one last time to defend David. "I struck him first in anger."

Christopher sighed. "Be that as it may, he should not have struck you in return. And I will never forgive him for calling you a whore. Now, go tend to Christin, sweet."

She put her face in her hands and dashed away from him. He followed not far behind, and he could hear her sobbing all the way up the stairs. He paused a moment in the great hall, and listened as the door of their bedchamber slam, and feeling enough grief and sorrow to flood England.

He was deeply shocked at his brother, and his behavior was inexcusable. Yet in his heart he would rather kill himself than take his brother's life. Torn, increasingly despondent, he made his way outside.

David was waiting for him in full armor.

CHRISTOPHER WAS UNARMED and without his protective gear, and he eyed his brother from a distance. Edward and Leeton had dismissed the men and stood with Jeffrey, Max, Anthony, Nicholas and Guy on the edge of the practice field, hardly believing what they were seeing. Edward was the first to approach Christopher.

"What in the hell is going on?" he demanded. "David said you called him out. Why?"

Christopher continued to eye his brother. "Because he called my wife a whore and accused her of bearing Burton's bastard."

"Christin?" Edward repeated with disbelief. "That is insane. Why would David say that?"

Christopher shrugged. "I do not know, and I furthermore do not care. He did it and he shall pay."

Edward grasped his arm. "You cannot kill your brother, Chris," he said firmly. "Banish him from your presence forever, disown him, but do not kill him. You shall never be able to live with yourself."

Christopher looked at Edward for the first time, mulling over his advice. True, he certainly did not want to kill David, and banishing him was indeed a viable alternative. "I must punish him, Edward. What he did was unforgiveable."

"Indeed, but discover his reasons and make your judgment," Edward replied. "Good God, he's your brother, Chris. Your very best friend, your flesh and blood. Can you, will you, truly kill him over one incident?"

"One incident?" Christopher repeated sharply. "Suppose I allow this to go unpunished and one incident becomes two, and Dustin suffers more than a bruise on the cheek? Suppose she suffers serious injury? Nay, Edward, I must punish my brother for his actions."

"He hit her?" Edward echoed, eyeing David. "My God, Chris, what is going on in his head?"

"I do not know." Pain inflected itself into his voice. "But mayhap you are correct in suggesting I should find out."

He left Edward and walked deliberately toward his brother, who raised his sword defensively. Christopher stopped a few feet away, glaring at his brother with a mixture of anger and sorrow.

"Before I pass judgment, David, I would hear why you committed such terrible sins against Dustin," he said quietly. "I would like to understand what provoked this event."

David did not lower the sword. "She has blinded you," he said. "Christin is Marcus' child as surely as I am Myles'. Can't you see how much she looks like him?"

"If that were true, then it is my problem to deal with, not yours to handle in my stead," his brother replied. "I told you once before that Dustin is my wife, not ours. If there is any revenge to be sought or any punishment to be dealt to her, it will come from me and not you. You have no right to interfere in my life."

"Interfere?" David spat, suddenly dropping the sword and tearing his helmet off. "Someone has to. She has turned you into a soft, gutless fool. The Christopher who used to be my brother would have killed Marcus the first time he laid hands on her. He would not have spared his life and allowed this liaison to continue. What has happened to you?"

Christopher understood a lot in that tirade. David simply didn't understand what it was to love more strongly than anything else on earth, a love that was forgiving and divine and complete. Marcus wasn't the issue here; it was David. David was jealous, perhaps feeling alone and left out, and he could not accept it.

"What has happened is that I have fallen in love with my wife and child, and for the first time in my life I am truly happy," Christopher replied softly. "David, I am sorry if you cannot understand that. Mayhap if you take a wife, someday you will understand. But my loving Dustin and Christin in no way diminishes my love for you. Perhaps you are trying to drive a wedge between Dustin and I simply because you feel left out of my life. Marcus, although you have always been jealous of him, is just an excuse."

David tried to glare at him, to hold his edge, but it was rapidly slipping. It always amazed him just how insightful his brother was. "Are you going to kill me or not? Get on with it."

"Do you hate my wife?" Christopher asked.

David looked confused. "I...she's made you weak, and...."

Christopher shook his head. "Answer me. Do you hate her?"

David's chin went up. "Aye."

Christopher studied his brother's face. "And when did you discover this? There seemed to be no problem until Christin was born." He took a few steps closer and slammed the sword away from David's hand. "You are jealous. You are jealous because I have a beautiful family and you do not. And you are trying to destroy it. Christ, David, why would you do this?"

David faltered, stammered. "It was only after Christin was born that I began to see what was truly going on. We had all been blind to it until she presented you with a dark-haired daughter. We did not want to think the worst until we saw the proof with our own eyes."

"There is no proof because nothing ever happened," Christopher said sharply. "As I told you, Dustin's mother had black hair. There is no mystery to it. You are the one who is being blind, David. I never expected this of you, little brother, and it pains me greatly. I always thought you were my greatest supporter."

David's hurt became evident in his face and he lowered his gaze, moving slowly to pick up his sword. "Kill me if you are going to."

Christopher was devastated that his brother was being so stubborn. He was having a difficult time accepting all of it.

"You will not apologize?" he asked.

"Nay," David said firmly. "I am not the one who is wrong."

Christopher ground his jaw, irritation and fury sweeping him. His obstinate brother was leaving him with no choice whatsoever.

"So be it," he growled. "I will not kill you, although God knows I should. You are my only brother and the bind of blood saves you from certain death. But I will exile you from Lioncross forever. You will never again be allowed near me, or my family, and you are banished from my service as Richard's Defender. I care not where you go, or what you do, because you no longer exist to me. Get out of my sight, David. I want nothing more to do with you."

He turned on his heel and left David standing in the courtyard, his young face a mask of rage and grief. Death would have been preferable than his brother's rejection. Within a half hour he had packed his things and was gone.

Christopher watched his little brother from the solar that used to be Lady Mary's. His twisted heart grieved him deeply and his torment was unimaginable, alternately raging and cursing his brother for his violent, sudden actions and then wondering why he did not have the foresight to see the storm coming.

He and David had always been so very close, as if they could read one another's thoughts, but this time Christopher had had no idea what David had been thinking, and he was overridden with shock. When David's white charger exited the gates, Christopher allowed himself the privilege of hot, bitter tears.

"He is going." Dustin stood in the doorway, having seen David load his destrier and turn for the gates. She went in search of her husband and found him in the private little room that her mother had favored.

Christopher's back was to her and she stood there a moment, wondering if she should leave him alone when she suddenly saw his shoulders heave. Shocked, she moved into the room and her ears met with a muffled sob.

Dustin rushed to him, throwing her arms around him and pressing herself against his back. She felt a warm hand gently grasp her arms and beneath her embrace, he began to shake with sobs.

"Oh, Chris," she murmured soothingly. "My love, my sweet husband, I am so very sorry. Please do not cry."

His sobs were unbridled, like a child's, and Dustin's face was soon wet with her own tears. She felt so guilty, so helpless, and so pained with his grief. She blamed herself for David's departure one moment, yet knew she had done nothing the next. She continued to hold her husband tightly and croon to him soothingly, hoping she would be able to comfort him somehow. His deep tears cut her to the bone.

He continued to stand by the window and weep. and she allowed him time to grieve before pulling him away from the sill and sitting him in a chair. She then sat on his lap and cradled his great head against her breast, caressing him tenderly until his crying ceased. Even after he stopped, they continued to sit together for an endless eternity, lost in their own thoughts. Both were devastated from the loss of a brother.

Canterbury

Late January

FROM THE SNOWS on the Welsh marches to the milder temperatures of Kent, David found that it was much more pleasant to travel the further south he went. But his fat horse, even with its heavy winter coat, still wore a blanket against the cold as David traveled closer to Canterbury. In fact, when he'd stopped for the night to rest during his travels, he'd slept in the stable with the beast to ensure the animal was warm enough. Also, the horse seemed to be his only friend these days. It was the only real contact he had with something living.

So much had been weighing heavily on his mind during his trip to Canterbury, mostly thoughts of his brother and his brother's wife. He hadn't been wrong about Dustin; he knew he hadn't been wrong. The child looked just like Burton and he knew without a doubt the baby was not his brother's. He was still devastated that Christopher didn't see it, that he sided with his wife, even when the evidence was clearly in front of him. Christopher was being made a fool of and he didn't seem to care.

David was so sure that he was right that he'd been willing to fight his brother to the death about it. Perhaps Christopher's death would have been better than the shame the man was living with a wife who was being bedded by the man's best friend. But the fight between Christopher and David had not come, and David had ridden from the gates of Lioncross resolute and furious in his position.

He *had* been right. But as the days and weeks passed, that anger turned into something else, something deep and mournful and regretful. Eventually, he had shed tears. Now, he was without his brother and he missed him. He had no idea what to do now that he'd been disowned. Should he go to William Marshal swear fealty? He knew that The Marshal would accept him without question. In fact, David knew that any house in England would take his fealty without question. But he wasn't particularly thinking about that now. He only had one thing on his mind other than his brother at this point, and that was Emilie.

He'd left her in sorrow to return to his brother. Now, he'd left Lioncross in sorrow as well. He tried not to be hard on himself for leaving devastation in his wake wherever he went. It wasn't his fault, after all... *was it?*

The truth was that he didn't know.

The closer he drew to Canterbury, the more thoughts of his brother faded, and thoughts of Emilie began to take precedence. The land surrounding Canterbury was without snow but was very cold and dead on this blustery day as heavy winds gusted in from the north. David could see Denstroude Castle off to the east and he knew that he would soon be seeing the village of Canterbury. Truth be told, his stomach was in knots. He was returning to Emilie because he told her he would, because he had nowhere else to go. But it was anyone's guess how she would receive him. After they had parted so terribly, perhaps she would simply turn him away, too. Turn away the man who loved her but couldn't tell her.

Jesus, he'd been an idiot.

He loved her. He'd always loved her. It was a feeling that had only grown stronger, even when he'd been away from her during his time at Lioncross Abbey. She was on his mind constantly, and even now as he crested the rise and saw Canterbury with its soaring cathedral in the distance, he was planning what he was going to say to her. He hoped it was enough. He sincerely hoped she didn't toss him out on his ear.

But there was more to it than an apology. Having been banished from Lioncross, he was a wandering man that didn't belong anywhere. He had no home, no heart. But he did here at Canterbury – his heart was with Emilie. He hoped he still had hers. After the manner in which they had previously parted, he wouldn't blame her for feeling otherwise but he prayed that was not the case. He wanted to come back to her, to come home to her, and to tell her of his feelings for her. He could no longer be fearful of appearing weak by declaring his love for a woman. He had to be brave enough to tell her and suffer the consequences if that love was no longer returned.

So he passed through the town of Canterbury, which was surprisingly busy in this cold weather. Villiens were bundled up in their woolen rags against the cold and he was somewhat the object of curiosity, a lone knight on an expensive horse, heading for Canterbury Castle. As he approached the castle on the muddy road that led to the iron-fanged gatehouse, he removed the scarf from covering his mouth and called up to the sentries.

Bundled-up soldiers looked down at him from the wall walk, but this time his name was quickly recognized, and the portcullis began to grind open, lifting slowly, before he even fully announced himself. When the portcullis was half-way up, he proceeded into the mud-filled ward beyond, only to be met by a very familiar face.

Brickley was blocking his path.

It was an unwelcome sight. David sighed faintly, bracing himself for yet another round with the man. He thought to try to ease the situation a bit by being pleasant, for truly, he was weary of fighting and arguing. He'd done enough of that with his brother, as of late, and he simply didn't have the strength in him to battle any longer. He had come to see Emilie and he hoped that Brickley wasn't going to provide a big barrier against that. But he assumed the worst before he even spoke. When it came to Brickley, he could do nothing less than be on his guard with the man, always.

"I see you made it home from the battles of the spring and summer," he said to Brickley, trying to be pleasant but professional. "Where did you see your last action?"

Brickley, his face pinched red from the cold, gazed steadily at him. "A skirmish in Nuneaton about five months ago," he said. "You?"

"A very small encounter near King's Lynn six months ago."

Brickley simply nodded, eyeing David for a moment. "I am assuming you have come to see Lady Emilie."

"I have."

Brickley lifted a gloved hand and motioned him off the horse. "I have sent word to her."

David was rather astonished at the so far non-threatening conversation. Silently, he dismounted the horse, passing him off to the same two stable boys who had taken the horse from him once before. They were a little bigger now, swathed in layers against the cold. As the boys led the horse away, this time avoiding the foaming lips, David pulled his saddle bags off of the animal before it could get away completely.

Slinging the heavy leather bags over one shoulder, he noticed that Brickley was watching him. He was still edgy with the man even though the conversation thus far had been calm. But it was a calm that could easily break; he supposed he'd better take charge and speak plainly so they could both get on with it.

"Well," he said, fixing Brickley in the eye. "Let us get this out in the open, de Dere. Lord Lyle betrothed me to Emilie this past summer. I intend to wed her so if you have anything to say about it, let us get it out in the open and out of the way. I do not intend to be doing battle with you at every turn for something you cannot change, so let us deal with the situation like men."

Brickley didn't really react other than a slight shift in his expression, one that suggested resignation. It was a quick flash, instantly gone. "I know you are betrothed to Emilie," he said. "Lord Lyle told me upon my return in September. Where have you been for the past four months? I would have thought you would have come back to see Emilie before now."

David thought back to Lioncross, to the turmoil there, turmoil that went beyond his conflict with Dustin. The past four months for him had been quite complicated and he didn't want to discuss it, and certainly not with Brickley.

"Within my brother's house, there is always something critical happening," he said vaguely. "I came as soon as I could. Has Emilie been well?"

Brickley nodded. "She is well," he said. "There has been a sickness going through town and many of the town's folk are here in the great hall so that the physic can tend to them all in the same place. Emilie has been helping him."

David eyed the man and his emotionless explanation. Brickley didn't seem anything like the confrontational knight David had known him to be when it came to Emilie. His manner was almost… calm. This, in fact, was the Brickley that David had known for years, an amiable man of good nature. David wanted to be relieved but he just couldn't quite manage it. He was still braced for any manner of confrontation. He wasn't willing to believe that Brickley had given up the pursuit of Emilie so quickly. Still, he found focus with the subject at hand. Emilie was more important at the moment than Brickley's behavior.

"What sickness do you speak of?" David asked, his brow furrowing. "I have not heard of a plague in this area."

Brickley shrugged and motioned for David to follow him. They headed in the direction of the big hall, tucked into the corner of the bailey near the gatehouse.

"Not a plague," Brickley said. "An infection of the chest. Nathalie and Elise had it, too. Elise has been extremely sick. She is still quite weak but both girls are able to get out of bed and move around now. Emilie has been very busy tending her sisters, as well as helping the physic with the villiens."

David nodded, concerned that Emilie should be around the sick, but in the same breath he knew that was the role of the lady of the castle, which she was. It would also be her role as his wife. He didn't like the idea but understood her duty. He was heading for the great hall with Brickley beside him when Emilie suddenly emerged from the structure.

Brickley made himself scarce almost immediately. David thought for sure the man would remain at his side, trying to muck up any manner of personal conversation with Emilie, but the moment she came forth, Brickley turned and headed for the gatehouse and left David alone, facing a woman he'd not seen in four months. David was genuinely grateful.

Emilie's expression as she faced David was one of great surprise. Clad in a heavy woolen gown of a deep shade of brown, her hair was rolled at the back of her head and pinned up. Somehow, she looked different from when David had last seen her. She was still as lovely, more so, but there was a maturity to her expression that David had never witnessed before. As if she had grown while he'd been gone, maturing somehow.

It was the most beautiful sight he'd ever seen.

Emilie came out of the great hall, wiping her hands with a rag, and looking at him quite earnestly.

"David?" she said with awe in her tone. "You... you have come back."

She said it with such astonishment and suddenly, David felt a lump in his throat. The sight of her, of this lovely and intelligent woman that he had hurt so deeply, brought tears to his eyes. After his battle with his brother, the estrangement, and now seeing Emilie after knowing how badly he'd hurt her, was too much for him. His emotions were raw and overflowing.

"I love you," he whispered as tears streamed down his face. "I am so sorry for what I've done, Emilie. I hurt you... I behaved terribly. Please know that I love you and will never again behave so atrociously. I pray you can forgive me, even just a little."

His feelings for her were the first words out of his mouth, unintentional as they were. He'd been thinking them, of course, but the moment he saw her, they were the first words that came to mind. He didn't hold back. The tears continued to fall and Emilie rushed to him, throwing her arms around him.

"Please don't cry," she hushed him soothingly. "There is nothing to forgive, David. I swear to you that there is nothing to forgive at all."

He held her tightly with one hand as the other held his saddle-bags, his face buried in her neck, and suddenly he erupted into gut-busting sobs. The sobs were meant for his brother, for their es-trangement, something he'd been holding back since it happened, but they were also for Emilie. They were for everything that had happened over the last four months and he simply couldn't control himself. David wasn't the crying kind but his exhaustion and emotions had the better of him. The sight of Emilie had been his undoing, and she held him tightly as he cried.

"Everything is well, my darling," she breathed. "I have never stopped loving you and I have waited for you to return. I have hoped for it. Surely you know that."

He could only nod his head. He held on to her with a death grip but Emilie noticed that some of the soldiers were watching, so she turned him for the keep. She didn't want the men, who feared and admired David, see him in his weakness.

"Come with me," she said softly. "You are simply exhausted. Come inside with me. I shall take care of you."

He let her shuttle him inside, clinging to her, feeling so incredibly weak and foolish. All of the terrible things he'd ever said to his brother about a woman making him weak were coming back to haunt him. It was if now he finally understood what it meant to have the love of a woman, and her comfort. Everything was spilling out of him, and into him, filling his heart more than he could imagine. It was as Emilie was his rock at the moment and he held to her tightly, as if she alone would save him.

Save him from himself.

Emilie whisked him into the keep, warmer against the chill tem-peratures outside, and took him through her father's solar into the small chamber where they'd made love those months ago. Taking charge, Emilie pulled his saddlebags off of his shoulder and set them down against the wall before taking him by the arms and pushing him down onto the bed, which had been repaired after Nathalie and Elise's prank.

David sat and wiped his eyes, struggling to gain control of himself, as Emilie ran into her father's solar and took his pitcher of wine and a cup off of his table. She scooted back into the small chamber, poured a cup for David, and put it in his hand.

Emilie stood over him, watching every move he made, as he drained the cup in three big gulps. Then she poured him more and watched him take another long gulp, wiping his mouth with the back of his hand.

"You are exhausted," she said gently, setting the pitcher aside and pulling his helm off his head. "Look at you, David; you are weary to the bone. How long have you been traveling?"

Tears under control, he felt drained and embarrassed for his outburst. He set the cup aside so he could remove his gloves.

"It seems like forever," he said. As he pulled on the fingers of a glove, she pushed his hands away and remove the gloves for him. "I have come from Lioncross."

Emilie set the gloves aside. "Stand up so that I can remove your cloak."

He obeyed. She pulled the heavy cloak free, hanging it on the peg next to the door. "Lioncross is weeks away," she said with concern. "Why have you been traveling for weeks in this weather?"

He looked at her, hanging up his wet cloak. "Because I had to come to you."

She paused, turning to look at him, a faint smile on her face. "You did not have to risk your life in this terrible weather to do it," she said. "But I am glad that you did."

His gaze drank her in, soaking in the lovely sight of her. "As am I," he said. "Now that I see you, I feel... I suppose I feel whole again. Something is missing when I am not with you, Emilie. Something has been missing for months."

Her smile grew and she turned for the hearth, which was cold and dark. When David saw what she was doing, trying to start a fire, he gently pushed her aside and began building the fire himself. Emilie was on her knees next to him, watching his pale face and slow movements. She was over the shock of his unexpected appearance but she sensed there was something more to his arrival because the man was not himself in the least. It was in his movement, his expression, and everything about him. Something was wrong. It concerned her.

"Then I am glad you came back to me," she said, going down onto her knees beside him. "I have missed you a great deal."

He turned to look at her. "You should not have," he said. "Not after the way I left things between us. You should be berating me at the very least."

She shook her head. "And yet I am not."

"Why?"

She lifted her shoulders. "Because there is no need," she said. "I forgot my anger against you long ago, I suppose. Time has a way of doing that. I should not have become angry because you did not speak the words I wanted to hear. In your own way you were trying to tell me of your love but I would not listen."

It was a magnanimous reaction, making David feel even more guilty about it than he already did about how he had behaved. This kind and gentle creature was far too forgiving. It was too good to believe.

"I do not know what to say," he said. "Your forgiveness... it is more than I had hoped for."

Emilie stroked his damp blonde hair. "Yet you have it," she said. "It is true that I was hurt. But I am quick to hurt and anger sometimes. I should have been more understanding."

He turned to look at her, kissing her hand when she put it on his cheek. "'Tis simply that it is very difficult for me to speak of my feelings," he said. "I have never had anyone to speak them to. When my brother married his wife, I accused him of being weakened by his emotions for her so I suppose there is some embarrassment for me to admit that I now understand how he feels. I feel for you what he feels for his wife, and it is difficult for me to admit that. I always thought that emotions, like love, make a man weak."

Her dark eyes glittered at him. "And now you do not?"

He shook his head. "Nay," he murmured. "I have been forced to swallow my pride in order to tell you that, but now I do not think emotions make a man weak. At this moment, with you by my side, I feel like the strongest man in the world."

Emilie put a soft hand on his cheek, kissing his cold lips sweetly. David wrapped his arms around her, holding her close as he kissed her deeply. He was so very grateful to be back in her arms again. It meant more to him then he could express.

"I am here to stay if you will have me," he said when they paused between heated kisses to catch their breath. "I will not be going back to Lioncross. If your father will accept my oath, I will swear fealty to Canterbury."

Emilie's brow furrowed with some confusion. "But what of your brother?" she asked. "You are sworn to him."

David shook his head, releasing her as he went back to building the fire. "Not any longer," he said. "We fought. I will not be seeing or speaking to my brother anymore."

Now Emilie was very concerned. "But why?" she asked. "Can you tell me what happened?"

He paused in stacking kindling into the hearth. He wasn't sure he should tell her everything, but the truth was that she would soon be his wife, and it was her right to know about her husband and his relationship with is family. Besides, he felt the need to confide in her. The only person he'd ever confided in was his brother, so this was something of a strange experience to bare his soul to someone else.

"We fought over his wife," he finally said. "She delivered a daughter a few months ago."

Emilie thought that sounded like good news; she wasn't sure why such a thing would distress him. "I think that is lovely," she said. "Is the babe healthy?"

He nodded. "She is very healthy," he said. "Her name is Christin and she looks just like my brother's best friend, Marcus Burton. It is his child and my brother will not see reason. Everyone knows it is not his child but him."

Emilie lifted her eyebrows, shocked at such scandalous news, but she tried to remain objective about it. She didn't want to say anything that might offend him. "And you told your brother your suspicions?"

He shook his head, striking the flint and stone and producing a small flame on the first try. "I confronted his wife and gave her the opportunity to confess," he said. "She denied it, of course, and the discussion became heated. She slapped me and I slapped her back. I should not have done it and I regret that I struck her, but you must understand Dustin to know that she is always willing to fight, no matter what the situation. I did not strike her first and I will swear to that, but hitting her in return… I am not one to strike a woman, in any case, but I did. It was very wrong."

Emilie was astonished to hear such a confession. "I do not believe it," she said staunchly. "You would no sooner hit a woman than… than my father would or Brick would. You are not that kind!"

He was feeling increasingly ashamed for his actions. "Mayhap not under normal circumstances, but I did slap her when she slapped me," he said. Then, he looked at her. "I do not offer excuses, Emilie, but mayhap an explanation. It was simply a heated argument that went out of control. When Chris found out what had happened, he banished me from Lioncross and from his service. I have been disowned."

Emilie was coming to see now why he'd been so emotional when he first saw her. There had been a good deal of angst and sorrow and regret building up inside of him, about many things. It didn't even bother her that he had slapped his brother's wife; given the situation, being struck first, she didn't put any blame on him. As far as she was concerned, he was provoked. She put her hand on his.

"It does not matter," she said firmly. "You have come back to me and here is where you shall remain. My father will be happy to have you and your sword."

David smiled wryly. "And Brick?" he asked. "I am sure the man will be thrilled to death to see me on a daily basis. He did seem rather pleasant when I arrived, however, unless it was a ruse. Mayhap is waiting outside for me even now with an ax in his hand."

Emilie grinned although she was thinking back to that September day when Brickley had returned from the skirmishes with John's mercenary army. It had been about a month after David had departed, after their betrothal and subsequent sorrowful parting. Brickley had returned, fully prepared to resume his pursuit of her, but both she and Lyle had informed him that such a thing was no longer possible because she had been betrothed to David.

At the time, Emilie had still been quite upset with David, hurt with his inability to speak of his feelings for her, but she never let on to Brickley. He was, in fact, hurt enough to know that his offer of marriage for her had been formally, and finally, rejected. So the two of them had lingered in their own worlds of hurt for a while, not speaking to one another, and the friendship between them forever changed.

Emilie wasn't sorry for the change but there were times she wished Brickley was still her friend and they could speak on things without the angst of emotion coming between them. But that friendship had been irrevocably damaged and something else had taken its place, something oddly cold and formal. Emilie could now speak to Brickley, and he to her, but their conversations were usually only necessary ones. The camaraderie was gone. And Brickley had changed as well, a man who seemed to have lost some of his joy in life. He kept to himself, resigned to a world without Emilie in it.

It had been a difficult change to watch.

"Brick is a changed man," Emilie finally said. "He knows of our betrothal and he is resigned to it. He knows that Papa will send him away if he does not behave."

David lifted his eyebrows in understanding. "Has it been awkward for you, being at Canterbury with him?"

Emilie shook her head. "Nay," she said honestly. "We simply do not speak anymore."

David had to admit he was glad to hear that. He was glad that the situation with Brickley had calmed down, because the last thing he wanted to do was fight the man off at every turn. He blew at the fire, sparking it into a healthy blaze, before standing up and pulling Emilie up with him. He wrapped his arms around her, gazing down into her sweet face.

"Then I am glad for a peaceful situation," he said. "And am looking forward to our life together more than you know. With everything that has happened with my brother, I am thankful that you are my way to happiness. I have longed for this moment more than you know. Have you considered a wedding date, then?"

She smiled, relishing the feel of the man against her, something she had hoped to feel again but, in spite of what she had told him, wasn't truly sure if she ever would. At the moment, she felt as if she was living a dream.

"I have not," she admitted. "But I would like for it to be soon."

"So would I."

"Mayhap in the spring when the weather is better? It will give me a chance to finish my wedding gown."

He kissed her. "Whatever you wish," he said. "I am completely at your whim."

Emilie liked hearing that. She put her arms around his neck, hugging him tightly. It was such a joyous embrace, because when she'd awoken that morning she had no idea that David would come back into her life on that very day. Therefore, the day itself had turned out most beautifully and unexpectedly. All of the hurt and sorrow she'd felt for the past four months had miraculously been erased.

Strange how those few words spoken by David, declaring his love for her, had worked such magic for her delicate heart.

All was well in the world again.

PART THREE
THE LION ROARS

"War, I say! – end as you well began!"

~ Song of Roland c. 1040 A.D.

CHAPTER NINETEEN

H E WAS TRACKING his prey.

After Emilie had left him to return to tend the sick in the great hall, David had laid down on his borrowed bed and taken a long nap. He'd slept like the dead, heavily and deeply, and when he had awakened, the sky outside was turning pink shades of sunset. He laid upon his bed for a few minutes, orienting himself and coming to the realization that he hadn't dreamed his reunion with Emilie.

He was here at Canterbury, and here to stay.

He could still feel the texture of her skin in his hands and the smell of her hair in his nostrils. No dream could compete with the reality of Emilie in the flesh and he lay there a moment, staring at the ceiling, wondering if he should thank God for the fact that Emilie didn't turn him away when he'd shown up. As he'd told Emilie once that he wasn't particularly pious, but in this case he might change his mind. After the terrible happening with Christopher, it was as if God knew he needed a haven and comfort. David had found both in Emilie. Perhaps a little prayer was indeed in order.

It was just a few words, really. Just enough to let God know he was grateful for his blessings. Then David thought that he should probably rise and seek Lyle out. He needed to speak with him about the situation with Christopher and he hoped that Lyle would accept his oath. He started to roll off the bed when two big black dog's heads suddenly popped up from the floor of the chamber, and before David realized it he was being smothered by those two hairy beasts that belonged to Emilie and her sisters. The dogs were as big as he was and they jumped into bed with him.

Quickly, David shoved them out of his bed, scolding them, and wondering how in the hell they had gotten into his chamber. They hadn't been there when he had fallen asleep. But the dogs were ill-behaved and kept jumping on to the bed next to them. The big slobbery dogs kissed his face as he kept shoving them off the bed. Then he grabbed at his boots next to the bed and shoved his feet in, preparing to make a swift exit from the over-excited dogs. But the moment he put his feet in his shoes, he knew that something was very wrong.

Pulling his feet out, that were now strangely slimy, he stuck his hand in and pulled out eggshells. Someone had put eggs in his shoes and it didn't take a great intellect to figure out who. Frustrated, and knowing he should have seen this coming, he shook the eggshells out of his boots. All the while, however, he was plotting his vengeance. Those two wicked devils that pretended to be little girls were about to meet their match. He'd vowed it before and had never had the chance to carry out his threat.

Now, he had the chance.

So he put his shoes back on and opened the door, letting the happy dogs out into Lyle's solar beyond. The room was empty, cold and smelling of smoke. The dogs were running around in Lyle's solar, jumping up on the table and knocking things around, but they didn't seem very willing to leave David behind. They seemed to want to stay close to him. David was fairly certain that Nathalie and Elise had let the dogs into his chamber just to annoy him, and in that realization, he knew what he was going to do to them.

He was going to make them pay.

Going back into his borrowed chamber, he flipped the straw mattress off the bed to reveal the new rope frame beneath. He untied the entire rope, long enough to tie two girls up with, and took it with him as he left the chamber. The dogs danced around him, happily, and he managed to coerce them back into his chamber. Once they were in, David shut the door and the hunt for his prey began. He was afraid if he didn't respond now, it would forever set the tone of their terror against him.

So he began to stalk. The keep was seemingly deserted at this hour and he suspected the girls might still be in the keep, being that they had been ill and more than likely would remain where it was warm. He also suspected that was how they knew he was here, since they were bottled up in the keep. They had crept into his room while he had been sleeping, put eggs in his shoes, and left the dogs behind to annoy him. Well, they were about to get their just rewards for poking the bear.

With rope tucked away in his hand, he made his way out of Lyle's solar, disgusted by the feel of the egg that was still in his boots, now squishing around his toes. The stairwell leading to the upper floors was directly across from him and he quietly made his way to the steps, slipping up the stairs to the floor above. The level was darkened and quiet, and he peered into the two chambers that were on this level, only to find them empty. He didn't even hear any sounds. The spiral staircase continued on to the floor above and he made his way up to that level in complete and utter silence.

The top level was dark, with another two chambers on either side of the landing. One chamber seemed to be empty but he could hear voices in the other chamber. The door was shut but light emitted from underneath the door jamb, and David pressed himself up against the wall, adjacent to the door, and listened very closely.

There were voices he didn't recognize, but they were young and female. He didn't hear Emilie in the mix, and truly had no idea where she was, but the chamber contained more than one young female and he was willing to bet it was Nathalie and Elise. *His victims!* He hoped it were them because he had something very special in store. Keeping himself pressed against the wall, he knocked. And then he waited.

The door opened rather swiftly after his first knock and he spied the youngest daughter, Elise, as she took a step out into the landing to see who was there. Immediately, he grabbed her, pulling her away from the door. Terrified, Elise shrieked and her cries brought Nathalie running. The middle Hampton sister rushed out of the room, only to be grabbed by David as well. Now, he had both of them, like two cats in a snare, and he shoved them both against the wall. He wasn't being rough with them but he was being firm. Nathalie, the stronger of the two, bellowed and fought.

"Unhand me!" she roared. "How dare you touch me! I will tell my father what you've done!"

David had her wrist and her sister's wrist together, wrapping the rope around the limbs. "Excellent," he said. "I hope you do. Then I will tell him about the dog shite in my helm, the egg in my shoe, and I will also tell him about the time you sabotaged my bed by cutting the ropes. Three times you have made a fool of me, ladies. There will not be a fourth."

Infuriated that David had the audacity to seek revenge, Nathalie began smacking him around the hand and shoulders with her free hand, struggling to break away, but David had her tied quite snuggly to her sister, who had stopped fighting back and was now standing there, weeping loudly. David dodged most of Nathalie's furious slaps as he secured one knot before grabbing that same flailing hand and holding it fast against Elise's free wrist. He wound the rope around the, back to back, tying up their arms and securing their bodies together. Soon enough, the girls were tied up to the point where they couldn't readily move except for their feet, but because of the way David had tied them, loose feet weren't doing them much good. Natalie continued yelling while Elise wept.

Once his quarry was trussed up, David stood back and took a look at his handiwork. He had tied them tightly but not tight enough to hurt; just enough so they couldn't really move. He folded his arms across his big chest smugly.

"Now," he said. "I want to hear an apology for the nasty things you have done to me. If it is sincere enough, I might untie you."

Nathalie, tied securely against her sister, was mad enough to spit. "You will be punished for this," she threatened. "You are an arrogant swine, David de Lohr! And I care not that my sister thinks she is in love with you! I would rather kiss a pig than marry someone like you!"

David cocked an eyebrow at her. "That can be arranged," he said. Then, he looked at Elise. "And you? What do you have to say for yourself?"

Elise had nothing to say. She simply wept. With Nathalie snarling and Elise refusing to speak, David unfolded his arms, picked up both girls together in a bundle, and carefully carried them down the spiral stairs.

At first, Nathalie started to kick, throwing him off balance, but he cautioned her from doing that lest they all fall down the steps to their deaths. She was less apt to kick at the walls after that but she kept trying to kick his knees, which amused him to no end. She was a fighter, this one, so he was careful in the way he handled her. He didn't want to make a mistake and end up dropping them both. Poor Elise would pay for her sister's resistance.

It was therefore slow going to the entry level of the keep. Once down the stairs, he headed across the foyer to Lyle's solar. It was still empty, fortunately, and David was able to make it to his chamber door without interruption. He set the girls on their feet and opened the door.

The big black dogs with the enormous tongues greeted them and David lifted the girls once more, carrying them into the chamber. The dogs were excited to see all of them and didn't try to run out, which made it easy for David to shut the door behind them. In the tiny chamber with the girls tied up and the two dogs, David managed to lay the girls into the floor where the dogs could lick their faces and they couldn't do anything about it. In fact, the dogs were particularly amorous and slobbered all over Nathalie and Elise's faces while the girls screamed and cried, begging David to release them so that they could at least defend themselves. He stood by the door, hands on his hips, watching the girls being licked to death.

"Consider this your punishment for the terrible tricks you have played on me," he said. "In fact, it is my understanding that no one has been safe from your antics so consider this vengeance from every man you have taunted and tricked over the years. I am quite sure they will award me with a prize when they hear of this."

One of the big dogs was licking Nathalie's face so vigorously that she was turning red. "You... beast!" she sputtered in between licks. "I will tell... my father! He will... punish you!"

David laughed, without humor. "Somehow, I think not," he said. "If you take your punishment like a man and not tell anyone, then I will consider this matter settled. You will never again play a trick on me or any other man at Canterbury. But if you cry to your father like a weak, silly child, know that what you are enduring now is only the beginning. You will know torture such as you have never comprehended and I will make it so. Now, what is your choice?"

Nathalie kept turning her face but every time she did, the dog's big tongue would find her. "I will get you for this," she yelped. "Do you hear me? You will not be safe!"

David had to admire the woman; she wasn't going to back down. A foolish quality, but a brave one.

"Is that your final answer?" he asked.

Nathalie screamed when the dog began licking at her ears. "Untie me *now!*"

David shook his head. "Mayhap later," he said. "If I were you, I would think very carefully about my next move. Consider my offer. If you do not, then you will be the one to suffer, not I. I am bigger and smarter than you are, Nathalie Hampton. Remember that."

Natalie only yelled. As David watched, the dog that had been furiously licking Elise suddenly lifted its leg and peed on her feet. Elise screamed and cried as David fought off the giggles. It was cruel, that was true, but for what those girls had done to him, to Brickley, and to any number of Canterbury soldiers, they deserved everything they were getting and more.

Leaving the girls on the floor with the happy, licking, and peeing dogs, he left the chamber and quietly closed the door on them. He would come back in a few minutes and release them, but for now, they deserved everything they were getting. Perhaps it was the start of all-out war between him and the girls, or perhaps it would be a ceasefire. In any case, he couldn't help the laughter as he stood at the door and listened to them wail in disgust.

He hadn't laughed so hard in years.

EMILIE COULDN'T FIGURE out why here sisters seemed to subdued.

The supper that evening was a warm and fragrant affair in the smaller hall, with her father, David, Brickley, Lillibet, Nathalie, and Elise present, only Nathalie and Elise, who were usually fairly active during their meals, simply sat and picked at their food. Emilie did notice that every time David moved, they would jump and look at him with big, frightened eyes. Emilie wasn't quite sure what it all meant, but she suspected something had happened between David and her sisters that she wasn't aware of. She made a mental note to ask him later, for Nathalie and Elise's behavior were very curious.

Elise had come to sup in the hall as she always did, with her box of people placed on the table next to her trencher. Usually, she took her people out but tonight they remained in their box. As Emilie's attention lingered curiously on her sisters and their behavior, Lyle and David had been having a rather detailed conversation about the winter weather and the dozens of winters they had known since their childhood. Brickley wasn't much in the conversation, nor was

Lillibet. Everyone else at the table seemed relatively quiet except for Lyle and David. Lyle seemed particularly talkative. After nearly an hour of conversation, he finally turned to the rest of the table.

"It seems that I have been doing all of the talking and monopolizing David's time," he said. "'Tis simply that I am glad to see him, as I am sure we all are. I am only sorry I was not here to greet him when he arrived but I understand that Brickley was most hospitable."

Everyone looked at Brickley, who seemed rather uncomfortable that all eyes were on him. He cleared his throat softly, reaching for his wine. "It was my duty, my lord," he said. "With you away at Denstroude, I greeted him in your stead."

Lyle nodded, sobering somewhat. "The entire garrison at Denstroude has this terrible illness that has passed through the town," he said. "I took more men to reinforce the ranks. It does no good to have a garrison that cannot defend itself."

Emilie was listening with concern. "Mayhap I should go to the garrison, Papa, and see to the men," she said. "This sickness is quite bad."

Lyle shook his head. "The garrison commander has his sister to tend them, Mistress Juliann," he replied. "You know the woman, of course."

Emilie nodded. "I do."

"She has the situation well in hand. You are needed here, Emilie."

Emilie couldn't disagree with him. "There *are* a lot of sick," she admitted. "I do not believe the physic has slept more than a few hours all week. Lillibet and I have been trying to give the man some relief by tending the ill so that he can sleep."

David, seated between Emilie and Lyle, spoke up. "And you?" he asked. "I hope you have not let yourself get too tired."

Emilie smiled at him. "I am not too tired," she said. "Do not worry about me."

He frowned, lightly done. "Of course I shall worry," he said. "It would not due for you to become ill before we are married."

Emilie shook her head, patting him on the hand that was on the tabletop. He grasped her fingers and they smiled at each other, a warmth radiating from them that everyone in the room could feel, even Brickley, who was trying not to notice any of it.

Brickley had his back partially to the happy couple as he sat back in his chair, nursing his wine. Lyle kept glancing at the man even though Brickley seemed resigned to his place in Emilie's life, in which it was clear he had no place at all. Still, Lyle didn't want the man deliberately hurt. He knew Emilie and David weren't holding hands to insult to Brickley, but Lyle could only imagine how the odd knight out was feeling, even if he wasn't showing it.

"Emilie," Lyle turned to his daughter. "David and Brick and I had a long conversation before sup whilst you were still tending the sick. I have accepted David's fealty, and Brickley will be taking command of Denstroude Castle. With David here, there is no need for two knights and Brickley is happy to command the garrison."

Emilie had not yet heard this news; she had been so busy with sick villagers up until supper time that she hadn't had much chance to speak with her father since his return from Denstroude.

"That is excellent news," she said, approval in her tone. "I am glad to see that you were able to come to a satisfying conclusion for everyone. As I recall, Brickley rather likes Denstroude. It is much closer to the sea and he likes the sea. Is that not correct, Brick?"

Brickley looked up from his wine, his expression rather dull. He didn't like it when she called him Brick; it sounded too informal, too affectionate as she used to be in days past, and it hurt his feelings. But he didn't voice his thoughts. He simply nodded.

"Aye, my lady," he replied. "I grew up by the sea. I have always been fond of it."

He didn't seem hugely excited but he didn't seem depressed, either. There seemed to be a tense peace around the table now that David had joined their family. At least, no one was arguing or glaring or seemingly upset about it – namely, Brickley. Emilie was quite relieved, to be truthful. But this was the first time they had all sat together since the betrothal announcement, so she was hoping for the best from Brickley's perspective. The man may have been resigned to the situation but that didn't mean he didn't have the right to be bitter about it. If he was, he wasn't showing it, thankfully.

"Speaking of growing up, Brick, you have not said much about the son you visited back in August," Emilie continued. "You mentioned it when you returned to Canterbury, but I have not had the opportunity to ask you how Huxley is faring."

The reality behind that entire statement is that she really wouldn't talk to him at all, fearful to strike up a conversation with him on any subject that wasn't absolutely necessary, for fear he would turn the focus back to his feelings for her. Somehow, he always found a way to do that. But here in front of David and her father, it was safe to ask him about his son. Plus, it was a way to include Brickley in a conversation that he'd so far been left out of.

But when Emilie spoke of Huxley, Brickley simply looked at her. *If she really cared about my son, she would not have waited three months to ask me.*

The bitterness was starting.

"He is well, my lady," he said. "He is already as big as I am and running Barnwell Castle. He even has a young lady he has his eye on."

Emilie smiled. "That is wonderful to hear," she said. "A man should get married young, I think. Don't you, David?"

David snorted into his cup. "A man should get married when he is ready to get married."

Brickley looked back to his wine and took a large gulp. "Some men are ready sooner than others," he said, wiping the back of his hand. "Some men are ready but there is no bride to be had."

Lyle, sensing the conversation might very well take a downturn at that moment, spoke up quickly.

"David, have you heard of any news from London," he said, even though he'd already asked the man that same question in their conversation before supper. He was just speaking on the first that came to mind but quickly amended his question. "Of Eleanor, I mean. She usually winters in the Aquitaine, does she not? I am curious to know if she is returning to London considering Richard's current status."

David knew very well that Lyle was trying to prevent him and Brickley from getting into a verbal tussle, so he graciously allowed the man to lead them along another subject. "As far as I have been told, she is still in France," he said. "I do not know if she will be coming to England. She hasn't for quite some time, even though Richard left her to rule in his stead as Regent. She has done so quite ably from France with the help of Richard's chancellor."

Lyle nodded. "Longchamp has not had an easy time of it, especially with John running amuck," he said. "I have lived a long time and I swear to you that I have never seen family dynamics such as those between Henry and Eleanor and their children. As a younger man, I fought with Henry against his sons, you know. It always seemed to me that Henry was rather hurt to have his sons turn on him as they did."

"And his wife," David put in.

Lyle chuckled in agreement. "*And* his wife."

"Speaking of family," Brickley said to David from across the table, "when you and Lyle spoke before supper you mentioned that you and your brother were at odds now. I thought the de Lohr brothers were unbreakable."

It was clear that Brickley had too much drink in him. In fact, that was what he had been doing most of the evening and now his tongue was loosened. Lyle spoke before David could.

"That is none of your affair, Brick," he said quietly. "It does not matter why David has sworn fealty to me. His relationship with his brother is none of your concern."

Brickley shrugged. "He spoke of it right in front of me when he was discussing the subject with you," he said. "If he wanted to keep it a secret, he would not have mentioned it in front of me. Now I am curious to know what happened that would drive him back here to Canterbury. It took him four months to come back to Emilie, but that is none of my concern, either. I was simply curious what happened, 'tis all."

So now Brickley's true feelings on David's return was starting to surface. Although the man appeared reconciled to the situation, some wine in his veins proved that he wasn't as resigned as he pretended to be. Lyle was growing quite annoyed with Brickley but David quieted him. This was directed at him, after all. Brickley could say all that he wanted, but the fact remained that Emilie belonged to him, so David kept that in mind. Nothing Brickley could say could hurt him or Emilie in any way.

"Do you have any brothers, Brick?" David asked after a moment.

Brickley shook his head. "I do not," he said. "It is just me and my son."

David toyed with is cup as he watched the man across the table. "I see," he said. "Then suffice it to say that sometimes there are misunderstandings. Sometimes it is best to put space between brothers. Men have strong opinions sometimes that are not easily changed. But that is not the real reason I came back to Canterbury; it was to be with Emilie. Surely you can understand that reason above all else."

It was a bit of a barb at Brickley, who frowned as David finished his sentence. He poured himself more wine. "I do," he said. "But what happens when your brother recalls you? Are you just going to leave her again?"

"That is not going to happen."

The conversation was on the verge of turning ugly. Lyle clapped his hands, calling for more food and wine and sweets to be brought to the table, and servants began to scurry. Emilie held David's hand under the table, smiling encouragingly at him when he glanced at her. She could see what was happening, too, and how difficult Brickley was being.

She wasn't the only one who noticed, however. Across the table, Nathalie was somewhat aware, too, but she'd stopped pining for Brickley long ago. He had made it clear he held no interest for her, so she had moved on now to a young farm boy, whom Brickley had brought in to help reinforce Canterbury's ranks when he left to fight against John. With nothing of interest to hold her attention at the supper table, she grew bored quickly with the subject of two knights vying for her sister's affections, especially when one of those knights was her archenemy, David de Lohr.

In spite of what had happened earlier in the day, Nathalie didn't consider the war between her and David over in the least. It was true that he had subdued and humiliated her, but she wasn't going to let that stop her. No man was going to get the better of her, and especially not a buffoon like David. Now that he was occupied with her father and sister, she would be free to leave the table and do as she pleased to his possessions. At least, that was the way she looked at it.

"Papa?" she asked politely from across the table. "May Elise and I be excused?"

Lyle eyed his younger daughters, who had come to the supper table this evening looking rather wet and dirty, and Elise smelled of dogs and piss. But he didn't give much thought to it, much as he didn't give much thought to the fact that the girls now wanted to leave the table. He waved a hand at them.

"Go," he said. "Take Lillibet with you. She will see you to bed."

Nathalie, rising from her feet, was clearly unhappy that her father had consigned them to Lillibet. It would mean her plans for revenge against David would be ended for the night, for Lillibet wouldn't let her out of her sight.

"Nay, Papa," she said, but when she noticed her father looked surprised at her refusal, she hastened to explain. "Lillibet spends so much time with us. I am sure she would like to spend time in adult conversation for a change."

Elise, with her box of wooden people in her arms, nodded. "She spends too much time with us!"

Lyle frowned at his daughters. "That is because you are young and foolish," he said. "Lillibet, go with them. Make sure they go to bed."

Lillibet was on her feet, already moving for the girls, who were very unhappy with the chaperone. They frowned at just about everyone at the table, Emilie and David included, but when they came to David, their expression seemed to change quite a bit. Elise looked away, swiftly, while Nathalie's eyes narrowed dangerous. David didn't react but he met her stare, boldly, as Lillibet shuttled them from the room.

Emilie hadn't noticed the glare her sister had given David, but she did notice that the Roland and Cid were not where they usually were under the table. By now they would be up and following the girls form the hall.

"Where are the dogs?" she wondered aloud. "It seems strange not to have them beneath the table."

Lillibet wasn't quite out of the room yet, trailing behind Nathalie and Elise. "They are in the barn," she said, spit flying out onto her clothing. "Nathalie and Elise are punishing them for some reason, so they are tied up in the barn. Do not worry; I made sure they had water and a bone. They will do well for the night."

Lyle scratched his head. "Why would the dogs be punished?" he wanted to know. "What did they do?"

Lillibet shrugged. "They would not tell me, my lord," she said. "They would only tell me that they do not want the dogs in their chamber tonight."

As Lyle and Lillibet discussed the mysterious reason behind the dogs' incarceration, David could hardly keep a straight face. At least Nathalie and Elise hadn't told of the incident this afternoon, instead they locked away the dogs that had been used as a torture device so David couldn't use them again. They were smarter than he gave them credit for.

Victory, at least for tonight, would be his.

"Now that the children are gone we can drink to excess and spout foul language," Lyle said, breaking David from his mental victory celebration. "It is probably better that Nathalie is gone. She seems to become quite strange when we discuss anything that has to do with Emilie's wedding. She seems to hate the mere mention of the word."

David looked at Emilie curiously, but she merely shrugged. "Not to worry, Papa," she said, thinking that her sister hated discussion of marriage because of her failure to attract Brickley. Even though that episode was over with, still, the bitterness lingered. "I am sure it is nothing at all. David, Papa asked you about Queen Eleanor earlier. Have you actually met the woman?"

The subject was gracefully changed away from anything painful or awkward, like weddings and unrequited love, expertly done by Emilie who seemed to have a knack for the art of conversation. She knew what would be a better issue to discuss and she moved the discussion in that direction. David was happy to comply.

"I have," he said, looking to Lyle. "Have you, my lord? I know you spent a good deal of time supporting Henry back in the day."

Lyle, reaching out to pick up one of the sweet cakes the servants had brought, shook his head. "I did not meet her personally," he said, shoving the cake in his mouth. "I have seen her on a number of occasions but I have never met her. An extremely powerful woman, she is. She has been married to kings and birthed at least one."

David thought on the rather tall and fair Eleanor, now in her advanced years. "She would have made an excellent king herself had she been born male," he said. "She seems to like my brother a great deal. Chris thinks she even tried to seduce him, once, although he fended her off and fled in terror."

That comment even brought a weak smile from Brickley as Lyle lifted a cup as if to salute Eleanor's lusty libido, even at her advanced age.

"Why not?" he said. "Your brother is young and handsome, and I heard rumor that Eleanor even seduced her own uncle once, so why not a handsome young knight?"

As he snorted, Emilie looked rather chagrined. "She did?" she said. "How shocking."

Lyle waved her off, still grinning, as David poured Emilie more wine. "Here," he said. "Drink this. It will make Eleanor's seduction not seem to terrible. See how much your father is enjoying it."

Emilie laughed softly because Lyle was rather giddy with drink at this point. She took the cup from David as the entry door opened and blustery cold wind snaked inside the keep, reaching into the hall. Emilie shivered as the wind gusted and one of the two soldiers who had entered shoved the door shut. Both men were heavily dressed against the elements as one soldier, who was in the lead, proceeded into the small feasting hall as the second soldier hung back by the entry.

Lyle, noting that two of his soldiers had entered, wasn't particularly happy to see them. Soldiers usually meant there was a message of some kind that he needed to attend to, and he genuinely did not want to go back out for the night. Therefore, he already decided that whatever it was, he would send David or Brickley. With two powerful knights at his disposal, he didn't have to lift a bloody finger anymore.

Lyle rather liked that idea.

"What is it?" he demanded.

The soldier in the lead produced a missive from beneath his heavy cloak. "A messenger brought this, my lord," he said. "He says that William Marshal has sent him."

Those few words erased any apathy Lyle might have had about any incoming message, and the mood in the room suddenly dropped from light and festive, to one of concern and even apprehension. There was no more humor or easy talk to be had. *The Marshal has sent a missive.* That meant it was serious, indeed. David was already on his feet, moving around the table and taking the missive from the soldier. David pulled it out of its leather casing and inspected the wax seal closely.

"It is the Marshal," he confirmed, glancing at Lyle. "May I open it, my lord?"

Lyle waved him on. "Aye," he said, "quickly, read it."

David did. He popped the seal on the vellum and unfolded it, as it had been folded over itself and sealed up. He moved over to the hearth to have more light to read by and the seconds ticked away as he read the contents. Those watching him could see a change in his face as he read; he went from concern to a hardness that was difficult to describe. Emilie saw it most of all in that face she loved so well.

"David?" she asked, fearful. "What does it say?"

David let out a hissing sigh. "Emilie, mayhap you should retire for the evening," he said. "This would not interest you."

Something told Emilie that David was quite wrong in that assessment. "I will stay," she said firmly. "Answer me, please. What does it say?"

David looked at her for a moment, realizing he couldn't get her out of the room without an argument, so he didn't try. He turned his attention to Lyle.

"Richard is being released," he said quietly. "Although this is excellent news, it seems to have prompted John into putting his full force into wresting England from his brother. The Marshal is calling for all men and all troops to converge in the middle of England, for it is feared that John is moving on Gowergrove Castle. Have you heard of it, my lord?"

Brickley, who had been listening intently, spoke before Lyle could. "I have," he said. "I have even spent time there. It is a beast of a fortress south of Nottingham that controls two major roads north. If John gains control of Gowergrove, he could essentially cut the north off from the south."

It was bad news, indeed. The men in the room seemed to automatically shift into battle mode now that the contents of the missive were known. David moved away from the hearth to hand Lyle the missive, who took it eagerly and read it, as Emilie took one of the small banks of tapers off the table and moved it closer so her father would have more light. As Lyle and Emilie read the missive, David looked at Brickley.

"What do you know of Gowergrove?" he asked the man. "If you have spent time there, then you know her strengths."

Brickley lifted his eyebrows thoughtfully. "Gowergrove has walls that are thirty feet high in some places," he said. "There is also a massive moat, which is more of a lake than a moat. One must cross the moat to get to those walls, and both the walls and the moat are nearly unbreachable."

David had only seen Gowergrove in passing because of the roads that passed near the castle. He'd never been there before, but he'd heard tale of the place. "But it is possible to get across the moat and over the walls?"

Brickley nodded. "It is," he said. "With enough men, it can happen."

David was thinking rapidly about the factors he knew, statistics already established that might give John the edge in capturing such a castle. "John has thousands of mercenaries," he said to Brickley. "We already know this."

Brickley wasn't in the command hierarchy as David was. Even Brickley would agree that David had much more knowledge about such things than he did.

"So I have been told," he said. "Surely your brother has received the same missive from William Marshal. That means that he will be heading to Gowergrove as well."

David, who had thus far seemed relaxed but concerned in the course of the conversation, seemed to tense up considerably at the mention of his brother. He turned away from Brickley at that point.

"I will make that assumption as well."

Brickley, who was trying to shake off too much drink now that there was a serious subject at hand, wasn't sensing David's mood. "We can bring at least eight hundred men north," he said, assuming David was going with him. "If we leave within the week, we can make it to the southern forests of Nottingham in about three weeks."

David thought on that. It was clear the call was going out to all of Richard's supporters to hold the kingdom for Richard, who was evidently on his way home. As thrilling as that news was that the king had apparently been ransomed, the fact was that the king's brother was now making his final and violent grab for the throne of England, and it was quite troubling. More than that, David knew for a fact that his brother was probably the first person to have received the Marshal's summons, and David was willing to bet that his brother was already on his way to Nottingham.

A brother who didn't want to see him. David moved back over to the hearth, pondering the situation between him and his brother. He didn't want to show up leading Canterbury troops because he wasn't entirely sure how his brother would react to his appearance. Christopher would be in charge of the battle and it would make it more than awkward for the man, perhaps even distracting him from his duties. Distraction in battle was deadly, and David wrestled with the very real possibility that he might cause more harm than good, were he to show up to fight. Christopher had made it quite clear that he didn't want to see him anymore.

A brother disowned.

But his heart inevitably began to ache. He and his brother had fought countless battles together. This would be the first one where they were not fighting side by side, and that knowledge hurt David to the bone. Christopher had so many knights around him – Edward, Leeton, Thomas Dudley, and any number of other knights that had sworn fealty to him. It wasn't as if he needed David.

He really didn't need him at all.

"You will take the troops, Brick," David finally said, pausing by the hearth. "I will not be going."

That brought a gasp from Emilie as both Lyle and Brickley looked at David as if the man had gone mad. "Why not?" Lyle demanded. "You have seen the summons. You cannot disobey."

David sighed heavily. "I am not on that summons, my lord," he said. "That summons is not addressed to me. Therefore, I am not violating anything. I do not wish to discuss my reasons for not riding north with the army, but suffice it to say that I cannot do it. I *will* not. My brother, and the rest of England, must fight this battle without me."

Brickley appeared puzzled, Lyle was gravely concerned, and Emilie rose out of her seat and walked around the table, making her way to David. Her expression was quite serious as she stood next to him, her gentle hand on his arm.

"Why not?" she asked softly. "Why will you not fight?"

He looked at her. "My reasons are my own," he said softly. "I would ask that you respect that for now until I am ready to speak more on the subject."

She was quite worried about his refusal and lowered her voice when next she spoke. "You said that you and your brother fought," she whispered. "Does it have to do with that?"

He nodded, once, and she let the subject go, her hand still on his arm as he stood by the hearth. Lyle, however, was still quite puzzled by the refusal.

"David, it is well known you are one of the best knights England has ever seen," he said. "You have sworn fealty to me. If I sent my army north, then I should expect you to go with them. Richard needs you now more than ever."

Emilie spoke up before David could. "Papa, please," she said. "David has given us his position on the matter and we must not question him. He has been fighting constantly for years. He fought for three years in the Holy Land only to return and continue fighting on English soil. If the man does not wish to fight this particular battle, it is his right. Has he not earned a rest?"

She was passionate in her defense of him, and Lyle wasn't sure what more to say. Still, it was clear that he wasn't happy about it. He stood up from the table, missive still in hand.

"I would say that now is not the time for him to rest," he said as he moved away from the table. "Although we will not discuss it tonight, David, you and I will revisit this in the morning. I am sorry, but it is necessary."

With that, he left the small hall, heading out into the darkness beyond. David and Emilie saw him disappear into his solar. As they stood there in tense silence, Brickley rose from his seat, grunting with the weariness he was feeling. Wine always made him weary. He, too, moved to quit the hall.

"I will bid you both a good eve, then," he said, not looking at them. "David, I never thought I would say this, but I would feel better if you went. There are not many knights in the world of your caliber and we would all be better served with you than without you."

He left before David could reply. David and Emilie watched him go, leaving the taper-lit hall and leaving the keep, out into the cold winter night. When they were finally alone, Emilie turned to David.

"I know you said that you did not wish to discuss it, but I am very concerned that you will not be going north to fight alongside your brother," she said softly. "Mayhap his anger against you has cooled by now. Don't you think he will be looking for you? Expecting you? How can he fight without you?"

David put his arm around her shoulders and turned her around, moving for the table where there was still plenty of wine and sweets. He helped her to sit before taking a seat beside her.

"He will not be expecting me," he said quietly. "Em, my brother is a very painful subject and I do not wish to discuss it right now. I told you all I can about what happened, at least for now. Please respect that."

She nodded. "I will," she said. "I am sorry. I am just concerned for you."

He kissed her cheek gently. "I know," he said. "I appreciate it. But suffice it to say that this new gathering, this battle at Gowergrove, will be fought without me. I will not go. Knowing my brother, he will have a massive army behind him. He doesn't need me, anyway."

Emilie let the subject go after that. It seemed there wasn't much more to say and David wasn't willing to speak of it, anyway. All Emilie knew was that David seemed much more subdued after that. Sad, even. It was very difficult for her not to speak on is mood or manner, but it was clear when the change had occurred. But he had asked her not to speak of his disagreement with Christopher, so she wouldn't.

After that they simply sat alone in the hall and sipped wine as David told her of the amazing cities he had visited on his way back from the Holy Land, simply to change the subject away from battle and Christopher de Lohr. It worked; she was particularly enamored with a city surrounded by mountains called Vienna and he promised to take her there one day.

When Canterbury's troops left Canterbury Castle five days later, David de Lohr was not with them.

CHAPTER TWENTY

February Year of our Lord 1194

*T*HE STOP IN LONDON *had been for the sole purpose of picking up the crown troops, now numbering nearly three thousand strong. Christopher viewed his huge army with satisfaction, knowing they would surely quell John easily and he could return home soon. Richard was crossing the channel as he met with the jubilant justices, but Christopher could not wait for the king. John had to be controlled as he laid siege to the mighty stronghold of Gowergrove Castle.*

Richard's return had indeed pleased Christopher, but with the focus his life had taken, he hadn't felt the excitement he once would have. He no longer lived solely for his king, but for his family, and he wondered how well Richard would receive that knowledge. Christopher intended to step down from his title as Defender and become a mere baron once again, leaving the duties of the realm to a successor he would surely hand-pick. Marcus was the first man that came to mind.

With the troops retrieved, the three-thousand-man army headed northwest to the great castle of Gowergrove, a favorite holding of Richard's, which was at the southern tip of Sherwood Forrest. John had always had his eye on the fortress, and if Gowergrove was under his command, 'twould be near impossible to pass from southern to northern England without passing through his territory. Christopher had to secure the castle at all costs, and early on the eleventh day after leaving Lioncross, he laid siege to John's troops at Gowergrove Castle.

John's mercenary army was dug in like a tick on a dog. The walls of Gowergrove were nearly thirty feet tall. The moat surrounding it was filled with nasty, rotting filth, which was very undesirable for the men-at-arms to go plunging into, to say nothing of the knights in their armor. Leeton set two hundred men to building ladders to mount the walls, but until that time, there was naught else to do but besiege Gowergrove with archers. These were fine Welsh archers whose accuracy was legendary.

Three days into the siege, the ladders were complete and after a day and a night of attempts, they were finally able to cap the walls and the battle truly began. When the bridge went down, Christopher was the first man inside.

The fighting went on for days, long and exhaustive days. Christopher saw barely five hours' worth of sleep, and he spent his entire time in the saddle dueling mercenaries. Ralph was nowhere to be seen, but he saw Sir Dennis on several occasions, and made it his focal point to seek the man out and destroy him.

The battle had spilled out into the surrounding areas and the moat was filled to overflowing with the bodies of the dead. Christopher had suffered tremendous losses, as had John, but he refused to withdraw because John's army was considerably weaker. He knew it would not be much longer and he would have Gowergrove secured.

As was usual in February, the winter weather turned extremely foul and the worst storm Christopher could remember doused them day and night. At night, the rain would turn to ice and pelt the armor like a thousand stones being thrown, but in the day, it was miserable freezing rain. The land outside the castle soon turned into a deep, mucky bog and the destriers were up to their knees in the stuff, making fighting extremely difficult.

Christopher was exhausted, as they all were. One morning, he found himself fighting outside of the great wall, trying to help Leeton subdue a particularly hearty band of criminals. They were trying to *steer them toward the moat, corner them in, but the unruly horde was proving to be most disobedient and Christopher was fed up with all of it. His frustration had reached a frenzied level when something huge and powerful tore into his body, plowing through his mail and shoving his breastplate aside as it invaded his midsection brutally.*

Stunned, Christopher's hand flew to his left side and he was anguished to feel the shaft of a great spear protruding from his torso. The rain had begun to fall again, in great blinding sheets, washing his life's blood down his saddle and onto the ground before it could collect on his armor.

He still retained enough of his wits and reined Zephyr around, heading with speed for the trees. He wanted to be away from the battle zone so there would be something left of his body to return to Dustin. And he knew, with great remorse and anger and agony, that he was going to die. He had seen wounds like this before and they were always fatal.

Christopher barely made it to the edge of the forest before weakness overcame him and he fell from his horse in a great, dying heap. He struggled through the haze of darkness that threatened to crawl further into the underbrush, his breathing coming in harsh gasps and feeling pain radiate throughout his body like nothing he had ever known.

His eyes burned with tears, but not for himself. He would never again know the sweetness of his wife's flesh, nor would he have the joy of watching his daughter grow into a beautiful young lady. The torment of cruel fate surged through him and he cursed himself the first day he ever picked up a sword. If he could have changed it, he gladly would have. He missed Dustin already. Goddammit, it just wasn't fair!

There was someone beside him and he recognized Leeton, rushing at him in panic.

"Jesus, Chris," Leeton's voice cracked. "The bloody bastards got you. Oh, Jesus, let me see!"

Christopher tried to wave him off, knowing any attempt to save him was futile, but Leeton roughly yanked off his breast plate and shoved his mail aside.

"A spear," Leeton spit with contempt. "Goddamn cowards could not get you with a sword, so they took to hurling spears. I have got to get this out."

Christopher started to shake his head, but he was far too weak to do anything but utter a strangled yelp when Leeton yanked the spear from his guts. Bright red blood gushed freely as Leeton slapped a few rags of linen on the spot, knowing they would be nearly useless against such a flow. He already felt the loss of his liege deeply and his handsome face was pale with sorrow.

"Leeton," Christopher groaned, grabbing at him.

"Aye, Chris, I am here," he said, grasping Christopher's hand and holding it tightly.

Christopher could barely speak. "Take....take my wedding ring," he whispered. "Take it back to my wife. Tell her....tell her what happened and tell her my last thoughts were of her. And tell her I love her, Leeton. I love her with all my heart."

Leeton, a seasoned veteran, found himself choking back tears. "Chris, I...."

"Take it!" Christopher tried to yell, but he had not the strength to press his point. His life was fading away and his strength with it.

He held up his left hand. Leeton hesitated for a tormented moment before ripping off the gauntlet and pulling off the ring. He did not know who was the more miserable; him or Christopher. He wanted to scream, to yell, to demand that God show pity and take him instead, but he could only focus on his liege with tears in his eyes. Christopher, satisfied that his last wish would be carried out, let his hand fall to the ground. His blue eyes closed and there was a faint smile on his lips.

"Thank you," he whispered.

Leeton heard a horn and turned his head in the direction of the battle. "Chris, they have got the mercenaries boxed in. I have got to go, but I swear I shall be back. Do you hear me? I shall be back. I shall find

Burwell and return. He will save you."

Christopher weakly grasped his wrist. "No one can save me, Leeton," Christopher murmured. "You and I both know this is the end of me. One more thing....find David and tell him that I am sorry for everything. Tell my brother that I love him and ask him to take care of Dustin and Christin for me."

Leeton could not stop the strangled sob, but he nodded his head furiously. "Aye, anything you say," he said tearfully, grasping Christopher's shoulders with his big hands. "Just... please hold on. Burwell ought to have something to patch up that hole."

Christopher did not reply; he had already slipped into unconsciousness and his breathing was slowing. Swallowing hard, Leeton took one last look at his liege, his grief overflowing, wishing he was not the one charged with the horrible duty of informing Lady de Lohr of her husband's passing. Already, he felt the agony to his bones.

But he would do what had been asked of him in one last show of obedience. He would have much rather stayed with Christopher as he breathed his last, but more pressing duties were calling and he answered reluctantly. Leaving Christopher lying beneath the trees to protect him from the rain, he put the wedding ring on his left hand for safekeeping and mounted Zephyr. His own destrier, suffering a huge gash to the chest, was left grazing on the edge of the forest.

Leeton reined Zephyr in the direction of the battle, taking one last glance at Christopher's still form under the trees. Dear God, it wasn't fair. Christopher was The Defender, entitled to immortality, deserving of divine grace. To die fighting the bastard prince was unworthy of such a great man, and Leeton felt a great surge of anger wash over him.

Leeton swore to himself that he would find Ralph and Dennis and John and run each one of them through on Christopher's behalf. If it took him the rest of his life, he would do it. Every one of those bastards would pay for what they had done to his beloved liege and friend. And with each stroke of the sword into their flesh, he would be sure to mention Dustin's name.

He made it several hundred yards from the wall, fighting alongside other knights in the blinding rain. Aboard Zephyr, the men thought he was Christopher and the fighting was furious. They were inspired by him. Yet they were not the only ones who thought he was Christopher; a barrage of crossbows unleashed arrows as plentiful as rain, and Zephyr went down in a scream of agony. Leeton tried to bolt free, but the horse fell quickly and with all of his armor, he was weighted severely. There was no chance for him to escape.

Twenty-five hundred pounds of horseflesh buried him face-first in the mud, and in Leeton's last wild thoughts, he never imagined he would actually drown on the field of battle.

THE BATTLE FOR GOWERGROVE was over.

Crown troops victoriously let Richard's pennant fly from the walls and took to killing any remaining mercenary soldiers. Word of The Defender's death hit everyone hard, as hard as if their own beloved father had been taken from them, and they were committed to doing everything they could to make John's army pay. As the men moved slowly and lethargically about their duties, as exhausted men usually do, disbelief filled every face.

Anguish and grief were hand in hand among the men, and especially the knights. But none were harder hit than Christopher's personal stable, and they set about their tasks mechanically, although each and every one of them had taken the time to view the body in the mud, half-burled underneath his destrier. Seeing had to be believing, yet none wanted to believe.

"We lost Leeton, too," Max mumbled, gazing down on the body of their great liege. "Has anyone even seen him?"

"Nay," Sean de Lara, another allied knight, replied and turned away from the rotting corpse underneath the horse. Sean was a knight sworn to Richard and had remained in London when Christopher had

gone to Lioncross last year, but then rejoined Christopher when the man had come to London to collect the crown troops. He had been by the baron's side for weeks. "He is probably buried underneath this muck, somewhere. I saw his horse three days ago, over by the line of trees."

Anthony de Velt had shown an amazing amount of responsibility in the past three days. A rotting hand, a wedding ring around the left finger, was jutting up out of the rancid mud and he reached down and plucked the gold band free. "For Lady de Lohr," he said softly. "She will want to keep it. Now, we must bury the body."

"We are not returning him to Lioncross?" Max stood up from his crouch and faced his brother. "To be buried on his soil?"

"Max, if we bring this sickening corpse back to Lioncross, you know Lady Dustin is going to want to view her husband," Anthony said pointedly. "We will try to prevent her, but you know she will gain her way. Do you truly want her to see Chris in this state? It will drive her insane."

Max glanced down at the corpse, so bloated and unrecognizable that the skin was splitting on the head where the helmet was restraining it. The only thing of any recognition was the blond hair, and the ring.

"Nay," he said after a moment, crossing himself and uttering a prayer. "God, no."

Anthony nodded curtly. "Then set up a detail to dig Chris a grave. Leeton one, too, if we can find his body. Pick a nice place, perhaps on that little rise up there."

Max tore his gaze away from the body and motioned to Guy de la Rosa. "Come on," he muttered. "Let's get to it."

Sean and Anthony were left gazing down at the grisly scene. "What in the world happened?" Walter asked. "I mean, look at the way the horse has fallen. Impaled through the heart, he is. Is it possible it fell on Chris and he drowned in the mud?"

Anthony shrugged. "Mayhap we shall know after we free the body.

Meanwhile, we have a whole keep to clean up." He glanced over at the men-at-arms who were beginning a funeral pyre and he stomped off in their direction. "Hey! You men over there! Do not burn bodies so close to the keep unless you want to render everyone in the castle ill!"

He was off shouting, leaving Sean standing a depressing watch over the remains of his liege. The thought that The Defender was gone was so overwhelmingly bleak, that the man hesitated to believe another day would dawn over England.

He glanced at the sky above, bleak and gray. That was the world to him at the moment without his liege; bleak and gray and colorless. He could not stand to look at the body anymore, and with a sting to his eyes, he went to help the others dig graves.

CHAPTER TWENTY-ONE

*W*ORD OF THE DEFENDER'S *passing spread through England like wildfire. Ralph and John, having been at Nottingham when Sir Dennis had brought them the news, partied for three days.*

Richard disembarked at the Tower to be met by the justices, welcoming him home to English soil with one breath and notifying him of the current situation with the next. John held fourteen castles and Christopher de Lohr was dead, killed in battle at Gowergrove Castle. Deeply distressed and seriously exhausted, Richard had shed public tears at his brave friend's passing. Sir Philip de Lohr, disembarking with Richard, crossed himself and went immediately to Winchester Abbey, where he prayed for two straight days.

David, now betrothed to Emilie Hampton and serving Lyle Hampton, heard from the earl of his brother's passing. His pain was so great that Lyle ordered David locked in his room with a constant guard on his person, terrified his future son-in-law would take his own life. He knew of Christopher and David's falling out, and he furthermore feared David would never be the same.

A violent argument between two brothers would now never be resolved, and David was inconsolable. Even Emilie could not bring him out of his depression. But David was made of strong blood, and after his initial shock and pain dulled, he kissed Emilie good-bye and set out for London to see Richard. He knew the king would want to see him, but his stay in London would be short. After that, he vowed to continue to Lioncross and beg Dustin's forgiveness, hoping she would allow him to comfort her.

And mayhap, she could comfort him as well. He could not deal with the fact that Christopher had gone to his grave hating him.

Canterbury Castle
March Year of our Lord 1194 A.D.

THE RAINS HAD been miserable for days and days, overflowing creeks and rivers and washing away some of the poorly-constructed homes in the town of Canterbury. Nearly everyone was flooded out to a certain extent and that included the keep at Canterbury, whose lower level – a storage level – was seeing several inches of water. As a result, the servants and soldiers had been forced to move a good deal out of the storage vault and it now cluttered the corners of the small hall and into Lyle's solar.

More rain poured that night from a storm that lit up the sky brilliantly for miles, thunder and lightning that created a spectacular show. Because part of the town nearest the river had been inundated, several dozen villiens had come to the castle seeking shelter, something that Emilie was in charge of providing. Between her, Lillibet, Nathalie, and even Elise, they were able to settle many people into the great hall comfortably. The servants kept a fire blazing in the hearth as families settled in, drying out their clothing near the fire and supping on bowls of gruel with dried currants and apricots in it. Everyone was warm, drying out, and fed.

Meanwhile, David had been in the town with about fifty of his men saving lives because part of the river bank had eroded away, and many homes had collapsed into the raging waters. David and his soldiers had been pulling people out of the mud and water for most of the evening, ever since the storm had rolled in, and now as things had settled Emilie went to the gatehouse, wrapped up against the weather to anxiously await David. Their wedding was finally scheduled for the following Sunday and she was very concerned for her soon-to-be-husband. When the call for help had come to the castle, he had fearlessly led his men out into the town, which was an admirable quality, but Emilie was terrified the man was going to end up down the river.

Fortunately, he returned to her after the crisis passed, covered in mud and soaked through to the skin. Emilie had taken him into the keep to help him clean off, and dry off, as Lyle, who had remained warm and cozy and out of danger for most of the crisis, went to the gatehouse to keep watch until David was in a better position to resume his duties. It was a night of chaos with the storms and flooding, and Lyle remained vigilant on the second floor of the gatehouse, monitoring the town from that position. It was also from that position that he saw the first signs of his returning army.

Like phantoms through the mist, they came in as wet and weary groups. Sentries on the walls were the first to see the army between lightning bursts, as they entered the town from the north. A sentry called out the sighting to his sergeant, who then waited for the next lightning strike to confirm the sighting before rushing to Lyle with the news. Lyle assumed it was his army returning from battle, for certainly, no army would be out in this weather to lay siege to Canterbury Castle. Moreover, he didn't even know anyone who would want to try, for he had no real enemies as far as he knew. So Lyle wait with great excitement as his army drew closer, illuminated by the lightning rolling through the sky.

But it took time. The roads were terrible and the army, mostly on foot, was moving slowly. As the first of the men began to trickle in, Lyle directed them to the great hall where there was still room for them to get out of the weather and dry out. The rest of them would have to go into the small hall in the keep, and Lyle ordered the hearth in the small hall stoked. Quickly, the room became cloyingly, and welcomingly, hot.

More men trickled in, dead tired and soaked to the bone, and Lyle found himself directing the disbandment with a few of the battle-weary sergeants. Finally, he spied a knight astride a charger towards the rear of the column and recognized Brickley's animal. He had to admit that he was glad to see the man. When Brickley passed beneath the iron-fanged portcullis, Lyle was there to greet him.

"Brick!" he said. "Why did you not send word that you were soon to be arriving? I've not heard from you in weeks!"

Brickley's face was pale, rain dripping off his face. He dismounted his charger, nearly collapsing when he hit the ground out of sheer exhaustion. Lyle steadied the man and tried to pull him away.

"Nay," Brickley said huskily. "My horse. He must be tended."

Lyle was already waving on the small pair of stable boys who always tended the horses. When the boys grabbed the reins and began pulling Brickley's horse, and other horses, away, Lyle tugged Brickley towards the keep.

"Come on, man," he said. "Let's get you out of this rain."

Brickley was moving, but not too easily. He was looking around, as if searching for someone. "Where is de Lohr?"

Lyle pointed to the keep. "The riverbank collapsed on the north side of town and he has been there most of the evening trying to keep people from drowning," he said. "He has just returned and gone inside."

Brickley came to a halt, grabbing on to Lyle so that he came to a halt, too. "Wait," Brickley said, hanging on to Lyle. "I must tell you something before we go inside. Has David received word about his brother?"

Lyle wasn't happy that he was standing out in the rain becoming wet. He wiped at his face. "What word?" he asked. "We have not received any word here, about anything, since you left. Why do you ask?"

Brickley fixed on Lyle. Water was pouring over his pale face as he spoke. "Christopher de Lohr was killed in battle last month," he said. "David has not been told?"

Lyle suddenly wasn't so concerned with the rain. His eyes widened with shock at the news. "Sweet Lord," he exclaimed softly. "Nay… nay, we have not received any word to that regard. Are you sure, Brickley? There is no mistake?"

Brickley shook his head, so exhausted he could hardly stand. "No mistake," he said hoarsely. "The entire country is in mourning. And David does not yet know."

Lyle put a hand over his mouth to hide his shock and sorrow. "He does not," he said, sounding oddly hollow. "Sweet Lord… he does not."

Brickley resumed his walk towards the keep, only he was very nearly staggering. "You must tell him."

Lyle was helping Brickley towards the stairs but his mind was reeling with the news; *Christopher de Lohr is dead*! He didn't want to be the one to break the news to David but there was no other choice. If what Brickley said was true, then the news had to come from Lyle, as David's liege. He turned to Brickley again.

"You are sure there is no doubt?" he asked again.

Brickley shook his head. "Although I did not see the body, one of de Lohr's men told me," he said. "They do not know that David is at Canterbury, you see. I told no one and no one asked. It was none of my business that David is here so it did not seem right to tell anyone where he was. Mayhap he did not want his brother or his brother's knights to know. In any case, I suppose no one would know where to send a missive, but I had to ask if you had received anything to that regard. It is my understanding that Richard is personally returning the body to Lioncross Abbey."

They had reached the keep stairs. The slippery stone was carefully climbed by the men as they made their way to the top. All the while Lyle was struggling with what he had been told. He could hardly believe it.

"I will tell David," he said, "but he will want to hear it from you, too, Brick. You were there. He will want to hear it from your own mouth."

Brickley shook his head. "My lord, it is not as if David and I are close," he pointed out. "In fact, this past year has seen us become adversaries and you know it. Although I am resigned to David's existence here at Canterbury, surely I cannot tell him such a thing. He already dislikes me. If I tell him of his brother, I am sure my life will be measured in minutes as the bearer of such news."

Lyle was holding on to the man as they made their way into the keep. "I told you that I will tell him," he repeated. "I am sure he will not try to harm you in his grief. But he may have questions I cannot answer. You will stand with me when I tell him. Please, Brick. I think it is important that you do."

Brickley didn't argue any further. Frankly, he was too exhausted to do so. They passed through the open entry door, propped open by the servants so that the returning army could come in and dry out. There were already men in the hall, stripping off wet clothing, so Lyle pulled Brickley into his solar where another fire burned. In the chamber beyond, the small room where David was settled, they could hear the voices of David and Emilie.

Lyle positioned Brickley by the fire so the man could begin drying out as he went to close the solar door. He didn't want anyone to see or hear David's reaction when the devastating news was delivered. Then, he went to help Brickley strip off his wet things, for the man was struggling. Lyle called out to David and Emilie in the room beyond.

"David?" he called. "The army is returning from the north."

David was suddenly in the doorway of his chamber, looking at Brickley with some surprise as Lyle pulled the man's gloves off. Naked from the waist up, David still had mud all over his neck that Emilie, following him with a rag, was trying to wipe off.

"You have returned," David said to Brickley, perhaps the warmest thing he could manage. "I suppose John's mercenaries have bad aim these days."

The statement, meant in humor, was like a shot to the gut for Brickley and Lyle. *Their aim was not so bad that they did not miss your brother.* In fact, Lyle closed his eyes briefly and grunted, knowing he could not delay what needed to be said. He was already sick to his stomach about it. The longer he delayed, the more difficult it would be to tell him.

"David," he said, somewhat subdued. "Come here."

David did, sensing absolutely nothing out of the ordinary. Emilie was tagging along behind him, trying to get the hardened mud off the nape of his neck. David's hair was wet where he had dunked it into a bucket of water to rinse out the mud, but he still had patches of dirt on him.

"What were the losses, Brick?" David asked.

Brickley wouldn't look at him as he and Lyle moved to remove him from his soaking tunic. Brickley was so cold that his fingers weren't moving correctly so Lyle was doing all of the work.

"I left with eight hundred and twelve men," he said, lips blue and quivering. "I have returned with six hundred and ninety-four."

David pondered that figure. "A loss of one hundred and eighteen men," he said, somewhat somber. "I suppose that ratio is not too bad, considering. Where did you see action?"

Brickley spoke through chattering teeth. "The missive we received from the Marshal said Gowergrove was the center of John's activity," he said. "We headed there and joined up with your brother's army as they headed north from London. He had evidently marched from Lioncross to London to pick up crown troops, so by the time we joined them, it was well over three thousand men. We headed north and saw action at Gowergrove as predicted. John's army had already captured it by the time we arrived, however, so it was a matter of purging them from the castle."

David was listening intently. "Did you see my brother?"

Brickley couldn't help but glance at Lyle, who was hanging the dripping tunic up on a peg next to the hearth. When Lyle simply nodded his head, as if to give Brickley permission speak on the subject of Christopher, Brickley continued. But it was becoming increasingly uncomfortable and painful.

"I did," he said. "I did not speak with him if that is what you mean. Knights such as I do not speak with the great Defender. We only do what we are told."

David didn't react to that statement. He seemed to be content that Brickley had seen the man. "Go on about Gowergrove," he said. "Were you able to reclaim the castle?"

Brickley nodded. "We did," he replied. "But it was a horrific battle. We fought for weeks in weather much like this. It poured and the mud was up to our hips in some places. Unfortunately for many of our dead, the mud swallowed them up and hardened. When I left Gowergrove there were several hundred men unaccounted for, including some you may know."

Lyle thought it was a rather brilliant lead-in to what was to come, as David seemed quite somber and serious about the situation. "Like who?" he asked quietly.

Brickley sighed heavily. "Leeton de Shera," he said. "I heard that the man was unaccounted for and presumed dead under all of that muck."

David closed his eyes briefly, greatly saddened to hear the news. "Jesus," he muttered, a hand going to his head in a gesture of strife. "He was a great knight but I suppose… I suppose he is happier now. He has not been the same since his wife died. Mayhap you knew Leeton, but if you did not, he was still in mourning for his wife who died in childbirth over three years ago now. I am happy for the man to have finally been reunited with her in heaven."

Brickley looked at Lyle at that point. It was the perfect opportunity to tell of his brother and Lyle caught the glance and took the hint. He moved away from the hearth to stand next to David.

"More were lost, David," he said as gently as he could. "It seems that your great and powerful brother has also joined those ranks, for Christopher was lost on the field of battle as well."

David stared at him. It was an odd stare, as if he was processing Lyle's words but not particularly comprehending them. In fact, he snorted, grinning as if it was all a big joke.

"That is not possible," he said. "My brother would not fall to John."

Lyle put his hand on David's big arm. "It is true, David," he insisted softly. "I am so terribly sorry. Your brother is gone."

The smile faded from David's face as he looked at Lyle. Something was going on behind those pale blue eyes because they suddenly widened and he looked at Lyle as if the man had just grievously lied to him. His brow furrowed, outrage evident on his face.

"It is *not* true!" he insisted. "Who told you such lies?"

At this point, Brickley spoke. He had to. "It is true, David," he said firmly. "I am very sorry to tell you what I was told. One of your brother's men, a man named Anthony de Velt, told a group of knights, me included, that Christopher was found buried in the mud, having fallen beneath his mortally wounded horse. There... there were no marks on his body that they could find. The best they could tell was that he had drowned in the mud when his charger was wounded and fell on him. All of England knows of his death by now, and I heard rumor that Richard himself was taking your brother's body back to Lioncross. That may or may not be true, but I thought you should know."

David was looking at Brickley as if the man was speaking in tongues, as if he couldn't comprehend what he was being told. He must have stopped breathing because he suddenly took an enormous gasp and stumbled back, tripping over the chair behind him and falling to the ground. As Emilie fell to her knees beside him, David sat up, knees bent and head in his hands, and began rocking back and forth like a madman.

"Nay," he muttered to himself. "It is not true. It cannot be true. He is not dead; *he is not dead!*"

Emilie was already in tears, her hands on David's bare shoulder. "I am so sorry, my darling," she whispered. "I am so, so very sorry."

David's rocking was growing worse, sharp little pants coming out of his mouth as if he was struggling to hold back the sobs that were determined to come forth.

"Nay," he said, shaking his head, hands clutching his skull. "It is not true. He cannot be gone!"

"He is, David," Lyle said, greatly concerned. "I am very sorry for your loss, lad."

David was on the verge of a breakdown of extreme limits. "Nay," he mumbled again. "*It is not true!*"

Emilie didn't know what to do; she looked to her father, tears streaming down her face. "Papa," she gasped. "Please help him!"

Lyle, watching David with perhaps the greatest sorrow he had ever felt, went to his knees beside the man as well. "David," he said, trying to sound comforting but firm. "God determines our time on earth. He sent Christopher here to do great things, but his time is over. God needs him back in heaven, mayhap to lead the heavenly hosts now. Your brother's great legacy will live on, I promise. It will live on through you. You are the last and greatest de Lohr now, and that is a responsibility I know you can bear. Your brother would have wanted you to bear it proudly."

David looked at Lyle, hearing the words that only seemed to make his grief worse. He couldn't even describe what he was feeling at the moment, because no words existed to flesh out the magnitude of anguish he was experiencing. He didn't even have the sense to know that Lyle had meant well; all Lyle had managed to do was make it all hurt more. David's face crumped and he put his hands over his mouth, tears streaming down his face.

"God help me," he whispered over and over. "*God help me!*"

It was like listening to a man who was losing his mind. David suddenly stopped rocking, burying his face in his hands, and weeping openly. Emilie threw her arms around his head and neck, hugging him tightly as he sobbed. Lyle, who could see that for the moment there was no comforting David, rose wearily to his feet and went to Brickley.

"Go find Lillibet," he muttered to the man. "Ask her for the poppy powder. Bring it back here with a full measure of wine. Hurry!"

Brickley, saddened to witness David's breakdown, regardless of the relationship between them, moved quickly to obey. Man to man, knight to knight, he greatly sympathized with David's grief. As Brickley fled, David continued to sob into his hands as Emilie tried desperately to comfort him. But there was no comfort to be found; he was wallowing in a world of sorrow that had swallowed him whole. The pain wracking through his body was just too great.

"He died hating me," David mumbled, his hands over his mouth. "Our last words were those of anger. I did not go to Gowergrove because I was afraid if I did, I would be a distraction to him. I was afraid he would be distracted from the battle and harm would befall him. But I should have gone! I could have saved him from this!"

Emilie squeezed him. "Mayhap," she said soothingly. "But it is equally as possible that there was nothing you could have done. You must not blame yourself for this. It was not your fault."

David shook his head, disagreeing with her. "I should have been there," he muttered. "Chris and I have never faced a battle without each other. Now see what has happened because I refused to go."

Emilie didn't know what to say to that. It seemed that anything she or her father said simply made it worse. It was evident that this was something David would have to work through on his own. There wasn't anything she could do and that was a difficult realization for her.

David wasn't sobbing so much anymore as he was simply grunting with emotion. Wiping his face of the tears, he simply sat there with his eyes closed and his hand over his mouth, laboring with every fiber of his being to regain his composure. But all he could see was his brother's face the last time he saw him and the words of anger kept rolling around in his head. Was it really possible that Christopher left the earth thinking so poorly of him? Was it really possible they would never have the chance to reconcile, a foolish argument that was now going to haunt him the rest of his life?

I care not where you go or what you do because you no longer exist to me. Get out of my sight, David. I want nothing more to do with you....

Those were the last words from his brother, the last thing he was to remember. All he could see was Christopher's angry face as he spouted those words of doom. Exhausted, and shattered, David dropped his chin to his chest and covered his eyes, hearing those words over and over again. It was difficult to shake them. Oh so difficult. He could feel Emilie beside him, her arms around him, and it gave him great comfort. But the truth was that he didn't want any comfort at the moment; his grief, his guilt, was his alone to bear. He welcomed the pain because he knew he deserved it. He invited the pain in, letting it wash over him, knowing he deserved every last barb and slash and prick.

He deserved it all.

As David wallowed in a grief bordering on madness, Brickley returned shortly with a full cup of wine and handed it to Lyle, who went to David and took a knee beside the man. He put his hand on David's shoulder.

"David, drink this," he said, holding the cup to him. "It will help you. Drink it all."

David shook his head, pushing the cup away, but Emilie wouldn't let him. "Please, David," she begged. "Please drink it. For me, drink it."

David lifted his head to look at her, seeing her devastated face, and reluctantly took the cup. He downed it in two big swallows, tasting some bitterness to it, but he didn't give it much thought. He hoped it was poison. Death, at this point, would have been preferable than suffering the loss of his brother.

My brother....

More than a brother, in fact. Since their parents had died when they were both young, it had always only been Christopher and David, so in a sense, they had been everything to each other – father, mother, as well as brother. David couldn't ever remember being without his brother and even in this silly argument between them, he knew it would not be permanent. He knew, at some point, they would reconcile, but now that reconciliation would never come. Already, the guilt of that had gutted him.

He knew he would never be the same.

Time rolled past, as tangible as the storm outside. There was something painful and loud about it now, something to hide from. Exhausted, overwhelmed, he began to grow very groggy as he sat there and wept. He thought to retire for a time, to sleep and forget, and hopefully regain some of his composure.

David tried to stand up but couldn't quite make it, so Lyle and Brickley had to haul him to his feet and nearly carry him into his borrowed chamber. David fell upon the bed, with Emilie right behind him, covering him up and making sure he was warm enough. But the truth was David didn't care about any of that; he simply wanted to sleep and forget.

Forget about death....

Very shortly, he was snoring heavily lying on his belly and Emilie watched him for a few moments, making sure he was all right, before turning to her father.

"Remove the weaponry from this room," she said quietly but urgently. "Remove anything he can hurt himself with."

Brickley was already moving, collecting David's broadsword and hunting down the assortment of daggers spread across the room. Lyle watched Brickley as he carefully gathered anything sharp and deadly.

"If he really wanted to hurt himself, he could use the bed linens and hang himself, Em," Lyle said. "What good will it do to remove his weapons? If a man wants to kill himself, he will find a way."

Emilie frowned at her father. "I will not make it easy for him," she said, looking down at David as the man snored. "I wonder how long he will sleep."

"Long enough," Brickley said. "Lillibet put a good deal of that powder in the wine. See how quickly it affected him."

Emilie watched David sleep for a few moments longer before pulling up a stool that was next to the hearth. She sat right next to the bed, right by his head. "I will sit with him," she said. "I do not think we should leave him alone."

Lyle agreed. "I will post a guard at the door as well, just in case he awakens and becomes too powerful for you to handle," he said. "Meanwhile, I will send a message to William Marshal to ask him if he knows of the funeral arrangements for Christopher, for I am sure David will want to know when he regains his senses. I have a feeling he will not miss the burial."

Emilie simply nodded, getting comfortable in her vigilant watch over David as her father and Brickley left the room. Brickley came in and out a few times, still collecting David's weapons, which were many. When the room was cleared out of anything sharp, he left Emilie alone with David, who was snoring like an old bear.

But at least he was at peace for the moment, which was all Emilie could hope for. Such shocking news on this night of nights and she felt horrible for David. Horrible that an argument between brothers might be something that affected David for the rest of his life. She began to think of her own sisters and how she would feel if something happened to them. She knew that her grief would be limitless, much as David's was. Even thinking about losing Nathalie or Elise brought tears to her eyes.

Until she started smelling something terrible. If she didn't know better, she thought it smelled like horse dung. She sniffed around the entire chamber, hunting for it, until she realized that it was coming from the bed. David had fallen on the coverlet without climbing beneath it so Emilie picked up the edges of it, hunting for the source of the smell, until she realized it was coming from his pillow. Peering into the pillow, she could see that the goose down had been replaced by horse manure.

Nathalie and Elise struck again in their endless pursuit to torment David. Fury filled Emilie's veins; leaving the chamber door open so her father, still in his solar, could go to David's aid in case he was needed, Emilie went to find her sisters. She had never been one to react to her sister's tricks, mostly because they had never been directed at her, but tonight she would make an exception. Tonight, she would not tolerate any manner of action against David, in any form. She would make it her business to respond to the dung pillow.

Hell hath no fury like a sister in defense of her lover.

Nathalie and Elise were out in the great hall on this stormy night helping tend the peasants who had sought shelter from the storm. Without a cloak on, Emilie charged out into the rainy night and on into the great hall, which was stuffed with people taking shelter from the storm. It was fairly quiet, as people settled in to sleep for the night, and the soft sounds of babies crying or adults whispering were the only thing to fill the stale air.

Spying Nathalie near the far end of the hall, Emilie made her way across the hall with a purpose. Nothing was going to stand in her way. She knew that Nathalie was always the brains behind any pranks, so it would be Nathalie she dealt with. Coming upon her sister, she grabbed the girl by the arm and yanked her back into an alcove behind a screen, a space used by the servants to prepare food presentations. Nathalie had outrage on her lips until Emilie started swinging.

The entire hall heard Emilie give her sister a spanking that left the girl unable to sit pain-free for days.

DAVID WASN'T ENTIRE sure how long he had been awake. It took him awhile to realize that he was staring up at the ceiling as he thought on his brother's passing. He'd slept dreamlessly but had awoken to images of his brother and the man drowning in the mud. Such an incredibly undignified way for him to die, in fact. Christopher, at the very least, should have gone out in battle, fighting off hordes of Saracens or French mercenaries. But he met his end beneath a horse, drowning in mud. It was horribly unfitting.

So David lay there, absorbing what was to be his life from this point forward. His brother was dead. There would be no more camaraderie, no more laughter, no more fighting side by side in battle. He felt the loss more deeply than anything he had ever felt in his life and it was something that sucked the wind out of him. At least, that was the way he felt – as if everything within him had been drained. Jesus, he hurt. He hurt more than he had ever hurt in his life.

But in that hurt came a decision. For the sake of his soul, he knew he had to leave Canterbury and go to Dustin. The issues started with her and they had to end with her. For his sake, he had to ask forgiveness of the woman because in doing so, he would be asking his brother's forgiveness as well. He couldn't go the rest of his life with this horrible guilt of an unresolved argument, and although he still believed Dustin bore Burton's child, the truth was that it didn't matter now. The baby was a de Lohr and would be treated as Christopher's offspring, his legacy.

Thinking back to that dark day in December when he'd confronted his brother's wife over her infidelities, he was willing to admit that he had overstepped his bounds. It wasn't as if it had been his issue to deal with, as if she had shamed him personally, with but he was truly concerned about his brother's reputation and how Dustin was playing the man for a fool. Perhaps she was; perhaps she wasn't.

But none of that mattered now. It all seemed so silly and childish in hindsight.

For his own peace of mind, he had to seek forgiveness for his actions.

He had to go to Lioncross.

Sighing heavily, he sat up in bed, feeling sluggish and disoriented. There was a fire burning in the hearth, making his room quite warm, and he wondered where Emilie was. He missed her, wanting to see her, wanting to feel some measure of comfort from her. He needed to hear her voice and feel her soft hands in his. In this horrible world of grief he existed in, he needed the comfort only she could bring him. He had to talk to her and tell her of his plans. As he struggled to stand up from the bed, a figure appeared in the chamber door.

"So you are awake," Brickley said. "I thought I heard you moving around."

David eyed the man, yawning and scratching his head. "I have not slept a full night in a very long time," he said. "Odd; I still feel exhausted."

Brickley leaned against the doorframe. "You have not only slept a full night but a full day as well," he said. "It is morning on the second day since my return to Canterbury. You have been out for nearly two days."

David looked at him, mildly surprised. "Jesus," he hissed. "I suppose I was more exhausted than I realize."

Brickley watched the man rub sleep from his eyes. "Lyle gave you a potion to make you sleep," he said. "You were so distraught... he thought it would help you."

David nodded briefly, understanding that he'd essentially been knocked out. He tried not to look too embarrassed. "I suppose was somewhat hysterical," he said, sheepish. Then, he looked around. "Where is everyone?"

Brickley came away from the door as David stood up and stumbled out into Lyle's solar beyond. "Emilie watched over you the night you fell asleep and well into the morning until Lyle took over," Brickley said. "She slept a little and then was back. She watched over you all night. I came in before sunrise and relieved her. She was quite worried about you; she would not leave you."

David wasn't sure how he felt about hearing that from the man he'd essentially stolen Emilie from. But Brickley said it with no emotion. David wasn't sure, had the situation been reversed, he could have been so unemotional about things.

"She would have done that for any of us," he said. "She is a compassionate woman."

Brickley simply nodded, heading towards the entry to Lyle's solar and sending a servant, who was in the small hall beyond, for some food for David. When he turned around, it was to see David standing next to Lyle's table, the one that held all of his missives and vellum and maps and ink.

David was just standing there, looking down at the desk, perhaps at the missive that was still there requesting troops to Gowergrove. It was right on the top of everything, that fateful and terrible missive. It seemed to Brickley that the man was still overwhelmed with everything; he simply had the look about him, stunned by the difficult event that life had dealt him.

Brickley cleared his throat softly.

"I would again express my sorrow at your brother's passing, David," he said. "I have known you and Chris for many years. We have fought for Richard for that long. We… well, we were friends, once. I am sorry… well, sorry for many things. I just wanted you to know."

David's choking, consuming grief was still simmering in his chest but at least he had some control over it today. After his breakdown two days ago, he was able to retain his fragile composure by sheer force of will. It was still a world where his brother was dead and he was still stricken with grief, but there was determination there, too. Focusing on what he had to do, the journey he needed to make to

Dustin, helped him fight off the urge to crumble.

He appreciated Brickley's condolences. Still, he had some questions for the man, a man who had been where his brother was. He hadn't been able to question him the night he'd been told of Christopher's death, but now, in the dawn of a new day, he was able to think more clearly.

"You mentioned that you saw my brother at Gowergrove," he said. "In what context? Was it in battle?"

Brickley thought back to the moments when Christopher de Lohr had crossed his path. "I saw him mostly in passing," he said. "He was at the head of the command and I was placed under East Anglia's command. A cousin of yours, I believe. At any rate, I did not see your brother much. But I will tell you this – the battle for Gowergrove is as bad as any battle I have ever seen. The weather, coupled with the difficulty in breeching the fortress, made for a truly miserable and costly battle. Had it been I, my sense would have been to walk away from it. One castle does not cost a king his crown. But that is simply my opinion; obviously, your brother felt otherwise."

David stood and listened, visibly subdued. His jaw ticked faintly, agreeing with Brickley on the fact that it had been a costly battle. It had cost England her greatest knight.

"And Anthony de Velt told you of my brother's passing," he muttered, more a statement than a question. "Yet you never saw the corpse?"

Brickley shook his head. "I did not," he said. Then, he hesitated a moment before continuing. "I did hear your name, however. Men wondered where you were when we first arrived at Gowergrove because it was obvious you did not ride with your brother. I did not tell anyone where you were and no one asked. I am quite certain they are frantically looking for you at this moment. The last I heard Richard was in London, but he had planned to go to Lioncross and return your brother's body."

David nodded, his movements lethargic and sad. "That would be logical," he said quietly. "He was quite fond of my brother. I am sure his passing has devastated the king."

Brickley simply nodded, preventing from speaking when a servant entered the solar with food for David. The kitchen servant set the wooden tray with cheese, bread, cold beef, and warmed wine on the edge of Lyle's table before fleeing the room. David just looked at the morsels meant for him; he wasn't hungry in the least.

"I must leave, Brick," he said, turning away from the table. "I must return to Lioncross. My brother's wife will need me. My brother had an empire that must now be governed."

"And you are the most logical one to do it," Brickley said. "I can only imagine what must be settled in the wake of his death."

David, too, could only imagine. Christopher had much that depended on him. He went to the hearth and held up his hands to the blaze. "You mentioned that Richard was in London," he said. "Do you know this for certain?"

Brickley shrugged. "I only know what was constant rumor on the campaign," he said. "We know that Richard has been returned and that he is in London, but I cannot confirm that."

David pondered that a moment. "Then I should go to London and see the king first," he said. "I am sure the man will want to see me."

"Who will want to see you?"

Emilie was standing in the doorway of her father's solar, looking sleepy but alert. She smiled timidly when David looked at her. "A servant came to tell me you were awake," she said. "You slept a long time. How do you feel?"

David didn't know why he felt so emotional at the sight of her. Perhaps because he was coming to depend on her for his strength as of late. "I am well," he told her, holding out a hand to her. "Come to me. Let me see you."

Emilie's smile broadened as she went to him, taking his hand and holding it tightly. "I heard you say that someone will want to see you but I did not catch the name," she said. "Who wants to see you?"

David held both of her hands in his. "Richard," he said quietly. "He and my brother were great friends. I was telling Brick that Richard will want to see me. I must leave Canterbury, Em. With my brother's death, there is much for me to see to. Much for me to resolve."

Her smile faded. "Of course," she said, although she sounded disappointed. "I understand. When will you leave?"

David squeezed her hands. "Today," he said. "As soon as I can. Much time has passed since my brother's death and I am sure a great many people are looking for me. No one knows I have come to Canterbury, or at least, I never told anyone. It is therefore imperative that I go to London and seek Richard. He and I have much to discuss."

Emilie was trying to pretend that talk of his departure did not upset her. "I am sure you do," she said. "May I go with you?"

He smiled faintly, touching her cheek. "Nay, sweetheart," he said. "You will stay here. I am not sure how long or difficult this journey will be and I do not want to subject you to it. I will return as soon as I can, as soon as my brother's affairs are settled."

Emilie just looked at him and all of her attempts to be understanding and positive left her. Her disappointment in yet another delay for their wedding was overtaking her.

"I assume we will not be married next week," she said.

David shook his head. "When I return, I promise."

"When will that be?"

"I told you that I do not know."

She didn't like that answer in the least and as she pulled her hands from David's grip, Brickley saw that as his cue to leave. In fact, he was going to find Lyle because if David was leaving, Lyle needed to know. But in the interim, David and Emilie needed to settle a few things between them, namely her disappointment. David seemed to do that a lot to her. David noticed that Brickley was slipping out but he didn't say anything; his focus was on Emilie and the tense mood between them.

"I am sorry, sweet," he said to her. "I would like to be married next week as much as you would, but I must return to Lioncross and see to my brother's widow. I must make sure she is taken care of."

Emilie was deeply upset about the situation, so much so that she wasn't beyond slinging barbs at him. "The same woman you and your brother fought over?" she pointed out. "The same woman you accused of bearing another man's child? I do not understand why it is so important to tend to her. Surely your brother had other men about, men who will see to her. Why is she suddenly so important to you?"

David knew she was upset and he really didn't blame her. "My brother had other men around him, of course, but I am his brother," he said. "How would it look if I never showed my face to Christopher's wife after his death? Emilie, listen to me – you know that my brother and I fought. A stupid argument has become the greatest regret of my life. I must return to Lioncross to seek some manner of absolution for it, something to ease this guilt that is eating me alive. The argument started with Dustin and it must end with her. Do you understand that?"

Emilie turned to him. "Aye, I understand," she said. "But I also understand that you have made it a habit of leaving me. You are back and forth, back and forth, and I always accept you back with open arms. I am not a priority for you, David; I am like a comfortable old cloak that you always know will be there when you need it, waiting and hoping for your attention. Is that fair to me to treat me like that?"

He frowned. "I do not treat you like an old cloak."

She nodded, frustrated. "You do," she insisted. "You have never once considered my needs and wants over your own. I know that you must tend to your brother's affairs and I accept that, but why must you do it before you marry me? Why can you not marry me first and then go? I do not understand why I must be pushed aside again because you have priorities greater than me."

He was becoming upset now, wracked with more guilt that perhaps she was correct in her assessment of the way he had treated her. His wants had always taken priority over hers, that was very true, but in this case, he was hurt that she couldn't see that, indeed, his brother's death was more important than their marriage.

"At the moment, my brother's death is the most important thing to me," he said. "I am sorry that you cannot understand that. There is a whole big world outside of these walls of Canterbury, Emilie Hampton, that do not revolve around you. You are not the center of the world. You *are* the center of my world, however, but right now, but you must step aside for something greater even than you. I must see to my brother's widow and I am sorry if you cannot accept that."

She crossed her arms angrily. "She is more important than I am?"

"For the moment, she is."

It was like a slap to her the face. Emilie didn't like being usurped in David's mind, not by anyone, not even the beautiful blond wife of Christopher de Lohr who was now a widow. *A widow....* That meant she was free to marry anyone, including her brother-in-law. Is that why David was so eager to return to her? Emilie turned her back on him.

"Go, then," she said. "But this is the last time I will allow you to push me aside. It is not fair to me and you know it. What happens to our plans, David? You cannot even remain here long enough to marry a woman you profess to love?"

His jaw was ticking unhappily. "Even if I marry you today, I will still leave," he said. "Why is it so important that you marry me before I go? Are you afraid I will not return so you seek to force me to return by making me marry you now?"

She looked at him, shocked. She was so angry now that she was starting to tremble. "I am more concerned why you refuse to marry me now," she said. "It would be easy enough to summon the priest.

But mayhap you are unsure of me now that your brother's wife is widowed."

He just stared at her. "What is that supposed to mean?"

She turned away from him again, sickened and full of anguish. "Go if you must," she said without answering his question. She knew he could figure it out for himself. "But if you do not marry me before you go, do not come back. I will not have you leave me again, only to return when you have nowhere else to go. I will not be a convenience, David. Do you understand me?"

David was infuriated, struggling not to let it show. He didn't need this kind of grief from her because it sounded spoiled and stubborn to him. He couldn't believe she would be so petty about him leaving to tend to dead brother's affairs. Demanding marriage before he left... he wouldn't be pushed into it. He wasn't going to let her emotionally manipulate him.

"I will not be threatened," he said, his voice low. "And I do not have time for your foolishness. I am going whether or not you like it, and I will be back whether or not you like it. We will continue this conversation when I return."

He moved away from the hearth and toward the entry to his small chamber. Emilie turned to watch him walk away, heading for the door.

"We will not," she said, turning for the main solar door that led out into the keep entry. "I am finished having this conversation with you. You have made it very clear with your actions that I am not a priority and I will accept that. But I do not have to accept you any longer. Go to Lioncross and wherever else you may go, but do not come back to Canterbury. You will not be welcome."

Emilie left the solar before he could say anything. The truth was that he wasn't sure what more to say; he knew she was hurt and he knew she felt as if he considered everyone else first before her. If he thought about it, *really* thought about it, perhaps there was some truth to that. Perhaps he did simply go about whatever he wished to do, knowing she would be waiting for him. Now, she was making it clear that she would no longer tolerate his gypsy behavior.

Infuriated at Emilie, and grief-stricken about Christopher, David rode from Canterbury that morning before speaking to Lyle on his plans. He simply left and didn't look back, heading for London in the hopes of meeting up with the king.

This time, Emilie didn't watch him from the window.

She couldn't bear to do it.

CHAPTER TWENTY-TWO

Lioncross Castle
April Year of our Lord 1194 A.D.

*B*EFORE SUNSET THAT EVENING, *an approaching army was sighted and Edward knew that it had to be Richard and David. There was no other alternative. With renewed vigor, he ordered the dinner portions doubled and the remaining unoccupied bedchambers prepared. He waited until everything was moving smoothly before seeking Marcus out.*

As he suspected, he and Dustin were holed up in Lady Mary's solar playing a game of Fox and Hounds. Marcus kept her very much to himself, very isolated from the others. Edward could not help the satisfaction that crept into his voice.

"Richard and David are approaching, my lord," he said evenly. "Mayhap you would like to greet them in the bailey?"

Marcus' lifted an eyebrow as Dustin shot to her feet. "Richard and David?" she repeated, agitated. "I do not want to see them."

"Mayhap so, but they are here nonetheless." Marcus put up a hand to calm her. "Why don't you go upstairs and change into one of your new surcoats? That would please me."

"Nay!" she yanked away from him, toppling the game board. "I do not want them here, either of them. They are to blame for my misery and I hate them."

425

Marcus stood up. "Calm down, honey," he said softly. "You shall only have to see them a moment and then never again. I promise I shall keep them away from you."

Edward did not like the wild look to her eye. All of the healing that had occurred with Marcus over the past week was rapidly slipping away.

"Richard killed Christopher," she said pointedly. "He is responsible for everything that has happened."

"Be reasonable, Dustin," Marcus said steadily. "Christopher served Richard of his own accord; no one forced him. He is not the first man to die in the service of his king, and he certainly won't be the last. Richard is not responsible in the least and I am sure his grief is great. Chris was his dear friend."

She eyed Marcus with doubt and agitation, knowing his words made sense but not wanting to admit it. She had to blame someone for her husband's death, and Richard was the most obvious target.

"I hate him," she seethed. "And I am going to beat David to a pulp if he sets foot in my keep."

Marcus never did ask what had happened between Christopher and David, but at this moment he decided to find out. Dustin was obviously very angry with her brother-in-law.

"What happened between Chris and David that you should hate him so?" he asked her.

She jutted her chin out, turning away from him. "He accused me of horrible things and we fought. Christopher banished him from Lioncross."

"You fought?" Marcus repeated with mounting disbelief. "Do you mean that you actually exchanged blows?

"I slapped him and he slapped me back," Dustin replied. "Christopher was going to kill him, but he exiled him instead."

Marcus shook his head. "What did he say to you that was so horrible? I know for a fact that David adored you, Dustin. What happened?"

She looked him in the eye. "He accused me of being your whore and of bearing your child. So I hit him."

Marcus was almost physically impacted by the statement. Edward watched him as he tried to keep his steady demeanor, but it was apparent he was shocked. After a moment, the veins on his throat throbbed.

"Then David does not set foot in this castle," he said in a low voice. "I shall run him through if he tries."

"You will have no choice," Edward informed him. "He comes with Richard, and Richard will gain him entrance. You cannot go against our king."

Marcus glared at Edward; he did not like the way this was going already. He could not take Dustin with him tomorrow as planned if Richard was here, and he did not want David near her, yet Edward was correct in that he had no power to deny him entrance to Lioncross.

Muttering a curse, he turned away. Horns sounded on the wall outside and they knew that the army's arrival was imminent. The huge outer gates were already swinging open.

Marcus turned to Dustin. "Honey, go upstairs. Wait for me there."

Dustin turned immediately and quit the room. Edward and Marcus exchanged glances before proceeding out into the foyer and onward to the bailey.

As they expected, David and Richard entered the courtyard side by side. Slightly behind them rode Sir Philip de Lohr, and a host of other distinguished knights that had come to pay their respect to Lady de Lohr. Edward and Marcus were stunned; they thought that only Richard and David and a few vassals were coming, when in fact, the army that had come with them were made up entirely of knights that had served with Christopher in the Holy Land. Marcus recognized every man he lay eyes upon, as did Edward, and they swapped awestruck gazes.

The courtyard was full of men in full armor and regalia, and even then the party still spilled out of the gates and down the road. The

*men-at-arms were astonished at the show of support for their liege;
they, of course, had always known the baron to be a great man. But
they could not imagine that the whole of Richard and his court
respected him as much as they did. It was an awesome sight to behold.*

*Dustin saw the men from her bedchamber window, her hate and
agitation fleeing when she saw all of the knights that had accompanied
the king. Without even being told she knew that they had come to pay
their respects to her for the loss of her husband, and all of her fortitude
and mental stability returned in one fell swoop. Out of their love and
respect for her husband, they had come to pay him homage and she
would not disappoint. They wanted to see the Lion's Claw's wife, and
see her they would. She could feel the reverence radiating from the
army, the very deep admiration they held for Christopher evident and
she was deeply touched. They would not see the crazy, dirty woman
who had run mad with grief for weeks on end, nay; they would see
regal, composed Lady de Lohr as befitting the baron's wife.*

Dashing from the window, she bellowed for rosewater and a towel.

*RICHARD, HIS TUNIC of scarlet with three fierce lions as clean as anyone
had ever seen it, held up a hand in greeting to Edward and to Marcus.*

*"Marcus, I thought you might be here," he said. "Ever the faithful
vassal to Chris, aren't you?"*

*Marcus nodded slowly. "Sire, our prayers were answered with your
safe return."*

*Richard raised a heavy eyebrow and dismounted stiffly. "Indeed.
Yet I come home to discord and chaos, even amongst my own ranks."
He removed his gauntlets and passed an eye over Edward. "De Wolfe,
you are looking well. I understand you have been taking care of Lady
de Lohr."*

*"In a sense, sire," Edward bowed. "I am making sure Lioncross is
running smoothly."*

Richard nodded shortly then glanced over his shoulder at David. "Are you going to sit there forever?"

David dismounted. His eyes were guarded against Edward, and were outright hostile on Marcus. Richard was no fool; he could plainly read the distrust and animosity between his men. All of his joviality and good feelings fled.

"Enough of this," he snarled. "When we were together in the Holy Land, you men were inseparable. There were no stronger bonds anywhere in my ranks, and I return home to find everyone at odds. I shall not stand for it any longer. I heard rumor that Dustin Barringdon is the root of this problem, but I refused to believe it. Since when does a mere woman come between my knights of the realm?"

The three men looked decidedly uncomfortable and Edward cleared his throat. "'Tis not that simple, sire, truly," he said softly.

Richard was impatient. "Then we shall discuss it later, but for now, I wish to see this woman on whom my kingdom hinges. Where is she?"

"Inside, sire," Marcus replied. "I shall retrieve her for you."

"No need," Philip walked up on the small group, his faded blue eyes gazing over their heads at the front door to the keep. "She has come."

All eyes turned to see Dustin emerging from the door, and not a man who laid eyes upon her beauty dared to breathe. She was dressed in royal blue silk, Christopher's color, the color that enhanced her gray eyes like nothing else. Her hair had been brushed within an inch of its life and pulled softly back from her face, revealing her true loveliness. Around her neck hung the huge cross Christopher had given her, and those closest to her noticed color to her lips. She looked as beautiful as ever, her head held high as she paused at the top of the steps.

Without introduction, the host of knights knew who she was. It was as if she possessed an aura about her that distinguished her from another mere lady. When she paused at the top of the stone stairs, waiting to be summoned forward to meet Richard, every man in armor dismounted and dropped to their knees, driving their swords into the dirt before them. It was a unified show of support and respect, a sea of mighty knights in armor displaying their undying devotion to the wife of their fallen Defender.

Dustin was stunned at the swift, decisive movement of the collective group. There were so many of them that it was a truly awesome sight to behold, and her eyes widened in astonishment. Every man was on his knees before her, some with their faces turned toward her, some with their heads bowed reverently in prayer. Dustin's chest swelled with pride, wishing Christopher could be here to see the show of force.

A smile crept onto her lips, a smile of pleasure and genuine hope. She could feel the respect coming forth and touching her, silently enveloping her weary body and helping to heal the gaping hole in her heart left by her husband's passing. Strange that it took no words, no magic, no medicine to start the healing process. A simple gesture, mighty as it was, became the catalyst.

It was completely silent, the only sounds being the nighthawk that was riding a draft somewhere high above. The sun sunk lower in the sky and a faint breeze had picked up, but Dustin stood frozen to the spot as the knights of Richard's realm paid mute homage to her fallen husband. Behind her, she heard sniffles and she recognized the source.

"Gowen," she said softly without turning around. "Get Christin. Hurry."

Frozen for a moment in time, she was entranced by the overwhelming support and continued to gaze back at the men until Gowen finally appeared at her side, holding Christin. Dustin took her daughter into her arms, murmuring softly and pointing to the bailey below, filled with hundreds of silent, powerful knights.

The baby chewed her fingers, wide-eyed. Dustin took the steps, coming upon Edward and Marcus, who had kneeled with the rest of them. In fact, they had all kneeled, even Richard, and when she came upon him, he took her hand and kissed it genteelly.

"Lady de Lohr," he said hoarsely. "Am I to assume this is Chris' daughter?"

"Her name is Christin, sire," Dustin answered.

Richard rose unsteadily to his feet, alternately eyeing her and the baby. Finally, he held out his hands. "May I?"

She handed the baby to him and the first thing Christin did was stick her finger in his eye. Richard laughed loudly and kissed the tiny fingers.

"She is beautiful," he responded, handing her back to Dustin. "I can see Chris in her face most definitely. Arthur would be proud, my lady."

Dustin nodded graciously, deeply pleased and in awe of the king's presence. Richard's gaze was open on her. "I came to meet you, Lady Dustin, and to extend my condolences on the passing of your husband."

"Thank you, sire," Dustin answered softly.

Behind him, Sir Philip rose from his crouch and smiled faintly at her, and Dustin instantly saw the family resemblance.

"You must be Sir Philip," she said. "Chris told me so much of you, I feel as if I have known you a lifetime."

"An honor to meet you, my lady," Philip replied.

Dustin glanced down at Philip's side and saw David's bowed head. Forgiveness filled her and she knew now that whatever had happened in the past, it had been foolish and ridiculous. She and David had always liked each other a great deal and the tiff had been a freakish event. She realized that now, for suddenly she realized everything with a clear, solid mind. Christopher was dead and she was forever altered, but life would continue and she was somehow stronger for it. Her strength was in the love they had once shared and for the character he had built in her through his devotion. She understood that now.

She moved past Richard and Philip and touched the top of David's head.

"David," she said softly. "Get up and greet your niece. It has been a long time since she saw you last."

He raised his head his entire face was wet with tears. Dustin *shushed him softly, encouraging him to his feet and then falling into his embrace. Against her, David let loose with his sobs as she whispered comfortingly to him. Forgiveness was more, and better, than he had ever hoped for.*

Not releasing David, she turned back to Richard. "Sire, we have refreshments for you and your party. Would you please come in?"

Richard smiled at her and cupped her chin gently between his fingers. She gazed up at him, watching his face ripple with emotion. At thirty-seven years old, he looked much older and haggard from his tumultuous life.

"I understand Chris found love with you, my lady," he said softly. "I can see why."

She flushed, the first color to her cheeks in weeks. Passing Christin to Marcus, she took Richard's arm and escorted him inside.

As Richard and Dustin headed for the keep, David didn't move. His gaze was on Marcus, as hostile and confrontational as ever. Marcus met his gaze, steadily, feeling the tension between them explode.

"How long have you been here?" David finally asked.

"Over a week," Marcus replied steadily.

David's jaw ticked. "You couldn't even wait until my brother was cold in his grave, could you?"

Marcus didn't want a fight on his hands, not with Christin in his arms, so he kept his manner calm. "It is not like that, David. Give me more credit than that."

David wouldn't back down. "Then you can leave – now."

Marcus' jaw ticked. "Not without Dustin. She is returning with me to Somerhill."

David's nostrils flared but he kept his cool because of Christin. "No," he said flatly. "She is staying here."

Marcus did not reply, knowing that if any more were said it could result in raised voices and frighten the baby. He simply turned away from David and started back toward the house, when a knight nearby called out to him.

"Lord Marcus?" The man stood up, taking a step forward. "I am Sir John de Monfort. I served with you and Lord Christopher during the siege of Arce."

Marcus nodded coolly. "I remember you. A fine knight."

The man nodded. "Thank you, my lord. I was wondering...the babe. She is Lord Christopher's, is she not?"

Marcus looked at the baby in his arms, who was still chewing furiously on her fingers. "The Lady Christin de Lohr."

The knight nodded faintly. Without another word, he approached Christin and fell to one knee, touching her little foot and bowing his head in a silent prayer. Abruptly, he rose and wandered off, but immediately behind him was another man to take his place. Marcus soon realized that the entire group of knights were falling into line to pay their respects to Lady Christin.

David stood behind him as the knights filed past, some touching her foot, some gently touching her head, and simply others making the sign of the cross before her and murmuring a prayer. And still others placed small medallions in her little hands, bright objects for her to play with, yet were undoubtedly expensive. Marcus was silent, protective, and deeply touched on Christopher's behalf.

Christin, being the good-natured baby that she was, thought all of it was great fun and cooed and babbled the entire time. She would grab the hair of the men who bowed before her or reach out and snag a piece of tunic. More than once Marcus had to pry her hands free of someone, to which she would scream baby talk and wave her wet hands angrily at him. More than once, she batted him in the face with her wet fingers, leaving damp streaks. But Marcus didn't flinch.

David, watching his niece with her developing personality, could not help thinking just how much like her mother she was. The more he watched her, the more he realized how very wrong he had been; except for the hair color, she looked nothing like Marcus and he, too, was beginning to see Christopher in her features. He only wished his brother was alive so he could tell him so.

The knights camped in and around Lioncross that night, their bonfires sending eerie blobs of fire glowing into the blackness of the March night and each man feeling closer to the Defender, walking the very earth that Baron de Lohr had come to love so well.

DUSTIN AND CHRISTIN *had sat with Richard and the knights for most of the evening, listening to the fighting men tell tales of battle upon the sands of the Holy Land and stories of valor involving Christopher. Even though Christin couldn't understand the stories, still, Dustin wanted the baby there, basking in the aura of her father's memory. It was as if he was holding her once again, so strong and vivid the tales. He was there, in spirit, if not in body.*

It had been evident since the meal commenced, however, that David and Marcus were deeply at odds. Edward sided with David, and Marcus seemed to be on his own island of righteousness. He was defensive when it came to Edward and David, yet warm and accommodating when it came to Dustin.

He told his own stories of Christopher, some involving Christopher, David, himself, and Christopher's cousin on his mother's side, a knight by the name of Kieran Hage. Another great knight on the quest, he had been killed by assassins before the quest had been complete. Christopher and David had grieved long the man who had been like a brother to them. When Marcus brought up his name, even Richard grew saddened.

"War is the widowmaker and kings, the executioner," he muttered philosophically. "I have seen many good men fall all in the name of religion or conquest. I do not believe that Christopher had gotten over the death of Kieran."

David reflected on his massive and intelligent cousin. "Nor I," he said softly. "To lose him as we did, to assassins no less, was tragic."

"We never recovered his body, did we?" Richard said before he could think. "The last I was told, he was tracked to Nahariya, but after that, he all but vanished."

David and Marcus, rather anxious, passed glances at Dustin, who was sitting next to Richard with the baby sitting on the table in front of her. Richard realized they were on to a very bad subject and quickly shifted focus.

"My lady, I understand your mother is a Fitz Walter," he said the first thing that popped to mind, watching David wince. Another bad subject. "I… I never met your mother. Arthur spoke very fondly of her."

Dustin looked up from the baby, whom she was playing patty-cake with. The subject of Christopher's cousin's missing body did not escape her; much like her own husband, they had nothing to bury. That was all she could seem to focus on. She was struggling not to linger on those morose thoughts as Richard attempted to engage her in other conversation.

She smiled weakly at the king. "My mother and father were married for over twenty years," she said. "They were quite fond of each other."

"No brothers or sisters?"

She shook her head. "Only me," she said. "If my father wanted a son, he never said so. He was very attentive to my mother and me."

Richard was growing worried; there didn't seem to be many safe subjects with Lady de Lohr, except for the baby. That one seemed safe enough. When Christin squealed happily as her mother played with her, Richard was glad for the diversion.

"The child is good natured," he said. "You are very blessed."

Dustin smiled at her daughter as the little girl slapped at her hands. "She is a happy lass."

The baby was animated, finding a used spoon from her mother's trencher and putting it in her mouth. Marcus, across the table, made little clucking noises and Christin turned to look at him. He smiled at the baby and she grinned back, broadly. Marcus set down his cup and *reached across the table, pulling her into his arms.*

He tickled the baby and made loud kissing noises on her fat little hands. Christin was delighted, but seated next to Marcus, David was clearly unhappy. He continued to watch as Marcus played with Christin until the baby grew fussy and Dustin called for Griselda. The old women whisked the baby from the hall and they could hear her crying upstairs, unwilling to settle down for sleep. As the sounds of her sleepy and unhappy daughter faded away, Dustin sat next to the king and sipped on her wine, thinking back to the stories of her husband's valor and trying not to miss him too much. It was a difficult struggle.

And it was not a struggle missed by David or Marcus. They were watching her as Richard was watching them. Now that the baby was gone, the tension at the table was increasing. They had behaved for the sake of the baby, but now that she was gone there was no longer any reason for good behavior. They ended up glaring at each other over the rim of their cups. Finally, Richard reached his limit.

"Enough of this," he snapped quietly. "This behavior will end. Am I clear?"

Marcus averted his gaze, but David continued to stare the man down. Richard slammed his cup on the table top to get David's attention.

"David," he hissed. "Do you hear me?"

"I hear you, sire."

"What is your issue with Marcus? Tell me now and let us get this out in the open."

David took his eyes off Marcus, then. He looked at the king, seeing the man's extreme displeasure.

"It is not a simple thing, sire," he said, realizing it was difficult to explain. "I do not think that...."

Richard cut him off. "Marcus," he addressed him. "You will tell me why you and David are at each other's throats."

Marcus was considerably less hostile when facing his king. "He is angry with me."

"Why?"

"Because… because I have come to Lioncross to take Lady Dustin away from here and marry her."

Richard wasn't surprised. It all but confirmed the rumors of Burton's attraction to lady de Lohr. "Is this so?" he said. "Do you intend to take her and the baby back to Somerhill?"

"I do."

Richard pondered that as he looked back to David. "And you disagree?"

David nodded his head, his eyes on Marcus. "Aye, sire, I do. Lady de Lohr belongs here at Lioncross."

"Alone? Or with you?" Richard demanded. "David, you are betrothed yourself, are you not? Do you intend to break your betrothal to Emilie Hampton and marry your dead brother's wife?"

David faltered. "Nay, my lord, I still intend to marry Emilie," he said. "But Lady Dustin's home is here, within these walls. And Chris would want his child to be raised in his own keep."

"So you would have her stay here, alone, simply to raise a child who will not even remember her true father?" Richard shook his head. "If that is truly Chris' desire, then it seems most selfish to me. Or is it that you object to Marcus personally, David? I am curious."

David looked at Richard. "Marcus is the best knight in the realm now that my brother is gone, but…."

Richard interrupted him. "That was not my question. Why do you object to Marcus marrying your brother's wife?"

David lowered his gaze, toying with his goblet. "Because she is Chris' wife, sire," he said softly. "She is his legacy. If she marries Marcus, she will cease to become Chris' wife. She will be Lady Burton, and it will almost be as if Chris was never married or never had children. Lioncross will be empty of his family and his legacy will die."

Dustin fought off the tears and lowered her head so no one could see her pain. But Richard saw her pain and he placed his palm over her soft, white hand.

"Christopher is a legend, David," he said quietly. "So long as there are a thousand knights to remember him and pass on his story, his legacy continues endlessly. And that beautiful babe in the nursery is the fruit of his loins, his legacy in the flesh. Marcus Burton would never change that."

David's head shot up sharply to Marcus, and then focused on Richard once more, and the king could see the doubt and grief.

"David, Christopher will live forever in our hearts," he said. "What Marcus is doing is offering to wed Lady Dustin and provide her with a stable, safe life. He is offering his companionship to her, and I for one think he is being quite selfless. I should think you would appreciate knowing Chris' wife would be well taken care of."

David lowered his gaze.

Down the table was the tall figure of Philip de Lohr. He had been listening closely to everything. He drew his nephew's sullen glance, and the attention of everyone else at the table, when he cleared his throat quietly.

"Every time I look at you, David, I see my brother," Philip said softly. "I know what it is like to lose a brother, someone I admired above anyone else. When Myles passed away, I felt toward Val much as you do toward Dustin. She was Myles' wife and I felt that she was my personal responsibility." He sat forward on the table, his handsome face weary. "But Val followed Myles shortly after in death. I honestly believe she could not live without him and allowed whatever ailment that claimed him to claim her. But if that had not been the case, I would have wished for someone to offer her a new life, someone I knew and respected, and someone who would treat her as my brother had treated her. I think Lady Dustin is very lucky to have Marcus as her savior."

"Savior is a strong word, Philip," Marcus replied softly.

David's hard wall was faltering and Philip faced him. "I suppose what I am saying, David, is this – I know how you feel. I lost my older brother, too. Had Val lived, I know he would have wanted her to be *happy. Allow Dustin her happiness, lad. If it is with Marcus, then be happy for them both."*

David's handsome face was tired and uncertain. Dustin's head was bowed, trying so hard to fight the tears that were nonetheless spilling onto her lap. Time ticked by as David mulled over his uncle's words.

Finally, David shook his head. "Uncle Philip, Chris loved her more than anything on this earth. I just cannot believe that he would want her to leave Lioncross and take Christin away." His eyes flicked up to Marcus. "I cannot in good conscience, let her go with Marcus. I just cannot."

Oddly enough, the tension had drained out of the room. Now there were only men trying to understand the position of each other. But Marcus wasn't leaving without Dustin, David or no David.

"She is going with me," he told David firmly. "If I have to cut through you and every other man here, she is going with me back to Somerhill, and I am going to marry her. I do not care if you approve or not, David. It is not up to you."

David had been very calm until Marcus' reply, which sounded suspiciously like a challenge. He stiffened in his chair.

"I am not surprised," he snarled. "Hell, you tried everything in your power to take her away from my brother. Why shouldn't I think you would kill me to get to her?"

He bolted to his feet and Marcus bolted to his feet. Marcus' knights followed suit, as did Christopher's until Richard was shouting above the clanging of armor and the unsheathing of swords to restore order.

"Sit down, all of you," he roared. "Damnation, sit down or I shall have you all thrown in irons. David, sheath that damn sword or I shall shove it down your throat."

The king was furious. Marcus stepped back from the table angrily, his chair toppling over as he paced aimlessly toward the hearth. The other knights obeyed their king, taking their seats again, except for David and Philip. Philip was trying to calm his nephew down, coaxing him back to his seat.

Dustin couldn't take it anymore. She was already emotionally brittle and spiritually spent and her breaking point was low. She stood up, marching over to her brother-in-law.

"You do not own me, David," she snapped. "I must decide what is best for me, not you. I hate it that you are constantly fighting with Marcus. You used to be the best of friends before I came along, I know. Edward told me that you and Chris and Marcus were inseparable. And now you are ready to kill him. I cannot take your hostilities any longer."

"I am thinking of your best interests, Dustin," David said. "You are still grieving, for God's sake. I do not want you making a quick decision you will regret."

"But it is my decision," she fired back. "Let me make my own mistakes, David. Let me live my own life, which happens to be a life without your brother." She spun around, gesturing to the heavens of the great hall. "This place is my home, my wonderful home until a year ago. Ever since then, I have seen the pinnacles of joy and the very depths of grief here. My family has lived here for five generations, but do you know that when I look at the dining table, I only see Christopher sitting at the head? And 'tis only him I see mounting the stairs to our bedchamber, or stoking the hearth because I am cold. David, the man lived here slightly over a year, yet he left his mark as indelibly as if he had lived here one hundred years. With every turn, with every flash of light, I see only him and I am haunted."

She suddenly realized she was giving this speech for every man present, opening up her soul as she hadn't opened it up for anyone. The fire crackled in the hearth as she took a cleansing breath and faced off against David and Marcus.

"I do not want to leave Lioncross," she said softly. "This is my home; it is Chris' home. But sometimes I feel as if I will go mad if I stay here a moment longer. Marcus is well aware of my feelings on the matter, and I accept his offer to go with him to his keep because I believe I need the change. I shall return to Lioncross, someday, mayhap

as Lady de Lohr, mayhap as Lady Burton. But it is my decision to make and my life to live. I have to do what is best for Christin and best for me."

David was clearly torn after her speech. "But why with him, Dustin?"

"Why not?" she asked him deliberately. "Why on earth not, David? Surely you do not want me; you have Emilie. And I will not go with your uncle to Lohrham Forest, for the man doesn't need me banging about there. Why is it so hard for you to let me leave this place? You are making a difficult decision even harder."

David was slipping. "Because...oh, hell, Dustin, I do not know. I cannot think on it anymore; I suppose I cannot fight you anymore. If you truly want to go, the truth is that I cannot stop you."

"Good," Dustin breathed, satisfied. Still, she could see the pain in his expression and it saddened her. "I appreciate your concern as my husband's brother, but you must let me do what I think is best."

David gave up in that moment. There was nothing more to fight and nothing more to say. He stared at Dustin for several long moments before walking to her, pulling her head against his lips and kissing her hair.

"Be happy, then," he whispered. "He would want you to be."

He left the hall, ascending the stairs wearily to his bedchamber. Dustin visibly relaxed, her gaze moving to Marcus where he stood handsome and strong, by the hearth. He smiled weakly at her but she did not respond, instead, facing against Richard.

"If you shall excuse me, sire, I shall be retiring," she said quietly.

Richard nodded faintly and Dustin curtsied, quitting the hall and going the same path of David to the second story. Only when she was in her bedchamber, the chamber she had shared with Christopher, did she let her guard down. She lay heavily on his side of the bed, on the linens she hadn't changed since he had left because she could still smell his musk in the sheets. Inhaling deeply, she again smelled the faint scent and it brought tears to her eyes.

With a ragged sigh, she lay her cheek on his pillow and let her mind wander to happier days.

MARCUS COULD NOT sleep that night. He found himself wandering the halls of Lioncross, feeling Christopher's presence like a ghost, following him everywhere. He paced the second floor completely, made his rounds on the third floor, and then found himself down on the ground floor, not even aware of his wandering because he was so deeply lost in thought.

Was he pushing Dustin to do something she did not want to do? Had he taken advantage of her weakened state for his own selfish reasons? Clearly, he was, but he was afraid if he did not take her now, then she would never go with him. She was an heiress and valuable to Richard as a commodity, and Marcus was deathly afraid if he did not marry her now, then Richard would find a husband for her to somehow strengthen his empire. He had to press his advantage now, while there was time. If he allowed her time to grieve and recover, then his chance might be past. And he could not stand the thought of Dustin in someone else's arms.

He found himself in the abbey. Curious for the first time of his surroundings, he glanced about the dark, forbidden place and wondered how in the hell he got there. As he turned to remount the stairs, there was an unmistakable ring of a sword as it was being unsheathed from its scabbard.

Marcus stiffened, not particularly surprised to see David looming several steps above him, a sword in his hand.

"I am unarmed, David," Marcus said quietly.

A sword suddenly landed at his feet with a clatter. "Not anymore," David replied. "Here and now, Marcus. We will end this here and now."

Marcus did not move for his sword just yet. "Why do you hate me so much, David? We used to be best friends. Is it truly Dustin, or is it something else I have done?"

"You changed, Marcus," David said in a low voice. "You coveted my brother's wife. You shamelessly pursued her and embarrassed yourself and the de Lohr name. You showed no restraint or control whatsoever. It was as if you would stop at nothing to have her, and even though Christopher overlooked it, I was deeply offended. And now, I am going to do what my brother should have done all along."

"Kill me?" Marcus said with raised brows. "Your devotion to your brother is touching, David, but do you truly think my 'pursuit', as you call it, is worth taking my life?"

David lowered his sword a bit, taking a step. "Then let's see it from a different angle, Marcus," he said. "Let's assume that it was you who married Dustin, and Christopher who was so madly consumed with her that he was not shy about his feelings in the least. Let's say that he kissed Dustin, your wife, and tried to hide the fact. Let's say that he was with her always, never actually voicing his feelings, but not having to because they were written all over his face. Let's say that he was so relentless that everyone began spreading rumors, but he did not care. He looked like a fool, you looked like a fool, and Dustin looked to be nothing short of a whore. Now, how would you react to such a thing?"

Marcus' face was dark. "I was never like that, David. I admitted my infatuation to Chris and banked it well. I was never shameless in my pursuit of Dustin until now."

David smiled thinly. "It hurts, doesn't it? If the situation were reversed, then you most certainly would not have been as forgiving as Christopher was. He overlooked everything you did because of his love and respect for you, and it made him look like an idiot. Now ask me again – why do I want to see justice served?"

Marcus inhaled deeply and looked to the ground where his sword was. Slowly, he reached down and picked it up.

"You won't kill me, you know," he said quietly. "I shall disembowel you first."

David shrugged faintly. "Tell me one thing, Marcus," he muttered. "Did you bed her?"

Marcus lifted his sword, examining the blade in the faint torch-light. "Does it matter?"

"Not really. Whether or not you did it physically, you have already done it in your mind a thousand times," David replied. "I was simply curious to know if you indeed followed through with your desires and if she responded."

Marcus was focused on the ridge of his blade. "It is none of your business."

A bolt of fury shot though David at the evasive answer. "Then you just answered my question."

Marcus glanced up at him, cocking a black eyebrow. "I did. I told you it was none of your affair, which it isn't. What goes on between Dustin and me isn't anyone's concern."

David's nostrils flared angrily. "Then I was right all along; she was your whore. And Christin? She's your daughter."

Marcus kept his calm. "Dustin was never, ever my whore, David. And Christin is Chris' daughter."

"Did you bed her?" David roared, enunciating each word and they reverberated off the thick abbey walls.

Marcus raised his sword slowly, moving it into a defensive position. "I did."

David was actually stumped at the short, precise answer. He had expected more denials, more maneuvering. But his shock was gone in a second, his fury returning tenfold.

"You bloody bastard," he growled. "You filthy son of a bitch. How could you do that to Chris? He trusted you, goddammit. He trusted you!"

Marcus could see David's pain more than his anger, and his own pain surfaced as well. "It wasn't that simple, David. When it happened... Dustin did not even know it was me. She thought I was Chris and she took me into her bed," his voice was a whisper. "I am a weak man, David, not at all as perfect as our Defender was. I could have stopped it, but I did not. I wanted to. Aye, I freely admit it to you. I took advantage of the situation. Never blame Dustin, David, for she thought I was her husband. Are you satisfied now that you have a confession? I have simply given you more reason to kill me."

David raised his sword, fighting back his considerable anger. If he lashed out and tired himself at the beginning, then Marcus would show no mercy and finish him off in his fatigue.

"I do not blame her," he said. "I have never blamed her. She's young and impressionable. But I fully blame you."

"As you should," Marcus gripped his sword with two hands on the hilt, preparing for the first strike. "You may try to kill me if you think you must, David. I am ready."

David did not reply. Instead, he came hurtling down from the stairs and met Marcus with the force of his fury. Metal met on metal, screaming at the pressure and sparks flew into the damp air of the abbey.

Marcus was fully prepared for the onslaught, and for David's fury. A whole year of anger and resentment and jealousy was releasing itself. David was faster than any man alive with a sword, but he could be reckless. Marcus, however, was far more controlled and more powerful than his opponent. It was dark in the abbey, working to neither man's advantage as they plowed their way through pieces of old furniture and bounced off the walls.

David tripped at one point and staggered against the stone wall, narrowly averting being decapitated by Marcus as the big man descended on him with all of his might. The clang of broadsword against broadsword echoed loudly and roused a few servants, instantly panicked at the fight in the abbey and Richard was awoken from a deep sleep.

Angry as hell, the King of England grabbed his serrated broadsword and marched for the bowels of the abbey. He had no doubt as to who was doing the fighting.

MARCUS AND DAVID *stood before Richard in the grand hall, a few of the king's officials surrounding the tired monarch as he glared back at his disobedient vassals. He was so damn tired all he wanted to do was sleep, but instead, found himself breaking up a serious fight. Had he not intervened when he did, David de Lohr would now be preparing for his burial.*

"I know why you were fighting," Richard said in a low voice. "I need no explanation. And from what I am told, it was a long time in coming. But I will tell you this now; I will hear no more of fighting between you two. There is no one in this world I am at peace with, including my brother, and I shall not stand for any goddamn fighting within my own ranks. I should like there to be just one minute measure of stability in my life right now, gentle knights, and I should like it to start with my loyal warriors, or I swear I shall take Lady Dustin with me and keep her at Windsor if you two cannot make peace with each other. Is that understood?"

Marcus and David nodded simultaneously. "Aye, sire."

"Good," Richard exclaimed, eyeing them both critically. "I will ask one thing, however; who started it?"

David piped up before Marcus could speak. "I did, sire. I sought Marcus out."

"David, you know better than to cause trouble." Richard jabbed his finger at him. "Good Lord, you are just like your father. Hot-headed and aggressive. But I will tell you now, no more of it. Christopher, thank God, controlled himself better than most men and you should have learned from him. And Marcus; you are David's superior officer. You should not have responded to his challenge."

"I was given little choice, sire," Marcus responded. "It was either defend myself or die."

Richard shot David a withering look. "Get hold of yourself, Sir Knight. Come to grips with your grief and the future will work itself out. It does not need your interference."

David lowered his gaze, his jaw ticking. Marcus didn't dare look at him, both of them feeling like naughty children being caught with their hand in the candy jar. Marcus didn't hate David, but he hated the animosity he was creating. If David would only surmount his guilt and anger, he was sure his feelings would calm.

"Back to Canterbury with you on the morrow, de Lohr," Richard said finally. "Go back and marry your Emilie, and I will hear no more about you and Marcus Burton."

"Aye, sire," David said softly, bowing as he quit the hall.

CHAPTER TWENTY-THREE

Canterbury Castle
July Year of our Lord 1194 A.D.

B RICKLEY WAS ON WATCH towards the end of this clear and rather warm day, as spring was beginning to warm and the summer months were on the horizon. The countryside was in bloom and the town, having recovered from the terrible rains of the spring and early summer, was still bustling, even at this hour. Shops were being closed for the night and the smell of cooking fires filled the air.

Brickley was on the wall walk near the gatehouse. From this position he could see the ward of Canterbury easily, and he could see the road leading to the gatehouse easily as well. The men were about to change shifts on the walls and he watched a senior sergeant deal with a young man who was evidently ill but still trying to assume his post. Brickley recognized it as a farm boy he'd recruited last year, the same boy whom Nathalie had her eye on.

In fact, the farm boy was a young man of fifteen years, uneducated but wise, who was very quick to learn the methods of soldiering. Brickley had taken the young man under his wing as of late because he saw a good deal of his own son in the young man, whose given name was Payn. Nathalie, unskilled in the art of flirting, simply called him 'farmer,' but in spite of that Nathalie and the lad had struck up a friendship of sorts. Brickley could not have been more thrilled that her thoughts were off of him and onto the young farm boy, who was slightly younger than she was. He continued to watch as the sergeant tried to send the young man away but Payn was resolute to do his duty, even coughing and wheezing as he was.

Brickley finally caught the sergeant's attention and waved the man off, who shrugged and allowed the young man to fill his post. Brickley was moving over to Payn to see just how sick he really was when he caught sight of a rider heading towards the gatehouse.

Even with the sun setting and the shadows cast, Brickley could still see rather clearly, and he noted right away that there was something familiar about the knight. Something *quite* familiar. A sense of foreboding settled about him as he watched the horse and rider approach, something ominous. He could feel the mood increase the closer the rider came and suddenly, recognition dawned. He flew down from the wall faster than he'd moved in a very long time.

Brickley came off of the narrow stairs leading down from the wall and nearly shoved over a soldier who got in his way. There was purpose in his movements, but there was also rage. Utter and complete rage. He bellowed for the portcullis to be lifted and kicked at the thing when it didn't move fast enough. The chains pulling up the heavy iron fangs creaked and groaned, and by the time Brickley had enough clearance to duck underneath it, the rider was nearly upon them.

"Halt!" Brickley said, throwing out a hand. "Stop right there, David. Come no closer."

David reined his big white horse to a halt. He was in full armor, complete with helm, and he was not wearing an identifiable tunic. He had worn the de Lohr tunic his entire life and for a short period, the yellow, gray, and black Canterbury, but on this day, he simply wore a light colored woolen tunic of no discernable color. Even so, he was still recognized because of his snow-white horse. He flipped up his visor, his concerned and stubbled face in full view.

"What is wrong?" he asked Brickley.

Brickley knew this moment would be coming. He had been waiting for it ever since David fled and Emilie, after having too much wine once night, had spilled the situation between her and David. Lyle and Brickley had listened with some shock, and perhaps anger, trying to be understanding of a man who had just lost his brother and felt there were other priorities in his life than the woman he was betrothed to. Lyle was far more understanding of it than Brickley was. In fact, Brickley had seen it as his opportunity.

Aye, he was an opportunist. Emilie felt that David did not feel she was important enough to marry and was convinced that David was returning to Lioncross to marry his brother's widow. Therefore, Brickley had permitted his feelings for Emilie to come forth again, hoping that, this time, she would be wounded enough or weak enough to respond to his suit. It was something he had prayed for daily.

But Lyle had quickly caught on to what Brickley was doing. He was still very much a supporter of David and told Brickley to leave Emilie alone. Brickley obeyed, but it was all for show. He hadn't really listened at all. He just became less obvious about it in front of Lyle.

But it hadn't exactly worked in his favor because whatever Emilie had thought of David's actions, it was clear that she still loved him. That made Brickley angry. He was finished watching David de Lohr ruin Emilie's life and, in a sense, his life as collateral damage. He wasn't going to let the man toy with her any longer. Therefore, Brickley was prepared for the moment when David returned to Canterbury because he knew for a fact the man would return. He always did. And then he always left again, breaking Emilie's heart.

It wasn't going to happen again.

Now David had returned, as Brickley had feared, and there was a show down going on in front of Canterbury's portcullis. Brickley refused to let the man pass.

"Did you marry your brother's widow?" he asked bluntly.

David's brow furrowed. "Of course not," he said. "Why do you ask?"

"Then what are you doing here?"

David, who was in no mood for Brickley's antics, leaned forward on the saddle. "I am here to see my betrothed," he said. "You are standing in my way."

Brickley didn't move. "Emilie does not want to see you," he said. "Turn around and go."

David saw where this was going. With a heavy sigh, he dismounted his horse and faced Brickley on his feet. "I am not going anywhere," he said flatly. "Where is Emilie?"

Brickley had a height advantage on David but that was all. Everyone in England knew that there was no one faster with a sword than David, so Brickley was already very much on his guard. David hadn't so much as made a move to unsheathe his weapon but Brickley knew he would probably do it and spear Brickley through the heart before he even saw it coming. That was his fear of David and he tried not to show it.

"She is inside the keep," Brickley said. Then, he forced himself to become a bit more conversational and not feed off of his anger so much. "David, she had made it clear she does not want to see you. You must respect her wishes."

David crossed his big arms, folding them over his chest as much as the mail and heavy garments would allow. "I will hear it from her and not you," he said. "Surely you can understand that."

Brickley's jaw ticked. After a moment, he hissed. "Why can you not simply leave her alone?" he asked. "You have been in and out of her life since you met her. You come back, make promises, and then something always happens where you find yourself leaving her again, and leaving her in tears. Do you have any idea how distraught she was when you left this last time? I realize you were grieving your brother, but for Christ's sake, you needed to give a thought to the living as well. To Emilie, in fact. She thinks you have gone back to marry your brother's widow."

David learned a lot in that slightly-hissed rant. He sighed heavily again, shaking his head. "I sent her several missives," he said. "Did she read any of them or did you intercept them again?"

Brickley shook his head. "I did not intercept them," he said. "I did not need to. I gave her every one and she burned every one without reading it."

David grunted unhappily. "That is unfortunate," he said. "Go and get her, Brickley. Bring her out here so that I may speak with her."

Brickley shook his head. "I will not," he replied. "I will not see you hurt her again."

David lifted his eyebrows. "Or what?" he asked. "Or you will kill me? I invite you to try, Brickley, I really do. Your attempts to protect Emilie are admirable but this is none of your affair. If you will not go and get her, then step aside or I will be forced to move you."

Brickley could see that something terrible was coming but he didn't back down. He couldn't. But he was starting to see his life flashing before his eyes and he didn't like that.

"Why can't you simply go away?" he wanted to know. "Surely your brother's empire and the politics of England will take enough of your time. I have no idea what you are dealing with and I am sure it is all quite difficult, but life has been peaceful here the past few months while you were away. You bring chaos here when you come and we do not need it. Emilie doesn't need it. You have hurt her badly, David. Do the honorable thing and leave."

David moved to unsheathe his broadsword and he swore he could hear a collective gasp from the soldiers on the wall, now watching his confrontation with Brickley. The blade from David's expensive sword gleamed in the late afternoon sun, flashing bolts of lightning for all to see. David stood there a moment, looking at the razor-sharp weapon.

"When I left here, I went to London to meet with Richard," he said. "I discovered that my brother's body was left at Gowergrove, buried with his men. Therefore, Richard was not returning the body to Lioncross in spite of the rumor you heard. But he was going to my brother's castle to pay his respects to his widow so I accompanied him, along with my uncle who was one of the men who had gone to escort Richard home from captivity. Yet when I arrived at Lioncross... well, as you said, dealing with it was all quite difficult. And do you know that they all knew I was at Canterbury? Someone must have told them, although I did not find out who. Mayhap... mayhap my brother simply knew I would return to Emilie. He knew of my feelings for her. In any case, after I arrived at Lioncross, I tried to kill my brother's best friend because the man is determined to marry my brother's widow. I tried to stop him. Richard sent me away because of it."

Brickley couldn't help but feel some sympathy for the turmoil of David's life since his brother's death, but that was frankly not his problem. David's issues were his own. Brickley was only concerned about Canterbury and what happened here. He didn't want David to throw everything into turmoil again.

"I have already told you that you have my sympathies for the passing of Chris," he said. "But that does not change the fact that I do not want you back at Canterbury."

David looked up from his sword. "What does Lyle say?"

Brickley seemed to lose some of his stubborn defiance. "This is not Lyle's decision," he said. "It is mine."

David was too weary to be standing here arguing with a jealous man. "I see," he said. "Where is Lyle?"

"Inside."

"Does he know I am here?"

"He does not."

David was starting to think that perhaps only Brickley didn't want him here. Furthermore, it was quite possible he was lying about Emilie. Perhaps she did read his missives and perhaps she *did* want him here. He would only know that if he was able to speak with her and, so far, Brickley wasn't about to let that happen.

"Move aside, Brickley," he said. "I will not tell you again."

Brickley took a defensive stance as the men on the walls hunkered down, trying to jockey for a better position to watch the coming sword fight. With David de Lohr involved, in promised to be spectacular.

"I will not."

David's features will like stone. "Are you sure you want to take that stance with me?"

Brickley's jaw ticked. "I will take any stance necessary," he said. "I am to blame for this, you know. I should have let Dennis le Londe kill you that day of the mass competition at Windsor but I foolishly saved your life. Had I to do it all over again, knowing what I know now, I would have let him kill you."

It was an insult that brought consequences. David's first strike sent Brickley onto his arse and from there, the fight was on.

"WHAT ARE YOU doing down here?"

Lyle was at the top of the stairs that led down into the storage vaults below Canterbury's keep. He asked the question of Emilie, who was standing on the floor below him with a pair of kitchen servants, a large fatted torch lighting up the vault and sending black smoke up to the ceiling. Emilie turned to look at her father when she heard his voice.

"The mice are into the grain again," she told her father. "They chewed through the sacks and now it is spilled out all over. We need to have barrels, Papa. Can the wheelwright make some for us? Otherwise, we are going to lose a good deal of stores."

Lyle couldn't really see what she was looking at so he shrugged his shoulders. "And we have to do this right now?" he asked. "I am hungry. Where is the evening meal?"

Emilie grinned at her father. "Papa, you are worse than a child," she said. "Sup will be ready at the usual time. You need not worry."

Lyle wasn't too pleased; being hungry always made him irritable. He could smell the food but there was nothing on the table, nothing prepared, so he came hunting for Emilie and found her down in the store room. He was greatly annoyed.

"Then come out of there and make it so," he told her. "Where are your sisters?"

Emilie came closer to him up on the narrow stairs that led down into the storage area. There used to be only a ladder but so many servants had hurt themselves lugging items up and down the ladder that Lyle commissioned a set of narrow stairs to be built out of stone. There was even the rarity of a railing built into them so it would be more difficult to fall off.

"The last I saw they were with Lillibet," she said patiently. "You know that Lillibet has had them making tunics for the poor for the past few months, ever since I told her what they did to… when the put horse dung in his pillow. You know that Lillibet has been putting their wicked energies to good use as of late."

Lyle simply nodded, noticing that Emilie couldn't even bring herself to say David's name after all of these months. The pain of his departure was still fresh. All that aside, he also knew that Lillibet was perpetually punishing Nathalie and Elise for their constant pranks, finally coming to a head when the girls turned their venom on David those months ago. Horse dung in the pillow of a man who had just found out his brother had perished had not been the smartest thing they'd ever done, although in their defense, they didn't know anything about David's brother.

Still, between Emilie and Lillibet, they had overridden any protests from Lyle and taken matters into their own hands. Nathalie and Elise were never alone, alone to concoct wicked plans, and were therefore put to work – they would help bake bread and churn butter, they helped the stable master with the horses (since they liked horse dung so much), and Lillibet had task after task lined up for them, mostly sewing or reading the bible out loud. That had curbed their wicked streak and the men of Canterbury rejoiced.

But his daughters' punishment wasn't a big concern of Lyle these days. His concern was, and had been, Emilie since David had departed after his brother had died. Her existence had been a painful one. Two days after David had been informed of his brother's passing, he suddenly left without a word to anyone except Emilie, and she couldn't even speak of it for days. Lyle finally stopped asking until one night, after she'd had too much wine, the story all came spilling out.

Refusal to marry... possible marriage to his brother's widow... affairs to settle... Emilie was not a priority. All of these things came spilling out of Emilie's mouth as Lyle and Brickley had sat in stunned silence. Neither one of them had any idea that all of this had gone on. Lyle had been somewhat dubious of his daughter's explanation on David's flight, but Brickley had believed her implicitly. And that's where the problems begin.

Lyle seemed to think that Brickley, with David perhaps gone for good, thought that he now stood a chance with Emilie again. His pursuit of her had been far subtler than it had been before, mostly agreeing with her assessment of David and being quite chivalrous to her when he happened to be around her. It wasn't anything strong, or obvious, but Lyle could tell that Brickley's interest in his daughter had resumed. He had reminded Brickley on more than one occasion that Emilie was still pledged to David, but Brickley tried to pretend he was quite innocent to Lyle's meaning. Lyle knew that he wasn't.

He knew that Brickley had a plan in mind.

Gazing down at Emilie as she looked up at him, Lyle had to shake thoughts of Brickley from his mind. Even if his daughter had given up on David, Lyle hadn't. He just didn't think the man was capable of what Emilie said he was capable of. Perhaps he was blinded by the de Lohr name, but he didn't think so. He simply thought there was more to the situation than Emilie had told him.

"Come out of there," Lyle said after a moment, waving her up the stairs as Roland and Cid, down in the storage room chasing rodents, barked behind her. "Come up to the hall and let us eat. I am famished."

Emilie obeyed, gathering her skirts to take the narrow stairs up to the floor above. She called to the dogs, who were lonely these days without Nathalie and Elise to play with. The younger girls were so busy with whatever Lillibet planned for them that they simply hadn't time. So Emilie mounted the steps with the bored dogs moving up behind her, climbing the stairs with their dog-paws. By the time she came to the level above, which was a small alcove in the small hall, her father was standing in the middle of the room speaking with a soldier. Upon second look, the soldier looked most frantic in expression and gesture. The man was pointing to the gatehouse. Emilie frowned.

"Papa?" she said. "Is anything the matter?"

Lyle looked at her, surprise registering in his expression. He waved the soldier along and the man fled from the hall, out of the keep. Lyle held his hand out to his daughter.

"Come with me," he said. "Hurry."

Emilie took his hand and together they raced from the keep with Cid and Roland running behind them. "Where are we going?" Emilie asked.

Lyle didn't answer her. He simply led her down the steps to the bailey and then ran towards the gatehouse, still clutching her hand.

"Papa?"

Emilie's voice was worried, inquisitive, but Lyle still didn't answer. Even as they approached the gatehouse as the night fell, they could hear the clash of swords. The gatehouse was shadowed, with soldiers gathered up near the half-open portcullis, but Lyle pushed his way through, dragging Emilie behind him, when he suddenly came face to face with the reality of it.

David de Lohr had returned and Brickley was trying to keep the man out of Canterbury.

Shocked, Lyle watched a very bad scene indeed; Brickley was bloodied and struggling from David having cut the back of one of his knees, severing tendons. Brickley was dragging the leg behind him, trying to fend off David, who was as swift as the wind as he repeatedly attacked Brickley, trying to beat the man down. It was a fight that wasn't long for the going; with Brickley badly injured, it was only a matter of time before David overwhelmed him and, more than likely, killed him. It was a graphic and heart-wrenching scene.

It was one not lost on Emilie. Upon seeing David, she started to cry out but Lyle slapped a hand over her mouth to quiet her. Any sound from her would distract one or both knights, possibly giving one of them the edge of the other. That being the case, someone was likely to be killed and Lyle didn't want his daughter to be any part of the scene playing out before him, a scene that had been years in the making, ever since that day in December when David first set eyes on Emilie. Aye, it had been that long in the making. Now, the very thing he had feared all along was coming to pass.

Brickley was in bad shape. His leg was uncontrollable from David's very wise tactic to disable his enemy early on in the fight, so he was fighting from a kneeling position as David struck at him again and again, kicking him over, and kicking him again when he was down. Somehow, Brickley would manage to keep his torso away from David's blade and use his good leg to shove the man away so he could regain his feet, but it wasn't pretty to watch. It was like watching death throes.

Lyle had a feeling that he was about to lose a good knight and the knowledge saddened him. In fact, the entire situation did, but he understood the bare bones of what he saw before him – a knight's pride. That was really all it was. Brickley had been foolish enough to believe Emilie and thought he was doing her a favor by keeping David away, while David believed that Brickley had no business in his affairs. David was in the right; Brickley had put himself into a situation that didn't involve him. One man's romantic pride over another man's chivalrous ego.

But it was a situation that involved Emilie. She'd spent the past three months trying to forget about David because she was convinced that he'd gone to Lioncross to marry his brother's widow. That was truly what she believed. Or perhaps she had simply talked herself into it because of the stress of the last conversation she'd had with David. He had refused to marry her before leaving and she took that to be a sign that he did not want to.

So she'd spent the past three months miserable with sorrow, struggling daily to forget about the man she loved, but the truth was that she couldn't forget about him. Even when he sent her missives, and he'd sent several, she'd simply burned them, and happily. She didn't want to read of a wedding announcement or, worse, perhaps even a statement that he had been sorry to ever agree to a betrothal. She'd told him not to come back and she truly hoped he wouldn't. She didn't know what reason he would have for coming back. He'd made it clear that she was not a priority.

… but here he was.

Stunned, and horrified, she watched as David beat Brickley down with his sword. Brickley was wounded, unable to move, and David was simply toying with him, but there seemed more to it than that. There was anger in David's movements and she watched, as they all did, as David finally wrested Brickley's sword from him and tossed it aside. At that point, everyone expected David to slay Brickley right in front of them. In fact, Emilie was so terrified that she was about to witness Brickley's death that she yanked her father's hand away from her mouth and called out to him.

"David, *don't!*" she cried. "Do not kill him!"

David, in full battle mode, suddenly came to a halt and turned in the direction of the half-open portcullis. It was darker now as the sun set, and fatted torches upon the wall illuminated the scene on the road below, casting shadows into the night.

A great battle of warriors had taken place in the road outside of the gatehouse, a great battle until David had cut the tendons behind Brickley's left knee. With Brickley down, the battle had turned into a death watch. But with Emilie's voice piercing the night, David turned to see her standing behind the portcullis with Lyle's arm around her shoulders. She appeared pale and frightened, but David had never seen a more beautiful sight. It also served to fuel his rage, knowing that Brickley had, since nearly the beginning of their association, tried to keep David from Emilie. He wanted her for himself.

He still wanted her for himself.

So David tossed his sword away, into the soft grass, and turned to Brickley in fury. His big fists, gloved, began to pound into Brickley's head and face, sending the man to the ground.

"That is for the slugging me the jaw at the mask at Windsor," he snarled, pulling Brickley up so he could slug him again. "And that is for pursuing Emilie even when she told you she did not want you. You are a foolish and idiotic man, de Dere. I should have taken your head off long ago but I didn't do it. I thought I was being magnanimous but I can see that you only thought I was being weak. Trying to keep me from Emilie tonight is the last nail in your coffin. Tonight, I am going to end this."

He pounded Brickley a few more times as the man tried to defend himself. David kicked at Brickley, too, in his bad leg, and Brickley struggled not to cry out. Over by the portcullis, Emilie was watching with such horror that she couldn't take anymore. She was sickened and frightened and overwhelmed with everything. Before Lyle could stop her, she darted underneath the portcullis and ran out onto the road.

"David, *stop!*" she begged. "Please – no more!"

Breathing heavily with rage and exertion, David turned around to see that she was only a few feet away. The fear on her face had an impact with him. He was in battle mode and fully prepared to beat

Brickley to death, but the sight of Emilie's face stopped him. He staggered back, away from Brickley and away from Emilie. Yanking his helm off, he tossed it aside as his pale eyes blazed.

"He told me that you do not wish to see me," he said, pointing to Brickley. "He told me that you burned all of my missives. I told him I would not go until I heard it from your lips, Emilie, so tell me now – do you want me to go? If you tell me to leave, I will and I will never come back. I will never bother you again."

Words of dismissal were on her lips; they really were. But the longer she gazed at David, the weaker she became. God, she loved him so. She knew she did. All of those months of separation were beginning to dissolve, mixing with fonder memories, until she couldn't really remember the anger and sadness she had towards him. The heart was funny that way. But there were unanswered questions that needed resolution before.

"Did you marry your brother's widow?" she asked.

He looked at her as if she had lost her mind. "I have no idea why you think I would do such a thing," he said, exasperated. "You said it before but I do not know why you did. I never said anything to make you think that was my intention."

She wouldn't back down. "You said you had to go and see to her," she said. "You refused to marry me before you left and by your own words you were going to tend to a woman without a husband. I did not misunderstand you when you said that."

He grunted, shaking his head. "Then you wrongly assumed," he said. "I will be honest with you, Emilie; I left Lioncross weeks ago. I have been traveling through England coming to terms with my brother's death and trying to understand if I have really been treating you as poorly as you say I have been. If I have, it was never intention-al. I do not love my brother's wife and no matter what sense of duty I have towards her, it is not in the romantic sense and it certainly had nothing to do with marrying her. It is you I adore. Is that clear enough for you?"

Emilie nodded, feeling somewhat subdued by his words. But it didn't erase the fact that he hadn't been willing to marry her before he left. Confused, and hurt, she simply nodded her head.

"It is," she said quietly. "But my assumption is not totally my fault. There has always been something in you that has been unwilling to commit to marriage. You told me when I first met you that you were not the marrying kind. We have been betrothed for quite some time and still no marriage. I will tell you this; if you intend to return to me now and not marry me, then I would have you not return at all. I will not be waiting for you until I am old and you are old and there is no point in marrying at all. I told you before I would not be a convenience, someone to come to when you are lonely or in despair. I would have a husband and children and a home of my own. If you are not willing to give me these things, then let me find someone who is."

David sighed heavily at her somewhat painful speech. "I did not want to marry you before I left for Lioncross because my focus, at that time, was solely on my brother's death," he said, his voice dropping in volume because people were listening. He felt as if he was laying his life out for all to hear but he had little choice at the moment. "I knew I could not give our marriage the attention it deserved. I would have been distracted and distraught. Is that how you would want our wedding to be? With the groom grieving his brother's death and unable to experience the joy of the wedding?"

Emilie's brow furrowed. "Then why did you not tell me that?"

"You did not give me a chance," he said. "You were so busy trying to force me to marry you before I left that you did not give me that chance."

He was right. Emilie was coming to realize that she had created some of the issue between them with her willingness to quickly assume the worst. It was a bad fault she had. Still, she knew she wasn't completely to blame.

"Mayhap that is true," she said softly. "But it was not as if you were willing and talkative on the morning you left. You did not say very much to me at all, only that you had to leave and see to your brother's widow. What was I supposed to think, David?"

David shook his head, realizing they both shared some fault at the situation. "I am sure you had no other choice than to think what you did," he said. He turned to look at Brickley, seated on the ground several feet away with his head in his hand. His attention returned to Emilie. "Did you really burn my missives?"

She nodded without hesitation. "I did."

"Why?"

"Because I did not want to read a wedding announcement."

He shook his head. "I would never marry Dustin," he said again. "Moreover, she and Christin do not need me. Marcus Burton has stepped forward to take care of them and they shall be his burden from now on."

Emilie felt much better after hearing that. "For their sake, I am glad."

He shrugged his shoulders, unwilling to go into the entire fiasco of the battle between him and Marcus and the reasons why Richard had sent him back to Canterbury. He gestured at Brickley.

"He needs a physic," he said. "Have someone tend him. But not you."

She turned to her father, gesturing frantically to the man and pointing to Brickley. When Lyle began to send men to Brickley's aid, she turned to David, fighting off a grin.

"Why can I not tend him?" she asked.

David was moving towards the swords and helm he'd tossed away. "Because if you do, I will kill him," he said. "Is that clear enough."

"It is."

"Did he try to woo you while I was gone?"

Emilie shook her head. "Not that I was aware of," she said. "Even if he did, I am sure you know me well enough to know that it would not have made a difference."

David bent down, picking up his sword and Brickley's, and then collecting his helm with his other hand. "I know you well enough to know that you are maddening and stubborn and bewildering at times," he said, looking her in the eye. "But I also know that you are sweet, intelligent, gentle, and kind, and I love you with all my heart. If you are still willing to marry me, I would very much be willing to marry you."

Emilie's lips blossomed with a full and beautiful smile, touched deeply by his words. God, she was so glad to have him back. Gazing into that handsome face seemed to melt away every sorrow and every disappointment he'd ever created, real or imagined.

"Aye," she murmured. "I am still willing. Happily so."

Bloodied, exhausted, and beaten, with two swords in one and a helm in the other, he walked up to her and bent down, kissing her quite lustily in full view of the entire castle of Canterbury. Men began to whistled and clap, encouraging David's show of affection, and Emilie threw her arms around David's neck and held him fast. Finally, he was back, and he was here to stay.

Finally, David had come home.

HE WASN'T GOING to stay.

In his second floor room of the gatehouse, Brickley had packed the last of his possessions into his saddle bags, crammed full of things he had accumulated over the years. Five days after his beating at the hands of David, he had determined he couldn't stay at Canterbury any longer. He couldn't watch the woman he loved marry a man who came and went as he pleased without any recourse. If Emilie wanted to be stupid with her life, then that was her affair. He didn't have to stick around to see it.

Limping from the injury to his left leg, he was still well enough to move around and he could certainly ride. He thought he might travel north to East Anglia and see if the earl could use another knight. He'd fought under East Anglia at Gowergrove and he rather liked the man. Besides, anything was better than remaining here.

So he packed his things and had his horse prepared. He hadn't seen Emilie or David since that fateful battle, and he'd only seen Lyle twice when the man had come to check on him. Leaving a note for Lyle on his bed, he collected his things and made his way down to the bailey, moving slowly on his injured leg, and headed across the ward to the stables.

It was a blustery day, and oddly cool for summer. The bailey had patches of grass growing in here and there, and he could see the soldier on the wall walk pacing their rounds. He passed through the shadow of the keep, glancing up to take his final look at the place before departing. He had come to love Canterbury and tried not to be sad about leaving, but he knew he had to go. There was no question in his mind.

The plans for David and Emilie's wedding were in full swing. It was set for the end of the month to give guests enough time to arrive. Brickley had heard, through some of the soldiers that had been running as messengers, that Emilie and David had sent out invitations to everyone important, including the king, but most particularly they had wanted David's Uncle Philip to attend. Since David no longer had his brother, Philip and his young son, Edward, were David's last true remaining family members and their attendance was important to David. So the wedding was essentially waiting for the man to appear all the way from Derbyshire.

A wedding. Brickley tried not to think about it or be bitter for the fact that he wished it was his wedding to Emilie. It should have been his. He had earned it, hadn't he? He had served Lyle flawlessly for years and he deserved to be rewarded with what he felt was his due. But things hadn't worked out as he had hoped. He was bitter about it, no doubt, but that was something he would have to deal with. He was nearly to the stables when he heard a voice from behind.

"Brickley? Where are you going?"

Emilie was standing behind him. Dressed in a linen dress the color of eggshell, her hair was bound back with a kerchief over her head and she looked as if she had been working. He turned to her, struggling to keep his expression neutral.

"Where did you come from?" he asked.

Emilie nodded her head in the direction of the kitchens. "I was in the kitchen yard," she said. "I saw you come from the gatehouse. Where are you going?"

Brickley had to steel himself against her; he always felt himself growing weak where she was concerned. "Away," he said. "I have left your father a note. It is in my chamber, on the bed."

Emilie was looking at him seriously. "I do not understand," she said. "Why are you leaving?"

He studied her a moment. "You must truly ask that question?" he said quietly. "Please don't make me answer it."

Emilie wasn't being foolish or deliberately daft; she suspected why the man was leaving, or at least she thought it was the reason. "Is it because of your fight with David?" she asked. "Brickley, he hasn't said anything more about it. I am sure he has put it out of his mind. You should not be embarrassed by it. Canterbury is your home; why would you leave?"

He was trying not to become exasperated with her. "Is that what you think?" he asked. "That I am leaving because I fought with David? Truly, Emilie, that has nothing to do with it. I am leaving because I cannot watch you make a fool of yourself any longer for a man who treats you no better than one would a loyal pet. Every time he treats you poorly, you simply wait for him to come back and pretend nothing has ever happened. I tried to protect you from him this last time but that effort was wasted. So I am leaving so I do not have to watch your idiocy any longer."

Emilie was a bit taken aback at his strong words. He was insulting her, that was clear. But it wasn't in her nature to let the man berate her like that.

"I never asked you to protect me," she pointed out. "You did that of your own accord so you cannot blame me for your failure. And what happens between David and I is none of your affair."

Brickley was put in his place. Offended, he simply nodded his head. "Very well, Lady Emilie," he said. "I wish you luck with David de Lohr. You are going to need it."

Now she was the one offended. "Why would you say that?"

"I told you why."

Emilie put her hands on her hips. "David and I will be fine," she said, "and if this is truly the way you feel, then we are better off without you. No one has asked you to leave Canterbury; you are doing this of your own accord. I always thought better of you, Brickley, but I guess I was wrong. I was wrong about you in many ways. Therefore, I wish you well on your travels and I pray you eventually find a woman who returns your feelings. I am sorry I couldn't."

"So am I."

"I think you should go."

Brickley did. He turned for the stables and collected his horse, riding past Emilie, who was still standing in the bailey, watching him leave. He wouldn't even look at her, focused on the gatehouse and the road beyond as if seeing his life spread out before him. A life that did not involve Emilie.

Emilie watched Brickley until he disappeared from view, wondering if it would be the last time she ever saw him. He was such a part of their lives that it was difficult to think of Canterbury without Brickley de Dere being a fixture there. She wondered if she shouldn't have tried to talk him out of leaving, but she supposed it was the best thing for them all. Brickley was beaten, and humiliated, and every time he saw David, he would remember those feelings. There was no chance for them to ever work peacefully together, and that was something that needed to happen if their lives were going to be pleasant. Given that situation, she was coming to agree with his decision.

It was better for him to go.

It was the end of a chapter in their lives and Emilie was saddened that things with Brickley had ended so poorly. It was his choice to leave, indeed, but the truth was that the man had little choice. To save his pride, and probably his heart, he had to go. For all of the good years they had together, Emilie genuinely wished him well. Lingering on this final conversation with Brickley, Emilie headed into the keep to tell her father of his departure.

Lyle wasn't surprised by Brickley's departure, either, but he was saddened much as Emilie was. He liked Brickley a great deal. He felt it was the end of an era, too, much as Emilie did, but he was also convinced it was for the best. A castle couldn't have two dominant knights and with David marrying into the family, there would be no place for Brickley.

And with that, Brickley de Dere rode from their lives.

Still, there was no lingering sorrow at his departure with a wedding on the horizon. Eight days later, Philip de Lohr and his son, Edward, arrived at Canterbury Castle along with a host of other guests including William de Ferrers, Earl of Derby and his son, also William, the young lord whom David had seen at the tournament at Windsor.

It was a friendly and festive gathering that finally happened on the last day of the month. At the door to Canterbury Cathedral Lady Emilie Hampton become Lady Emilie Hampton de Lohr. The sun was setting behind the couple, creating a hallow from which to watch the start of the mass. Emilie faced David in her pink silk gown and accepted him as her husband, and he accepted her as his wife. Then, they went into the cathedral to finish the mass.

The wedding feast lasted all night and into the next day, a joyous and lovely occasion that gave no hint that six weeks later, they would all receive the greatest surprise conceivable.

It was one that would change the course of their lives forever.

CHAPTER TWENTY-FOUR

Canterbury Castle
September Year of our Lord 1194 A.D.

DAVID'S HANDSOME FACE was white as he stood by the ornate glass window, looking over the inner courtyard of Canterbury Castle. Beside him, Philip de Lohr sat motionless.

"He's alive," Philip whispered in disbelief.

David was overwhelmed with the contents of the missive, so much so that he did not trust himself to speak immediately after reading it. But now, having had the chance to mull it over in his frazzled mind, he would speak.

"Dustin is with Marcus," he murmured. "And I let her go. After he kills Marcus, he is going to come and kill me."

"Do not be ridiculous," Philip snapped softly. "You were obeying a direct order from Richard. He ordered you away, and you had to go. If Chris is going to kill anyone, let it be our king. He gave Marcus his blessing.

David turned away from the window, his face sunburned from an entire afternoon of practicing in the late spring sun. The past three days had been the most cataclysmic of his life, getting married and learning that his late brother was not at all dead. It was almost more than he could take.

"How is it that he was mistaken for dead?" David wondered aloud.

"I do not understand how Anthony could have made such a mistake. Even Burwell declared him dead. I do not understand any of this."

Philip picked up the missive from Edward; it had come alongside the message from Christopher. "'Twould do you well to ride for the north and prevent your brother from tearing Marcus apart. Edward seems to think it will be a full scale war."

"Edward likes to overreact," David said flatly. "But he is right in assuming I would want to know of my brother's plans. If anyone can stop him, I can."

"He rides with Richard by his side, and you cannot stop our king," Philip said. "According to Edward, Christopher is riding to Windsor to seek reinforcements, and then on to Somerhill to retrieve Lady Dustin, who by now is probably Lady Burton."

David eyed Philip for a moment before turning away. "This is all madness. Jesus, if Christopher had just killed Marcus the first time he made a move on Dustin, none of this would be happening. Now the whole goddamn country is going to fall apart because my brother and his former best friend cannot keep their hands off the same woman."

"What are you going to do?" Philip asked softly.

David thought a moment. "Take a couple of hundred men with me and ride for Somerhill, I suppose, but I do not know what good it will do. Lord Hampton may want to go, even though he considers himself retired after turning his troops over to me." He glanced at Philip. "What about you? You have a hundred men lodged here in Canter-bury. Will you go with me?"

"You forget, I brought Edward here for the wedding, and I shall not allow my twelve-year-old son to ride into battle," Philip said. "Nay, when I leave, it will be to return to Lohrham Forest. I shall let you deal with Christopher; I never could. The only man who could remotely handle him was Richard."

"Christopher respects you, Uncle," David said. "He always listened when you spoke."

Philip snorted. "Listened to me and then did exactly as he pleased, *anyway. Nay, David, whatever happens is between Christopher and Marcus. Richard is likely to be torn in two if he intervenes."*

There was a soft rap on the solar door and the Lady Emilie de Lohr stuck her head in, smiling tenderly at her new husband.

"Mother is serving refreshments in the smaller hall. I promised I'd tell you."

David smiled back at his new wife, truly in love with the woman. And why not? She was a soft, gentle beauty and a tremendous flirt. He liked that.

"You did, my sweet," David replied. "Tell Mother we shall be there in a moment."

Emilie nodded, then cocked her head quizzically at her husband. "Is something wrong? You do not look well."

David snickered ironically. "No, sweet, nothing is wrong. We shall be along."

Emilie took the hint like a good wife and closed the door behind her. David glanced at Philip. "Now, if that were Dustin, she'd be in here beating me to a pulp until I let her read the missive. I was terrified to take a wife because I was afraid they were all like her."

Philip laughed. "And this is the woman a country is tearing itself apart over? Most confusing."

David was jesting, of course, trying to alleviate some of the tension. As he turned to his uncle again, the door to the solar flew open and a tall, gangly blond youth appeared.

"Father!" he exclaimed. "The mare is foaling. Lord Hampton promised I could have the foal."

"So he did," Philip rose, eyeing his son critically. "Eddie, are you old enough to see an actual birth?"

Edward de Lohr scowled at his father. "I have seen worse. Come quickly. David, you come, too."

David waved him off, watching his uncle and cousin quit the room.

When they were gone, he sighed heavily and sank into the nearest chair. He could scarcely believe that Christopher was alive, but all the more thankful that the rumors of his death had been untrue. He could only imagine the turmoil his brother was going through, knowing his wife was with another man, and there were so many unanswered questions that David was wildly confused.

He knew he had to go north, if nothing more than to show support for his brother. He would apologize to Christopher for the things he had said about Dustin and prayed his brother would forgive him. He could only hope that with all of his other troubles, Christopher would be willing to put theirs aside. Dustin had forgiven him and he hoped his brother was in the same spirit.

Emilie was waiting for him in the hall. He saw her sweet, rounded face and took her into his arms. She blushed as he kissed her, feeling flushed and warm.

"Ah, let me guess," David said seductively. "You cannot wait for me to bed you again."

"David," Emilie gasped in mock outrage. "Do not say such things. My sisters are apt to hear and…."

He frowned. "They hear everything, Emilie, no matter if it is whispered or shouted. Nathalie and Elise have ears all over this damn place. They are probably around the corner right now, giggling their heads off."

Emilie smiled at the mirth of it. "They are only children, for God's sake. Do not get so angry."

"Children? Ha! You mean the Devil's own offspring," he snorted. "At fourteen and sixteen years of age, I would hardly call them children."

Emilie kissed him softly, making him forget all about her annoying sisters. "No wonder your father was so glad when I came along," he purred against her cheek. "He has had his fill of women."

David rolled his eyes as he rubbed his cheek against hers. "The poor man is outnumbered."

"You have evened out the odds somewhat."

"Not enough."

Emilie giggled, letting him hold her and kiss her for a few moments. "What did the missives from Lioncross say?" she asked casually.

He pulled back and cocked an eyebrow. "You little minx, using affection to gain information."

"I am not," she replied indignantly. "I simply wanted to know if it said something about Dustin and Christin."

He looked at her a moment before releasing her from his embrace and taking her hand. "Let's go find your father, then. I think he would like to hear this, too."

"Here," Emilie said, handing him two clean tunics, tightly rolled for easier packing. "I washed these for you yesterday. They are dry enough now for you to pack them."

David kissed her in thanks as he took. "You washed these with your own hands?"

She grinned, batting her eyelashes at him. "Of course I did," she said. "Do you think I would let someone else touch your clothing?"

He laughed softly as he shoved the rolled-up tunics into the corners of his saddlebags. "Thank you," he said sincerely. "I will wear them next to my heart, knowing that your hands were the last that touched them."

Emilie grinned, her cheeks flushing at his sweet flattery. He winked at her as he continued packing for his trip to rendezvous with his brother and Richard, his mind already ahead to seeing the brother he thought was dead. He still couldn't believe it, as he said repeatedly. But Emilie could see the joy in his manner since last week when he had been delivered the missives regarding Christopher's miraculous resurrection. Emilie was quite sure he hadn't slept much for the excitement of it. She'd never seen the man quite so happy about anything but, of course, their marriage a few weeks earlier had left his mood perpetually pleasant. So had bedding her every night and awakening to her sweet face.

It was that intimate act between them that had come to fruition. With his wife a few weeks pregnant, that was something else for David to be overjoyed about. He would put his hands all over her belly, speaking to his son, even though her belly was still flat. Nonetheless, he knew a child grew inside of her based upon what she had told him – her menses had stopped and her breasts were growing uncomfortable and round. David could see the changes in her body and it thrilled him. Therefore, there was much for him to be joyful of as of late.

Emilie was joyful, too. Their days were perfect and their nights even better. Marriage to David was everything she had ever hoped it would be. Even Nathalie and Elise, in spite of what David had said about them, seemed to be accepting him. Due to Nathalie's blossoming friendship with Payn, the frequency and severity of pranks had dropped off tremendously. They still weren't beyond little tricks, for instance, putting honey on his pillow or putting Cid and Roland to good use by admitting the dogs into the garderobe that David was using so that the animals rushed in and licked his arse as he was relieving himself and unable to fend them off.

Even that prank had drawn giggles from Emilie when David, red-faced, told her what they'd done. David had promptly retaliated by capturing both girls and stringing them up by the ankles in the stable, where the horses tried to eat Elise's long blond hair and slobbered all over Nathalie's head. David had stood outside with the stable master, an older man who had been the victim of pranks before, and giggled his head off. It was Payn who eventually saved the pair that night by hearing their cries and lowering them into the hay below, untying their ankles and being generally nice to them. After that, fearful of David's nasty revenge tactics, all tricks and pranks against the man had ceased.

Which made for a very bucolic life at Canterbury after that. With their days of tricks seemingly over, Nathalie and Elise were turning into proper young women as their married elder sister doted on her husband. Even now, Emilie bustled around their chamber, the one she used to share with Nathalie, to help David as he finished packing.

More missives had come to Canterbury over the past few days, missives from Christopher stating that Dustin had been abducted by Prince John and that the man was holed up with her at Nottingham Castle. Christopher had stated that he was heading in that direction to reclaim his wife but there was still mention of Somerhill Castle, Marcus Burton's seat.

The missives had been conflicting and confusing for the most part, feeding David's sense of urgency to ride to his brother's aid. His destination was still Somerhill. So Emilie sat on the bed and watched David finish up with his packing, feeling his urgency and determination. This time, she strangely didn't mind him leaving her. It seemed to be a habit with him, as Brickley had once said, but it also seemed to be a habit for him to return to her. She knew in her heart that David would always return to her, no matter what, and it wasn't even the marriage or her pregnancy that fed that opinion. It was the character of the man himself.

The man she had finally married.

"Is there anything more to take with you?" she asked. "I had the cook pack food for you, so you should be well stocked on things to take with you on your travels. Am I missing anything?"

He shook his head. "I do not think so," he said, looking over the contents of his saddlebags, which also contained all of the missives he had received. "I think I have everything."

Emilie, too, looked at the things he intended to take. "Do not forget your rain cloak," she said. "The weather is turning colder now. The rains will come soon and if you are gone into winter, you must contend with the snow."

He began to seal up his saddlebags. "I will not be gone into winter," he said. "I am not entirely sure what is going on, given the missives I've received as of late, but all indications are that John has abducted Dustin and Chris is riding to retrieve her. I cannot imagine such a task taking too long, so I would expect to be back well before the snows come."

Emilie watched his handsome face as he finished off with his saddlebags. "I wonder how he was able to abduct her?" she asked softly. "Did you not say that she had gone with Marcus Burton to Somerhill? Surely the man would have protected her against such things."

David could only shrug. "I cannot imagine how the prince was able to gain control of her," he said. "But I am sure I will find out."

Emilie put her hand on his arm. "You will be careful," she said. "I would have my son know his father."

He smiled, kissing her on the cheek. "He will," he said. "You needn't worry. It is my suspicion that the army marching on Nottingham is one of the biggest England has ever seen. It will make laying siege a simple thing."

"How many Canterbury men are you taking with you?"

"About three hundred."

There wasn't much more to say to that. David was packed and Emilie had her information, information that would sustain her until he returned. She was trying not to show her sadness in his departure.

"So you will leave me once again," she teased, watching him grin sheepishly. "It seems all you ever do is leave me."

He leaned forward, kissing her on the lips. "And all I ever do is come back to you, too," he said. "I am sorry to leave again, Emilie, truly, but...."

She cut him off. "Do not be ridiculous," she scolded lightly. "Your brother has returned from the dead and now you must help him reclaim his wife. Of course you must go; I insist that you do. It is your duty."

He nodded, slinging the saddlebags over one broad shoulder. "It is," he said, his warm gaze lingering on her. "But so are you. How are you feeling today?"

Emilie shrugged. "Well enough, I suppose," she said. "I have had some odd pains in my groin and back for the past few days but Lillibet said that is normal in pregnancy to have a few aches and pains, especially at the beginning."

"And how would she know? She has never had children."

Emilie lowered her voice. "I am not so sure that is true," she said. "I have never told you this before, mostly because it has been such a normal thing in our family that it has not yet crossed my mind to tell you, but my father and Lillibet are lovers."

David looked at her, shocked. "They are?"

Emilie nodded. "You have not noticed?"

David shook his head, wide-eyed. "I haven't," he admitted. "How long as this been going on?"

"Since my mother passed away," she said. "It has been a very long time. Papa thinks that we do not know, but we do."

David chuckled at the mental picture of Lyle bedding the buxom nurse that sprayed spit like a fountain when she spoke. "How *do* you know?" he asked.

Emilie gave him a rather reproachful look. "Because we have all lived together for a very long time," she said. "When Lillibet would think we were asleep, she would sneak into Papa's chamber. We have seen her. And then we would hear Papa panting, as if he was breathless, so we knew that something was going on."

David laughed again. "If that is true, then I applaud the man for seeing to his needs for all of these years, conveniently, with his children's nurse," he said. "But why do you say that Lillibet knows about pregnancy?"

Emilie's tone dropped even more, fearful that her sisters or Lillibet herself might be close enough to hear her. The keep was a close, small place at times, even with the thick walls.

"Because many years ago she put on weight and then she left us, saying that she had to go and visit family," she said. "I was mayhap five years of age, Nathalie was three, and Elise was still a baby, but I remember because I was quite traumatized when she left. I had just lost my mother, you see, and I was fearful in general of people leaving me. When Lillibet returned a few months later, she was much thinner than when she left. It did not occur to me at the time but in thinking back, I think she had a child."

David shrugged. "If she did, where is it?"

Emilie shook her head. "I do not know," she said. "Mayhap she left it with her family or mayhap it died. I have not asked her because it is not my business. But I will admit that I have wondered."

David shook his head at the secrets from the family he had married in to. It wasn't unusual for a man to have illegitimate children, but he seriously wondered that if, indeed, Lyle had a child, why he had not let it grow up with the rest of his children.

But he put those thoughts out of his mind, for they weren't anything to linger on unless, in the years to come, some young man came forth and claimed to be the heir to the Canterbury earldom. David would deal with that if, and when, the time every came. At the moment, he had family issues of his own to deal with that would take all of his attention.

"Well," he grunted as he heaved up his scabbard and broadsword from its' peg on the wall. "I suppose someday all secrets shall come out and you shall know. Until then, will you go with me down to the stables? I must see to my horse and I do not want to spend any more time away from you than I have to."

Emilie was more than happy to accompany him but as she stood up, the pain in her groin and back increased to the point where she actually had to rub at her belly to try and ease the ache. David saw her rubbing.

"Are you well?" he asked, concerned.

Emilie nodded although something just didn't feel right to her. The pains were very achy, radiating down her legs a bit. "Aye," she assured him. "Just the aches and pain of a pregnant woman."

He smiled at her. "A beautiful woman," he corrected. "If you'd rather stay here and rest, I will return as soon as I can."

Emilie shook her head. "Nay," she said firmly. "You will be gone for an unknown length of time. I will be spending enough time alone while you are away."

David didn't argue with her. He led her from their chamber and took her down to the stables were there were several horses being prepared for the march northward, and the three hundred men to accompany David were in the ward being supplied and outfitted by their sergeants and the quartermaster. It was all quite busy as David and Emilie passed by the men, heading to the stables. Cid and Roland came out of nowhere, rushing Emilie with their big, happy bodies, and David was forced to push the dogs aside so they wouldn't bowl her over. Just as they reached the mouth of the stable, Lyle appeared.

He wrestled back Cid and snapped at Roland when the dog wouldn't listen. "Sorry, Emilie," he said. "They are spending the day with me because Nathalie and Elise are too busy for them. I fear I cannot control them as you and your sisters do."

Emilie grinned, petting Roland's big head. "Not to worry," she said, kissing the dog on the head. "Do you want me to take them back inside, Papa?"

Lyle nodded gratefully. "Do you mind?"

Emilie shook her head but David stopped her. "Wait," he said. "Those dogs are big enough to run you down. Let me take them back."

Emilie laughed as Lyle spoke. "Let her do it, please," he said. "I have a need to speak with you before you go, David."

David wasn't happy but he allowed his wife to lead the dogs back to the keep so long as she didn't try to wrestle with them or manhandle them. Those were his terms because he didn't want her to somehow be hurt, and Emilie agreed. As she called the dogs and headed for the keep with the big black mutts trailing her, David turned to Lyle.

"What is your wish, my lord?" he said. "How may I be of service?"

Lyle cleared his throat softly, suddenly looking uncomfortable. "Walk with me for a moment. I have something to tell you."

David followed and they proceeded to move away from the stables and the gathering men. They were heading towards the gatehouse and David was increasingly curious about the subject at hand, since it seemed to have Lyle slightly uneasy. They were nearing the gatehouse and Lyle looked up to the wall, searching for something. He finally came to a halt and pointed.

"Do you see that young soldier up there?" he said.

David looked at what he was pointing at. "I think so," he said, peering up to the parapet near the gatehouse. "That is Nathalie's friend. I think his name is Payn."

Lyle cleared his throat again. He was having difficulty looking David in the eye, it seemed. "Aye," he muttered. "His name is Payn. David, it is not easy to speak of this but I must. You must not tell anyone."

"You have my oath."

Lyle eyed the young man on the wall. "That young soldier is my son," he muttered. "He does not know it. He is the result of liaison between myself and another woman, and he has been living with an elderly farm couple on the edge of the village since birth. I told Brickley to retrieve the boy when he was recruiting reinforcements for my army last spring, but I did not tell Brickley who he was. All was well and good until Nathalie decided to befriend him and I fear... I fear her friendship for him may turn into something else. You know that she has romantic inclinations for nearly every man she meets. Therefore, I want you to take him with you when you leave. I would consider it a favor if you would make him your squire. Train him. He is the son of an earl and due such consideration. But, most of all, get him away from Nathalie before she does something we will all regret."

David kept himself quite neutral as Lyle spoke, but inside, he was quite shocked. It was so strange that he and Emilie had been speaking on this exact same subject not a few minutes earlier, so Lyle's confession was quite coincidental. Providence, even. David looked up on the battlements to where the tall young man stood, looking out to the countryside beyond.

"He is a fine boy, my lord," he said. "Who is his mother?"

"That is not important."

"Is it Lillibet?"

Lyle looked at him, stunned. He didn't respond right away, perhaps debating just how to answer, but it was clear that he seemed unable to put up a good denial. He finally shook his head, reconciled to the inevitable.

"How... how did you know that?" he asked quietly.

David smiled faintly. "Call it a hunch," he said, holding up a hand when Lyle tried to press him. "It does not matter how I knew, truly. It was really just a guess. Does Lillibet know the boy is hers?"

Lyle shook his head. "I have not told her he is here," he said reluctantly. "She does not ask of him and she does not ask of my business. If I want her to know, I will tell her."

David thought of his own son whom Emilie was carrying. "That is your decision, of course," he said. "But she is his mother, after all. It would be the right thing to tell her."

Lyle simply shrugged, feeling unsettled by the conversation. The illegitimate son had always been an awkward point with him, fathered with his children's nurse, and he had tried to hide the boy away as if hiding an unsavory secret. But the truth was that he had been thrilled to see his son when Brickley had brought the boy back those months ago. Lyle thought the lad looked just like his father.

In any case, he still wasn't sure how he felt about revealing his weaknesses and shortcoming and admitting he'd fathered a bastard with a woman who was nothing more to him than a concubine. Still, he could see David's point.

"Mayhap I will at some point," he said. "But for now, take the lad with you and train him. I would consider it a personal favor."

David simply nodded and whistled to the nearest soldier, who came on the run. He sent the man up to the wall to send the young man to him as Lyle, still nervous and unsure to be around the lad, made himself scarce.

As David became acquainted with young Payn, who happened to have Emilie's eyes, up in the keep Emilie was dealing with something quite devastating.

The end of a dream.

BY THE TIME EMILIE reached the keep with the dogs, the pain in her belly, back, and legs was intense. As the dogs ran into the smaller hall to sniff the floor for scraps, she went up to the chamber she shared with David and pulled the chamber pot out from under the bed. She felt as if she had to piss and she lifted her skirts and squatted over it, relieving herself.

But it was more than piss that went into that pot. Emilie could see a great deal of blood in it, too, with dark clots. Terrified, she put a cloth over the pot and went to find Lillibet, who was sitting in the next room with Elise, sewing on a garment of some kind. Emilie stuck her head into the room, motioning to Lillibet to come to her.

It was a rather secretive gesture and Lillibet complied, her plain features twisted in confusion. She came to Emilie where the woman stood at the door but then Emilie pulled her through, into the chamber she shared with David, and shut the door. Once the door was shut, Emilie pressed her hand to her belly and lowered herself onto the bed.

"Look," she pointed to the chamber pot. "In there. Something is terribly wrong."

Lillibet went to the pot and uncovered it, faced with the sight of blood. Quickly, she turned to Emilie. "How are you feeling?" she demanded, spit flying from her lips. "Are you in pain?"

Emilie nodded, her face pale and her expression miserable. "I have some pain," she said. "My belly and back ache a good deal."

Lillibet looked at her with sorrow. Covering up the chamber pot, she pushed Emilie back on the bed. "Lay, child," she said. "You must lay down."

With fear in her expression, Emilie looked up at the woman. "Why?" she asked. "What is wrong?"

Lillibet sat down beside her, taking her hand. "This happens sometimes," she said as Emilie wiped spraying spit off of her arm. "I will send for the physic. He will know what to do."

Emilie was puzzled. "*What* has happened?" she demanded. "You said that pains were part of childbearing. Why is there blood?"

Lillibet shook her head sadly. "Because I suspect your child is no more," she said. "We will send for the physic and he will tell us."

Emilie stared at the woman for a moment before her eyes started to well with tears. "My... my son is gone?"

"He is."

"Are you sure?"

Lillibet glanced over at the chamber pot. "I believe so," she said. "You are not meant to bleed when you are with child. The loss of blood means the loss of the child."

Emilie's face crumpled and she put a hand over her face, covering her tears. "It cannot be," she whispered tightly. "I do not believe it!"

Lillibet patted her shoulder. "Do not despair," she said soothingly. "I know it seems terrible, but it is God's will that this should happen. It was not meant to be. There will be more children for you, Emilie. Take heart, sweetling."

Emilie began to sob softly as Lillibet bent over and tried to hug her, trying to give her some comfort. But in this case, there was no comfort to be had. The swift and shocking loss of the pregnancy had both women reeling but in Lillibet's opinion, there was no doubt what had happened. God's will would be done.

Quietly, Lillibet rose and went to the wardrobe where all manner of personal products was kept. Among those were linen pads with moss stuffing for a monthly cycle, with ties that would go about the waist to keep the pad in place. Lillibet simply handed the pad to Emilie and turned her back for a moment, for Emilie knew what to do with it. She didn't want to bleed all over the bed.

The mood of the chamber was quite sorrowful with Emilie's soft sniffing filling the air. While she was taking care of personal matters, seeing more blood and mourning her loss, Lillibet took the chamber pot and put it away, beneath the wardrobe, for the physic to inspect to see if the child was in those dark blood clots. When she turned around, Emilie was back on the bed, laying down, her hand at her belly as if to comfort herself for the emptiness now inside her. It was a rather sad sight to see.

"Are you in terrible pain, Em?" Lillibet asked softly.

Eyes closed, Emily lay still and pale upon the bed. "It aches, but it is not terrible," she said. "It has eased somewhat. It is manageable."

Lillibet felt as badly as she possible could for the young wife. She and David had been so thrilled about the child, about the new life they had created and the legacy of a new de Lohr on the horizon. Now that dream was dead. She went to the bed and put her soft, warm hand on Emilie's head.

"I will send for the physic," she said quietly. "You will lay there and rest."

Emilie reached up and grasped Lillibet's hand before the woman could get away. "Wait," she said. "Do not send for him now. Wait… wait until David leaves."

Lillibet lifted her eyebrows in mild surprise. "Why?" she asked.

Emilie shook her head, her watery eyes opening. "Because this child is all he can speak of," she said, sniffing. "Right now, David is happy and preparing to see a brother whom he thought he had lost. If… if I tell him of this, it will crush him. He may not even go. And he must go. There is nothing he can do if he remains with me, although he will want to. I know he will."

"Then you will not tell him?"

"Not now."

Lillibet simply touched her forehead in a comforting and understanding gesture. "As you wish," she said. "He will not hear of it from me."

Emilie closed her eyes again. "Thank you."

"I will fetch you a hot brew now. You need your rest."

Emilie didn't say anything more. She knew that David would soon be looking for her, as he would be ready to depart, and she was feeling particularly weak and achy. More than that, she was still trying to absorb the fact that she was no longer with child.

It was true that she had been moderately achy for a few days and had mentioned it to Lillibet, as she had told David. But clearly she had not considered that her aches and pains were a sign of things to come. It had never crossed her mind. But it was evident that those aches were a harbinger of doom, the death of something that was very important to bot her and David. She hoped that he wouldn't blame her for the loss or, worse, somehow blame himself. But she knew the man well enough to know that he would not become angry with her, for it was not her fault. As Lillibet said, it was God's will.

God's will that her son should die.

So she lay upon the bed, silent tears falling for the child she would never hold in her arms. She was so sad and very miserable, and at some point must have dozed off because she awoke to David entering their chamber. His expression upon her was one of great concern.

"What are you doing up here?" he said. "I have been looking everywhere for you. We are about to depart and I want you to see me off."

Emilie didn't want to get up; the ache was still there, although considerably lessened, but she was afraid of what would happen if she stood up. Already, Lillibet thought she'd lost her child but what if she hadn't? What if he was barely hanging on and standing up might dislodge him completely? They were wild thoughts, but thoughts nonetheless. She smiled wanly at David's serious face.

"I am so very tired," she said. "I fear the child is taxing me greatly. May… May I see you off right now? Would that disappoint you terribly?"

David shook his head and went to his knees beside the bed, wrapping her up in his big arms, which were cold because of the mail he wore.

"It would not disappoint me at all," he said. "I am sorry you are feeling so poorly. Is there anything you need before I go?"

Emilie had her arms around his neck, hugging him tightly. "Nay," she murmured. "Lillibet is here. She will take great care of me. And you must leave, my darling. Your brother is waiting."

He pulled his face from the crook of her neck, looking down into her pale face. Her eyes were red, he noticed, and he peered more closely at her. "What is wrong?" he asked, stroking her cheek. "You look as if you have been weeping."

A lump came to Emilie's throat but she fought it. "I have not," she lied, her voice hoarse. "I… I am simply weary. A baby is very tiresome."

He smiled and kissed the tip of her nose before kissing her lips, sweetly. "I am sorry, my sweet," he said, hearing no real hint in her voice of the distress that was in her heart. "You are a strong and brave woman. I will send you a message as soon as I meet up with my brother. Jesus, even as I say it I can still hardly believe it. It does not seem real that I will be seeing my brother soon."

"It will be real enough when you see him."

He chuckled. "I suppose so," he said. His humor faded. "You will rest and take care of yourself. Do you understand? I want you and my son healthy when I return."

The tears came then but she pulled him close, hugging him to hide the tears as she blinked them away. "I will do my very best," she said. "And you will take great care of yourself and return to me sound and whole. I will be very angry if you do not."

He laughed softly, kissing her cheek and lips again before letting her go and standing up. Emilie looked him over; he was dressed for battle in his mail and Canterbury tunic. Her heart was so proud that she thought it might burst, aching for this man, this knight, that meant everything to her.

"My steel warrior," she murmured in approval. "You look as if you are made of steel. You look invincible."

The smile never left his face as he tightened his gloves. "I am," he said. "I have you and my son to come home to. That makes me indestructible."

Emilie lifted a finger to her lips, blowing him a kiss. "Be safe, my darling," she murmured. "I love you very much."

His smile softened. "And I, you," he said. "Take great care. I shall return as soon as I can."

"Safe travels."

"Thank you."

With that, he was gone, through the door and down the stone steps. She could hear his boots as he made his way down, crashing against the stone, until the sound finally faded. Then, and only then, did she let more tears for their loss fall.

As the army departed Canterbury under the command of Sir David de Lohr, Baron Broxwood, Emilie found herself praying steadily for him. Prayers that would keep him safe so that he would return to her, as he'd promised. She didn't regret not telling him about the child, because she knew it had been the right thing to do. He would find out soon enough and he would mourn soon enough. For now, she let him be joyful with the return of his brother. That was the way she looked at it.

Let the man feel the elation with his brother's resurrection before knowing the pain of a child lost.

PART FOUR
AND SO, IT ENDS....

"Recks not, sire, by what death we die:
Good never came from counsel of pride,
List to the wise, and let madmen bide."
~ Song of Roland c. 1040 A.D.

CHAPTER TWENTY-FIVE

South of Nottingham
October Year of our Lord 1194 A.D.

*N*EVER WAS A *mightier army to be assembled.*

Christopher, Marcus and Richard intercepted the army riding from Somerhill and took command of the nine-hundred-man force. With the additional fifteen hundred men riding north from Windsor, they would not only lay siege to Nottingham; they would mow it to the ground.

Richard made the decision to wait for his army from Windsor. Christopher highly disapproved of the conclusion, but he was unsuccessful to convince his king otherwise. Marcus actually became quite irate and he and Richard had exchanged angry words. For a change, Christopher had had to separate the two of them.

Richard's logic was simple; he believed Dustin to be fairly safe and saw no need to go charging in and risk a great number of casualties. With the troops from Windsor, mayhap the casualties would be minimal simply because of the sheer number of men. Additionally, Dustin was not the primary concern; Richard intended to regain Nottingham for the crown and he knew he must show overwhelming force. When mercenary French soldiers returned to Philip Augustus after seeing battle with the returned King of England, he wanted the French king to know that Richard the Lionheart would not tolerate

French meddling in his country.

So they waited outside of the village of Grantham, a little over twenty miles to the east of Nottingham. Camp was set up and the wait for the army from Windsor was met with impatience by all. Christopher was nearly insane with grief and worry, but he knew that within two days, they would be marching for Nottingham and for his family. Until then, he was helpless.

Marcus got a grip on himself and was handling the wait better than Christopher. He and Christopher would talk of items that related to the battle, but that was the extent of their contact. For two men who had shared a tent for three years, it was a little strange being without the camaraderie and support of one another. They would gaze at each other across the compound, eyes meeting sometimes, but with no emotion. Yet even with the hurt and jealousy and anger, each man sensed an unfillable void the other had left within him, although they would not admit it. The pain of losing one's best friend was too deep for words.

On the second day of camp, an army was sighted riding in from the south and immediately the battle cry went up. Marcus expertly set up skirmish lines under the eagle-eyes of Richard and Christopher as they studied the incoming troops.

"Now who in the hell could this be?" Richard mumbled.

Christopher could see colors being flown, but they were too far away. He tightened his reins. "We shall soon find out."

The dark brown destrier charged forward, kicking up great clods of dirt as Christopher ran at break-neck speed down the slight incline before leveling out on the flat, grassy land. As Christopher drew closer, he could see that there were no more than three hundred men and he was truly curious. Who would be riding a small army this far north?

The answer came to him when he spied the yellow and gray and black of Lord Lyle Hampton, Earl of Canterbury. David! His little brother had come.

David met Christopher well in front of his army, the familiar white destrier he rode catching Christopher's eye. Christopher was so damn glad to see his brother that he was off his destrier before the horse even came to a halt, pulling his brother into a great bear hug in spite of the bulky armor they both wore. His anger, his grief, his disgust with David was dissolved in an instant.

"David," he managed to choke after an emotional minute. "What in the hell are you doing here?"

David wiped at his eyes, not ashamed to let his brother see how caught up he was. "Here to support you, of course," he said, then gestured to the massive army on the rise. "What is all of this?"

Christopher was so emotional he was ready to crack. He cuffed his brother affectionately on the side of the head.

"Dustin was taken to Nottingham," he said hoarsely. "How did you know we were here?"

"Because I received missives to that effect and, knowing you would be heading to Nottingham to collect Dustin," he replied, his blue eyes drinking in his brother's face. "I came to help."

Christopher laughed softly. "And so you have," he murmured, his hand still on his brother's shoulder as if incapable of letting him go. "We are waiting for reinforcements from Windsor before we go charging in and raze the place. Christ, David, you do not know how good it is to see you."

David's face was lit up like a candle. "What about you? Jesus, you were dead. What in the hell happened to you?"

Christopher waved at him. "It is a long story. I was severely wounded and it took me three months to find my way back home again, but we shall delve more into that later," he said. "What matters now is retrieving my wife and daughter."

David shook his head, still reeling with emotion. "What about Marcus?"

Christopher shrugged. "A truce, for now. At least until we get Dustin back."

"That's why I came, you know," David said. "I thought you were

going to have an all-out war with Marcus and I wanted to fight with you. Even if you did not want me."

"Did not want you...?" Christopher repeated, realizing how very foolish they had both been. "You are my brother, David. My only brother. What happened....well, we both said and did things in the heat of anger that we should not have."

David shook his head hard. "I am all to blame, Chris. You did nothing but protect your wife," his voice lowered regretfully. "You were right when you said I was jealous. I was jealous, of everything you had. When you first married Dustin, it was a sort of game to try and get you to like her. You didn't, you know. You and I had much the same view of marriage. But when you came to love her, I felt left out. I guess I had to find something wrong with her to make you not love her so that things would be as they had been. Can you ever forgive me?"

Christopher's eyes were warm. "I understand you returned to Lioncross to act as her protector. That proves to me how sorry you were for what happened."

David snorted ironically. "A lot of good I did. She married Marcus anyway."

"Richard said you tried to kill Marcus in a sword fight," Christopher said. "Very brave of you, little brother. I spent half the day yesterday trying to do the same thing."

David shrugged, not voicing what he was thinking. That their friendship had come to this still bothered him greatly. He glanced back at his troops after a moment.

"I have three hundred men to reinforce your ranks," he said, "if you shall have me."

Christopher smiled broadly. "I would have no other." He slugged his brother again and moved toward his destrier. "What is this I hear that you have taken a wife?"

David snickered at his brother's disbelieving tone. "I did, and a lovely woman she is. But she came with two sisters and they are driving me crazy."

Christopher crowed with laughter as he mounted. "You deserve all that and more. You never could handle a woman."

David mounted his dancing animal. "They are not women. They are the spawn of Satan."

"Not Nathalie," Christopher said. "She is an obedient, thoughtful girl."

"That is what she wants you to believe," David sneered. "She puts on a prim and proper front, and then when your guard is down – boom. And Elise, the youngest, is even worse. Do you know that they put honey on my pillow? And charcoal in my helmet? I went for half a day with black hair and had no idea why my men were laughing at me."

Christopher laughed heartily at the mental picture of his high-strung brother dealing with two disobedient children. "David, I think I like these girls. You must tell me more sometime."

David made a face. "Later."

Christopher waved at him and they turned tail on one another, returning to their respective armies. For them both, the world suddenly seemed a little brighter, a little more hopeful.

David's men set up camp and it was truly like old times. Richard had his inner circle of knights about him and he could not have been more pleased. In spite of the tension in the air, David and Marcus had barely acknowledged one another and kept their distance, dampening Richard's mood a bit, but it could not be helped. He would have rather had them ignoring each other than trying to slit one another's throats.

The army from Windsor was expected on the morrow and Richard took leave of his men and went to bed early. Christopher and David were standing around the massive pyre, watching the sparks fly into the dark night and speaking of insignificant things. Christopher wanted to know more of his new sister-in-law, Emilie, and was eager to hear of David's exploits with her younger sisters. He laughed until he cried, picturing his brother trying to handle two spirited young girls.

They were laughing about something or another when Marcus

strolled past the fire, eyeing the two brothers impassively. Christopher gazed back, as did David, and immediately the tension rose. Harold, at Christopher's feet, rose and snarled menacingly.

"Marcus," he greeted formally.

Marcus merely nodded his head, crossbow strung over his shoulder, and continued on his way. David watched him disappear into the night before letting out a hissing sigh.

"Be mindful that he doesn't use that thing on your back," he referred to the crossbow. "Marcus is the best archer in the realm."

Christopher nodded. "I am well aware of his skill," he looked at his brother and slugged him playfully. "That is why I have you here – to cover my back."

David grinned, gazing at his brother a moment. "I told you once that you had changed. I cannot believe how much you have changed."

"How so?" Christopher raised his brows.

"Jesus, Chris, how haven't you changed?" David snorted. "The Lion's Claw I knew had little sense of humor, and ate, drank, and slept war on the field. The only time I ever saw you relax was with a woman in your arms. But right now…I mean, look at us. Since when did we laugh and slug each other like a couple of lads? And that ugly dog is constantly with you; you always hated animals. Furthermore, you smile all the time. You never used to smile at all. I wondered at times if you even knew how. You have taken on a dimension I never knew you had."

Christopher shrugged. "There is much in life to be happy over, I suppose. I love my wife and my daughter. Why shouldn't I smile?"

David grinned at him and shook his head. "Then you were right. Love hasn't made you weak; it has made you invincible."

Christopher nodded deliberately, pleased his brother was seeing the truth of it. "And Emilie? Do you love her?"

David looked embarrassed, kicking at the ground. He thought if he admitted he did, he'd sound like a hypocrite. "I am very fond of her, God knows. But love… well, it scares me."

"As it frightened me," Christopher looked thoughtful. "I seem to remember a close relative of mine, male of course, tell me once that if I would only allow my wife to love me that everything in this world would right itself. Quit fighting her, I was told. Now I wonder who told me that?"

David looked away sheepishly. "Some idiot, I am sure."

Christopher smiled. "A wise idiot, who happened to be my brother. He should follow his own advice."

David crossed his thick arms and drew in a deep breath. "Mayhap. But I swear I am going to kill her sisters one of these days."

Christopher chuckled. "Don't you dare! I am pleased that they are proving to be a thorn in your arrogant side."

"Arrogant," David choked. "Now look who's calling me arrogant. Jesus, out of the mouth of the man who invented the term."

They grinned at each other, watching the fire burn in comfortable silence. Bootfalls caught their attention and they both looked through the flames to see Marcus appearing out of the darkness.

"Posts are secured, my lord," he told Christopher formally.

Christopher nodded slightly. "Very good."

Marcus gave a slight bow and turned on his heel, but Christopher stopped him. He did not know why he should, but somehow, it just wasn't right for them to hate each other. It was as if the earth was out of balance, or the stars out of alignment. It was unnatural and went against the grain. With everything that had happened, he still yearned for his friend.

"You did not eat," he said.

Marcus' face was unreadable. "I wasn't hungry."

Christopher sighed. "Will you join us?"

Marcus' eyes widened a bit and he eyed David. "Nay, my lord, I do not think so."

Christopher sat on the log behind him and rested his ankle on his knee. "Sit down, Marcus."

David took his own seat, not looking at Marcus. Marcus looked at *the two brothers, once his very best friends, and he, too, yearned for the way things had once been. But there was so much hurt and anger in his heart that it was difficult to see past it. Yet he could see that Christopher was making some sort of effort to be civil, and he decided to reciprocate. But he wondered if David was hiding a dagger in his belt with his name on it.*

Slowly, he lowered his big body onto an upturned log and sat stiffly, his hands clasped in front of him. Harold growled threateningly at him and Christopher admonished the dog sternly.

"Have you seen your father since you have returned?" Christopher asked.

Marcus shook his head. "Nay, even though Leicester is less than a day from Somerhill," he said. "The last I heard of my father, the earl, he and his new wife were busy on a family of their own. He has no time for his second son from his first wife."

"What of your brother? Surely you have seen him?" Christopher asked.

"My brother, the monk?" Marcus said with some contempt. "The man will inherit the earldom when my father dies and doesn't know a damn thing about running it. As far as I know, he's still at Westminster. I did not even see him when I was in London."

Christopher looked at him a moment before staring back into the flames. It began to occur to him that Marcus felt alone in the world, abandoned by his father and forgotten by his brother. He had no one at all, which was probably why he was so determined to hang onto Dustin. He needed the security of a family from her desperately, and Christopher wondered if he was even aware of it.

"Tell me something, Marcus," he said after a moment. "Are you so resolved to keep Dustin because you love her or because you have no family ties whatsoever? Is she and Christin your ready-made family or are they the love of your life?"

Marcus' features grew dark. "How in the hell can you ask me that? I told you once and I shall tell you again – I love her."

Christopher kept calm; he truly wasn't trying to rile Marcus, but simply help him think. "It could not be because your mother died when you were young and your father deposited you on the Earl of Derby when you were five? You have never had the closeness or strength of a woman or a family as I have. Is she somehow filling a role for you, a role you have forced upon her whether or not she is willing?"

Marcus stood up, his big fists clenched. "To hell with you," he snared. "How dare you judge me."

David sighed heavily and shook his head. Christopher glanced at his brother, pleased that he was keeping his calm, but knew it was difficult for him.

"I am not judging you," he said softly. "I did not mean to upset you, Marcus. I am just trying to understand. Please sit and we shall speak no more about it."

Marcus did not sit, but he did not leave, either. "How dare you probe me, Chris," he hissed. "How dare you try and analyze my actions. By what right?"

"'Tis my right because it is my wife you married," Christopher reminded him.

Marcus' jaw ticked. "And my daughter she bore."

"You bastard." David could hold still no longer. He snarled at Marcus. "You are the most...."

"Shut up, David." Christopher cut his brother off, returning his gaze to Marcus with less calm than before. "If she is your child, kindly explain how it is she looks like me?"

"We all see what we want to see," Marcus said quietly. "You see yourself, and I see me. But I know without a doubt that she is my flesh and blood."

"Wishful thinking," David snapped. "She's not your child, Marcus. She is as much your daughter as Dustin is your wife, which is not at all."

"Stay out of this, David," Marcus warned. "This does not concern you."

"The hell it doesn't!" David snarled. "Anything that concerns Chris concerns me. I should have spilled your guts when I had the chance."

"You never had the chance," Marcus said smoothly. "If you recall, I was winning our bout when Richard separated us. If anyone's guts were to be spilled, it would have been yours."

"Arrogant son-of-a-bitch," David rumbled. "Jesus, Marcus, what has Chris ever done to you that you would try and destroy his life?"

Marcus stopped in his tracks. He was preparing for an all-out verbal fight with the two brothers when David's words suddenly struck him. Faltering, he turned away from the two of them because he honestly could not reply. He never thought of the situation in that context; what had Christopher ever done? My God, was he being vindictive for the fact that Christopher had earned a greater reputation, or had found more favor with the king, and he did not even realize it? Confusion swept him.

"Is...is that what it looks like? That I am seeking some sort of revenge?" he murmured, turning back around to face Christopher. "That I am out to destroy you?"

Christopher just looked at him, not replying. Marcus had asked the question with such bewilderment that it was difficult not to feel his honesty. The white-hot tension that had surrounded them was draining away and even David began to relax.

"What do you think?" David said earnestly. "Of course it looks like you are trying to take everything away from my brother. His wife, his child, his life... why, Marcus? Did he wrong you somehow?"

Marcus shook his head vehemently, his puzzlement overwhelming. "Nay," he breathed. "I am not trying to punish him for a wrong against me. We just happen to love the same woman."

Christopher sighed, leaning forward with his arms resting on his knees. "Marcus, she is my wife and Christin is my daughter. Your marriage to her is void anyway because I was alive when you married her. She was never your wife, and she was always mine." He looked up at him. "I have tried to be patient, I have tried to become angry, I have threatened you, and I have fought you. Dustin has even told you that she doesn't want you. What will it take, then, for you to leave us in peace?"

Marcus, a man of considerable pride, lowered his gaze uncertainly. Everything that was said, albeit unpleasant, made sense even to him. He did not want to admit it, any of it, but it was clear even to him that he was in the wrong. As if a fog had lifted and revealed a scene as clear as heaven itself, he suddenly realized how very terrible he had been.

But, God, he loved her. His motives had always been very sincere toward Dustin; he simply loved her. But David's words, Christopher's words, seeped into his brain and even as he tried to fight off their meaning, his common sense and moral character could not deny their correctness. They were right; they had always been right, and he had been selfish and absorbed. He had been right when he told Christopher that both of them saw what they wanted to see. He only saw his love for Dustin and completely disregarded her feelings, as well as Christopher's. Only his wants had mattered to him because he was used to having his desires fulfilled.

But Dustin did not want him; she had told him that, but he had chosen to believe that he could make her love him if he tried hard enough. Mayhap for the first time in his life Marcus realized he could not manipulate the situation to his advantage. With a stab of pain to his chest, he realized that he had indeed been self-indulgent and ignorant. God help him, he did not want to let her go, but as much as he loved her, he knew he had to.

His strength drained from his body and he collapsed on the up-turned log. He stared into the flames of the pyre for an endless amount of time, weary and defeated.

"I love her," he murmured slowly. "I was blinded by her beauty, her innocence, her charm. She made me forget all that I am and all that I stand for, and I will tell you now that I am deeply ashamed to admit my guilt. I took it for a game, at first, but my obsession with her grew and I could not control it." He looked up at Christopher's sad eyes. "I will not fight you for her anymore, Chris. I can see now that I have already done enough damage."

David was shocked to see Marcus fold so quickly. He blinked at his brother, whose expression was one of sorrow.

"I trusted you once and you betrayed me," Christopher said hoarsely. "I am having difficulty believing you."

"No doubt," Marcus said with defeat. "I could swear to you on the Bible, but I think mayhap even that would not be strong enough. If I swear to you on my oath as a knight, will you believe me?"

Christopher looked at the fire, not wanting to doubt Marcus' oath, for the man was the best knight in the realm. But he was bitter and weary and tired of deceit.

"Mayhap in time," he whispered. "Mayhap your actions will speak louder than words."

Marcus was bewildered and frustrated, at himself, at everything. "I am not completely guilty in all of this," he said. "You proved to be spiteful and irrational, too. If there is any betrayal to be felt, I should be allowed a small portion."

Christopher's head came up. "What are you talking about?"

"In London, Chris. Do you remember how crazed jealous you were when I was around your wife? We had done absolutely nothing at that time, yet you were wild with envy," Marcus reminded him.

"You had kissed her," Christopher returned.

Marcus threw up his hands. "An innocent taste, I swear to you. I felt nothing for her at the time. It was, as I said – a game. My feelings for her followed shortly thereafter."

Christopher let out a laborious sigh. "I do not know, Marcus. I just do not know what to think or believe anymore."

Marcus watched his former friend as he stared at his hands. "Do you know that even after I married her, she refused to take your wedding rings off?" he said. "I am not daft, Chris. I knew she did not love me, but I hoped with time that things would change. And they would have, but with you returned, even I know that there is no hope."

With that, Marcus stood up walked away, leaving Christopher drained and David astonished.

"Do you think he is sincere?" David asked.

Christopher ran a hand through his hair. "Oh, hell, David, I do not know," he sighed heavily. "I would like to hope so, but he has lied to me before where Dustin was concerned. I will not allow myself to be sucked in again. We shall just have to wait and see."

David puffed out his cheeks and sat down, shaking his head in wonder. He never thought he would live to see the day when Marcus Burton backed down from anything. Surprisingly, he wasn't leery as his brother was.

He believed him.

On the morrow, the siege of Nottingham Castle commenced and the Defender, after a long and drawn-out battle, triumphed over Prince John and reclaimed his family.

THE DAY AFTER the siege of Nottingham, the grounds surrounding the castle were muddy and desolate, with smoke from smoldering cooking fires still rising in the damp morning air as Richard's army organized the dead and wounded for the return home.

David was already prepared to depart. He hadn't suffered any injury during the battle, which had been an overwhelming thing with so many crown troops and the king in the midst of it.

Truthfully, David was satisfied with the entire event and pleased that his brother had managed to reclaim is wife and daughter. Both Dustin and Christin were unharmed and even now, they were still sleeping in Christopher's tent as Christopher, awake and going about his duties, made sure to tell the men to keep their voices down and steer clear of his tent. Dustin, whom he had discovered to be pregnant with their second child, was sleeping the sleep of the dead, with her daughter cradled against her.

Nottingham was back in Richard's hands now, with John and the Sheriff of Nottingham having escaped Richard's nets. They were on the run with a small portion of their mercenary army, as nearly half of that army had been decimated in the siege and conquest of the castle. There were a lot of enemy dead laying around, giving the air a rotten stench that mixed with the smoke, and Richard had his prisoners of war collect the bodies of their colleagues for burial in a mass grave outside of the castle.

The armies were preparing to depart, the dead were being buried, and everything had happened as it should. David couldn't have been more grateful or relieved. Now, he was looking forward to returning home to his wife. It was all he could think of as he packed the remainder of his belongings.

"Greetings, David."

David turned around at the sound of the voice and was faced with a sight he never thought he'd see again. Brickley was standing behind him, looking weary and beaten. Their eyes met, they gazed at one another, and a brittle peace filled the air between them. Old friends, now enemies, but evidently still comrades in arms.

It was difficult to describe the moment.

"Brick?" David said, astonished. "I did not know you were here. Where did you come from?"

Brickley smiled weakly. "I am with East Anglia's army these days," he said. "We were holding the bridge while you and the rest of Richard's knights gained entrance."

In that brief explanation, David realized he was glad to see the man. He didn't know why, but he was. Maybe it was because he and Brickley had been friends long before the situation with Emilie. David had always known Brickley to be a wise and noble knight. But maybe he was in a position to be magnanimous because he had emerged the victor in the battle for Emilie's heart. Whatever the case, he was genuinely glad to see the man. When Brickley had left Canterbury without telling anyone, David felt as if there was something left open between them. Good or bad, it needed to be dealt with. He needed some closure.

Now was his chance.

"You and your men held it well," David said. "I should have guessed someone you like were in charge. Are you well, then? Did you suffer any injury?"

Brickley shook his head. "I did not," he said. "In fact, my son is here somewhere, too. He came with Barnwell and Lord Huston. He is only fifteen but I am told he actually fought with a sword when the gatehouse was breached and the mercenaries began fleeing. I saw him after the battle and I swear to you that you have never seen a happier lad. I think he killed someone."

David laughed softly. "I have never met your son," he said. "But if he is anything like is father, I am sure he will be a fine knight."

Brickley nodded, feeling rather awkward with the conversation. He didn't even know why he had approached David, but he had. Mayhap it was because David reminded him of something he missed very much – Canterbury. Maybe it was because he, too, felt as if he needed some closure. He and David had been friends, once. But much had happened, on both sides, to damage that. After a moment, he forced a smile.

"Well," he said, starting to back away. "I am glad to hear that your brother's death was misreported. I saw him earlier and even spoke to him. But I wanted to tell you that I am glad he is not dead."

He was turning to leave and David stopped him. "Wait," he said. "Brick... I am not going to ask you why you left Canterbury, for I know. But in hindsight, I wish you hadn't. Lyle misses you. He was very fond of you, you know. I wish you felt as if you could have stayed. I would have done my best to ensure there was peace between us."

Brickley cleared his throat softly, feeling embarrassed now that the touchy subject of his departure had been introduced.

"I am sure you will understand when I say that I couldn't stay and watch the woman I had once loved marry another man," he said. He shrugged weakly. "There was a war between us, a war over Emilie, and you won. To the victor goes the spoils. But I didn't want to stay and watch you claim your prize."

David nodded. "I understand," he said. "I really do. I am simply sorry that you and I could not maintain a friendship through this all."

Brickley shook his head. "Our friendship as knights and colleagues is still there in spite of everything," he said. His pale eyes twinkled. "I cannot say that I would hoist an ale with you any time soon, but as an ally, I will be there for you. I… I did not mean it when I said I should have let Dennis le Londe kill you. I do regret that."

David waved him off. "We say things in the heat of the moment that do not mean anything," he said. "I always assumed that was one of those times. Besides, Dennis died in the siege. I saw his body in the castle."

Brickley turned to look at the dark-stoned castle behind the, torn up by the ravages of the siege. "Is that so?" he said, mildly surprised. "Then this battle accomplished two good things – reclaiming your brother's wife and the death of le Londe. The man was an evil bastard."

"Indeed he was."

Brickley's gaze lingered on the castle a little while longer before returning his focus to David, who was looking at him rather intently. Feeling awkward again, Brickley scratched at his bearded face and began to move away.

"Give my regards to Lyle and his daughters," he said. "And to your wife. I am assuming that Emilie is your wife by now."

"She is. And I will tell her that I saw you. She will be pleased to know you are alive and well."

Brickley simply nodded his head, moving away from David and giving the man a brief wave of the hand as if to beg his leave. But David called out to him as he walked away.

"You will come and visit sometime, won't you?" he said. "I am certain Lyle would like to see you. I can make myself scarce when you come so you won't have to sit and look at my ugly face across the feasting table."

Brickley was still walking, now turning around and walking backwards as he looked at David. He was grinning and trying not to. "You can stay," he said. "I just won't look at you."

"Fair enough," he said as Brickley turned around and continued walking away. "Make it soon, will you?"

Brickley simply lifted a hand and waved at him as if acknowledging the request. David watched the man go, a faint smile on his lips, thinking that he was glad they'd had the conversation. Things weren't the same between them, and probably never would be, but at least the situation was civil. That was the best he could hope for at this point. But he truly hoped Brickley would come back to Canterbury at some point, at least to visit.

It was his home, after all.

Gathering the last of his possessions and putting them on his horse, David had the sergeants gather the Canterbury army as he went to bid farewell to his brother.

Christopher knew that David wanted to return soon to see his wife, but after everything that had happened and the fact that the brothers hadn't seen each other in so long, Christopher managed to talk David into accompanying him back to Lioncross Abbey. It would only be a few weeks out of his way, at most, but David wasn't hard-pressed to go along. He knew that Emilie would understand. And he very much wanted to spend time with his brother, the man he thought he'd lost. God was giving him a second chance to strengthen those brotherly ties.

He didn't want to miss it.

He was Lioncross-bound.

CHAPTER TWENTY-SIX

Canterbury Castle
January Year of Our Lord 1195 A.D.

E VERYONE WAS SICK again.
The cold and wintery time of year seemed to breed disease and once again, half of the town was ill with a cough and fever. The town's physic knew the routine and gathered the sick into the great hall of Canterbury Castle so he could tend everyone all at once. More sick were brought in every hour.

Emilie was in the hall assisting the physic with the sick, giving them medicine made with horehound to ease their cough or boiled water to ease their thirst. A widowed woman who made wooden fabric fasteners, selling them from her home, brought her entire family in because all five children were feeling so poorly. So was she. As the woman got some much-needed rest, Elise sat with the children over near the hearth and allowed them to play with her wooden people. Elise was usually so protective over the wooden people but it was a sign of her growth that she was actually letting children play with her toys. She had even given a couple of them away.

Emilie and Nathalie had paused in their duties to watch their little sister share her most prize possessions, which was something that made them both smile. Cid and Roland had taken up station near Elise, and near the hearth, and Roland eventually turned into a pillow for two of the sickly children laying against them. But the dogs were happy, and not lonely anymore, snoring away as the children played around them. It made for a rather heartwarming scene.

And then there was Nathalie. David took her friend Payn away, but she very quickly forgot about the young man when another soldier, young and handsome, began to turn her head. He was well-liked by the sergeants of Canterbury, and he and Nathalie had struck up a rather sweet romance. Payn had vanished from her thoughts over the past three months, much to Lyle's relief. He therefore encouraged her latest romantic obsession, even if it was a simple foot soldier. Nathalie was much like Emilie had been at that age, liking men and with suitors coming about, so Lyle resigned himself to that fact that he would soon have to find a husband for his middle daughter.

But he didn't mind. It could have been worse; he could have been fending her off of Payn, who was in truth her half-brother, so he didn't mind encouraging her interest with other young men. As for Payn, Lyle had received a missive from David not long ago informing him of the army's whereabouts, their future plans, and telling him that Payn was a very sharp young man with a good deal of military potential. That was a prideful thing for Lyle, very prideful. One evening after the girls had gone to sleep and Lillibet was in his bed, he told her of the son they had, who was now with David de Lohr in the north fighting at Nottingham Castle.

Lillibet had wept with joy at the news. Lyle knew, for a fact, that the woman was eager to see her son for the first time. She hadn't seen him since birth because Lyle had forbidden it. Now, he was coming to think he'd been too hard on the long-suffering Lillibet. Even in these days of growth and maturity for his daughters, Lyle seemed to be growing as well. Family, he realized, was more important than pride or secrets.

Therefore, on this blustery night, Lyle lingered in the warmth of the keep with thoughts of his son on his mind, as the women of the family were in the hall aiding with the sick. All was peaceful within the walls of Canterbury, and the doors were closed to the hall to keep the heat in, which meant the ladies didn't hear the sentries take up the call for the approaching army. Lyle, buried up in his bedchamber behind thick walls, didn't hear the cry either.

Having come all the way from Dartford, which is where they had stopped to rest the previous night, David had pushed his weary army on the last day of the journey all the way home. It had been a very long day, and a ridiculous amount of miles traveled, but he figured the men wanted to get home just as badly as he did, so no one complained.

Onward they trudged through the cold and muddy roads all day and into the darkness, finally seeing the castle in the distance beneath a bright and silver moon. It had been like a beacon in the darkness, the castle and the enormous cathedral of Canterbury, and the men picked up the pace until they heard the chains of Canterbury's portcullis lifting for them.

Then, they started to run, literally, running through the gatehouse and into the bailey beyond, thrilled to be home, and exhausted to the bone. The sergeants bellowed at them, telling them not to run, but they weren't listening. When David charged beneath the portcullis on his fat white horse, he nearly ran several men over because they weren't watching where they were going. They were aimlessly, wandering children, happy to have made it back to their place of origin.

Happy to be back in the fold.

And none happier than David. He thundered over to the stables where the two young stable boys were there to meet him, holding his horse steady as he wearily dismounted and collected his saddlebags. The horse was foaming, as usual, and the boys pulled the animal along to cool him off before tending him, but no one escaped the foaming lips this time. David had to laugh when, once again, a frothy horse mouth came down on two small dark heads. This time, both boys groaned.

Jesus, it was good to be home. David was so weary that his legs felt like water, but he headed for the keep on quivering legs, heading for Emilie until he saw Lyle emerging from the keep and heading straight for him. Having been informed of the army's arrival by a servant, Lyle was glad to see him but told him that Emilie was in the hall because there was more sickness in town this winter, and the sick townsfolk had been moved into the hall, once again, for convenience sake. Exasperated to hear that his pregnant wife was tending the sick, David growled.

"Why must she tend the ill?" he asked Lyle, although it was more of a rhetorical question born of frustration. "She risks herself and my son by exposing herself to all manner of sickness like that. How long has this been going on?"

Lyle gave him a very queer expression followed by one of surprise and then sadness. Reaching out, he grasped David by the arm. "Your son...?" he asked, trailing off. "David... she sent you at least two missives that I know of. Did you not get them?"

David nodded, not particularly paying note to the tone of Lyle's voice. "I did," he said. "Why do you ask?"

Lyle blinked in confusion. He scratched his chin, muttering more to himself than to David. "I thought sure that she told you."

"Told me what?"

Lyle could see, in that instant, that David had no idea that Emilie was no longer pregnant. If he had known, then he certainly would not have made a comment about Emilie jeopardizing the health of his son. Clearing his throat softly, Lyle knew he should not be the one to tell him. He reached up and pulled David's saddlebags off of his shoulder.

"Go find Emilie," he said. "She will tell you."

Puzzled, but still unconcerned at this point, David allowed Lyle to take his saddlebags. He watched his liege head for the keep. "When I am finished with Emilie, I have news for you," he called after him.

"I saw Brick, among other things. He was at the siege of Nottingham serving East Anglia."

Lyle paused and turned to David. Somehow, he looked very old on this night. Old and weary. But he forced a smile at the mention of Brickley.

"That is good to know," he said. "You spoke with him?"

"I did. I will come in and tell you about it in a moment."

Lyle's gaze lingered on him. His expression was strange, almost sympathetic in nature. "Welcome home, David," he finally said.

"Thank you, my lord."

Shrugging off Lyle's seemingly odd behavior, David headed for the great hall as Lyle returned to the keep to put David's possessions away. As David approached the hall, one of the enormous doors swung open and Lillibet suddenly emerged, seemingly quite interested in the return of the army. She saw David right away and she went to him, her manner nervous and urgent.

"My lord," she said respectfully as the spit flew and hit David in the chest. "Lord Lyle told me that you took a young man with you as your squire. His name is Payn. Did he return with you?"

David nodded, taking a step back from the woman to avoid the smattering of spit. "He did," he replied. "He is somewhere with the men."

"But he made it home?"

"He did."

"Would you be kind enough to point him out to me, my lord?"

David turned around, looking through the crowd of men now filling the bailey. There was ambient light from torches on the wall, and a few of them at the entry to the keep and entry to the great hall, but it was still difficult to see through the darkness. Impatient to get to his wife, David scoured the gang of men collecting in the bailey, finally coming to the pale head of tall and gangly Payn. He pointed the lad out to Lillibet.

"There," he said. "The tall lad with the blond hair. See him near the end of the great hall?"

Lillibet was straining to see what David was pointing out, finally spying what he was indicating. "That young man?" she asked. "The one with the blonde hair?"

"That one."

She gave her thanks and scurried off. As David watched with curiosity, she went to the young man and a few words were exchanged. He thought he might have even seen an embrace, but he couldn't really see more than that in the darkness. Lillibet and Payn were surrounded by other soldiers in heavy clothing and all of the fabric and darkness was blending into each other. But he swore that, through the dim light and the bustle, he saw the two of them embrace.

Yet he didn't let his attention linger on the pair any longer, for thoughts of his wife again took priority. He was desperate to see her. Turning for the entrance to the great hall, he entered the warm, stuffy room.

Immediately, he wrinkled his nose, sniffing the air. It smelled as if someone had been burning bodies because the physic was evidently burning herbs that were supposed to help the sick. But to David, it simply stank. Increasingly frustrated that his wife should be subjecting herself to such smells and disease, David pushed through the crowd of sick people, his gaze seeking out Emilie's blond head.

In his quest, he saw Elise over near the hearth with her wooden people out of their box, playing with some small children, and he couldn't help but notice the big dogs were sleeping next to her. It was actually quite a charming sight to see and when Elise saw him, she actually waved at him. Shocked, David waved back. Thinking that perhaps Elise's brain had been affected by illness, because she had never once waved to him in the entire time he'd known her, he pushed further into the hall. The quest to find Emilie was gaining in urgency.

The cavernous room was heavy with sick people, coughing and

miserable, and David was seriously thinking of berating his wife for risking her health, and the health of their son, even before he greeted her. He was genuinely furious. As he neared the end of the hall, he began to hear Emilie's voice mingled with Nathalie's. There was a servant's entrance back here, and an alcove where food was prepared or stored, and he thought the sounds were coming from there. With hope and relief in his heart, he pushed straight back into the alcove to be rewarded by a most welcome sight.

Emilie and Nathalie were facing away from him, evidently preparing something on a table against the wall. It seemed to be hot wine or something like it for the sick, to help with their coughs. He could hear Emilie tell Natalie that the physic wanted her to put a goodly measure of clove in the wine along with horehound, and serve it promptly. Nathalie was trying to do just as her sister was telling her, carefully stirring up an earthenware pitcher of something steaming.

"I have been returned for nearly ten minutes and I am the one who has to come and find you?" he said, watching both women jump and turn to him. "I am deeply hurt, Em. I thought at the very least you would be at the gatehouse to greet me."

Only Emilie's head had turned to look at him; the rest of her was still facing the mixing table for the most part. Nathalie, upon seeing David, fled with the steaming pitcher in her hand without saying a word. That was more of the reaction he was used to from Nathalie and Elise, so he didn't feel quite so disoriented after that. He watched Nathalie run, and with a grin on his face he turned his attention to his wife. Then his features softened.

"Greetings, wife," he said. "Have you no better greeting for me than to simply stare at me?"

Emilie was looking at him with an expression between great joy and great sorrow. It was difficult to describe. She was bundled up against the cold in heavy layers, including a heavy woolen robe that was draped over her, with big sleeves meant to be layered upon heavy clothing. It was warm and bulky. Therefore, she was quite covered up, and her belly concealed, when she fully turned to him.

"Oh… David," she breathed. "Thank God you have returned."

He lifted his eyebrows at her. "That is the only greeting you can give me?" he asked, insulted. "Where are the cries of happiness? Why are you not throwing yourself at me? You may yet do it, but be mindful of my son when you do."

She sighed heavily, making her way towards him. Emilie had known this moment would come; she'd been anticipating it for months. Months of knowing she would have to face her husband and tell him of the child they had lost. Still, she had no idea how to tactfully couch the news so it was best she simply come out with the truth, in any format. Tactful or not, he needed to know. It wasn't as if she could keep it from him, but she was genuinely fearful of his reaction.

God, she was dreading this.

"I am so glad you have come home," she said, reaching out a hand to him which he caught and brought to his lips. His tender kiss to the palm of her hand brought tears to her eyes. "Are you well, my darling?"

He nodded, kissing her hand again before pulling her against him and kissing her lips tenderly. With the layers of clothing she was wearing and his armor, he couldn't much feel her body against his, at least not in detail. Not enough to know his precious son was gone.

"I am well," he told her, kissing her again. "Jesus, I've missed you. Are you well? Is my son well?"

The tears came then and she struggled to blink them away. "I am well," she said hoarsely. "But your son… I am so sorry, David, but it was not meant to be this time. Forgive me for not telling you sooner but it was not something I wanted to put in a missive. I did not want you grieving whilst on a battle campaign. I knew you would come home and there would be time for us to grieve our loss together."

She watched the light go out of David's face as she spoke. The blue eyes, which had been glimmering warmly at her, were now a dull echo of what was in his heart. He simply stared at her for a moment, not speaking, clearly trying to absorb what she was saying.

"The baby?" he finally asked. "What happened to the baby?"

Emilie put her hands to his face, her soft flesh against his stubble. "He is gone," she whispered.

Realization registered at her blunt words and a wave of sorrow washed over David's face. "Jesus…," he hissed. "Nay. Tell me it is not true."

"It is. I am so sorry, but it is."

He swallowed hard, laboring to come to grips with the fact that there would be no son in the spring. He continued to stare at her, a million dreams he had for his boy being shattered in the reflection of his eyes. Emilie gazed up at him sadly, seeing his despair.

"I did not want to tell you while you were off to battle," she said quietly. "You were engaging in a joyful reunion with the brother you thought you'd lost. You were with him, fighting side by side with him again. I did not want to ruin that happiness with news that your son was lost. I wanted to tell you in person."

His brow furrowed, great anguish on his face. "Did you think you could not tell me?" he asked. "Did… did you truly think my reunion with my brother was more important than you?"

She shrugged. "It was very important to you," she said. "I did not wish to burden you with this."

He just stared at her, agony filling his expression. "Emilie, please," he whispered. "Did you truly think you were not the most important thing in the world to me? That our son was not the most important thing to me? You told me once that you believed you were not a priority to me. God forgive me if you still feel that way because I have tried to show you that you are. Is that why you did not tell me?"

She was starting to tear up, feeling the grief that was pouring out of him and into her. "I told you why," she said. "It was the truth. It was not that I felt this situation was unimportant. It was that…

David, you have had such agony in your life. Losing your parents at a young age, feeling as if you had no home. You told me that; do you recall? And then you lost your brother, who was miraculously discovered to be alive. I made the choice to let you experience that joy, the reconnection with someone you thought you had lost. My withholding the information was not about feeling that I was not a priority to you; it was about loving you enough to let you experience some joy for a little while. Losing our son… we would grieve for him soon enough."

David closed his eyes to her words, feeling every one of them as if she was pounding them into his brain. He couldn't even become angry that she had kept the news from him; in truth, he understood why she did it. It was the most selfless thing he had ever heard of. It was the greatest sacrifice he'd ever known.

At that moment, he came to realize what it truly meant to love and be loved. Emilie had showed him that. It was enough to bring tears to his eyes. He took her hands between his two big gloved ones, holding them to his lips.

"I have done many things in my life that I am not proud of," he murmured. "I never thought I have lived a particularly pious life. But, at this moment, I am coming to think that somehow, someway, I must have done something extremely good to warrant a woman like you. For the times I have made you weep, I throw myself at your feet and plead forgiveness. For the times I haven't shown you or told you what you mean to me, I beg your mercy. I have lived my life the way I have seen fit, only thinking of myself, until I met you. Now I know what it means to have a good woman by my side, for I never truly thought I would. You have changed that for me, Emilie. You have changed everything. I am more of a man than I ever was because of you. And I am home to stay, forever. I hope you can stand me for that long."

Emilie laughed softly, tears of joy streaming down your face. "I can stand you," he said. "And you are the greatest man I have ever known. I consider myself the most fortunate woman in the world to call you my husband."

He kissed her again, passionately. "I never thought I would like to hear that term when it came to me."

"And now?"

"I bear it more proudly than any man ever has."

David wrapped his arms around her, pulling her close, knowing that no matter what came, he and Emilie were strong together. They had suffered through events and situations that would have destroyed lesser people, but they were made of strong stuff. Too strong to destroy. Too strong to break.

As strong as a heart of steel.

Both of them.

EPILOGUE

Canterbury Castle
Year of our Lord 1208 A.D.

IN THE SMALL HALL of Canterbury, David was being watched. Stared at, scrutinized, and picked apart. He could feel the eyes on him, reaching out to him, pulling at him, demanding his attention. In truth, he was giving them as much attention as he could, given the circumstances. His mind was elsewhere.

Seated at the big, scrubbed table that Lyle Hampton's grandfather had commissioned, he glanced over at the eyes that were watching him. Big, blue eyes, three pairs of them, were seated across from him. The eyes were his color because his wife's eyes were brown; therefore, he was the one to blame for the eyes watching him. He had created them.

With the help of his wife, he had. Three little girls sat and watched him from across the table; Christina de Lohr, named for his brother, Christopher, Colleen de Lohr, named because Emilie had liked the name, and little Michaela de Lohr. Lyle had picked that name because he'd always wanted to name his son Michael.

But a son was not to be for Lyle, at least a legitimate one, and so far, a son was not to be had for David, either. Seven years into a childless marriage that had produced three miscarriages in those seven years, Emilie finally became pregnant and carried to term a daughter. Christina Valeria was born one snowy winter night, a fat baby who screamed constantly, and David and Emilie had been overjoyed. When Christina was two years of age, Emilie found herself pregnant again and delivered Colleen Willow on the eve of the summer solstice. Colleen was much better behaved than Christina was, and she was very much her father's daughter. David adored his girls.

But there were more to come. Michaela Maud was born a year after Colleen's birth and David found himself with three blond-haired cherubs to sit on his lap and call him "Papa." He couldn't have been happier. He never once wished for them to be boys, although Lyle put it in his head that Canterbury was evidently cursed with girl-only offspring. Maybe it was true, maybe it wasn't. Lyle was basing his statement on the fact that he'd had three daughters and now David and Emilie had three daughters. But David didn't much care; he was quite happy with his little chicks, as he called them, for they seemed to follow him everywhere in a gaggle. Life with his beautiful Emilie and three young daughters was good.

But then came another pregnancy two years after Michaela was born and hope for a son was not lost. Canterbury rejoiced. Lyle even had a special mass said in the cathedral, praying for a grandson.

It was now that David was waiting for that child to be born, as his three little daughters watched him over the tabletop. He sat in the small hall with them and with Lyle, while Lillibet and Nathalie and Elise were upstairs, helping deliver Emilie's baby. The child was quite large and Emilie had been in labor all day and into the night, straining to bring forth the infant, and David was trying not to become concerned about it. Emilie had never had short labors so it wasn't anything unusual as far as that went. But he was still on edge, more for her health than for the sex of the child. He just wanted her to emerge unscathed. That was really all he prayed for.

"Papa?"

David was diverted from his thoughts as little Christina spoke to him. She had a voice that sounded like a choir of angels. "Papa, is Mama done with her baby yet?"

David smiled at his eldest. "She is not," he said. "Not yet, but soon. Then we shall all go and see the baby."

Lyle, who was sitting in a sling-back leather chair near the hearth, mumbled. "A son," he muttered, half-asleep from the late hour and the warmth of the fire. "I have donated hundreds of coins to the cathedral this year. God must reward me for my tithing. It had better be a son."

At the sound of his voice, little Michaela, who was very attached to her grandfather, slithered off of her seat at the table and toddled over to him. He picked the child up, holding her against him as he began to rock back and forth, rocking her to sleep. Christina and Colleen remained at the table because the cook had placed all manner of sweet treats before them, and they were picking at a sweet tart with honey and blackberries and cream. It was David and Lyle's job to tend the girl while the rest of the women were upstairs. David didn't find it much of a task, however. He liked spending time with his girls.

"Papa, I want to see Mama!" Colleen declared, a plump berry in her mouth, turning her lips purple. "I will go *now!*"

Colleen had a bit of a stubborn streak in her, and David shook his head, stood up, and moved around the table. "Nay," he said, picking up Colleen as Christina climbed down from her seat. David led the girls over to the hearth. "We will wait here until it is time to see the baby. I will tell you a story. What would you like to hear?"

He sat down with Colleen on his lap as Christina sat down at his feet, nearly sitting on Roland, who was pushed up close to the fire. Cid had died the year before, leaving Roland alone, and he was growing old and gray around the mouth. David admonished Christina to be careful of the old dog as he settled into his chair.

"Be mindful of Roland," he told her. "He is very old. You must be kind to him."

Christina loved the old dog, as they all did, and she lay back, using him for a pillow. The mutt hardly cared. "Tell a story!" she demanded.

David usually told the girls things he made up, things he couldn't really remember when they asked for it again, so all of his stories were usually versions of things he'd said before. No two stories were the same. He thought on his repertoire as Christina made literary demands.

"Do you want to hear about dragons?" he asked. "Or fairies?"

"Fairies!" Christina and Colleen cried.

David grinned as he started a story, saying the first thing that came to mind. "Do you remember that I told you that Uncle Chris and I went to a land where Jesus lived?"

The girls nodded eagerly and David continued. "It is a magical land," he said. "It is covered with golden dust, called sand, and there are no trees, only rocks, but sometimes there are lakes and around the lakes grow strange and mysterious trees. One day your Uncle Chris and I were riding in a land with no water and no shade. It was very hot. But we saw something flittering in the golden sand and we thought it was a bird. But it moved very quickly and Uncle Chris said that it had legs and a white dress. Do you know what we saw?"

The girls were grinning broadly. *"A fairy!"* they shouted.

David had told a version of this story before so the girls knew that they would see fairies in it. He nodded to their jubilant cry. "Aye," he confirmed. "It was a fairy with wings made from spun gold and hair of silver floss. We followed her to a lake in the middle of the sand, surrounded by trees and grass, and in this grass, her family of fairies lived. We...."

"David!"

The call came from behind and David turned sharply to see Lillibet standing in the hall entry. She waved him over frantically and he leapt up from his chair, handing Colleen over to Lyle. He dashed towards the old woman, excitement and fear in his features.

"Emilie?" he asked. "Is she well?"

Lillibet was fighting off a grin. "She is well," she said, spit hitting David on the arm. "She wants to see you."

David didn't even ask if the child had arrived, which he probably should have. All he was focused on was the fact that his wife wanted to see him. He wanted to see her, too, so he took the spiral steps faster than he should have, racing to the third floor of Canterbury's keep where his chamber was. When he hit the third floor landing, he nearly plowed into Elise, who was leaving his chamber with a bundle of soiled linens in her arms. She grinned at him but said nothing as she continued down the stairs. David charged forward, into his chamber.

The door was partially open and he swung it back on its hinges in his haste. It banged against the wall and a baby began wailing. Startled, David looked at Emilie on the bed, who was sitting up and holding a crying infant in her arms. His face lit up with surprise and wonder.

"The baby is here!" he gasped as he made his way towards the bed. "Mother told me that you wanted to see me but she did not tell me that the child had arrived."

Emilie grinned, patting the bed beside her so he would sit. He did, and promptly held out his arms. "Give her to me," he demanded.

Emilie handed the child over and he took the baby easily. He had become quite comfortable with infants over the past few years and was an excellent and competent father. He looked down at the red face and tufts of white hair.

"Perfect," he said softly. "She is perfect."

Emilie continued to giggle. "Aye," she said. "Perfect. But you should know that the child has something that is seriously different from our other children. I suggest you unwrap the babe and see what I mean."

He looked at her, his smile fading. "What is wrong?"

Emilie patted the bed again, the space between them. "Unwrap the child," she said again. "You will see what I mean. I am not sure I should tell you."

David didn't like the sound of that at all. He lay the child down and began to unwind the tight swaddling, the work of Lillibet. Feather-soft wool began to become undone as the child screamed angrily. What was it he would find beneath? A third leg? Another head? Concerned, David peeled the layers away until he came to the fat, naked body beneath. It was then that he saw what he wife meant.

A difference, indeed.

Tears of joy sprang to his eyes and he burst out laughing. *"A boy!"* he cried. *"I have a son!"*

Emilie's laughter joined him. "You do, indeed," she said. "I wanted you to see for yourself."

He leaned over the red-faced infant and grasped her face in his hands, kissing her eagerly. But then he realized the baby was naked, and was probably cold, so he quickly wrapped the child back up as best he could and, very carefully, handed him over to his mother.

"Feed him," he ordered softly. "He is starving. Do not keep the lad waiting!"

Emilie grinned at her overexcited and demanding husband, who was clearly the proudest father in England. Obediently, she pulled back the top of her shift and placed the child on the nipple, which he took to eagerly. As the baby began to suckle fiercely, David moved closer and put his arms around the two of them, watching the infant feed against his wife's breast. The tears were still in his eyes, tears of gratitude and awe.

"I cannot believe it," he murmured as he watched. "A son. I finally have a son!"

Emilie nodded, looking up from the baby at her breast to kiss her husband on the cheek. "He is handsome and perfect, like his father," she said softly. "But he must have a name. You would not discuss male names with me at all, so we must decide what to name him. Do you have any ideas?"

David shrugged. "I did not want to discuss names because I did not want to curse our chances of having a son," he admitted. "But when you were carrying Christina, we discussed naming a son Daniel. I still like the name."

Emilie looked down at the downy-haired infant nursing against her breast. "Daniel was my grandfather's name," she said quietly. "That would make my father very happy. But I would also like to name him for your father as well."

David stroked her arm affectionately. "Daniel Myles de Lohr," he said. "I like it very much."

Emilie looked up at him because of the awe she heard in his voice when he spoke their son's name. It was enough to bring tears to her eyes. "Daniel de Lohr," she murmured. "He has a great legacy to live up to."

David nodded, his gaze still on the baby. "He will be the greatest de Lohr of all."

Emilie kissed his cheek again. "Of course he will," she said. "Now, go down and tell my father that his prayers have been answered. He will want to see him, of course, so you will bring him up here in a few minutes when I am finished feeding him. And bring the girls; they will want to see their little brother."

Little brother. Wasn't that what Christopher had always called David? Another de Lohr little brother. David grinned at that thought, kissing the infant's head before rising from the bed, off to deliver the good news to Lyle. He knew the man would be thrilled.

It was the culmination of a dream, of a life complete. With the addition of little Daniel, David felt as if he were walking on air. He had his beloved son, a man to carry on his name and legacy, and he was quite certain life couldn't get any sweeter. He thought back to the heartache and strife and pain he and Emilie had suffered through the years, both before their marriage and after, and with the birth of little Daniel, he realized that none of that pain really mattered anymore.

Everything had happened for a reason and everything had happened when it was supposed to. David was a believer in the winds of fate that way. He believed that everything always happened the way it should, but in this case, he was coming to think that God may have just had a hand in it. Perhaps God, for once, had shown him a little favor in the blessing of little Daniel.

David, for once, was willing to put a little faith in that belief.

He wasn't the only one given to faith. Upon hearing he finally had a grandson, Lyle fell to his knees and praised God for his mercy. Naming the child after his father had brought the man to tears, and he was so happy to finally have a male heir that he sat up most of the night, watching the infant sleep.

David knew this because he sat up, too, also watching his son sleep, and he and Lyle had many discussions about Daniel's future and the greatness he would achieve. Lyle was willing to believe that Daniel would be the greatest de Lohr of all while David, in fact, was sure of it.

Daniel embodied the best of all worlds. In that night, in that space of consciousness and time, David knew that the dynasty of the House of de Lohr would continue to live on.

The legend, for them, would prove immortal.

THE END

CANTERBURY'S ELDERFLOWER SAMBOCADE

A lovely recipe for a festive Medieval feast, a pie that David de Lohr loved very much.

1 nine-inch pie shell

1 ½ lbs. of cottage cheese (or a mixture of cottage and ricotta)

1/3 cup sugar

Whites of 3 eggs

2 tbs. dried elderflowers

1 tbs. rosewater

Combine all ingredients and blend thoroughly (a food processor or blender will do nicely). A Medieval cook would pulverize with a mortar and pestle. Pour mixture into pie shell and back at 350 degrees for 45 minutes to an hour, or until filling has set and the crust is golden brown. Let cool and serve to the hungry knights at your table.

(Elderflowers can be found at natural food stores, herb and spice specialty shops, etc. Don't use a substitution – the flavor of elderflowers is unique and the overall flavor of the final product depends on the real thing.)

About Kathryn Le Veque

Medieval Just Got Real.

KATHRYN LE VEQUE is a USA TODAY Bestselling author, an Amazon All-Star author, and a #1 bestselling, award-winning, multi-published author in Medieval Historical Romance and Historical Fiction. She has been featured in the NEW YORK TIMES and on USA TODAY's HEA blog. In March 2015, Kathryn was the featured cover story for the March issue of InD'Tale Magazine, the premier Indie author magazine. She was also a quadruple nominee (a record!) for the prestigious RONE awards for 2015.

Kathryn's Medieval Romance novels have been called 'detailed', 'highly romantic', and 'character-rich'. She crafts great adventures of love, battles, passion, and romance in the High Middle Ages. More than that, she writes for both women AND men – an unusual crossover for a romance author – and Kathryn has many male readers who enjoy her stories because of the male perspective, the action, and the adventure.

On October 29, 2015, Amazon launched Kathryn's Kindle Worlds Fan Fiction site WORLD OF DE WOLFE PACK. Please visit

Kindle Worlds for Kathryn Le Veque's World of de Wolfe Pack and find many action-packed adventures written by some of the top authors in their genre using Kathryn's characters from the de Wolfe Pack series. As Kindle World's FIRST Historical Romance fan fiction world, Kathryn Le Veque's World of de Wolfe Pack will contain all of the great story-telling you have come to expect.

Kathryn loves to hear from her readers. Please find Kathryn on Facebook at Kathryn Le Veque, Author, or join her on Twitter @kathrynleveque, and don't forget to visit her website at www.kathrynleveque.com.

Made in the USA
Lexington, KY
03 February 2017